Jonathan Kellerman is one of the world's most popular authors. He has brought his expertise as a clinical psychologist to more than two dozen bestselling crime novels, including the Alex Delaware series, *Bones*, *The Butcher's Theatre*, *Billy Straight*, *The Conspiracy Club* and *Twisted*. He is the author of numerous essays, short stories, scientific articles, two children's books and three volumes of psychology, including *Savage Spawn: Reflections On Violent Children*. He has won the Goldwyn, Edgar and Anthony awards, and has been nominated for a Shamus Award. Jonathan lives in California and New Mexico with his wife, writer Faye Kellerman and their four children, which include the novelist Jesse Kellerman.

Praise for Jonathan Kellerman's novels:

'When they're this good, it's impossible to get enough' *Mirror*

'Kellerman has shaped the psychological mystery novel into an art form' *Los Angeles Times Book Review*

'An alert eye for detail . . . Engrossing' *New York Times*

'Plot and sub-plot coalesce satisfyingly in high octane entertainment that never loses its characters' vulnerability' *The Times*

'A fast, professional read, with strong insights into the quirks of human and criminal nature' *Guardian*

By Jonathan Kellerman

THE BUTCHER'S THEATRE
THE CONSPIRACY CLUB

Alex Delaware Novels

WHEN THE BOUGH BREAKS
BLOOD TEST
OVER THE EDGE
SILENT PARTNER
TIME BOMB
PRIVATE EYES
DEVIL'S WALTZ
BAD LOVE
SELF-DEFENCE
THE WEB
THE CLINIC
SURVIVAL OF THE FITTEST
MONSTER
DOCTOR DEATH
FLESH AND BLOOD
THE MURDER BOOK
A COLD HEART
THERAPY
RAGE
GONE
OBSESSION
COMPULSION
BONES
TRUE DETECTIVES

Novels featuring Petra Connor

BILLY STRAIGHT
TWISTED

With Faye Kellerman

DOUBLE HOMICIDE
CAPITAL CRIMES

JONATHAN KELLERMAN

MONSTER

headline

First published in the United States in 1999
by Random House, Inc.

First published in Great Britain in 2000
by Little, Brown and Company

This edition published in 2009
by HEADLINE PUBLISHING GROUP

10 9 8 7 6 5 4 3 2 1

Cataloguing in Publication Data is available from the British Library

ISBN 978 0 7553 4287 7

Typeset in Fournier MT by Palimpsest Book Production Limited,
Grangemouth, Stirlingshire

Printed in the UK by
CPI Mackays, Chatham ME5 8TD

HEADLINE PUBLISHING GROUP
An Hachette UK Company
338 Euston Road
London NW1 3BH

www.headline.co.uk
www.hachette.co.uk

To the memory of
Kenneth Millar

Special thanks to Dr Spencer Eth and Dr Shoba Srinivasan

1

THE GIANT knew Richard Nixon.

Towering, yellow-haired, grizzled, a listing mountain in khaki twill, he limped closer, and Milo tightened up. I looked to Frank Dollard for a cue. Dollard appeared untroubled, meaty arms at his sides, mouth serene under the tobaccoed gray mustache. His eyes were slits, but they'd been that way at the main gate.

The giant belched out a bass laugh and brushed greasy hair away from his eyes. His beard was a corn-colored ruin. I could smell him now, vinegarish, hormonally charged. He had to be six-eight, 300. The shadow he threw on the dirt was ash-colored, amoebic, broad enough to shade us.

He took another lurching step, and this time Frank Dollard's right arm shot out.

The huge man didn't seem to notice, just stood there with Dollard's limb flung across his waist. Maybe a dozen other men in khaki were out on the yard, most of them standing still, a few others pacing, rocking, faces pressed against the chain link. No groups that I could see; everyone to himself. Above them, the sky was an untrammeled blue, clouds broiled away by a vengeful sun. I was cooking in my suit.

The giant's face was dry. He sighed, dropped his shoulders, and Dollard lowered his arm. The giant made a finger gun, pointed it at us, and laughed. His eyes were dark brown, pinched at the corners, the whites too sallow for health.

'Secret service.' He thumped his chest. 'Victoria's Secret service in the closet underwear undercover always lookin out for the guy good old Nixon RMN Rimmin, always rimmin wanting to be rimmed he liked to talk the walk cuttin outta the White House night house doing the party thing all hours with Kurt Vonnegut J. D. Salinger the Glass family anyone who didn't mind the politics heat of the kitchen I wrote *Cat's Cradle* sold it to Vonnegut for ten bucks *Billy Bathgate* typed the manuscript one time he walked out the front door got all the way to Las Vegas big hassle with the Hell's Angels over some dollar slots Vonnegut wanting to change the national debt Rimmin agreed the Angels got pissed we had to pull him out of it me and Kurt Vonnegut Salinger wasn't there Doctorow was sewing the Cat's Cradle they were bad cats, woulda assassinated him any day of the week leeway the oswald harvey.'

He bent and lifted his left trouser leg. Below the knee was bone sheathed with glossy white scar tissue, most of the calf meat ripped away. An organic peg leg.

'Got shot protecting old Rimmin,' he said, letting go of the fabric. 'He died anyway poor Richard no almanac know what happened rimmed too hard I couldn't stop it.'

'Chet,' said Dollard, stretching to pat the giant's shoulder.

The giant shuddered. Little cherries of muscle rolled along Milo's jawline. His hand was where his gun would have been if he hadn't checked it at the gate.

Dollard said, 'Gonna make it to the TV room today, Chet?'

The giant swayed a bit. 'Ahh . . .'

'I think you should make it to the TV room, Chet. There's gonna be a movie on democracy. We're gonna sing "The Star-Spangled Banner," could use someone with a good voice.'

'Yeah, Pavarotti,' said the giant, suddenly cheerful. 'He and Domingo were at Caesars Palace they didn't like the way it worked out Rimmin not doing his voice exercises lee lee lee lo lo lo no egg yolk to smooth the trachea it pissed Pavarotti off he didn't want to run for public office.'

'Yeah, sure,' said Dollard. He winked at Milo and me.

The giant had turned his back on all three of us and was staring down on the bare tan table of the yard. A short, thick, dark-haired man had pulled down his pants and was urinating in the dirt, setting off a tiny dust storm. None of the other men in khaki seemed to notice. The giant's face had gone stony.

'Wet,' he said.

'Don't worry about it, Chet,' Dollard said softly. 'You know Sharbno and his bladder.'

The giant didn't answer, but Dollard must have transmitted a message, because two other psych techs came jogging over from a far corner. One black, one white, just as muscular as Dollard but a lot younger, wearing the same uniform of short-sleeved sport shirt, jeans, and sneakers. Photo badges clipped to the collar. The heat and the run had turned the techs' faces wet. Milo's sport coat had soaked through at the armpits, but the giant hadn't let loose a drop of sweat.

His face tightened some more as he watched the urinating man shake himself off, then duck-walk across the yard, pants still puddled around his ankles.

'Wet.'

'We'll handle it, Chet,' soothed Dollard.

The black tech said, 'I'll go get those trousers up.'

He sauntered toward Sharbno. The white tech stayed with Chet. Dollard gave Chet another pat and we moved on.

Ten yards later, I looked back. Both techs were flanking Chet. The giant's posture had changed – shoulders higher, head craning as he continued to stare at the space vacated by Sharbno.

Milo said, 'Guy that size, how can you control him?'

'We don't control him,' said Dollard. 'Clozapine does. Last month his dosage got upped after he beat the crap out of another patient. Broke about a dozen bones.'

'Maybe he needs even more,' said Milo.

'Why?'

'He doesn't exactly sound coherent.'

Dollard chuckled. 'Coherent.' He glanced at me. 'Know what his daily dosage is, Doctor? Fourteen hundred milligrams. Even with his body weight, that's pretty thorough, wouldn't you say?'

'Maximum's usually around nine hundred,' I told Milo. 'Lots of people do well on a third of that.'

Dollard said, 'He was on eleven migs when he broke the other inmate's face.' Dollard's chest puffed a bit. 'We exceed maximum recommendations all the time; the psychiatrists tell us it's no problem.' He shrugged. 'Maybe Chet'll get even more. If he does something else bad.'

We covered more ground, passing more inmates. Untrimmed hair, slack mouths, empty eyes, stained uniforms. None of the iron-pumper bulk you see in prisons. These torsos were soft, warped, deflated. I felt eyes on the back of my head, glanced to the side, and saw a man with haunted-prophet eyes and a chestful of black beard staring at me. Above the facial pelt, his cheeks were sunken and sooty. Our eyes engaged. He came toward me, arms rigid, neck bobbing. He opened his mouth. No teeth.

He didn't know me but his eyes were rich with hatred.

My hands fisted. I walked faster. Dollard noticed and cocked his head. The bearded man stopped abruptly, stood there in the full sun, planted like a shrub. The red exit sign on the far gate was five hundred feet away. Dollard's key ring jangled. No other techs in sight. We kept walking. Beautiful sky, but no birds. A machine began grinding something.

I said, 'Chet's ramblings. There seems to be some intelligence there.'

'What, 'cause he talks about books?' said Dollard. 'I think before he went nuts he was in college somewhere. I think his family was educated.'

'What got him in here?' said Milo, glancing back.

'Same as all of them.' Dollard scratched his mustache and kept his pace steady. The yard was vast. We were halfway across now, passing more dead eyes, frozen faces, wild looks that set up the small hairs on the back of my neck.

'Don't wear khaki or brown,' Milo had said. 'The inmates wear that, we don't want you stuck in there – though that would be interesting, wouldn't it? Shrink trying to convince them he's not crazy?'

'Same as all of them?' I said.

'Incompetent to stand trial,' said Dollard. 'Your basic 1026.'

'How many do you have here?' said Milo.

'Twelve hundred or so. Old Chet's case is kinda sad. He was living on top of a mountain down near the Mexican border – some kind of hermit deal, sleeping in caves, eating weeds, all that good stuff. Couple of hikers just happened to be unlucky enough to find the wrong cave, wrong time, woke him up. He tore 'em up – really went at 'em with his bare hands. He actually managed to rip both the girl's arms off and was working on one of her legs when they found him. Some park ranger or sheriff shotgunned Chet's leg charging in, that's why it looks like that. He wasn't resisting arrest, just sitting there next to the body pieces, looking scared someone was gonna hit him. No big challenge getting a 1026 on something like that. He's been here three years. First six months he did nothing but stay curled up, crying, sucking his thumb. We had to IV-feed him.'

'Now he beats people up,' said Milo. 'Progress.'

Dollard flexed his fingers. He was in his late fifties, husky and sunburnt, no visible body fat. The lips beneath the mustache were thin, parched, amused. 'What do you want we should do, haul him out and shoot him?'

Milo grunted.

Dollard said, 'Yeah, I know what you're thinking: Good riddance to bad rubbish, you'd be happy to be on the firing squad.' He chuckled. 'Cop thinking. I worked patrol in Hemet for ten years, woulda said the exact same thing before I came here. Couple of years on the wards and now I know reality:

Some of them really *are* sick.' He touched his mustache. 'Old Chet's no Ted Bundy. He couldn't help himself any more than a baby crapping its diaper. Same with old Sharbno back there, pissing in the dirt.' He tapped his temple. 'The wiring's screwy, some people just turn to garbage. And this place is the Dumpster.'

'Exactly why we're here,' said Milo.

Dollard raised an eyebrow. '*That* I don't know about. Our garbage doesn't get taken out. I can't see how we're gonna be able to help you on Dr Argent.'

He flexed his fingers again. His nails were yellow horn. 'I liked Dr Argent. Real nice lady. But she met her end out there.' He pointed randomly. 'Out in the *civilized* world.'

'Did you work with her?'

'Not steadily. We talked about cases from time to time, she'd tell me if a patient needed something. But you can tell about people. Nice lady. A little naive, but she was new.'

'Naive in what way?'

'She started this group. Skills for Daily Living. Weekly discussions, supposedly helping some guys cope with the world. As if any of 'em are ever getting out.'

'She ran it by herself.'

'Her and a tech.'

'Who's the tech?'

'Girl named Heidi Ott.'

'Two women handling a group of killers?'

Dollard smiled. 'The state says it's safe.'

'You think different?'

'I'm not paid to think.'

We neared the chain-link wall. Milo said, 'Any idea why

someone in the civilized world would kill Dr Argent? Speaking as an ex-cop.'

Dollard said, 'From what you told me – the way you found her in that car trunk, all cleaned up – I'd say some sociopath, right? Someone who knew damn well what he was doing, and enjoyed it. More of a 1368 than a 1026 – your basic lowlife criminal trying to fake being crazy 'cause they're under the mistaken impression it'll be easier here than in jail. We've got two, three hundred of *those* on the fifth floor, maybe a few more, 'cause of Three Strikes. They come here ranting and drooling, smearing shit on the walls, learn quickly they can't BS the docs here. Less than one percent succeed. The official eval period's ninety days, but plenty of them ask to leave sooner.'

'Did Dr Argent work on the fifth floor?'

'Nope. Hers were all 1026's.'

'Besides total crazies and ninety-day losers, who else do you have here?' said Milo.

'We've got a few mentally disordered sex offenders left,' said Dollard. 'Pedophiles, that kind of trash. Maybe thirty of 'em. We used to have more but they keep changing the law – stick 'em here, nope, the prison system, oops, back here, unh-uh, prison. Dr Argent didn't hang with them, either, least that I noticed.'

'So the way you see it, what happened to her couldn't relate to her work here.'

'You got it. Even if one of her guys got out – and they didn't – none of them could've killed her and stashed her in the trunk. None of them could plan that well.'

We were at the gate. Tan men standing still, like oversized chess pieces. The faraway machine continued to grind.

Dollard flicked a hand back at the yard. 'I'm not saying these guys are harmless, even with all the dope we pump into them. Get these poor bastards delusional enough, they could do anything. But they don't kill for fun – from what I've seen, they don't take much pleasure from life, period. If you can even call what they're doing living.'

He cleared his throat, swallowed the phlegm. 'Makes you wonder why God would take the trouble to create such a mess.'

2

TWO CORPSES in car trunks. Claire Argent was the second.

The first, found eight months earlier, was a twenty-five-year-old would-be actor named Richard Dada, left in the front storage compartment of his own VW Bug in the industrial zone north of Centinela and Pico – a warren of tool-and-die shops, auto detailers, spare-parts dealers. It took three days for Dada's car to be noticed. A maintenance worker picked up the smell. The crime scene was walking distance from the West LA substation, but Milo drove over to the scene.

In life, Dada had been tall, dark, and handsome. The killer stripped off his clothes, bisected him cleanly at the waist with a tooth-edged weapon, dropped each segment in a heavy-duty black plastic lawn bag, fastened the sacks, stashed them in the Volkswagen, drove to the dump spot, most probably late at night, and escaped without notice. Cause of death was loss of blood from a deep, wide throat slash. Lack of gore in the bags and in the car said the butchery had been accomplished somewhere else. The coroner was fairly certain Dada was already dead when cut in half.

'Long legs,' Milo said, the first time he talked to me about the case. 'So maybe cutting him solved a storage problem. Or it was part of the thrill.'

'Or both,' I said.

He frowned. 'Dada's eyes were taken out, too, but no other mutilation. Any ideas?'

'The killer drove Dada's car to the dump spot,' I said, 'so he could've left on foot and lives close by. Or he took the bus and you could interview drivers, see if any unusual passengers got on that night.'

'I've already talked to the bus drivers. No memory of any conspicuously weird passengers. Same for taxi drivers. No late-night pickups in the neighborhood, period.'

'By "unusual" I didn't mean weird,' I said. 'The killer probably isn't bizarre-looking. I'd guess just the opposite: Composed, a good planner, middle-class. Even so, having just dumped the VW, he might've been a little worked up. Who rides the bus at that hour? Mostly night-shift busboys and office cleaners, a few derelicts. Someone middle-class might be conspicuous.'

'Makes sense,' he said, 'but there was no one who stuck in any of the drivers' memories.'

'OK, then. The third possibility: There was another car ready to take the killer away. Extremely careful planning. Or an accomplice.'

Milo rubbed his face, like washing without water. We were at his desk in the Robbery-Homicide room at the West LA station, facing the bright orange lockers, drinking coffee. A few other detectives were typing and snacking. I had a child-custody court appearance downtown in two hours, had stopped by for lunch, but Milo had wanted to talk about Dada rather than eat.

'The accomplice bit is interesting,' he said. 'So is the local angle – OK, time to do some footwork, see if some joker who learned freelance meat-cutting at San Quentin is out on parole. Get to know more about the poor kid, too – see if he got himself in trouble.'

Three months later, Milo's footwork had unearthed the minutiae of Richard Dada's life but had gotten him no closer to solving the case.

At the half-year mark, the file got pushed to the back of the drawer.

I knew Milo's nerves were rubbed raw by that. His specialty was clearing cold cases, not creating them. He had the highest solve rate of any homicide D in West LA, maybe the entire department for this year. That didn't make him any more popular; as the only openly gay detective on the force, he'd never be invited to blue-buddy barbecues. But it did provide insurance, and I knew he regarded failure as professionally threatening.

As a personal sin, too; one of the last things he'd said before filing the murder book was 'This one deserves more. Some felonious cretin getting bashed with a pool cue is one thing, but this . . . The way the kid was sliced – the spine was sheared straight through, Alex. Coroner says probably a band saw. Someone cut him, neat and clean, the way they section meat.'

'Any other forensic evidence?' I said.

'Nope. No foreign hairs, no fluid exchange . . . As far as I've been able to tell, Dada wasn't in any kind of trouble, no drug connections, bad friends, criminal history. Just one of those stupid kids who wanted to be rich and famous.

Days and weekends he worked at a kiddie gym. Nights he did guess what.'

'Waited tables.'

His index finger scored imaginary chalk marks. 'Bar and grill in Toluca Lake. Closest he got to delivering lines was probably "What kind of dressing would you like with that?"'

We were in a bar, ourselves. A nice one at the rear of the Luxe Hotel on the west end of Beverly Hills. No pool cues, and any felons were wearing Italian suits. Chandeliers dimmed to orange flicker, spongy carpets, club chairs warm as wombs. On our marble-topped drink stand were two leaden tumblers of Chivas Gold and a crystal pitcher of iced spring water. Milo's cheap panatela asserted itself rudely with the Cohibas and Churchills being sucked in corner booths. A few months later, the city said no smoking in bars, but back then, nicotine fog was an evening ritual.

All the trim notwithstanding, the reason for being there was to ingest alcohol, and Milo was doing a good job of that.

I nursed my first scotch as he finished his third and chased it with a glassful of water. 'I got the case because the Lieutenant assumed Dada was gay. The mutilation – when homosexuals freak, they go all the way blah blah blah. But Dada had absolutely no links to the gay community, and his folks say he had three girlfriends back home.'

'Any girlfriends out here?'

'None that I've found. He lived alone in a little studio place near La Brea and Sunset. Tiny, but he kept it neat.'

'That can be a dicey neighborhood,' I said.

'Yeah, but the building had a key-card parking lot and a

security entrance; the landlady lives on the premises and tries to keep a good clientele. She said Dada was a quiet kid, she never saw him entertain visitors. And no signs of a break-in or any burglary. We haven't recovered his wallet, but no charges have been run up on the one credit card he owned – a Discover with a four-hundred-dollar limit. The apartment was clean of dope. If Dada did use, he or someone cleaned up every speck.'

'The killer?' I said. 'That fits with the clean cut and the planning.'

'Possibly, but like I said, Dada lived neat. His rent was seven hundred, he took home twice that a month from both jobs, sent most of his money back home to a savings account.' His big shoulders dropped. 'Maybe he just ran into the wrong psychopath.'

'The FBI says eye mutilation implies more than a casual relationship.'

'Sent the FBI the crime-scene data questionnaire, got back double-talk and a recommendation to look for known associates. Problem is, I can't locate any friends Dada had. He'd only been out in California for nine months. Maybe working two jobs prevented a social life.'

'Or he had a life he hid.'

'What, he *was* gay? I think I would've unearthed that, Alex.'

'Not necessarily gay,' I said. 'Any kind of secret life.'

'What makes you say that?'

'Model tenants just don't walk out on the street and get sawed in half.'

He growled. We drank. The waitresses were all gorgeous

blondes wearing white peasant blouses and long skirts. Ours had an accent. Czechoslovakia, she'd told Milo when he asked; then she'd offered to clip his cigar, but he'd already bitten off the tip. It was the middle of the summer, but a gas fire was raging under a limestone mantel. Air-conditioning kept the room icy. A couple of other beauties at the bar had to be hookers. The men with them looked edgy.

'Toluca Lake is a drive from Hollywood,' I said. 'It's also near the Burbank studios. So maybe Dada was trying to make acting connections.'

'That's what I figured. But if he got a job it wasn't at a studio. I found a want ad from the *Weekly* in the pocket of one of his jackets. Tiny print thing, open casting call for some flick called *Blood Walk*. The date was one month before he was killed. I tried to trace the company that placed the ad. The number was disconnected, but it had belonged at that time to some outfit called Thin Line Productions. That traced to a listing with an answering service, which no longer serviced Thin Line. The address they had was a POB in Venice, long gone, no forwarding. No one in Hollywood's heard of Thin Line, the script's never been registered with any of the guilds, no evidence a movie ever got made. I talked to Petra Connor over in Hollywood. She says par for the course, the *industry's* full of fly-by-nights, most casting calls go nowhere.'

'*Blood Walk*,' I said.

'Yeah, I know. But it was a full month before, and I can't take it any further.'

'What about Richard's other job? Where's the kiddie gym?'

'Pico and Doheny.'

'What'd he do there?'

'Played games with toddlers. Irregular work, mostly birthday parties. The gym owner said he was great – patient, clean-cut, polite.' He shot back whiskey. 'Goddamn Boy Scout and he gets bisected. There has to be more.'

'Some homicidal toddler who resented waiting in line for the Moon Bounce.'

He laughed, studied the bottom of his glass.

'You said he sent money home,' I said. 'Where's that?'

'Denver. Dad's a carpenter, Mom teaches school. They came out for a few days after he was killed. Salt of the earth, hurting bad, but no help. Richard played sports, got B's and C's, acted in all the school plays. Did two years in junior college, hated it, went to work for his father.'

'So he's got carpentry skills – maybe he met the killer at some woodworking class.'

'He never went to classes of any type that I can find.'

'A carpenter's kid and he gets band-sawed,' I said.

He put down his glass, careful to do it silently. His eyes fixed on me. Normally startling green, they were gray-brown in the tobacco light. His heavy face was so pale it looked talced, white as his sideburns. The acne pits that scored his cheeks and chin and brow seemed deeper, crueler.

He pushed black hair off his forehead. 'OK,' he said very softly. 'Besides exquisite *irony*, what does it mean?'

'I don't know,' I said. 'It just seems too cute.'

He frowned, rolled his forearm along the edge of the table as if rubbing an itch, raised his glass for a refill, thanked the waitress when he got it, sipped his way through half the whiskey, and licked his lips. 'Why are we even talking about it? I'm not gonna close this one soon, if ever. I can just feel it.'

I didn't bother arguing. His hunches are usually sound.

Two months later, he caught the Claire Argent homicide and called me right away, sounding furious but sparked by enthusiasm.

'Got a new one, some interesting similarities to Dada. But different, too. Female vic. Thirty-nine-year-old psychologist named Claire Argent – know her, by any chance?'

'No.'

'Home address in the Hollywood Hills, just off Woodrow Wilson Drive, but she was found in West LA territory. Stripped naked and stashed in the trunk of her Buick Regal, back of the loading dock behind the Stereos Galore in that big shopping center on La Cienega near Sawyer.'

That side of La Cienega was West LA's eastern border. 'Barely in your territory.'

'Yeah, Santa loves me. Here's what I know so far: The shopping center closes at eleven, but there's no fence at the dock; anyone can pull in there. Real easy access because an alley runs right behind. West of the alley is a supplementary indoor lot, multiple levels, but it's closed off at night. After that, it's all residential. Private homes and apartments. No one heard or saw a thing. Shipping clerk found the car at six A.M., called for a tow, and when the driver winched it up he heard something rolling around inside and had the smarts to worry about it.'

'Was she cut in half?' I said.

'No, left in one piece, but wrapped in two garbage bags, just like Dada. Her throat was slashed, too, and her eyes were mangled.'

'Mangled how?'

'Chopped into hamburger.'

'But not removed.'

'No,' he said irritably. 'If my storage theory about Richard is correct, it would explain why she wasn't cut in half. Dr Argent was five-five, folded easily into the Buick. And guess where she worked, Alex: Starkweather Hospital.'

'Really,' I said.

'Ghoul Central. Ever been there?'

'No,' I said. 'No reason. None of my patients ever killed anyone.'

3

In the spring of 1981, Emil Rudolph Starkweather died in his bed in Azusa at the age of seventy-six, unmarried, leaving no heirs, having dedicated fifty years to public service, ten as a Water and Power engineer, forty as a state senator.

Tightfisted in every other regard, Starkweather campaigned relentlessly for mental-health funding and pushed through construction of scores of community treatment centers throughout the state. Some said living with and caring for a psychotic sister had made him a one-issue humanist. The sister died five months before Starkweather's massive nocturnal coronary. Soon after her burial, Starkweather's health seemed to rot away.

Not long after his funeral, state auditors discovered that the veteran senator had systematically embezzled four decades of campaign funds for personal use. Some of the money had been spent on the sister's twenty-four-hour nursing care and medical bills, but most went into real estate: Starkweather had amassed an empire of over eleven thousand California acres, primarily vacant lots in run-down neighborhoods that he never developed.

No racehorses, no Swiss accounts, no secret mistresses.

No apparent profit motive of any kind. People started questioning Emil Starkweather's mental health.

The rumors intensified when the will was made public. Starkweather had bequeathed everything to the State of California, with one proviso: At least one hundred acres of 'his' land was to be used for construction of a 'major mental hygiene facility that takes into account the latest research and progress in psychiatry and allied disciplines.'

Legal experts opined that the document was probably worthless, but the knots Starkweather had tied might take years to unravel in court. Yet, in one sense, the timing was perfect for the newly elected governor. No admirer of Starkweather – whom he'd long considered an annoying, eccentric old fart – he'd campaigned as a crime-crusher, condemning revolving-door justice that spat dangerous maniacs back onto the street. Frenzied consultations with legislative bosses produced a plan that cut through the morass, and aides were dispatched from Sacramento to search for worthless publicly owned real estate. The perfect solution emerged quickly: A long-unused parcel of county land well east of the LA city line, once a gas company fuel station, then a garbage dump, now a toxic swamp. Poisoned soil, pollutants seeping past bedrock. Only eighty-nine acres, but who was counting?

Through a combination of executive order and rammed-through legislation, Starkweather's purloined plots reverted to the state, and construction of a 'major mental hygiene facility' for criminals judged incompetent to stand trial was authorized. Secure housing for spree murderers, blood drinkers, cannibals, sodomizers, child-rapers, chanting zombies. Anyone too crazy and too dangerous for San Quentin or Folsom or Pelican Bay.

It was an odd time to build a new hospital. State asylums for the retarded and the harmlessly psychotic were being closed down in rapid succession, courtesy of an odd, cold-hearted alliance between right-wing misers who didn't want to spend the money and left-wing ignoramuses who believed psychotics were political prisoners and deserved to be liberated. A few years later, a 'homeless problem' would appear, shocking the deacons of thrift and the social engineers, but at the time, dismantling an entire inpatient system seemed a clever thing to do.

Still, the governor's storage bin for maniacs went up in two years.

He stuck the old fart's name on it.

Starkweather State Hospital for the Criminally Insane was one main building – a five-story cement-block and gray stucco tower hemmed by twenty-foot-high electrified barbed-wire chain link, streaked with mineral deposits and etched by pollutive grime. Punitively ugly.

We'd gotten off the 10 Freeway, sped past Boyle Heights and several miles of industrial park, traversed a series of dormant oil wells frozen like giant mantis specimens, greasy-gray slaughterhouses and packing plants, abandoned freight yards, several more empty miles that stank of stillborn enterprise.

'Here we go,' said Milo, pointing to a narrow tongue of asphalt labeled Starkweather Drive. Another sign said STATE FACILITY AHEAD.

The road drew the unmarked into a gray-green fringe of eucalyptus maybe seventy trees deep that blessed us with mentholated shade before we reemerged into the August sun and a white glare so piercing it rendered my sunglasses useless.

Up ahead was the high fencing. Electric cables thick and black as water snakes. A collection of English and Spanish warning signs in approved state colors presaged a glassed-in booth and a steel gate arm. The guard was a chunky young man of indeterminate mood who slid open a window, listened to Milo's explanation, took his time coming out. He examined our ID with what seemed like pain, took all the papers back to his glass closet, returned, asked how many firearms or knives we were carrying, and confiscated Milo's service revolver and my Swiss Army knife.

Several minutes later, the gate opened very slowly and Milo drove through. He'd been unusually quiet during the trip. Now he looked uneasy.

'Don't worry,' I said. 'You're not wearing khaki, they'll let you out. If you don't say too much.'

He snorted. What he was wearing was an old maroon hopsack blazer, gray wide-wale cords, gray shirt, wrinkled black poly tie, scuffed beige desert boots with soles the color of pencil erasers. He needed a haircut. Black cowlicks danced atop his big head. The contrast with the now-white side-burns was too strong. Yesterday, he'd made some comment about being Mr Skunk.

The road tilted upward before flattening. We came to an outdoor parking lot, nearly full. Then more chain link, broad stretches of earth, yellow-tinged and sulfurous.

Behind the fence stood a solid-looking man in a plaid sport shirt and jeans. The sound of the unmarked made him turn and study us.

Milo said, 'Our welcoming party,' and began searching for a spot. 'Why the hell would anyone want to work here?'

'Are you asking in general or about Dr Argent?'

'Both. But yeah, her. What would make her choose this?'

It was the day after he'd called me, and I hadn't yet seen the Argent file. 'There's something for everyone,' I said. 'Also, managed care's tightened things up. Could be she had no choice.'

'She had plenty of choice. She quit a research position at County General, neuro-something.'

'Maybe she was doing research here, too.'

'Maybe,' he said, 'but her job title was Psychologist II, pure civil service, and the director – some guy named Swig – didn't mention research. Why would she quit County for this?'

'You're sure she wasn't fired?'

'Her ex-boss at County told me she quit. Dr Theobold.'

'Myron Theobold.'

'Him you know?'

'Met him a few times at faculty meetings. What else did he say?'

'Not much. Like he didn't know her well. Or maybe he was holding back. Maybe you should talk to him.'

'Sure.'

He spotted an opening, swung in sharply, hit the brakes hard. Yanking off his seat belt, he looked through the windshield. The man in the plaid shirt had unlocked the second fence and come closer. He waved. Milo returned the gesture. Fifties, gray hair and mustache.

Milo pulled his jacket from the back seat and pocketed his keys. Gazed beyond the man in the plaid shirt at the chain-link desert. 'She spent eight hours a day here. With deranged, murderous assholes. And now she's dead – wouldn't you call this place a detective's happy hunting ground?'

4

DOLLARD UNLOCKED the rear gate and took us out of the yard and across a short cement path. The gray building appeared like a storm cloud – immense, flat-roofed, slab-faced. No steps, no ramp, just brown metal doors set into the block at ground level. Small sharp-edged letters said STARKWEATHER: MAIN BLDG. Rows of tiny windows checked the cement. No bars across the panes. The glass looked unusually dull, filmed over. Not glass. Plastic. Thick, shatter-proof, wind-whipped nearly opaque. Perhaps clouded minds gained nothing from a clear view.

The doors were unlocked. Dollard shoved the right one open. The reception area was cool, small, ripe with a broiled-meat smell. Pink-beige walls and black linoleum blanched under blue-white fluorescence. Overhead air-conditioning ducts emitted a sound that could have been whispering.

A heavyset, bespectacled woman in her thirties sat behind two old wooden desks arranged in an L, talking on the phone. She wore a sleeveless yellow knit top and a picture badge like Dollard's. Two desk plaques: RULE ONE: I'M ALWAYS RIGHT. RULE TWO: REFER TO RULE ONE. And L. SCHMITZ. Between them was a stack of brochures.

Her phone had a dozen lines. Four lights blinked. On the

wall behind the desk hung a color photo of Emil Starkweather flashing a campaign smile full of bridgework. Above that, a banner solicited employee contributions for Toys for Tots and the United Way. To the left, a small, sagging shelf of athletic trophies and group photos trumpeted the triumphs of 'The Hurlers: Starkweather Hosp. Staff Bowling Team.' First prize for seven years out of ten. Off to the right stretched a long, bright hallway punctuated by bulletin boards and more brown doors.

Dollard stepped up to the desk. L. Schmitz talked a bit more, finally got off. 'Morning, Frank.'

'Morning, Lindeen. These gentlemen are Mr Swig's ten o'clock.'

'He's still on a call, should be right with you. Coffee?'

'No, thanks,' said Dollard, checking his watch.

'Should be soon, Frank.'

Milo picked up two brochures and gave one to me. Lindeen watched him, then got back on the phone and did a lot of 'uh-huh'ing. The next time she put down the receiver, she said, 'You're the police about Dr Argent, right?'

'Yes, ma'am,' said Milo, hovering by the desk. 'Did you know her?'

'Just hello and goodbye. Terrible thing.' She returned to the phone.

Milo stuck around for a few more minutes. Lindeen looked up once to smile at him but didn't interrupt her conversation. He gave me a pamphlet. We both read.

Brief history of Starkweather State Hospital, then a boldtype 'Statement of Purpose.' Lots of photos: More shots of Emil the Embezzler; the governor breaking ground with a gold-tipped shovel, flanked by nameless dignitaries. Construction chronology from excavation to completion. Cranes, earth movers, hard-hatted worker ants. Finally a long view of the building set against a gorgeous sky that looked as false as Starkweather's chompers. The block walls were already stained. The hospital had looked weary on its birthdate.

The mission statement was written by William T. Swig, MPH, Director, and it stressed humane treatment of inmates while safeguarding the public. Lots of talk about goals, directives, objectives, interfaces. Who taught bureaucrats how to write?

I folded the brochure and slipped it in my pocket just as Lindeen said, 'Okey-doke, he's free.'

We followed Dollard down the hall. A few of the brown doors bore name signs in slide-out slots; most were blank. The bulletin boards were layered with state paper: Notices, legislation, regulation. No other people walked the corridor. I realized the place was silent except for the sibilance from the ducts above us.

Swig's door was no different from the rest, his sign no more permanent. Dollard knocked once and opened without waiting for a reply. Outer office. Another receptionist, older and heavier than Lindeen – 'Go right in, Frank.' Three vases of huge yellow roses, obviously homegrown, sat on her desk. Her PC monitor featured a Mona Lisa screen saver. Smiling, frowning, smiling, frowning . . .

Dollard pushed through to the inner sanctum. Swig was on his feet with his hand out as we entered.

He was younger than I'd expected, maybe thirty-five,

sparely built, with a soft, round baby face under a bald dome and several ominous moles on his cheeks and chin. What little hair he did have was blond and cottony. He wore a short-sleeved blue shirt, plaid tie, navy slacks, moccasin loafers.

'Bill Swig.' Introductions all around. Swig's hand was cool and small-boned. His desk was a bit larger than his secretary's, but not by much. No joke plaques here, just a pen-and-pencil set, books and folders, several standing picture frames, their felt backs to us. A photo on the right-hand wall showed Swig in a dark suit with a curly-haired, pointy-chinned woman and two pretty girls around four and six, both Asian. A few books and lots of rubber-banded paper in a single case. Swig's plastic window offered an oily view of the yard.

Dollard said, 'Anything else?'

Swig said, 'No thanks, Frank,' and Dollard hurried out.

'Please, sit. Sorry to keep you waiting. Tragedy, Dr Argent. I'm still shocked.'

'I guess you'd be a hard one to shock, sir,' said Milo.

Swig looked confused.

'Working here,' said Milo. 'The things you see.'

'Oh. No, not really, Detective Sturgis. This is generally a peaceful place. Probably safer than the streets of LA. Especially since the air-conditioning's fixed. No, I'm as shockable as anyone.'

'The air-conditioning?'

'We had a problem,' said Swig. 'The condensers went out a few years ago. Before I arrived.' He raised his hands, palms up. 'My predecessor couldn't get them fixed. As you might imagine, the comfort of our patients isn't a high priority in Sacramento. Staff attrition's what finally did it. People started quitting. I filed a report, we finally got a new system. Today's a perfect example – can you imagine it without AC?'

'How did the inmates handle it?'

Swig sat back. 'It was a bit of a . . . challenge. So . . . how can I help you?'

'Any ideas about Dr Argent's murder?'

Swig shook his head. 'I can understand your thinking it might be work-related, but I term that impossible. Because of one simple fact: Dr Argent's patients are here, and she was murdered out there.' He pointed at the window. 'Add to that the fact that her tenure was totally trouble-free, and there's nothing to work with, is there?'

'Model employee?'

'I was very impressed with her. Calm, level, thoughtful. Everyone liked her. Including the patients.'

'That makes the patients sound rational,' said Milo.

'Pardon?'

'The patients liked her, so they wouldn't hurt her. I thought the men here didn't operate out of any logical motive pattern. So what's to say one of them didn't hear a voice telling him to cut Dr Argent's throat?'

No mention of the eyes. He was keeping that confidential.

Swig tightened his lips. 'Yes. Well, they are psychotic, but most of them are very well maintained. But what's the difference? The main point is, they don't leave here.'

Milo took out his pad and scrawled for a while. That almost always gets a reaction. Swig raised his eyebrows.

They were pale blond, nearly invisible, and the movement created two crescent-shaped wrinkles above his clear blue eyes.

Milo's pen stopped moving. He said, 'No one *ever* gets out?'

Swig shifted in his chair. 'I won't tell you never. But *very*, *very* rarely.'

'How rare?'

'Only two percent even attempt to obtain release, and most of those never make it past our review committee. Of those who are reviewed, perhaps five percent succeed in obtaining conditional release. That means placement in well-supervised board and care, regular outpatient treatment, and random urinalysis to monitor medication compliance. Additionally, they must continue to show absolutely no symptoms of dangerous decompensation. Any minor infraction lands them back here. Of those who do leave, the revocation rate is still eighty percent. Since I've been here, never has a released patient committed a violent felony. So, for all practical purposes, it's a non-issue.'

'How long have you been here?'

'Five years.'

'Before that?'

'Before that, there were a few problems.'

'So,' said Milo, scanning his notes. 'With so few men released, it should be easy enough to track those who've gotten out.'

Swig clapped his hands together very softly. 'Yes, but that would require a court order. Even our men have rights – for example, we can't monitor their mail without clear evidence of infraction.'

'You can dose them, but no snooping?'

'The difference is that dosing them is for their own good.' Swig wheeled his chair forward. 'Look, I'm not trying to make your job difficult, Detective, but I really don't get this line of questioning. I can understand your initial assumption: Dr Argent worked with dangerous individuals, and now she's been murdered. On the face of it, that's logical. But as I said, it's probably safer at Starkweather than on your beat.'

'So you're telling me I need to file papers to find out who's been released.'

'I'm afraid so. Believe me, if there was some obvious risk, don't you think I'd let you know? If only for our sake. We can't afford errors.'

'OK,' said Milo with an ease that made me glance at him. 'Let's move on. What can you tell me about Dr Argent's personality?'

'I didn't know her well,' said Swig, 'but she was competent, quiet, businesslike. No conflicts with staff or patients.' He picked up a folder and scanned the contents. 'Here's something I can give you. Her personnel file.'

'Thank you, sir.' Milo took it and handed it to me and resumed jotting notes. Inside were Claire Argent's job application, an abbreviated résumé, and a headshot photo. The résumé was five pages thick. Several published studies. Neuropsychology. Reaction time in alcoholics. Solid journals. A clinical appointment as a lecturer. Why *had* she quit to come here?

The picture revealed a pretty, slightly broad face brightened by a shy half-smile. Thick, dark hair, shoulder-length, flipped at the edges, feathery bangs, white hairband, baby blue crewneck top. Clear skin, very little makeup, big dark eyes. The first adjective that came to my mind was 'wholesome.' Maybe a little too ingenue for someone her age, though she looked closer to thirty than the thirty-nine established by her birthdate.

No date on the photo, so maybe it had been snapped years earlier. She'd gotten her PhD ten years ago. Graduation shot? I continued to study her face. The eyes were lustrous, warm – her best feature.

Now mangled. Someone's trophy?

'I'm afraid I can't tell you much,' said Swig. 'We've got a staff of over a hundred, including more than twenty psychologists and psychiatrists.'

'The others are psych techs like Mr Dollard?'

'Techs, nonpsychiatric physicians, nurses, pharmacists, secretaries, cooks, plumbers, electricians, custodians.'

'And you don't know if any of them had some kind of relationship with Dr Argent away from work?'

'I'm afraid not.'

'Did she work with any staff members consistently?'

'I'd have to check on that.'

'Please do.'

'Certainly. It will take a few days.'

Milo took the file from me, opened it, flipped pages. 'I appreciate your letting us have this, Mr Swig. When I saw her she looked quite different.'

As if warding off the comment, Swig turned to me. 'You're a psychologist, Dr Delaware? Forensic?'

'Clinical. I do occasional consulting.'

'Have you worked much with dangerous psychotics?'

'I rotated through Atascadero as an intern, but that's about it.'

'Atascadero must have been pretty tough back then.'

'Tough enough,' I said.

'Yes,' he said. 'Before us, they were the toughest place. Now they're handling mostly MDSO's – sex offenders.' His tone was dismissive.

'You have some of them, too, right?' said Milo.

'A few,' said Swig. 'Incorrigibles who happened to come up for sentencing when the law-of-the-week said hospitalization. Nowadays, they go to jail. We haven't accepted any in years.'

That made the hospital sound like a college. I said, 'Are the sex offenders housed with the regular population or up on the top floor with the 1368's?'

Swig touched one of his moles. 'Regular population. The 1368's are a completely different situation. They're boarders, not residents. The court orders us to screen them. We keep them totally isolated on the fifth floor.'

'Bad influences on the 1026's?' said Milo.

Swig laughed. 'I don't think the 1026's can be influenced too easily. No, it's all the traffic and the escape risk. They come in and out on sheriff's buses – what they really want isn't treatment, it's out.' He sat back, touched some of the moles on his face. Fingering them carefully, like a blind man reading braille. 'We're talking about malingering criminals who think they can drool and avoid San Quentin. We evaluate them, ship them back.'

His voice had climbed and his skin had pinkened.

'Sounds like a hassle,' I said.

'It's a distraction from our main goal.'

Milo said, 'Managing the 1026's.'

'Treating insane murderers and keeping them invisible. From the public. Every one of our men has committed the proverbial "senseless crime." On the outside, you hear nonsense like "Anyone who kills has to be crazy." Doctor, you of course know that's garbage. Most murderers are perfectly sane. Our men are the exception. They terrify the public – the apparent randomness of their crimes. They have motives, but not the kind the public can relate to. I'm sure you understand, Dr Delaware.'

'Voices in the head,' I said.

'Exactly. It's like sausage making. The less the public knows about what we do, the better off we and the public are. That's why I hope Claire's murder doesn't put us in the spotlight.'

'No reason for that,' said Milo. 'The sooner I clear the case, the faster I'm out of your life.'

Swig nodded and worried another mole. 'Is there anything else?'

'What, specifically, did Dr Argent do here?'

'What any psychologist would do. Behavior modification plans for individual patients, some counseling, some group work – truthfully, I don't know the details.'

'I heard she ran a group called Skills for Daily Living.'

'Yes,' said Swig. 'She asked permission to start that a few months ago.'

'Why, if the men don't get out?'

'Starkweather's also an environment. It needs to be dealt with.'

'How many men were in the group?'

'I have no idea. The clinical decisions were hers.'

'I'd like to meet with them.'

'Why?'

'In case they know something.'

'They don't,' said Swig. 'How could they – no, I'm afraid I can't let you do that. Too disruptive. I'm not sure any of them even realize what happened to her.'

'Are you going to tell them?'

'That would be a clinical decision.'

'Made by who?'

'The clinician in charge – probably one of our senior psychiatrists. Now, if that's all—'

'One more thing,' said Milo. 'Dr Argent had a good position at County Hospital. Any idea why she switched jobs?'

Swig allowed himself a small smile. 'What you're really asking is why would she leave the glorious world of academic medicine for our little snakepit. During her job interview she told me she wanted a change of pace. I didn't discuss it further. I was happy to have someone with her qualifications come aboard.'

'Did she say anything else during the interview that would help me?'

Swig's mouth puckered tight. He picked up a pencil and tapped the desktop. 'She was very quiet – not shy. More like self-possessed. But pleasant – very pleasant. It's a terrible thing that happened to her.'

He stood. We did, too. Milo thanked him.

'I wish I could do more, Detective.'

'Actually,' said Milo, 'we wouldn't mind taking a look

around – just to get a feel for the place. I promise not to disrupt anyone clinically, but maybe I could chat with some of the staff Dr Argent worked with?'

The white eyebrows climbed again. 'Sure, why not.' Swig opened the door to the front room. His secretary was arranging roses.

'Letty,' he said, 'please call Phil Hatterson down. Detective Sturgis and Dr Delaware are going to get a little tour.'

5

Phil Hatterson was short, pear-shaped, middle-aged, with Silly Putty features and thinning brown hair. His mouse-colored mustache was feathery and offered no shelter to plump, dark lips.

'Pleased to meet you,' he said, offering the firm, pumping handshake of a club chairman.

His eyes were hazel, alert, and inquisitive, but soft – like those of a tame deer.

His shirt and pants were khaki.

We followed him at a distance.

'First floor's all offices,' he said cheerfully. His walk was odd – small, neat, dancelike steps that forced us to slow down. 'Not docs' offices, just administration. The docs circulate through offices on the wards.'

His smile begged for approval. I managed an upturned lip. Milo wasn't having any part of it.

Toward the end of the hall, at the right, were two double-width elevators, one key-operated that said STAFF ONLY, the other with a call button, which Hatterson pushed. Milo watched Hatterson intently. I knew exactly what he was thinking: *The inmates run the asylum.*

The elevator didn't respond but Hatterson was unbothered, bouncing on his feet like a kid waiting for dessert. No floor-number guide above the doors, no grinding gears. Then a voice came out of the wall – out of a small square of steel mesh surrounding the button.

'Yes?' Male voice, electronically detached.

'Hatterson, Phillip Duane.'

'ID.'

'Five two one six eight. You just let me down to see Administrator Swig. Administrator Swig just called to authorize me back up.'

'Hold on.' Three beats. 'Where you heading?'

'Just up to Two. I've got two gentlemen taking a tour – a police officer and a doctor.'

'Hold on,' the voice repeated. Seconds later, the elevator doors slid open. Hatterson said, 'After you, sirs.'

Wondering whom I was turning my back on, I complied. The lift was walled with thick foam. Interior key lock. Sickly-sweet disinfectant permeated the foam.

The doors closed. As we rose, Hatterson said, 'Up up and away.' He was standing in the middle of the car. I'd pressed myself into a corner, and so had Milo.

The elevator let us out into another pink-beige hallway. Brown double doors with plastic windows. Key locks. Wall speaker similar to that near the elevator. A sign above the door said A WARD. Hatterson pushed a button, talked to someone, and the doors clicked open.

At first glance, the second floor resembled any hospital ward, except for a nursing station completely encased by plastic. A sign said MED LINE FORM HERE, NO PUSHING. Three white-uniformed women sat inside, talking. Nearby, a gurney was pushed to the wall. Brown stains on white cotton sheeting.

The same black linoleum and brown doors as the first floor. Very low ceilings – no higher than seven feet. Khaki'd figures roamed the halls. Many of the taller inmates stooped. So did some short men. A few inmates sat on white plastic benches. Bolted to the floor. Others rocked in place; several just stood there. The arms of the chairs were drilled through with one-inch-diameter holes. Handcuff slots.

I tried to look around without being conspicuous.

Black men, white men, brown men, yellow men.

Young men with surfer-blond hair and testosterone posture, callow enough for acne but ancient around the eyes. Old men with toothless, caved-in faces and hyperactive tongues. Gape-jawed catatonics. Ragged, muttering apparitions not much different from any Westside panhandler. Some of the men, like Hatterson, looked relatively normal.

Every one of them had destroyed human life.

We passed them, enduring a psychotic gauntlet, receiving a full course of stares. Hatterson paid no notice as he dance-stepped us through.

One of the young ones smirked and took a step forward. Patchy hair and chin beard, swastika tattoo on his forearm. White welted scars on both wrists. He swayed and smiled, sang something tuneless, and moved on. A Hispanic man with a braid dangling below his belt drank from a paper cup and coughed as we neared, splashing pink liquid. Someone passed wind. Someone laughed. Hatterson sped up a bit. So many brown doors, marked only by numbers. Most bore small, latched rectangles. Peephole covers.

Halfway down the hall, two black men with matted hair – careless dreadlocks – faced each other from opposite sides. From a distance their stance mimicked a conversation, but as we got closer I saw that their faces weren't moving and their eyes were distant and dead.

The man on the right had his hand in his fly and I could see rapid movement beneath the khaki. Hatterson noticed it too, and gave a prissy look. A few feet away, an avuncular type – seventyish, white-haired as Emil Starkweather, wearing rimless eyeglasses and a white cardigan sweater over his beige shirt – leaned against the wall reading *The Christian Science Monitor*.

Someone cried out. Someone laughed.

The air was frigid, a good deal colder than down in Swig's office. We passed an obese, gray-haired man sitting on a bench, soft arms as thick as my thighs, face flushed and misshapen, like an overripe melon. He sprang up and suddenly his face was in mine, blowing hot, sour breath.

'If you're lost, that's the way out.' He pointed to one of the brown doors.

Before I could respond, a young woman appeared and took him by the elbow.

He said, 'If you're lost—'

The woman said, 'It's OK, Ralph, no one's lost.'

'If you're lost—'

'That's enough, Ralph.' Sharp voice now. Ralph hung his head.

The woman wore a green-striped badge that said H. OTT, PT-I.

Claire's group-therapy tech. She wore a long-sleeved chambray shirt, rolled to the elbows and tucked into snug jeans that showed off a tight shape. Not a large woman – five-six and small-boned. She looked maybe twenty-five, too young to wield authority. Her dishwater hair was gathered in a tight knot, exposing a long face, slightly heavy in the jaw, with strong, symmetrical features. She had wide-set blue eyes, the clear, rosy complexion of a farm girl. Ralph had six inches and at least a hundred and fifty pounds on her. He remained in her grasp, looking remorseful.

'OK, now,' she told him, 'why don't you go rest.' She rotated him. Her body moved smoothly. Taut curves, small bust, long smooth neck. I could see her playing volleyball on the beach. What did the men in khaki see?

Ralph tried again: 'If you're lost, that's the way . . .' His voice caught on the last word.

Heidi Ott said, 'No one's lost.' Louder, firmer.

A tear fell from Ralph's eye. Heidi Ott gave him a gentle push and he shuffled off. A few of the other men had watched, but most seemed oblivious.

'Sorry,' she said to us. 'He thinks he's a tour guide.' The blue eyes settled on Hatterson. 'Keeping busy, Phil?'

Hatterson drew himself up. 'I'm giving them a tour, Miss Ott. This is Detective Sturgis from the LAPD, and this is a doctor – sorry, I forgot your name, sir.'

'Delaware.'

Heidi Ott said, 'Pleased to meet you.'

Hatterson said, 'The thing about Ralph is, he used to cruise the freeways, pick up people having car trouble. He'd offer to help them and then he'd—'

'Phil,' said Heidi Ott. 'You know we respect each other's privacy.'

Hatterson let out a small, tight bark. Pursed his lips. Annoyed, not regretful. 'Sorry.'

Heidi Ott turned to Milo. 'You're here about Dr Argent?' Her lips pushed together and paled. Young skin, but tension caused it to pucker.

'Yes, ma'am,' said Milo. 'You worked with her, didn't you?'

'I worked with a group she ran. We had contact about several other patients.' The blue eyes blinked twice. Less force in her voice. Now she seemed her age.

Milo said, 'When you have a chance, I'd like to—'

Screams and thumps came from behind us. My head whipped around.

The two dreadlocked men were on the floor, a double dervish, rolling, punching, clawing, biting. Moving slowly, deliberately, silently. Like pit bulls.

Other men started to cheer. The old man with *The Christian Science Monitor* slapped his knee and laughed. Only Phil Hatterson seemed frightened. He'd gone white and seemed to be searching for a place to hide.

Heidi Ott snapped a whistle out of her pocket, blew hard, and marched toward the fighters. Suddenly, two male techs were at her side. The three of them broke up the fight within seconds.

The dreadlocked men were hauled to their feet. One was

bleeding from his left cheek. The other bore a scratch on his forearm. Neither breathed hard. Both looked calm, almost serene.

The old man with the newspaper said, 'By golly fuck!'

Heidi took the bleeder by the arm and led him to the nurses' station. Button-push, click, and she received something from a slot in the front window. Swabs and antibiotic cream. As she ministered to the bleeder, some of the men in khaki began to come alive. Shifting position, flexing arms, looking in all directions.

The hallway smelled of aggression. Phil Hatterson sidled closer to Milo. Milo stared him still. His hands were fisted.

One of the male techs, a short, husky Filipino, said, 'OK, everyone. Just settle down *now*.'

The hallway went quiet.

Hatterson gave out a long, loud exhalation. 'I hate when stupid stuff happens. What's the point?'

Heidi hustled the bleeder around the nursing station and out of sight.

Hatterson said, 'Gentlemen?' and we resumed our tour. Most of his color had returned. I wouldn't have picked him for any pathology worse than oily obsequiousness – Eddie Haskell misplaced among the lunatics, annoying but coherent. I knew many psychotics were helped mightily by drugs. Could this be chemistry at its best?

He said, 'Here's my favorite place. The TV room.'

The ward had ended and we were facing the open doorway of a large bright space filled with plastic chairs. A big-screen TV stood at the front like an altar.

Hatterson said, 'The way we choose what to watch is with democracy – everyone who wants to vote, votes. The majority rules. It's pretty peaceful – picking shows, I mean. I like news but I don't get to watch it too often, but I also like sports and almost everyone votes for sports, so it's OK. There's our mailbox.'

He pointed to a hard plastic box fastened to the wall. Rounded edges. Chain-locked. 'Our mail's private unless there's a mitigating circumstance.'

'Such as?' I said.

The question frightened him. 'Someone acts out.'

'Does that happen often?'

'No, no.' His eyelids fluttered. 'The docs do a great job.'

'Dr Argent, too?' said Milo.

'Sure, of course.'

'So you knew her.'

Hatterson's hands made tiny circular motions. He licked his lips and turned them the color of raw liver. 'We didn't do any counseling together, but I knew who she was. Very nice lady.' Another lip-lick. 'I mean, she seemed very smart – she was nice.'

'Do you know what happened to her?'

Hatterson stared at the floor. 'Sure.'

'Does everyone?'

'I can't speak for anyone, sir. It was in the paper.'

'They let you read the paper?' said Milo.

'Sure, we can read anything. I like *Time* magazine, you get all the news in a neat little package. Anyway, that's it for A Ward. B and C are mostly the same. There's a few women on C. They don't cause any problems.'

'Are they kept to themselves?' I said.

'No, they get to mingle. There's just not too many of them. We don't have problems with them.'

'What about the fifth floor?' said Milo.

'Oh,' said Hatterson. 'The 13's. Naw, we never see them except to look out the window when a sheriff's bus brings them in. They wear jail blues, go straight up their own elevator. They're . . .'

He shrugged.

'They're what?' I said.

'Fakers. Got no stake here. Anyway, we've got some pretty nice rooms, let me show 'em to you – here's an open one we can take a look at.'

The space was generous, totally bare, clean as a Marine barracks. Four beds, one for each corner: Mattresses set into white molded-plastic frames attached to the floor. Next to each one, a nightstand of the same material.

A single clouded window offered a few square inches of cottony light.

Three of the beds were made up neatly, top sheets tucked tight. One was jumbled. No closets. A doorless entry led to a tiny white lav. Lidless white toilet, white sink. No medicine cabinet, no toiletries, no toothbrushes. Anything was a potential weapon.

'They give us disposables,' said Hatterson, as if following my thoughts. 'Aftershave, brushes, shaving cream, safety razors under supervision. Guys who want to shave use electrics that are sterilized and reused.' He looked disapprovingly at the unmade bed. 'Someone must be having a bad day . . . We can't hang anything on the wall because it could be set on fire. So there's no family pictures or anything like that. But it's not bad, right?'

Milo grunted.

Hatterson flinched, but persisted: 'We get our three squares, the food's pretty tasty.'

Chapter president of the Starkweather Chamber of Commerce. I could see why Swig had picked him. He led us out of the room. 'And that's about all she wrote, folks.'

'Are all the rooms multiple occupancy?' I said, wondering how roommates were chosen.

'Except for the S&R's – Suppression and Restraint. Those come one to a customer. You can tell which ones they are because they have an S after the number.' He pointed. 'They're basically the same, except smaller, 'cause it's only one patient.'

'Does Suppression and Restraint mean straitjackets?' said Milo. 'Padded walls like the elevator?'

Hatterson's mustache vibrated. 'No padding, but sure, if someone needs a straitjacket, we've got 'em. But hopefully, if you behave yourself after you earn an S&R, you earn out of there in a jif. I couldn't say from direct experience, but that's what I imagine.'

Pride of ownership; he gave denial new meaning. I saw the revulsion in Milo's eyes.

We stood in the empty room as Hatterson prattled on about the food. Fridays were still fish, even though the pope said meat was OK. Vitamin pills, too. The patients were well taken care of.

An operator; there's one in every setting. A gossip, too, eager to tell us about Ralph's criminal history. Was he Swig's stoolie? Risky business on a ward full of murderers.

Might as well take advantage. I said, 'What wards did Dr Argent work on?'

Hatterson stopped. 'I guess she worked all over the place. The docs all do – they move around. Most of them don't even have permanent offices, they just share desks for charting.'

'Where are the charts kept?'

'In the nursing station.'

'What exactly did Dr Argent do here?' I said.

'I guess counseling.'

'What do you know about her group – Skills for Daily Living?'

'Just that she started it a few months ago. Picked some weird guys for it.'

'Weird in what way?'

'Messed-up guys,' said Hatterson. He tapped his temple. 'You know, low-functioning guys.'

Milo said, 'What was the point? No one gets out of here, right?'

Hatterson whitened. His head began to droop and remained low, as if straining under impossible weight. The plump lips rotated.

'Right,' he said.

'It's not right?'

'No, no, yes it is.'

'Did joining Dr Argent's group help someone *earn* release?' said Milo.

'Not that I heard, sir.'

'Did any of the group members get out?'

Hatterson shook his head. 'No, it was just about – learning

to do things for yourself. I guess Dr Argent wanted to help them feel better about themselves.'

'Improve their self-esteem,' said Milo.

Hatterson brightened. 'You got it. You can't love others 'less you love yourself. She knew what she was doing, the docs here are smart. OK, I'll call and get us up to B.'

The two upper wards were laid out identically to A. On C the hallway teemed, but no female inmates were in sight. We walked through quickly. No fights, nothing untoward; the same mix of degraded muscles, stupor and self-absorption, occasional dark stares rife with paranoia, a few serpentine tongue-flicks and jumpy muscles that said phenothiazine drug side effects. Hatterson moved us through quickly, no more happy chatter. He seemed defeated, almost peevish.

With his chatter gone, the corridors were stripped of conversation. No discourse among the inmates.

Here, every man *was* an island.

I supposed Swig was right; his charges would be easier to control than simple criminals. Because once the violent impulses were held in check, psychosis was a custodian's friend, neurochemically suppressing and restraining as the disease blunted initiative, squelched the spark of freshness and novelty.

Medication helped, too. To handle violent psychotics, the trick was to find a drug that soothed the occasional fried synapse, squelched rage, hushed the little voices that commanded mayhem.

But take away the violence and you didn't have serenity. What remained were what psychiatrists labeled the negative symptoms of psychosis: Apathy, flat mood, deadened voice, blunted movement, impoverished thinking, language stripped of nuance and humor. An existence devoid of surprise and joy.

That explained the ambient silence. The lack of noise wasn't peaceful. The ward felt like a crypt.

A psych tech came by wheeling a food cart. I found myself welcoming the jangle.

Hatterson took us to the C Ward elevator. Milo said, 'Let's go up to Five.'

'Sorry,' said Hatterson. 'I'm not authorized. No one is, not even the docs unless they get an order to evaluate a 13.'

'You know a lot about this place,' I said.

Hatterson shrugged. As we waited for the lift to arrive, I peered through the plastic panels on the door and watched the traffic on the ward. Techs moving around confidently, unarmed; a black nurse emerging from the station with a clipboard and making her way down the corridor with a high-hipped trot. Inmates not doing much of anything.

I thought of how Heidi Ott had handled Ralph and the fighters. In a jail, a skirmish like that could have led to full-scale rioting.

So Starkweather was indeed a tight ship. Full of one-way passengers.

Meaning the chance that Claire Argent's work had anything to do with her murder *was* remote.

But had the system broken down somehow? A released man 'acting out' in the worst way?

Maybe Heidi could tell us. She'd worked with Claire Argent on the Living Skills group . . . low-functioning men, according to Hatterson. What had Claire had in mind when setting up the sessions?

Why had she *come* here?

Hatterson said, 'Here's some docs.'

Three men came through the door. Shirts and ties, no white coats, badges with yellow bars. No outward sign that a colleague had been slashed to death and stuffed in a car trunk.

Milo said, 'Excuse me,' showed his badge, explained his purpose. The man in the middle was tall, sandy-haired, weathered-looking, in his sixties. Green plaid shirt, yellow knit tie. He said, 'Terrible thing. I wish you luck.' V. N. Aldrich, MD, Psychiatrist III.

Milo said, 'If there's anything anyone can tell me that might help . . .'

No responses. Then a bald, dark-bearded man said, 'Claire seemed very nice, but I can't say I knew her.' C. Steenburg, PhD.

The third man was short and ruddy. D. Swenson, MD. He shook his head. 'She was comparatively new, wasn't she, Vern?'

Aldrich said, 'Just a few months. I was her nominal supervisor on a few cases. Her work was fine.'

'Nominal?' I said.

'I'm the senior psychiatrist on day shift, so, officially, she reported to me. But she didn't need much supervision. Very bright. I'm terribly sorry about what happened. We all are.'

Nods all around.

'What kind of work did she do here?' I said.

'Mostly behavior modification – setting up contingency schedules – rewards for good behavior, withdrawal of privileges for infractions. That kind of thing.' Aldrich smiled. 'I won't claim to be an expert on her work product. We're pretty autonomous around here. Claire was very well trained, used to work at County General.'

'Any idea why she transferred?' I said.

'She said she needed a change. I got a sense she didn't want to talk about it. My feeling is that she'd simply had enough of what she was doing. I used to be in private practice, retired, got bored with golf, came here.'

'Did you get the sense that she needed more human contact than neuropsych provided?' I asked. It was a psychologist's question, not a cop's, and Aldrich studied me.

'I suppose,' he said. 'In any event, I don't imagine any of this has much to do with what happened to her.'

'Why's that?' said Milo.

'She got killed out there.' Aldrich pointed to a wall. 'The wonderful, democratic, *normal* world.' He looked over at Hatterson as if first noticing the little man, laced his hands behind his back, scanned Hatterson from toe-tip to head. 'Circulating, Phil?'

'Mr Swig asked me to show them around, Dr Aldrich.'

'I see. Well, do that, then.' Aldrich faced Milo. 'I wish we could help you, Detective, but we're all stymied.'

'So you've discussed what happened?'

The three of them exchanged looks.

'Yes, of course,' said Aldrich. 'We were all upset. What we found out is that none of us knew Dr Argent. It spurred us to be more social with each other. Good luck getting to the bottom of it.'

'One more thing,' said Milo. 'The group Dr Argent ran,

Skills for Daily Living. Would it be possible to meet with the patients?'

'You'd have to check with administration on that,' said Aldrich.

'Would you see a problem with it? Medically speaking.'

Aldrich tugged at his tie. 'Let me look into that. I want to make sure we don't . . . upset anything.'

'Appreciate it, Doctor.' Milo gave him and the others business cards.

The elevator arrived. Aldrich said, 'You three ride down first. We'll catch it next time.'

As we descended, Hatterson said, 'Dr Aldrich is very, very smart.'

Milo said, 'How long have you been here, Phil?'

Hatterson's head drew back like that of a turtle poked with a stick. His reply was inaudible.

'What's that, Phil?'

Hatterson began smoothing his mustache. Chomped his lower lip with his upper teeth. 'A long time.'

He stayed in the car and waved us out.

'Goddamn weenie,' said Milo, as we walked back toward the reception area. 'Didn't get a chance to speak with the Ott girl – better get her home number and follow up. Everyone here spouts the same line: "This place is as safe as milk." You buy it?'

'They broke up that fight pretty fast.'

'Yeah, OK, let's assume they've got the lunatics well controlled. You see anything that would lure Claire away from County?'

'Maybe all the structure,' I said. 'No more applying for grants or having to play the academic game. Aldrich said she talked about needing a change.'

'Structured or not, the place creeps me out . . . We didn't even scratch the surface, did we?'

'Maybe there's nothing below the surface.'

He didn't answer. We passed Swig's office. The door was closed. 'OK, I'll get Ms Ott's number, then we fly out of here. If you've got time, I can show you Argent's house. Out in the evil, messy, *normal* world. The longer I stay here, the more I crave the insanity out there.'

Lindeen Schmitz was back on the phone and she barely looked up. Milo stationed himself in front of her desk and leaned forward, imposing on her space. Where does a frustrated, six-three, 240-pound cop stand? Anywhere he wants.

She tried to 'uh-huh' her way through a conversation that was clearly personal, finally said, 'Gotta go,' and hung up.

'Yes, sir?'

Milo grinned down at her. 'I need to do some follow-up with one of your staffers. Heidi Ott. May I have her home number, please?'

'Um, I'm not sure I can do that without authorization. And Mr Swig's gone – Oh, what the hey, you're the police. You can always get it anyway, in one of those backwards directories, right?' Batting her lashes, she left her desk, sashayed up the hall to the closest brown door, came back with a message blank, and gave it to Milo. Neatly printed name and number, 213 area code.

Milo gave a small bow. 'Thank you, ma'am.'

'No problem, *sir*.' More eyelash aerobics. 'I hope you find whoever did it.'

Milo thanked her again and we headed for the main doors.

Lindeen said, 'Why do you want to speak to Heidi?'

'She worked with Dr Argent.'

Lindeen picked up a pencil and tapped the edge of her desk. 'I don't think they were friends or anything. Dr Argent didn't have any friends that I saw. Real quiet. When a bunch of us went for margaritas or something we asked her along, but she always said no, so we stopped asking. I figured she was shy. But still, it's so horrible what happened to her. When I heard, I just couldn't believe it, someone you see every day and then they're just . . .' She snapped a finger. 'She used to walk right past me every morning at eight, pronto, say good morning, walk on like she had a big plan for the day. It's so . . . horrible.'

'Yes it is,' said Milo. 'So she didn't have any pals at all?'

'Not that I saw. She always seemed like work, work, work. Nice, but work, work, work. Hope you solve it.'

She reached for the phone. Milo said, 'Pardon me, ma'am. Just one more thing I'm curious about.'

Her hand rested on the receiver. 'What's that?'

'The guy who took us around – Hatterson. What's he in for?'

'Oh, *him*,' she said. 'Why, was there some kind of problem?'

'No. Does he cause problems?'

She snorted. 'Not hardly.'

'The reason I'm asking is, he didn't seem very crazy.

I'm just wondering what kind of guy gets to be a tour guide.'

'Phil,' she said, pronouncing the name with distaste. 'Phil raped a child so bad she needed reconstructive surgery.'

6

Frank Dollard was waiting for us, outside. He walked us across the yard without comment. Giant Chet stood in a corner, staring at chain link. Sharbno the urinator was gone. A few men palsied, a few men sat in the dirt. The sun was even hotter.

Dollard waited as we retrieved Milo's gun and my knife. The outer gate swung open.

Milo said, 'Let me ask you a question, Frank. A guy like Hatterson – in prison he'd be lunch meat.'

Dollard smiled. 'So what's his status here? Low. Same as everyone. For all I know, the other guys don't even know what he did. They don't care much about each other – that's the point. They're not *connected*.'

Driving through the eucalyptus grove, Milo began to laugh.

'What?' I said.

'How's this for a story line: We catch the bad guy; he's some joker they let out by mistake. He pleads insanity, ends up right back here.'

'Sell it to Hollywood – no, not stupid enough.'

We left the grove, passed into white light. 'Then again,

you tell me our boy probably doesn't act or look crazy, so maybe I should forget about this place.'

'My guess is our boy is probably more like a fifth-floor resident.'

'So do I bother looking for a recently released Starkweather alum? And what's with that group Claire ran? Why do low-functioning guys need daily living skills? Unless she had a notion some of them would end up on the outside.'

'Maybe it was altruism,' I said. 'Misguided or otherwise. Heidi Ott might be able to shed some light on it. She'd also be able to tell you if any of Claire's patients have been released recently.'

'Yeah, she's definitely high on my list. Tough kid, the way she handled that Ralph guy. Can you imagine a female coming in here, day in and day out?' He drove off Starkweather Drive and back onto the connecting road. The bare gray acreage appeared, then the first of the packing plants, gigantic and soot-stained. Behind the shadowy columns, the blue sky seemed like an insult.

Milo said, 'I'm neglecting basic detective dogma: Lay your foundation. Get to know the vic. Trouble is, I'm getting the same feeling about Claire that I did about Dada. Grabbing air. She lived alone, no obvious kinks so far, no pals I can locate, no local family. You heard the way everyone at Starkweather described her: Nice, did her job, stayed to herself. Offended no one. Richard's spiritual sister. So what do we have here, a psychopath who goes after *inoffensive* people?'

'Assuming the cases are related, maybe someone who goes after lonely people.'

'Then half of LA's at risk.'

'Where is Claire's family?'

'Pittsburgh. Just her parents – she was an only child.' He chewed his cheek. 'I did the notification call. You know the drill: I ruin their lives, they cry, I listen. They're coming out this week; maybe I'll get more than I did over the phone, which was: Claire had no enemies, terrific daughter, wonderful girl. They're always wonderful girls.'

We cut through industrial wasteland. Mounds of rotting machinery, slag heaps, muddy trenches, planes of greasy dirt. Under a gray sky, it could have passed for hell. Today, it just looked like something you kept from the voting public.

Milo wasn't noticing the scenery. Both his hands were back on the wheel, tight-knuckled, white.

'Lonely people,' he said. 'Let me show you her house.'

He drove much too fast all the way to the freeway. As we swooped up the on-ramp, he said, 'I was up there for a good part of yesterday, checking out the street, talking to neighbors. Home's the big killing spot for females, so I told the crime-scene guys to take their time. Unfortunately, it looks like time ill spent. Got some prelims this morning: No blood or semen, no evidence of break-in or disruption. Lots of prints all over the place, which you'd expect in anyone's house, but so far, the only matches are to Claire's. Final autopsy's scheduled for tomorrow if we're lucky and no drive-bys stuff up the pipeline.'

'What did the neighbors have to say?'

'Take a guess.'

'"She kept to herself, never caused problems."'

'I'm hanging with the Answer Man.' He pressed down on the accelerator. 'No one spoke two words to her. No one even knew her name.'

'What about visitors?'

'None that anyone saw,' he said. 'Just like Richard. She did have an ex-husband, though. Guy named Joseph Stargill. Lawyer, lives down in San Diego now. I put a call in to him.'

'How'd you find him?'

'Came across some divorce papers she kept in her home office. I called Dr Theobold this morning; he'll be happy to engage in shrink talk with you. He had some vague recollection of Claire getting divorced. Only reason he found out is each year staff members update their résumés. In the past, Claire had put "Married" in the marital-status blank. This year she whited it out and typed "Divorced."'

'So it was recent,' I said. 'Theobold didn't ask her about it?'

'He said she just wasn't the type you got personal with.'

'Maybe that's why she took the job at Starkweather.'

'What do you mean?'

'Great escape. Show up on time, don't make waves, no one bugs you. Like Dr Aldrich said, the staff gets leeway. Maybe she wanted to do clinical work but was afraid of having to relate to patients. Surrounding herself with psychotics took the pressure off, and as long as none of her patients got violent, she could do what she wanted with them. The perfect escape.'

'Escape from what?'

'Academia. And emotional entanglement. Her divorce was recent. Just because she didn't talk about it doesn't mean she wasn't still hurting. People going through life changes sometimes try to simplify.'

'You see Starkweather as simple.'

'In a sense, it is.'

He didn't answer, put on even more speed.

A few miles later, I said, 'On the other hand, she got entangled with *someone*. The person who cut her throat.'

The house was like so many others.

Single-story white stucco aged to a spoiled-milk gray, roofed with black composite shingle. Attached single garage, double parking space instead of a front yard. One of those unadorned late-fifties hillside knockups posing as intentionally contemporary but really the product of a tight construction budget. The street was called Cape Horn Drive – a short, straight afterthought of a slit into the north side of Woodrow Wilson, dead-ending at a huge tipu tree. Matching trees tilted over the pavement. The sidewalk was bleached and dry where the branches didn't hover.

Second lot in, third from the end. Eight neighboring residences in all, most like Claire Argent's, with minor variation. Very few cars at the curb, but closed garage doors made it hard to assess what that meant. No major intersections or nearby commercial district. You'd have to intend to come up here.

This high, the air was moving. In the summer light, the tipu trees were filmy, their fern-shaped leaves swishing in the breeze. Contrary creatures: They lost their leaves in the spring, when everything else bloomed. When other branches began to shed, the tipus were a riot of yellow blossoms. Not yet. The only sparks of color shot from flower boxes and potted plants. Other houses, not Claire's.

We made our way up to the front door. Nice views all around. The freeway was miles away, but I could hear it. Nowadays, you always seem to hear it.

LAPD seal on the door. Milo had a key and let us in. I followed him into a tight, bare space too small to be called an entry hall. Two white walls right-angled us into the living room.

Not a lived-in room.

Unmarked walls, empty hardwood floors, not a single piece of furniture.

Milo took three echoing steps and stood in the center. Over his head was a light fixture. Cheap frosted dome; it looked original.

Chenille drapes browned the windows. The walls looked clean but were turning the same gray-white as the exterior.

The floors caught my attention – lacquered shiny, free of scuff marks, dents, drag furrows. As if the inhabitants had floated, rather than walked.

I felt short of breath. The house had no odor – neither the stench of death nor the aromas of tenancy. No food, sweat, perfume, cut flowers, air freshener. Not even the must of disuse.

A *vacant* place; it seemed airless, incapable of sustaining life.

I made myself take a deep breath. Milo was still in the center of the room, fingers drumming his thighs.

'Cozy,' I said, understanding why he'd wanted me to see it.

He turned very slowly, taking in the open area to the left that led to a small kitchen. A single oak stool at an eat-in counter. White Formica laced with a gold thread-like design, also bare except for white fingerprint-powder smudges. Same for the other counters and the cabinets. On the far wall hung an empty wooden spice rack. Four-burner white stove at least twenty years old, refrigerator of matching color and vintage. No other appliances.

He opened the fridge, said, 'Yogurt, grapes, two apples, baking soda . . . baking soda for freshness. She liked things neat. Just like Richard . . . simplifying.'

He began opening and closing cabinets. 'White ironstone dishes, Noritake, service for four . . . Ditto stainless-steel utensils . . . Everything full of fingerprint powder . . . One skillet, one saucepan, containers of salt, pepper, no other spices . . . Bland life?'

On to the stove burners. Lifting the grill, he said, 'Clean. Either she never cooked or she was really compulsive. Or somebody else was.'

I stared back at the empty front room. 'Did Crime Scene take furniture back to the lab?'

'No, just her clothing. This is the way we found it. My first thought was someone cleaned the place out, or she'd just moved in or was in the process of moving out. But I can't find evidence of her leaving, and her deed says she's been here over two years.'

I pointed to the virgin floor. 'Either she was planning to redecorate or never bothered to furnish.'

'Like I said, grabbing air. C'mon, let's take a look at the rest of the place.'

A hall to the left led to one bath and two small bedrooms, the first set up as an office. No carpeting, the same pristine hardwood, harsh echoes.

Milo kneeled in the hallway, ran his finger along the smooth, clean oak. 'Maybe she took off her shoes. Like in a Japanese house.'

We started with the bedroom. Box spring and mattress on the floor, no headboard, four-drawer pecan-veneer dresser, matching nightstand. On the stand were a tissue box and a ceramic lamp, the base white, ovular, shaped like a giant cocoon. Swirls of white fingerprint powder, the telltale concentrics of latent prints.

'Her linens are at the lab,' said Milo, 'along with her clothes.'

He moved the mattress around, slid his hand under the box spring, opened the closet. Empty. Same for the dresser.

'I watched them pack her undies,' he said. 'No hidden stash of naughty things, just your basic white cotton. Small wardrobe: Dresses, sweaters, skirts, tasteful stuff, Macy's, some budget-chain stuff, nothing expensive.'

He righted the mattress, looked up at the ceiling, then back at the empty closet. 'She wasn't moving out, Alex. This is where she lived. If you can call it that.'

In the office, he put his hands together prayerfully and said, 'Give me something to work with, Lord.'

'Thought you already went through it.'

'Not thoroughly. Couldn't, with the criminalists buzzing around. Just that box.' He pointed to a cardboard file on the floor. 'That's where I found the divorce papers. Near the top.'

He approached the desk and studied the books in the cheap plywood cases that covered two walls. Shelves stuffed and sagging. Volumes on psychology, psychiatry, neurology, biology, sociology, bound stacks of journals arranged by date. White powder and prints everywhere.

Milo had emptied the top drawer of staples and paper clips, bits of paper and lint, was into the second drawer, rummaging. 'OK, here we go.' He waved a red leatherette savings account passbook. 'Century Bank, Sunset and Cahuenga . . . Well, well, well – looks like she was doing OK.'

I went over and looked at the page he held out. Balance of $240,000 and some cents. He flipped to the front of the booklet. The initial transaction had taken place three years ago, rolled over from a previous passbook, when the balance had been ninety-eight thousand less.

Accrual of nearly a hundred thousand in three years. The deposit pattern was repetitive: No withdrawals, deposits of three thousand at the end of each month.

'Probably a portion of her salary,' I said.

'Theobold said her take-home was around four, so she probably banked three, took out a grand for expenses. Looks like it didn't change during the time she worked at Starkweather. Which makes sense. Her civil service job classification puts her at a comparable salary.'

'Frugal,' I said. 'How'd she pay her bills? And her taxes? Is there a checking account?'

He found it seconds later, in the same drawer. 'Monthly deposits of five hundred . . . last Friday of the month – same day she deposited into the savings account. The woman was a clock . . . Looks like she wrote mostly small checks – probably household stuff . . . Maybe she had a credit card, paid the rest of her bills in cash. So she kept five hundred or so around the house. Or in her purse. To some junkie that could be a sizable score. And the purse hasn't been found. But this doesn't feel like robbery, does it?'

I said, 'No. Still, people have been killed for a lot less. Without her purse, how'd you identify her?'

'Car registration gave us her name. We ran her prints, matched them to her psychologist's license . . . A stupid junkie robbery, wouldn't that be something? She's out shopping, gets mugged for her cash. But what junkie mugger would bother stashing her in trash bags, driving her to a semi-public spot, and leaving her car behind, when he could have thrown her somewhere dark, gotten himself some wheels for the night? Then again, most criminals take stupid pills . . . OK, let's see what else she left behind.'

He got to work on the rest of the desk. The money showed up in a plain white envelope, pushed to the back of the left-hand bottom drawer. Nine fifty-dollar bills, under a black leatherette appointment book issued as a gift by a drug company. Three-year-old calendar, blank pages in the book.

'So maybe she had fifty or so with her,' he said. 'Big spender. This does *not* feel like robbery.'

I asked him for the bankbook, examined every page.

'What?' he said.

'So mechanical. Exact same pattern, week in, week out.

No sizable withdrawals also means no vacations or unpredictable splurges. And no deposits other than her salary implies she got no alimony, either. Unless she put it in another account. Also, she maintained her individual account throughout her marriage. What about her tax return? Did she file jointly?'

He crossed the room to the cardboard file box. Inside were two years of state and federal tax returns, neatly ordered. 'No outside income other than salary, no dependents other than herself . . . nope, individual return. Something's off. It's like she was denying being married.'

'Or she had doubts from the beginning.'

He came up with a stack of stapled paper, started flipping. 'Utility bills . . . Ah, here's the credit card . . . Visa . . . She charged food, clothing, gasoline for the Buick, and books . . . Not very often – most months there're only three, four charges . . . She paid on time, too. No interest.'

At the bottom of the stack were auto insurance receipts. Low premium for no smoking and good driving record. No financing on the Buick meant she probably owned the car. No way for her to know it would end up being a coffin on wheels.

Milo scribbled notes and placed the paper back in the carton. I thought of what we hadn't found: Mementos, photographs, correspondence, greeting cards. Anything personal.

No property tax receipts or deductions for property tax. If she rented, why no record of rent checks?

I raised the question. Milo said, 'So maybe the ex paid the mortgage and taxes. Maybe that was his alimony.'

'And now that she's gone, he's off the hook. And if he's maintained some ownership of the house, there's a bit of incentive for you. Any idea who gets the two hundred forty? Any will show up?'

'Not yet. So you like the husband?'

'I'm just thinking about what you always tell me. Follow the money.'

He grunted. I returned to the bookcase, pulled a few books out. Foxed pages, neatly printed notes in margins. Next to five years' worth of *Brain* was a collection of journal reprints.

Articles Claire Argent had authored. A dozen studies, all related to the neuropsychology of alcoholism, funded by the National Institutes of Health. The writing was clear, the subject matter repetitive. Lots of technical terms, but I got the gist.

During graduate school and the five years following, she'd filled her hours measuring human motor and visual skills under various levels of intoxication. Easy access to subjects: County Hospital was the treatment center of last resort for physically wasted alcoholic paupers who used the emergency room as their private clinic. ER docs called them GOMER's – Get Out of My Emergency Room.

Her results had been consistent: Booze slowed you down. Statistically significant but hardly profound. Lots of academics drudged through undistinguished careers with that kind of stuff. Maybe she *had* tired of the grant game.

One interesting fact: She'd always published solo –

unusual for academic medicine, where chairmen commonly stuck their names on everything underlings produced.

Maybe Myron Theobold had integrity.

Letting Claire do her own thing.

Claire going it alone from the very beginning.

A rattling sound made me turn. Milo had been handling the objects on the desktop and a pen had dropped. He retrieved it and placed it next to a small calendar in a green plastic frame. Another drug company giveaway. Empty memo pad. No appointments, no indentations on the pad.

Such a spare life.

Several books trumpeting the virtues of serene simplicity had recently gone best-seller. I wondered if the newly rich authors practiced what they preached.

This house didn't seem serene, just blank, hollow, null.

We left the office and moved to the bathroom. Shampoo, soap, toothpaste, multiple vitamins, sanitary napkins, Advil. No birth control pills, no diaphragm. The travertine deck around the tub was clear of niceties. No bath beads or bubble bath or loofah sponge – none of the solitary pleasures women sometimes crave. The porcelain was streaked with amber.

Milo said, 'Luminol. No blood in the tub or the drain. No semen on the towels or sheets, just some sweat that matches Claire's blood type.'

Wondering if anyone but Claire had ever set foot in this house, I thought of the work pattern she'd chosen for herself. Five years with drunks, six months with dangerous psychotics. Perhaps, after days immersed in delusion and warp, she'd craved silence, her own brand of Zen.

But that didn't explain the lack of letters from home, not

even a snapshot of parents, nieces, nephews. Some kind of *contact.*

The ultimate Zen triumph was the ability to lose identity, to thrive on nothingness. But this place didn't bespeak any sort of victory. Such a sad little box . . . or was I missing something? Projecting my own need for attachment?

I thought of what Claire *had* hoarded: Her books and her articles.

Maybe work had been everything and she *had* been content.

Yet she'd abandoned her first job impulsively, relinquishing grant money, trading dry but durable science for the chance to school psychotic murderers in the art of daily living.

To what end?

I kept searching for reasons she'd traded County for Starkweather, but the shift continued to bother me. Even with comparable salaries, a civil service position was a comedown from the white-coat work she'd been doing at County. And if she'd craved contact with schizophrenics, County had plenty of those. Dangerous patients? The jail ward was right there.

If she was tired of the publish-or-perish grind, then why not do some private practice? Neuropsych skills were highly prized, and well-trained neuropsychologists could do forensic work, consult to lawyers on injury cases, bypass the HMO's and earn five, ten times what Starkweather paid.

Even if money hadn't been important to her, what about job satisfaction? Why had she subjected herself to shift after shift in the ugly gray building? And the drive to Starkweather – day after day past the slag.

There had to be some other reason for what I couldn't stop thinking of as a self-demotion.

It was almost as if she'd punished herself.

For what?

Or had she been fleeing something?

Had it caught up with her?

7

IT WAS just after two P.M. when we left the house. Outside, the air felt alive.

Milo connected to Laurel Canyon, headed south to Sunset, drove west on the Strip. An accident near Holloway and the usual jam of misery ghouls slowed us, and it was nearly three by the time we crossed through Beverly Hills and over to Beverly Glen. Neither Milo nor I was saying much. Talked out. He zoomed up the bridle path to my house. Robin's truck was in the carport.

'Thanks for your time.'

'Where are you headed?'

'Hall of Records, look for real estate paper, see what else comes up on Mr Stargill. Then a call to Heidi Ott.'

He looked tired, and his tone said optimism was a felony. I said, 'Good luck,' and watched him speed away.

I walked up to my new house. Three years, and I still thought of it as a bit of an interloper. The old house, the one I'd bought with my first real earnings, had been an amalgam of redwood and idiosyncrasy. A psychopath out to kill me torched it to cinders. Robin had supervised the construction of something white, airy, a good deal more spacious and practical, undeniably charming. I told her I loved it. For the most part, I did. One day, I'd stop being secretly stodgy.

I expected to find her out back in her studio, but she was in the kitchen reading the morning paper. Spike was curled up at her feet, black-brindle pot-roast body heaving with each snoring breath, jowls flowing onto the floor. He's a French bulldog, a miniature version of the English breed, with upright bat ears and enough vanity for an entire opera troupe. He lifted one eyelid as I entered – *Oh, you again* – and let it drop. A subsequent sigh was laden with ennui.

Robin stood, spread her arms, and squeezed me around the waist. Her head pressed against my chest. She smelled of hardwood and perfume, and her curls tickled my chin. I lifted a handful of auburn coils and kissed the back of her neck. She's a charitable five-three but has the long, swan-like neck of a fashion model. Her skin was hot, slightly moist.

'How'd it go?' she said, putting her hand in my hair.

'Uneventful.'

'No problem from the inmates, huh?'

'Nothing.' I held her closer, rubbing the taut musculature of her shoulders, moved down to delicate vertebrae, magical curves, then back up to the clean line of her jaw and the silk of her eyelids.

She stepped away, took my chin in one hand. 'That place made you romantic?'

'Being out of there makes me romantic.'

'Well, I'm glad you're back in one piece.'

'It wasn't dangerous,' I said. 'Not even close.'

'Five thousand murderers and no danger?'

'Twelve hundred, but who's counting.'

'Twelve hundred,' she said. 'How silly of me to worry.' At the last word, her voice rose a notch.

'Sorry,' I said. 'But really, it was fine. People go to work there every day and nothing happens. Everyone seems to think it's safer on the wards than out on the streets.'

'Sounds like rationalization to me. Meanwhile, that psychologist gets stuffed in a car trunk.'

'There's no indication, so far, that her work had anything to do with it.'

'Good. The main thing is, you're back. Have you eaten yet?'

'No. You?'

'Just juice in the morning.'

'Busy day?'

'Pretty busy, trying to finish that mandolin.' She stretched to her full height. She had on a red T-shirt and denim overalls, size six Skechers. Small gold hoops glinted from her ears. She took them off when she worked. Not planning to return to the studio.

'I'm hungry now,' she said. 'Hint, hint.'

'Let's go out,' I said.

'A mind reader!'

'Just call me the Answer Man.'

We gave Spike a chewbone and drove to an Indian buffet in Santa Monica that was open all afternoon. Rice and lentils, kulcha bread stuffed with onions, curried spinach with soft cheese, spicy eggplant, hot milky tea. Some sort of chant played in the background – a single male voice keening, maybe praying. The two ectomorphs in the next booth got up and left and we were the only patrons. The waiter left us alone.

Halfway through the pile on her plate, Robin said, 'I know I'm harping, but next time you go somewhere like that, please call the minute you get out.'

'You were really that worried?'

'Ax murderers and vampires, Lord knows what else?'

I covered her hand with mine. 'Rob, the men I saw today were submissive.' Except for the bearded fellow on the yard who'd come toward me. The fight in the hall. Plastic windows, S&R rooms.

'What makes them submit?'

'Medication and a structured environment.'

She didn't seem comforted. 'So you learned nothing there?'

'Not so far. Later we went to Claire Argent's house.' I described the place. 'What do you think?'

'About what?'

'The way she lived.'

She drank tea, put the cup aside, thought awhile. 'Would I want to live like that? Not forever, but maybe for a short stretch. Take a nice vacation from all the complications.'

'Complications?' I said.

She smiled. 'Not you, honey. Just . . . circumstances. Obligations, deadlines – life piling up. Like when I was handling all the construction. Or now, when the orders stack up and everyone wants results yesterday. Sometimes life can start to feel like too much homework, and a little simplicity doesn't sound bad at all.'

'This was more than simplicity, Robin. This was . . . bleak. Sad.'

'You're saying she was depressed?'

'I don't know enough to diagnose her,' I said. 'But the feeling I got from the place was – inorganic. Blank.'

'Did you see any evidence she was neglecting herself?' she said.

'No. And everyone describes her as pleasant, dependable. Distant, but no obvious pathology.'

'So maybe inwardly she was fine, too.'

'Maybe,' I said. 'The only things she did amass were books. Maybe intellectual stimulation was what turned her on.'

'There you go. She trimmed things down to concentrate on what mattered to her.'

I didn't answer.

'You don't think so,' she said.

'Pretty severe trim,' I said. 'There was nothing personal in the entire house. Not a single family photo.'

'Perhaps she wasn't close to her family. Or she had problems with them. But even so, how different does that make her from millions of other people, Alex? She sounds to me more like . . . someone cerebral. Living in her head. Enjoying her privacy. Even if she did have social problems, what does any of that have to do with her murder?'

'Maybe nothing.' I spooned more rice onto my plate, played with grains of basmati, took a bite of bread. 'If she wanted intellectual stimulation, why switch from a research job to Starkweather?'

'What kind of research was she doing?'

'Alcoholism and how it affects reaction time.'

'Anything earth-shattering?'

'Not to me.' I summarized the studies. 'Actually, it was pretty mundane.'

'Could be she came to a realization: She'd been a good little girl, doing what was expected of her since grad school. She got tired of hacking it out. Wanted to actually help someone.'

'She didn't pick a very easy group to help.'

'So it was the challenge that motivated her. That, and tackling something new.'

'The men at Starkweather don't get cured.'

'Then I don't know. All out of guesses.'

'I'm not trying to be contentious,' I said. 'She just really puzzles me. And I think there's a good deal of truth in what you're saying. She got divorced within the last year or so. Maybe she was trying to cut free on several levels. Maybe for someone who'd been grinding out studies year after year, Starkweather seemed novel.'

She smiled and stroked my face. 'If knitted brows are any kind of measure, Milo's getting his money's worth out of you.'

'The other thing I wonder about is the first case – Richard Dada, the would-be actor. On the surface, he and Claire have little in common. But what they do seem to share is negative space – an absence of friends, enemies, quirks. Both of them were very neat. No entanglements. Maybe we're talking about loneliness and an attempt to fill the void. Some sort of lonely-hearts hookup with the wrong person.'

'A man and a woman?' she said. 'A bisexual killer?'

'That would make Dada gay, and Milo never found any indication of that. Or maybe it had nothing to do with sex – just companionship, some kind of common-interest club. On the other hand, the cases could be unrelated.'

I raised her hand to my lips, kissed the fingertips one by one. 'Mr Romantic. I'd better switch gears before I drive *you* into isolation.'

She grinned, waved languidly, kissed air, put on her Bette Davis voice. 'Pass me the spinach, dahling. Then you can pay the check and sweep me off my feet to the nearest Baskin Robbins for some jamoca almond fudge. After that, hi-ho all the way home, where you ah cawjully invited to add some entanglement to my life.'

8

AT EIGHT P.M. Milo called. 'Am I interrupting anything?'

He'd missed interrupting by an hour. Robin was reading in bed and I'd taken Spike for a short walk up the canyon. When the phone rang, I was sitting out on the terrace, trying to rid my mind of question marks, struggling to concentrate on the sound of the waterfall that fed the fishpond. Grateful because I couldn't hear the freeway.

'Not at all. What's up?'

'Got the info on Claire and Stargill. Married two years, divorced nearly two, no kids. I reached Stargill. He says the split was amicable. He's a partner in a ten-lawyer firm, remarried three months ago. He just learned about Claire. San Diego papers didn't carry it, but one of his partners was up here, read about it.'

'What was his demeanor?'

'He sounded pretty upset over the phone, but what the hell does that mean? Said he doubted there was anything he could add but he'd talk to me. I set up an appointment for tomorrow morning at ten.'

'San Diego?'

'No, he's driving up.'

'Very cooperative fellow.'

'He has business here anyway. Some commercial property closings – he's a real estate lawyer.'

'So he comes up to LA regularly.'

'Yeah, I made note of that. Let's see what he's like face-to-face. We're meeting at Claire's house. Which she owns. It was his bachelor place, but after the divorce he signed it over to her and agreed to pay the mortgage and taxes in lieu of alimony and her dipping into his stocks and bonds.'

'Who inherits the property now?'

'Good question. Stargill wasn't aware of any will, and he claims neither of them took out insurance on the other. I never came across any policies; Claire was thirty-nine, probably wasn't figuring on dying. I suppose a lawyer would know how to play the probate process – he might make a case for mortgage payment constituting partial ownership. But my guess is her parents would come first. What do you think a place like that is worth?'

'Three hundred or so. How much is equity?'

'We'll find that out tomorrow if Mr Cooperative stays cooperative . . . Maybe he got tired of paying her bills, huh?'

'It could chafe, especially now that he's remarried. Especially if he's got money problems. Be good to know what his finances are like.'

'If you want to meet him, be there at ten. I left a message with Heidi Ott's machine, no callback yet. And the lab sent another report on the prints: Definitely only Claire's. Looks like she really did go it alone.'

The next morning I called Dr Myron Theobold at County Hospital, left a voicemail message, and drove to Cape Horn Drive, arriving at nine-forty-five. Milo's unmarked was already there, parked at the curb. A deep-gray late-model BMW sedan sat in front of the garage, ski clamps on the roof.

The house's front door was unlocked, and I entered. Milo had reassumed his position at the center of the empty living room. Near the kitchen counter stood a man in his forties wearing a blue suit, white shirt, yellow pin-dot tie. He was just shy of six feet, trim, with short, curly red hair and a matching beard streaked with gray. Skinny gold watch on his left wrist, wedding band studded with small diamonds, shiny oxblood wingtips.

Milo said, 'This is Dr Delaware, our psychological consultant. Doctor, Mr Stargill.'

'Joe Stargill.' A hand extended. Dry palms but unsteady hazel eyes. His voice was slightly hoarse. He looked past me, into the empty room, and shook his head.

'Mr Stargill was just saying the house looks pretty different.'

Stargill said, 'This wasn't the way we lived. We had wall-to-wall carpeting, furniture. Over there was a big leather sofa; that wall held a chrome cabinet – an étagère, I think it was called. Claire taught me that. I'd bought a few things when I was single but Claire filled it in. Pottery, figurines, macramé, all that good stuff.' He shook his head again. 'She must have gone through some major changes.'

'When's the last time you spoke to her, sir?' said Milo.

'When I U-Hauled my things away. Maybe a half-year before the final decree.'

'So you were separated before the divorce.'

Stargill nodded, touched the tip of his beard.

Milo said, 'So your last contact would be around two and a half years ago.'

'That's right.'

'You never talked about the divorce?'

'Well, sure. A phone call here and there to wrap up details. I thought you meant a real conversation.'

'Ah,' said Milo. 'And after the divorce you never came back to visit?'

'No reason to,' said Stargill. 'Claire and I were over – we'd been over long before we made it official. Never really started, actually.'

'The marriage went bad quickly.'

Stargill sighed and buttoned his jacket. His hands were broad, ruddy, coated with beer-colored hair. 'It wasn't a matter of going bad. The whole thing was essentially a mistake. Here, I brought this. Found it this morning.'

He fished out a crocodile wallet and removed a small photo, which Milo examined, then handed to me.

Color snapshot of Claire and Stargill arm in arm, 'Just Married' banner in the background. He wore a tan suit and brown turtleneck shirt, no beard, eyeglasses. His nude face was bony, his smile tentative.

Claire had on a long, pale blue sleeveless dress printed with lavender pansies, and she carried a bouquet of white roses. Her hair was long, straight, parted in the middle, her face leaner than in the headshot I'd seen, the cheekbones more pronounced.

Full smile.

'Don't really know why I brought it,' said Stargill. 'Didn't know I even had it.'

'Where'd you find it?' said Milo.

'In my office. I went in early this morning before driving up here, started going through all the paperwork Claire and I had in common: Divorce documents, transfer of ownership for the house. It's all out in the car – take whatever you want. The picture popped out from between some pages.'

Stargill turned to me. 'Guess a psychologist could interpret that – still having it. Maybe it does mean something on a subconscious level, but I sure don't remember holding on to it intentionally. Seeing it again was bizarre. We look pretty happy, don't we?'

I studied the photo some more. A flimsy-looking altar flecked with glitter was visible between the newlyweds. Glittering red hearts on the walls, a pink Cupid figurine with Dizzy Gillespie cheeks.

'Vegas?' I said.

'Reno,' said Stargill. 'Tackiest wedding chapel you ever saw. The guy who officiated was an old geezer, half blind, probably drunk. We got into town well after midnight. The geezer was closing up and I slipped him a twenty to do a quickie ceremony. His wife had already gone home, so some janitor – another old guy – served as witness. Afterward Claire and I joked that they were both senile – it probably wasn't legal.'

He placed his hands on the counter, stared blankly into the kitchen. 'When I lived here, we had appliances all over the place – juicer, blender, coffee maker, you name it. Claire wanted every gizmo invented . . . Wonder what she did with the stuff – looks like she was stripping everything away.'

'Any idea why she'd do that?' I said.

'No,' he said. 'Like I said, we weren't in touch. Truth is, even when we were together I couldn't have told you what made her tick. All she ever really liked was going to the movies – she could see a flick a night. Sometimes it didn't seem to matter what was on the screen, she just liked being in the theater. Beyond that, I never knew her at all.'

'Where'd the two of you meet?'

'Another major romantic story: Hotel cocktail lounge. Marriott at the airport, to be specific. I was there to meet a client from the Far East who never showed up, and Claire was attending a psychology convention. I'm sitting at the bar, irritated because this guy does this to me all the time, and now I've wasted half a day. Claire glides in looking great, sits a few stools down.'

He pointed at the picture. 'As you can see, she was an eyeful back then. Different from my usual type, but maybe that's what did it.'

'Different, how?' I said.

'I'd been dating legal secretaries, paralegals, a few models, wannabe actresses – we're talking girls who were into fashion, makeup, the whole body-beautiful thing. Claire looked like exactly what she was: A scholar. Great structure, but she didn't mess with herself. That afternoon she was wearing granny glasses and one of those long print dresses. Her whole wardrobe was those dresses and some jeans and T-shirts. No makeup. No high heels – open sandals, I remember looking down at her feet. She had really pretty feet, adorable white toes. She saw me staring and laughed – this low chuckle that struck me as being really sexy, and then I started to look past the glasses and I realized she was great-looking. She ordered a ginger ale, I was well into the Bloody Marys. I made some crack about her being a wild party girl. She laughed again and I moved closer and the rest is history. We got married two months later. At the beginning, I thought I'd died and gone to heaven.'

He had a redhead's typical milky complexion and now it pinkened.

'That's the whole sordid story,' he said. 'I don't know why I came here, but if there's nothing else—'

'Died and gone to heaven?' said Milo.

Pink turned to rose. 'Physically,' said Stargill. 'I don't want to be vulgar, but maybe this will help you in some way. What drew Claire and me together was one thing: Sex. We ended up getting a room at the Marriott and stayed there till midnight. She was— Let's just say I'd never met anyone like her, the chemistry was incredible. After her, those other girls seemed like mannequins. I don't want to be disrespectful, let's leave it at that.'

I said, 'But the chemistry didn't last.'

He unbuttoned his jacket, put a hand in his pocket. 'Maybe it was too much too quickly. Maybe every flame burns out, I don't know. I'm sure some of the blame was mine. Maybe most. She wasn't my first wife. I'd gotten hitched in college – that one lasted less than a year; obviously I wasn't good at the matrimony thing. After we started living together, it was like . . . something sputtered. No fights, just . . . no fire. Both of us were really into our work, we didn't spend much time together.'

The beard hair under his lip vibrated a bit. 'We never

fought. She just seemed to lose interest. I think she lost interest first, but after a while it stopped bothering me. I felt I was living with a stranger. Maybe I had been all along.'

The other hand went in a pocket. Now he was slouching. 'So here I am, forty-one, working on my third. Happy honeymoon so far, but who knows?'

I noticed that he tended to shift the focus to himself. Self-centered, or an intentional distraction?

I said, 'So Claire was really into her work. Did that ever change?'

'Not that I saw. But I wouldn't have known. We never talked about work. We never talked about anything. It was weird – one moment we're getting hitched, having hurricane sex, then we're each going about our business. I tried. I invited her to the office a couple of times, but she was always too busy. She never invited me to her lab. One time I dropped in on her anyway. What a zoo, all those drunks lurching around. She didn't seem happy to see me – like I was intruding. Eventually, we were avoiding each other completely. Easy to do when you're both working seventy hours a week. I'd get home when she was already asleep; she'd wake up early, be over at the hospital by the time I was in the shower. Only reason we stayed married for two years is each of us was too busy – or too lazy – to file the papers.'

'Who ended up filing?' I said.

'Claire did. I remember the day she announced it to me. I came home late, but this time she was up, in bed doing a crossword puzzle. She pulls out a stack of papers, says, "I thought it was about time, Joe. How do you feel about it?"

I remember feeling relieved. But also hurt. Because she didn't even want to try to work it out. Also, for me it was the second time, and I was wondering if I'd ever pull off the whole relationship thing. I moved out, but she didn't actually file for six months.'

'Any idea why?' said Milo.

'She said she hadn't gotten around to it.'

'What was the financial agreement?' said Milo.

'Polite,' said Stargill. 'No hassles; we worked the whole thing out with one phone call. I give Claire big points for fairness, because she refused to hire a lawyer, let me know she had no intention of cleaning me out. And I was the vulnerable one, I had the assets – investments, pension plan, I had some real estate things cooking. She could've made my life miserable, but all she asked was for me to deed her the house, finish paying it off, and handle the property taxes. Everything else was mine. I left her the furniture, walked away with my clothes and my law books and my stereo.'

He rubbed an eye, turned away, tried to speak, cleared his throat. 'The paperwork was easy – we never filed a joint tax return. She never changed her name. I thought it was a feminist thing, but now I wonder if she ever intended to stay with me.'

'Did that bother you?' said Milo.

'Why should it? The whole marriage didn't feel like a marriage. More like a one-night stand that stretched out. I'm not saying I didn't respect Claire as a person. She was a terrific woman. Considerate, kind. That was the only downer: I *liked* her – as a person. And I know she liked me. My first wife was twenty when she left me, we'd been together eleven months and *she* tried to enslave me for the rest of my life. Claire was so damn decent. I wouldn't have minded remaining her friend. But it just didn't go down that way . . . I can't understand why anyone would want to hurt her.'

He rubbed his eyes.

'When did you move to San Diego?' said Milo.

'Right after the divorce. A job opportunity came up, and I'd had it with LA, couldn't wait to get out.'

'Fed up with the smog?' said Milo.

'The smog, the congestion, the crime. I wanted to live near the beach, found myself a little rental near Del Mar. The first year, Claire and I exchanged Christmas cards, then that stopped.'

'Did Claire have any enemies you were aware of?' said Milo.

'No way. I never saw her offend anyone – maybe some nutcase at County got an idea in his head, stalked her or something. I still remember those drunks leering, smelling of barf, leaking all over the place when they walked. I couldn't see how Claire could work with them. But she was real businesslike about it – giving them these tests, doing research. Nothing grossed her out. I'm no expert, but I'd concentrate on County.'

He folded his handkerchief and Milo and I used the split second to exchange glances. Stargill didn't know about the job switch to Starkweather. Or wanted us to think he didn't.

Milo shook his head. *Don't bring it up now*.

He said, 'How much is owed on the house, Mr Stargill?'

Quick change of context. It throws people off balance. Stargill actually stepped backward.

'Around fifty thousand. By now the payments are mostly principal; I was thinking of paying it off.'

'Why's that?'

'Not much of a tax deduction anymore.'

'Who gets the property in the event of Dr Argent's death?'

Stargill studied him. Buttoned his coat. 'I wouldn't know.'

'So you and she didn't have any agreement – in the event of her demise, it reverts to you?'

'Absolutely not.'

'And so far, no will's turned up – do you have a will, sir?'

'I do. Why is that relevant, Detective Sturgis?'

'Just being thorough.'

Stargill's nostrils expanded. 'I'm the ex, so I'm a suspect? Oh, come on.' He laughed. 'What's the motive?' Laughing again, he stuffed his hands in his pockets and rocked on his heels – a courtroom gesture. 'Even if I did get the house, three hundred thousand equity, tops. One of the things I did when I moved to SD was invest in seaside property. I've got a net worth of six, seven million, so murdering Claire for another three hundred thousand, before taxes, would be ludicrous.'

He walked to the bare kitchen counter and rubbed the Formica. 'Claire and I were never enemies. I couldn't have asked for a better ex-wife, so why the hell would I hurt her?'

'Sir,' said Milo, 'I have to ask these questions.'

'Sure. Fine. Ask. Hearing about Claire made me sick to my stomach. I felt this stupid urge to do something – to be useful.

That's why I drove up, brought you all the documents. I should've figured you'd see me as a suspect, but still it's . . .' Shrugging, he turned his back on us. 'All I can say is, glad it's your job and not mine. Anything else you want to quiz me on?'

I said, 'What can you tell us about Claire's family background, her social life?'

'Nothing.'

'Nothing about her family?'

'Never met her family. All I know is she was born in Pittsburgh, did undergrad at the University of Pittsburgh, went to Case Western for her PhD. Only reason I know that is I saw her diplomas in her office. She refused to talk about her past.'

'Refused, or avoided?' I said.

'Both.'

'And she never talked at all about her family?'

Stargill pivoted and stared at me. 'That's right. She was a closed book. Claimed she had no brothers and sisters. Her parents ran some kind of store. Other than that, I don't know a *thing*.'

He shook his head. 'I talked plenty about my family, and she listened. Or pretended to. But she never met my side, either. *My* choice.'

'Why's that?' I said.

'Because I don't like my family. My mother was OK – a quiet drunk – but by the time I met Claire, she was dead. My father was a violent, drunken sonofabitch I wouldn't have tossed a stick at, let alone introduced to my bride. Same for my brother.'

He gave a sick smile. 'Get it? I'm one of those adult children of alcoholics et cetera, et cetera. Never developed a drinking problem myself, but I watch myself, went through the whole therapy thing after my mother killed herself. When I saw Claire with that ginger ale I wondered if maybe she had some history with alcohol, maybe we had something in common. I ended up telling her about my colorful background.' The smile acquired teeth. 'Turned out, she just liked ginger ale.'

'Not a mention of her family in two years of marriage,' I said. 'Amazing.'

'Like I said, it wasn't your typical marriage. Every time I tried to get personal, she changed the subject.' He rubbed his scalp and the corners of his mouth curled up – outward trappings of another smile, but his mood was hard to read. 'And she had an interesting way of changing the subject.'

'What's that?' I said.

'She took me to bed.'

9

STARGILL WAS eager to leave but Milo convinced him to tour the rest of the house. The bathroom provoked no comment. In the office he said, 'Now, this looks exactly the same. This was Claire's place, she spent all her time here.'

'Where was your office?' said Milo.

'I didn't like bringing work home, used a small desk in the bedroom.'

That room widened his eyes. 'No memories left here. We had a king-size bed, brass headboard, down comforter, antique nightstands. Claire must have really wanted a change.'

His expression said he still took that personally. He looked into the empty closet. 'Where are all her clothes?'

'At the crime lab,' said Milo.

'Oh, man . . . I've got to get out of here.' Grabbing his beard for support, he left the room.

Outside, he got the carton of documents from his BMW, handed them over, revved noisily, and barreled down the hill.

'What's your take on the guy?' said Milo.

'He's got his share of problems, but no bells are ringing. And unless Claire wasn't as financially benevolent as he made out – or he's not as rich – where *is* the motive?'

'Three hundred even after taxes is still serious bread. And guys with big net worth can still get into trouble. I'm going to take a crash course on his finances. What do you mean, problems?'

'Bleeding in public – telling us his life history. Maybe that's what attracted Claire to him. Someone so self-absorbed he wouldn't try to get into *her* head. Their marriage sounds like a passion-with-a-stranger fantasy gone stale. That shows an impulsive side to Claire, sexually and otherwise. Stargill says they avoided each other for most of the marriage, meaning both of them could've had multiple affairs. Maybe Claire's been dating strangers for years, and finally met the wrong one.'

'The neighbors never saw anyone.'

'Neighbors don't notice everything. Pick someone up in a bar, bring them back in your car late at night, who's to know? Or she had liaisons away from home. That would fit with no prints except hers in the house.

'Stargill described her the same way everyone else has: Nice but detached,' I went on. 'But there's one thing he did add: A touch of dominance. She moves into his house, takes over the office; he gets a desk in the bedroom. He shares *his* past, but she refuses to reciprocate. When she tires of him, *she* decides they're going to divorce. And what the settlement is going to be. The fact that Stargill didn't press her on anything tells us something about him.'

'A submissive lawyer? That's a novel concept.'

'Some people keep work and play separate. Think of the specifics of the settlement: Claire ends up with the house, gets him to carry the mortgage and the taxes, and he feels grateful because she didn't take more. Even their first meeting has that same lopsided feel: She's sober, he isn't. She's in *control*, he isn't. He spills his guts about his drunken father and brother, alcoholic tendencies of his own that he keeps in check. The guy's her polar opposite: Turns every conversation into therapy. Some women might be put off. Claire goes upstairs with him and gives him the time of his life. Later on, whenever she wants to shut him up, she uses sex. She was clearly drawn to people with serious problems. Maybe she left County because she needed a bigger dose of pathology.'

'So,' he said, 'maybe she found a nutcase who'd gotten out of the hospital, tried to dominate him, pushed the wrong button – I've got to see if anyone was released from Starkweather during the last six months. But if nothing turns up, then what?'

He looked worn out. I said, 'You ask me to theorize, I theorize. It could still turn out to be a carjacking gone really bad.'

We walked to the Seville.

'Something else,' he said. 'The big taboo she had on talking about her family. To me that says rotten background. Only, unlike Stargill, she kept the bandage on.'

'When are her parents coming out?'

'Couple of days. Why don't you meet them with me?'

'Sure.' I got in the car.

He said, 'She starts out as your basic nice lady, and now

we're thinking of her as some kind of dominatrix . . . So all I have to do is find some highly disturbed joker with sadistic tendencies who held on to her credit card. Speaking of which, better call Visa.'

He looked back at the house. 'Maybe she did have visitors no one saw. Or just one sicko loverboy . . . Her living room woulda been a great playpen, wouldn't it? Plenty of space to roll around in – those floors are baby smooth. No body fluid traces on the wood, but who knows?'

'What's easier to clean than lacquered hardwood?' I said.

'True,' he said. 'Carpet would have yielded something.'

'Stargill said she took the carpeting out.'

He rubbed his face. 'Ex-patient or ex-con, some bad boy she thinks she can control.'

'Both would fit with the fact that she was found in her own car. Someone without his own wheels.'

'Putting her in the driver's seat, again.' Faint smile. 'A late-night pickup – we know from Stargill that she wasn't opposed to being picked up. They go somewhere, things go bad. No semen in her, so it never got to hanky-panky . . . Bad Boy cuts her, puts her in the trash bag, stashes her in the trunk and drives her over to West LA. Doesn't steal the car, because that's a sure way to get busted. Smart. Meticulous. Not a Starkweather fellow.' He grimaced. 'Meaning I'm wasting my time over there. Back to square one.'

His cell phone chirped. Snapping it off his belt, he said, 'Sturgis . . . Oh, hi . . . Yes, thank you— Oh? How so? Why don't you just tell— OK, sure, that would be fine, give me directions.'

Cradling the phone under his chin, he produced his pad, wrote something down, clicked off.

'That,' he said, 'was young Miss Ott. She does the night shift today at Starkweather, wants to talk before work.'

'Talk about what?'

'She wouldn't say, but I know scared when I hear it.'

She'd asked to meet at Plummer Park in West Hollywood. I followed Milo, connecting to Laurel, turning east on Melrose. On the way, I passed a billboard advertising a kick-boxing gym: Terrific-looking woman in a sports bra drawing back a glove for a roundhouse. The ad line was 'You can rest when you're dead.' Theology everywhere.

The park was scrubby, crowded, more Russian spoken than English. Most of the inhabitants were old people on benches, heavily garbed despite the heat. A sprinkle of kids on bicycles circled a dry oval of grass in the center, sleepy-looking dog walkers were led by the leash, a few scruffy types in designer T-shirts and cheap shoes hung out near the pay phones trying to radiate Moscow Mafia.

Heidi Ott stood by herself under a sad-looking carrot-wood tree, arms crossing her chest, checking out the terrain in all directions. When she spotted us, she gave a small wave and headed for the only vacant bench in sight. A pile of fresh dog turd nearby explained the vacancy. Wrinkling her nose, she moved on and we followed her to a shady spot near the swing set, under an old Chinese elm. The surrounding grass was bruised and matted. A lone young woman pushed her toddler in a gently repeating arc. Both she and the child seemed hypnotized by the motion.

Heidi leaned against the elm and watched them. If I hadn't been looking for the fear, I might not have noticed it. She wore it lightly, a glaze of anxiety, hands knotting then releasing, eyes fixing too intently on the swinging child.

'Thanks for meeting with us, ma'am,' said Milo.

'Sure,' she said. 'My roommate's sleeping, or I would've had you come to my place.'

She moistened her lips with her tongue. She wore low-slung jeans, a ribbed white T-shirt with a scalloped neck and high-cut sleeves, blunt-toed brown boots. Her hair was drawn back, just as it had been at Starkweather, but in a ponytail, not a tight bun. Dangling earrings of silver filigree, some eye shadow, a smear of lip gloss. Freckles on her cheeks that I hadn't noticed on the ward. Her nails were clipped short, very clean. The T-shirt was form-fitting. Not much meat on her, but her arms were sinewy.

She cleared her throat, seemed to be working up the courage to speak, just as a tall, thin man with long hair came loping by with a panting mutt. The dog had some Rottweiler in it. The man wore all black and his coarse hair was a dull ebony. He stared at the ground. The dog's nose was down; each step seemed to strain the animal.

Heidi waited until they passed, then smiled nervously. 'I'm probably wasting your time.'

'If there's anything you can tell me about Dr Argent, you're not.'

Squint lines formed around her eyes, but when she turned to us they disappeared. 'Can I ask you one thing first?'

'Sure.'

'Claire – Dr Argent – was anything done to her eyes?'

Milo didn't answer immediately, and she pressed herself against the tree trunk. 'There was? Oh my God.'

'What about her eyes concerns you, Ms Ott?'

She shook her head. One hand reached back and tugged her ponytail. The man with the dog was leaving the park. Her eyes followed him for a second before returning to the swinging child. The boy squalled as the young woman pulled him off, struggled to stuff him into a stroller, finally wheeled away.

Just the three of us now, as if a stage had been cleared. I heard birds sing; distant, foreign chatter; some traffic from Fuller Avenue.

Milo was looking at Heidi. I saw his jaw loosen deliberately and he bent one leg, trying to appear casual.

She said, 'OK, this is going to sound weird but . . . three days ago, one of the patients – a patient Dr Argent worked with – said something to me. The day before Dr Argent was killed. It was at night, I was double-shifting, doing bed check, and all of a sudden he started talking to me. Which by itself was unusual, he's barely verbal. Didn't talk at all until Dr Argent and I began—'

She stopped, pulled the ponytail forward so that it rested on her shoulder, played with the ends, squeezed them. 'You're going to think I'm flaky.'

'Not at all,' said Milo. 'You're doing exactly the right thing.'

'OK. This is the situation: I'm just about to leave his room and this guy starts mumbling, like he's praying or chanting. I pay attention because he hardly ever talks – never really talks at all. But then he stops and I turn to leave again. Then all of a sudden, he says her name – "Dr A." I say, "Excuse me?" And he repeats it a little louder. "Dr A." I say, "What *about* Dr A.?" And he gives this strange smile – till now, he never smiled either – and says, "Dr A. bad eyes in a box." I say, "What?" Now he's back to looking down at his knees the way he always does and he's not saying anything and I can't get him to repeat it. So I leave again and when I reach the door he makes this sound I've heard him make a few times before – like a bark – *ruh ruh ruh*. I never knew what it meant but now I get the feeling it's his way of laughing – he's laughing at *me*. Then he stops, he's back in space, and I'm out of there.'

Milo said, '"Dr A. bad eyes in a box." Have you told anyone about this?'

'No, just you. I planned to talk to Claire about it, but I never got to see her because the next day . . .' She bit her lip. 'The reason I didn't mention it to anyone at the hospital was because I figured it was just crazy talk. If we paid attention every time someone talked crazy, we'd never get any work done. But the next day, when Claire didn't come to work, and later in the afternoon I heard the news, it freaked me out. I still didn't say anything, because I didn't know where to go with it – and what connection could there be? Then when I read the paper and it said she'd been found in her car trunk, I'm like, "'Boxed up' could be a car trunk, right? This is freaky." But the paper didn't mention anything about her eyes, so I thought maybe by "bad eyes" he meant her wearing glasses, it probably *was* just crazy talk. Although why would he say something about it all of a sudden when usually he doesn't speak at all? So I kept thinking about it, didn't know what to do, but when I saw you yesterday, I figured I should call. And now you're telling me something *was* done to her eyes.'

She exhaled. Licked her lips.

Milo said, 'I didn't exactly say that, ma'am. I asked why Dr Argent's eyes concerned you.'

'Oh.' She slumped. 'OK, so I'm making a big deal. Sorry for wasting your time.' She started to walk away. Milo placed a big hand on her wrist.

'No apologies necessary, Ms Ott. You did the right thing.' Out came his pad. 'What's this patient's name?'

'You're going to *pursue* it? Listen, I don't want to make waves—'

'At this point,' said Milo, 'I can't afford to eliminate anything.'

'Oh.' She picked some bark from the tree trunk and examined a fingernail. 'The administration doesn't like publicity. This is not going to earn me gold stars.'

'What's the problem with publicity?'

'Mr Swig believes in no-news-is-good-news. We depend on politicians for funding and our patients aren't exactly looked upon kindly, so the lower the profile, the fewer the budget cuts.' She flicked bits of bark from under her nail. Slender fingers twirled the ponytail again. Shrug. 'I opened the can, what did I expect. No big deal, I've been thinking about leaving anyway. Starkweather's not what I expected.'

'In what way?'

'Too repetitious. Basically, I baby-sit grown men. I was looking for something a little more clinical. I want to go back to school to become a psychologist, thought this would be a good learning experience.'

'Dr Delaware's a psychologist.'

'I figured that,' she said, smiling at me. 'When Hatterson said he was a doctor. You wouldn't exactly be taking a surgeon around on the ward, would you?'

'This patient,' I said. 'Is there any particular reason he'd pay attention to Dr Argent?'

'Not really, except she worked with him. I was helping her. We were trying to raise his verbal output, getting him to interact more with his surroundings.'

'Behavior modification?' I said.

'That was the ultimate goal – some kind of reward system. But it didn't get that far. Basically, she just talked to him, trying to build up rapport. She had me spending time with him, too. To bring him out of his isolation. No one else bothered with him.'

'Why's that?'

'Probably no one wanted to. He's got difficult . . . personal habits. He makes noises in his sleep, doesn't like to bathe. He eats bugs when he finds them, garbage off the floor. Worse stuff. He doesn't have roommates because of that. Even at Starkweather, he's an outcast.'

'But Claire saw something workable in him,' I said.

'I guess,' she said. 'She told me he was a challenge. And actually, he did respond a bit – the last few weeks, I got him to pay attention, sometimes nod when I asked yes-or-no questions. But no real sentences. Nothing like what he said that day.'

'"Dr A. bad eyes in a box."'

She nodded. 'But how could he know? I mean, it doesn't make sense. This is nothing, right?'

'Probably,' I said. 'Did this man associate with anyone who could've planned to hurt Claire? Maybe someone who's been discharged?'

'No way. He didn't associate with anyone, period. And no one's been discharged since I've worked there. No one gets out of Starkweather.'

'How long have you worked there?'

'Five months. I came on right after Claire did. No, I wouldn't be looking for any friends of this guy. Like I said, no one hangs out with him. On top of his mental problems, he's physically impaired. Tardive dyskinesia.'

Milo said, 'What's that?'

'Side effects. From the antipsychotic drugs. His are pretty bad. His walk is unsteady, he sticks his tongue out constantly, rolls his head. Sometimes he gets active and marches in place, or his neck goes to one side, like this.'

She demonstrated, straightened, kept her back to the tree trunk. 'That's all I know. I'd like to go now, if that's OK.'

Milo said, 'His name, ma'am.'

Another tug on the ponytail. 'We're not supposed to give out names. Even *our* patients have confidentiality. But I guess all that changes when . . .' Her arms went loose and her hands joined just below her pubis, fingers tangling, remaining in place, as if protecting her core.

'OK,' she said. 'His name's Ardis Peake, maybe you've heard of him. Claire said he was notorious, the papers gave him a nickname: Monster.'

10

MILO'S JAW was too smooth: Forced relaxation. 'I've heard of Peake.'

So had I.

A long time ago. I'd been in grad school – at least fifteen years before.

Heidi Ott's calm was real. She'd been a grade-school kid. Her parents would have shielded her from the details.

I remembered the facts the papers had printed.

A farm town named Treadway, an hour north of LA. Walnuts and peaches, strawberries and bell peppers. A pretty place, where people still left their doors unlocked. The papers had made a big deal out of that.

Ardis Peake's mother had worked as a maid and cook for one of the town's prominent ranch families. A young couple. Inherited wealth, good looks, a big old frame house, a three-story house – what was their name? Peake's name was immediately familiar. What did that say?

I recalled snippets of biography. Peake, born up north in Oregon, a logging camp, father unknown. His mother had cooked for the tree men.

As far as anyone could tell, she and the boy had drifted up and down the coast for most of Ardis's childhood. No school registrations were ever found, and when Peake and his mother Greyhounded into Treadway, he was nineteen and illiterate, preternaturally shy, obviously different.

Noreen Peake scrubbed tavern floors until landing the job at the ranch. She lived in the main house, in a maid's room off the kitchen, but Ardis was put in a one-room shack behind a peach orchard.

He was gawky, mentally dull, so quiet many townspeople thought him mute. Unemployed, with too much time on his hands, he was ripe for mischief. But his sole offenses were some paint-sniffing incidents out behind the Sinclair store, broad-daylight acts so reckless they confirmed his reputation as retarded. The ranch owners finally gave him a job of sorts: Rat catcher, gopher killer, snake butcher. The farm's human terrier.

His territory was the five acres immediately surrounding the house. His task could never be completed, but he took to it eagerly, often working late into the night with pointed stick and poison, sometimes crawling in the dirt – keeping his nose to the ground, literally.

A dog's job assigned to a man, but by all accounts Peake had found his niche.

It all ended on a cool, sweet Sunday morning, two hours before dawn.

His mother was found first, a heavy, wide woman sitting in a faded housedress at the kitchen table, a big plate of Granny Smith apples in front of her, some of them cored and peeled. A sugar bowl, white flour, and a stick of butter on a nearby counter said it would have been a pie-baking day. A pot roast was in the oven and two heads of cabbage had been chopped for coleslaw. Noreen Peake was an insomniac, and all-night cooking sprees weren't uncommon.

This one ended prematurely. She'd been decapitated. Not a neat incision. The head lay on the floor, several feet from her chair. Nearby was a butcher knife still flecked with cabbage. Another knife from the same cutlery set – heavier, larger – had been removed from the rack.

Bloody sneaker prints led to a service staircase. On the third floor of the house, the young rancher and his wife lay in bed, covers tossed aside, embracing. Their heads had been left on, though severed jugulars and tracheas said it wasn't for lack of effort. The big knife had seared through flesh but failed at bone. Facial crush wounds compounded the horror. A gore-encrusted baseball bat lay on the floor in front of the footboard. The husband's bat; he'd been a high school slugger, a champ.

The papers made a big deal about how good-looking the couple had been in life – what was their *name* . . . Ardullo. Mr and Mrs Ardullo. Golden couple, everything to live for. Their faces had been obliterated.

Down the hall, the children's bedrooms. The older one, a five-year-old girl, was found in her closet. The coroner guessed she'd heard something and hid. The big knife, badly bent but intact, had been used on her. The papers spared their readers further details.

A playroom separated her room from the baby's. Toys were strewn everywhere.

The baby was a ten-month-old boy. His crib was empty.

Fading sneaker prints led back down to the laundry room and out a rear door, where the trail lightened to specks along a winding stone path and disappeared in the dirt bordering the kitchen garden.

Ardis Peake was found in his shack – a wood-slat and tar-paper thing rancid with the stink of a thousand dogs. But no animals lived there, just Peake, naked, unconscious on a cot, surrounded by empty paint cans and glue tubes, flasks bearing the label of a cheap Mexican vodka, an empty filled with urine. A plastic packet frosted with white crystal residue was found under the cot. Methamphetamine.

Blood smeared the rat catcher's mouth. His arms were red-drenched to the elbows, his hair and bedding burgundy. Gray-white specks in his hair were found to be human cerebral tissue. At first he was thought to be another victim.

But he stirred when prodded. Later, everything washed off.

Fast asleep.

A scorching smell compounded the reek.

No stove in the shack, just a hot plate powered by an old car battery. A tin wastebasket serving as a saucepan had been left on the heat. The metal was too thin; the bottom was starting to burn through, and the stench of charring tin lent a bitter overlay to the reek of offal, putrid food, unwashed clothes.

Something else. Heady. A stew.

The baby's pajamas on the floor, covered by flies.

Ardis Peake had never been one for cooking. His mother had always taken care of that.

This morning, he'd tried.

* * *

Heidi Ott said, 'I never heard of him till I came to Starkweather. Way before my time.'

'So you know what he did,' said Milo.

'Killed a family. It's in his chart. Claire told me about it before she asked me to work with him, said he'd been nonviolent since commitment but I should know what I was dealing with. I said fine. What he did was horrible, but you don't end up at Starkweather for shoplifting. I took the job in the first place because I was interested in the endpoint.'

'The endpoint?'

'The extreme – how low people can go.'

She turned to me, as if seeking approval.

I said, 'Extremes interest you?'

'I think extremes can teach us a lot. What I'm trying to say is, I wanted to see if I was really cut out for mental-health work, figured if I could handle Starkweather, I could cope with anything.'

Milo said, 'But the job ended up being repetitious.'

'There's a lot of routine. I guess I was naive, thinking I was going to see fascinating things. Between their medication and their disabilities, most of the guys are pretty knocked out – passive. That's what I meant by baby-sitting. We make sure they get fed and stay reasonably clean, keep them out of trouble, give them time out when they pull tantrums, the same as you'd do with a little kid. Same thing over and over, shift after shift.'

'Dr Argent was new to the job,' I said. 'Any idea if she liked it?'

'She seemed to.'

'Did she talk about why she'd transferred from County General?'

'No. She didn't talk much. Only work-related stuff, nothing personal.'

'Was she assigned to Ardis Peake, or did she choose to work with him?'

'I think she chose to – the doctors have a lot of freedom. We techs are pretty much bound by routine.'

'Did she say why she wanted to work with Peake?'

She stroked her ponytail, arched her back. 'All I remember her saying about him was that he was a challenge. Because of how low-functioning he was. If we could increase his behavioral repertoire, we could do it for anyone. That appealed to me.'

'Learning from the extreme.'

'Exactly.'

'What about the Skills for Daily Living group?' I said. 'What was her goal there?'

'She wanted to see if the men could learn to take better care of themselves – grooming, basic manners, paying attention when someone else spoke. Even with their psychosis.'

'How were men picked for the group?'

'Claire picked them. I was just there to assist.'

'See any progress?'

'Slow,' she said. 'We only had seven sessions. Tomorrow would've been eight.' She swiped at her eyes.

'Any particular disciplinary problems in the group?'

'Nothing unusual. They have their moods; you have to be firm and consistent. If you're asking if any of them resented her, not at all. They liked her. Everyone did.'

Tug. She chewed her cheek, arched her back again. 'It really stinks. She was a good teacher, very patient. I can't believe anyone would want to hurt her.'

'Even though she didn't get personal,' said Milo, 'did she tell you anything about her life outside work?'

'No. I'm sorry – I mean, you just didn't sit down for coffee with her.'

Yet she referred to Claire by her first name. The instant familiarity of Gen X.

She said, 'I really wish I could tell you more. The thing about Peake – it's nothing, right?'

'Probably nothing,' said Milo. 'But I will want to talk to him.'

She shook her head. 'You don't talk to him. Not in any normal way. Most of the time he's totally spaced. It took Claire and me months just to get him to pay attention.'

'Well,' said Milo, 'we'll see what happens.'

She reached back, pulled a leaf from the tree, and ground it between her fingers. 'I guess I expected that. Better brace myself for a lecture from Swig. I probably should've gone through him first.'

'Want me to run interference for you?'

'No, I can handle it. At least I know I did the right thing – time to move on, anyway. Maybe do some work with children.'

'How much more school do you have?' I said.

'One more year for a bachelor's, then graduate work. I'm paying for it all, so it'll take time. One thing about Starkweather, the pay's good. But I'll find something.'

Milo said, 'So you're definitely leaving?'

'Can't see any reason not to.'

'Too bad. You might be able to help some more.'

'Help how?'

'By trying to draw Peake out again.'

Her laugh was skittish. 'No thanks, Detective Sturgis. I don't want to get any more involved. And he doesn't really talk to me, either.'

'He did the day before Claire was killed.'

'That was – I don't know what that was all about,' she said.

Milo smiled. 'I can't convince you, huh?'

She smiled back. 'I don't think so.'

'Think of it as learning more about extremes – a challenge.'

'If I want a challenge now, I rock-climb.'

'A climber,' said Milo. 'I'm afraid of heights.'

'You get used to it. That's the point. I like all sorts of challenges – physical things – climbing, parasailing, sky-diving. Getting physical's especially important when you work in a place like Starkweather. Having to watch yourself all the time, but no exercise, no movement. Anyway . . .' She looked at her watch. 'I'd really like to go now, OK?'

'OK.'

She shook our hands, walked away with an easy athletic stride.

Milo said, 'So what the hell is this thing with *Peake* all about?'

'Probably nothing,' I said. 'He muttered something; normally Heidi wouldn't have noticed. After Claire was murdered, she got scared.'

'Little Ms Daredevil?'

'Jumping out of planes is one thing. Murder's another.'

'"Dr A bad eyes in a box,"' he said. 'What if it's not pure gibberish? What if Peake had a buddy who got out? Someone who told him he was gonna do something bad to Claire?'

'It doesn't sound as if Peake has buddies. Heidi said he rooms alone, no one wants to associate with him. But maybe. Let's have a closer look at him.'

'Ardis Peake,' he said. 'Long time since he did his thing. Sixteen years ago. I know exactly, because I'd just started Homicide, first thing they hand me is a screwed-up whodunit, I'm sweating over it, not getting anywhere, wondering if I went into the wrong line of work. A few days later Peake does his thing over in Whateverville, some local yokel sheriff solves it the same day. I remember thinking some people have all the luck: Asshole just hands himself over on a platter with garnish. Few years later, when I took that VICAP course at Quantico, the Fibbies used Peake as a teaching case, said he was typical of the disorganized spree killer, just about defined the profile: Raving lunatic with poor hygiene, mind coming apart at the seams, no serious effort to hide the crime. "Bad eyes in a box" – so now he's gone from psycho to prophet?'

'Or he overheard another patient say something and repeated it. I just can't see him involved in Claire's murder. Because he *is* disorganized. Borderline intelligence. And whoever murdered Claire – and Richard – planned meticulously.'

'That's assuming Peake really is that messed up.'

'You think he's been faking all his life?'

'You tell me – is it possible?'

'Anything's *possible*, but I'd say it's highly unlikely. You're saying he's part of some murderous duo? Then why would he brag about it? On the other hand, a guy like that, withdrawn, never talks, someone might figure he's not tuned in, let down their guard around him, say something interesting. If that's what happened, maybe Peake can focus enough to tell you who it was.'

'Back to Bedlam,' he said. 'Peachy.'

We headed out of the park, toward our cars.

I said, 'One thing's consistent with what we were just saying about Claire. Picking Peake as a project because she wanted serious pathology. But what if something else happened along the way? In her attempt to open Peake up, she opened *herself* up – had the poor judgment to talk about herself. In therapist jargon, it's called self-disclosure, and we're taught to be careful about it. But people mess up all the time – focusing on themselves instead of the patient. Claire's specialty was neuropsych. As a psychotherapist, she was a novice.'

'She never got personal, but with Peake she related?'

'Precisely because Peake couldn't relate *back*.'

'So,' he said, 'she tells him something about a box, bad eyes . . . whatever the hell that means, and he spits it back.'

'Maybe a box refers to some kind of bondage game.'

'Back to dominance . . . You really see her that way?'

'I'm just throwing out suggestions,' I said. 'Maybe Claire selected Peake out of some great sense of compassion. Robin disagrees with my impression of Claire's house. She says it just sounds like Claire wanted privacy.'

'Something else,' he said. 'Something that made my little

heart go plink-a-plink when Heidi mentioned Peake's name. At Quantico, his case summary was passed around. I remember relatively seasoned guys looking at the photos and groaning; a couple had to leave the room. It was beyond butchery, Alex. I wasn't a hardened bastard yet. All I could do was skim.'

He stopped so suddenly that I walked past him several steps.

'What?' I said.

'One of the photos,' he said. 'One of the kids. The older one. Peake took the eyes.'

11

William Swig said, 'You think that *means* something?'

It was just after four P.M. and we were back in his office. Milo's unmarked was low on gas, so he left it at the park and I drove to Starkweather.

On the way, he made two calls on the cell phone. An attempt to reach the sheriff of Treadway, California, resulted in a rerouting to the voicemail system of a private security firm named Bunker Protection. Put on hold for several minutes, he finally got through. The brief conversation left him shaking his head.

'Gone,' he said.

'The sheriff?'

'The whole damn town. It's a retirement community now, called Fairway Ranch. Bunker does the policing. I talked to some robocop with an attitude: "All questions of that nature must be referred to national headquarters in Chicago."'

The call to Swig connected, but when we arrived at the hospital's front gate, the guard hadn't been informed. Phoning Swig's office again finally got us in, but we had to wait awhile before Frank Dollard showed up to walk us across the yard. This time he barely greeted us. Impending evening hadn't tamed the heat. Only three men were out on the yard, one of them Chet, waving his huge hands wildly as he told stories to the sky.

The moment we passed through the end gate, Dollard stepped away and left us to enter the gray building alone. Swig was waiting just inside the door. He hurried us into his office.

Now he tented his hands and rocked in his desk chair. 'A box, eyes – this is obviously psychotic rambling. Why would you take it seriously, Doctor?'

'Even psychotics can have something to say,' I said.

'Can they? I can't say I've found that to be the case.'

'Maybe it's no big lead, sir,' said Milo, 'but it does bear follow-up.'

Swig's intercom buzzed. He pressed a button and his secretary's voice said, 'Bill? Senator Tuck.'

'Tell him I'll call him back.' Back to us: 'So . . . all this comes via Heidi Ott?'

'Does she have credibility problems?' said Milo.

Another beep. Swig jabbed the button irritably. The secretary said, 'Bill? Senator Tuck says no need to call him back, he was just reminding you of your aunt's birthday party this Sunday.'

'Fine. Hold my calls. Please.' Rolling back, Swig crossed his legs and showed us his ankles. Under his blue trousers he wore white sweat socks and brown, rubber-soled walkers. 'State Senator Tuck's married to my mother's sister.'

'That should help with funding,' said Milo.

'On the contrary. State Senator Tuck doesn't approve of this place, thinks all our patients should be hauled outside and shot. His views on the matter harden especially during election years.'

'Must make for spirited family parties.'

'A blast,' Swig said sourly. 'Where was I . . . yes, Heidi. The thing to remember about Heidi is she's a rookie, and rookies can be impressionable. Maybe she heard something, maybe she didn't, but either way I can't believe it matters.'

'Even though it's Ardis Peake we're talking about?'

'Him or anyone else. The point is, he's here. Locked up securely.' Swig turned to me: 'He's withdrawn, severely asocial, extremely dyskinesic, has a whole boatload of negative symptoms, rarely leaves his room. Since he's been with us he's never shown any signs whatsoever of any high-risk behavior.'

'Does he receive mail?' said Milo.

'I'd tend to doubt it.'

'But he might.'

'I'd tend to doubt it,' Swig repeated. 'I'm sure when he was first committed there was some of the usual garbage – screwed-up women proposing marriage, that kind of thing. But now he's ancient history. Obscure, the way he should be. I'll tell you one thing: In the four years I've been here he's never received a visitor. In terms of his overhearing something, he has no friends among the other patients that I or anyone else on the staff is aware of. But what if he did? Anyone he might have overheard would be confined here, too.'

'Unless someone's been released recently.'

'No one's been released since Claire Argent came on board. I checked.'

'I appreciate that.'

'No problem,' said Swig. 'Our goal's the same: Keep the citizens safe. Believe me, Peake's no threat to anyone.'

'I'm sure you're right,' said Milo. 'But if he was receiving mail or sending it, no one on the staff would be monitoring it. Same with his phone calls—'

'No one would *officially* be monitoring content unless Peake acted out, but—' Swig held up a finger, punched four digits on his phone. 'Arturo? Mr Swig. Are you aware of any mail – letters, packages, postcards – anything arriving recently for Patient Three Eight Four Four Three? Peake, Ardis. Even junk mail . . . You're sure? Anything at all since you can remember? Keep an eye out, OK, Arturo? No, no authority for that, just let me know if anything shows up. Thanks.'

He put the phone down. 'Arturo's been here three years. Peake doesn't get mail. In terms of phone calls, I can't prove it to you, but believe me, nothing. He never comes out of his room. Doesn't talk.'

'Pretty low-functioning.'

'Subterranean.'

'Any idea why Dr Argent chose to work with Peake?'

'Dr Argent worked with lots of patients. I don't believe she gave Peake any special attention.' His finger rose again. Springing up, he left the office, closing the door hard.

Milo said, 'Helpful fellow, even though it kills him.'

'As Heidi said, he thinks publicity's the kiss of death.'

'I was wondering how such a young guy got to be in charge. Now I know. Uncle Senator may not approve of this place, but how much you wanna bet he had something to do with nephew getting the gig.'

The door swung open and Swig bounded in, carrying a brown cardboard folder. Bypassing Milo, he handed it to me and sat down.

Peake's clinical chart. Thinner than I'd have predicted. Twelve pages, mostly medication notes signed by various psychiatrists, a few notations about the tardive dyskinesia: 'TD, no change.' 'TD intensifies, more lingual thrust.' 'TD. Unsteady gait.' Immediately after arriving at Starkweather, Peake had been placed on Thorazine, and for fifteen years he'd been kept on the drug. He'd also received several medications for the side effects: Lithium carbonate, tryptophan, Narcan. 'No change.' 'No behav. change.' Everything but Thorazine had been phased out.

The last two pages bore four months of nearly identical weekly entries written in a small, neat hand:

'Indiv. sess. to monitor verb., soc., assess beh. plan. H. Ott assist. C. Argent, PhD.'

I passed the chart to Milo.

'As you can see, Dr Argent was monitoring his speech, not treating him,' said Swig. 'Probably measuring his response to medication, or something like that.'

'How many other patients was she monitoring?' said Milo.

Swig said, 'I don't know her total load, nor could I give you specific names without going through extensive review procedures.' He held out his hand for the folder. Milo flipped pages for a second and returned it.

Milo said, 'Did Dr Argent seek out severely deteriorated patients?'

Swig rolled forward, placed his elbows on the desk, expelled a short, pufflike laugh. 'As opposed to? We don't house mild neurotics here.'

'So Peake's just one of the guys.'

'No one at Starkweather's one of the guys. These are dangerous men. We treat them as individuals.'

'OK,' said Milo. 'Thanks for your time. Now, may I please see Peake?'

Swig flushed. 'For what purpose? We're talking barely functioning.'

'At this point in my investigation, I'll take what I can get.' Milo smiled.

Swig made the puffing sound again. 'Look, I appreciate your dedication to your job, but I can't have you coming in here every time some theory emerges. Way too disruptive, and as I told you yesterday, it's obvious Dr Argent's murder had nothing to do with Starkweather.'

'The last thing I want to do is disrupt, sir, but if I ignored this, I'd be derelict.'

Swig shook his head, poked at a mole, tried to smooth the fluff atop his bald head.

'We'll keep it short, Mr Swig.'

Swig dug a nail into his scalp. A crescent-shaped mark rose on the shiny white skin. 'If I thought that would be the end of it, I'd say sure. But I get a clear sense you're hell-bent on finding your solution here.'

'Not at all, sir. I just need to be thorough.'

'All right,' Swig said with sudden anger. He seemed to hurl himself upward. After fiddling with his tie, he took out a chrome ring filled with keys.

'Here we go,' he said, jangling loudly. 'Let's peek in on Mr Peake.'

On the ride up the elevator, Milo said, 'Heidi Ott's not in any hot water, is she, sir?'

'Why would she be?'

'For telling me about Peake.'

Swig said, 'Am I going to be vindictive? Christ, no, of course not. She was doing her civic duty. How could I be anything other than a proud administrator?'

'Sir—'

'Don't *worry*, Detective Sturgis. Too much worry is bad for the soul.'

We got out on C Ward. Swig opened the double doors and we walked through.

'Room Fifteen S&R,' he said. The halls were still crowded. Some of the inmates moved aside as we approached. Swig paid them no attention, walked briskly. Midway down the hall, he stopped and inspected the key ring. He was wearing short sleeves, and I noticed how muscled his forearms were. The bulky, sinewed arms of a laborer, not a bureaucrat.

Double dead bolts fastened the door. The hatch was also key-locked.

Milo said, 'Fifteen S&R. Suppression and Restraint?'

'Not because he needs it,' said Swig, still shuffling through the keys. 'The S&R rooms are smaller, so when a patient lives alone we sometimes use them. He lives alone because his hygiene's not always what it should be.' Swig began shoving keys up the ring. Finally, he found what he was looking for and stabbed both locks. The tumblers clicked; he held the door open six inches and looked inside.

Swinging it back, he said, 'He's all yours.'

Six-by-six space. Unlike the hallways, generous ceilings – ten feet high or close to it.

More of a tube than a room.

High on the walls were mounted thick metal rings – fasteners for the iron shackles now coiled up against the plaster like techno-sculpture.

Soft walls, pinkish white, covered with some kind of dull-looking foam. Faint scuff marks said the material couldn't be ripped.

Dim. The only light came through a tiny plastic window, a skinny, vertical rectangle that aped the shape of the room. Two round, recessed ceiling bulbs under thick plastic covers were turned off. No internal switch, just the one out in the hall. A lidless plastic toilet took up one corner. Precut strips of toilet paper littered the floor.

No nightstand, no real furniture, just two plastic drawers built into the foam walls. Molded. No hardware.

Music came from somewhere in the ceiling. Sugary strings and belching horns – some long-forgotten forties pop tune in a major key, done by a band that didn't care.

On a thin mattress attached to a raised plastic platform sat . . . something.

Naked from the waist up.

Skin the color of whey, blue-veined, hairless. Ribs so deeply etched they evoked a turkey carcass the day after Thanksgiving.

Khaki pants covered his bottom half, bagging on stick legs, stretching over knees as knobby as hand-carved canes. His feet were bare but dirty, the nails untrimmed and brown. His head was shaved clean. Black stubble specked his chin and cheeks. Very little stubble on top said he'd gone mostly bald.

His cranium was strangely contoured: Very broad on top, the hairless skull flat at the apex, furrowed in several places, as if a child's fingers had dragged their way through white putty. Under a bulging shelf of a brow, his eyes were lost in moon-crater sockets. Gray lids, caved-in cheeks. Below the zygomatic arch, the entire face tapered radically, like a too-sharpened pencil.

The room smelled foul. Vinegary sweat, flatulence, burning rubber. Something dead.

The music played on, nice bouncy dance tune in waltz time.

'Ardis?' said Swig.

Peake's head stayed down. I bent low, caught a full view of his face. Tiny mouth, pinched, lipless. Suddenly it filled: A dark, wet tongue tip showing itself as a liver-colored oval. The tongue retreated. Reappeared. Peake's cheeks bellowed, caved in, inflated again. He rolled his neck to the left. Eyes closed, mouth open. Lots of teeth missing.

Swig stepped closer, came within three feet of the bed.

Peake's head dropped and he looked down at the floor again. His nose was short, very thin – not much more than a wedge of cartilage – and bent up to the left. More putty, the child twisting capriciously. Large but lobeless ears flared battishly. Narrow, vein-encrusted hands ended in tentacle fingers that curled over his knees.

Living skeleton. I'd seen a face like that somewhere . . .

Peake's tongue darted again. He started to rock. Moved his head from side to side. Rolled his neck. Blinked spasmodically. More tongue thrusts.

The mouth had flattened, gone two-dimensional. Moistened by saliva, the lips materialized – port-wine slash in the center of the triangle, vivid against the doughy skin.

It opened again and the tongue extended completely – thick, purplish, mottled, like some cave-dwelling slug.

It hung in the air. Curled. Wagged from side to side. Zipped back.

Out again. In again.

More neck-rolling.

I knew where I'd seen the face. Poster art from my college days. Edvard Munch's *The Scream*.

Hairless melting man clutching his face in primal mental agony. Peake could have posed for the painting.

His hands remained in his lap, but his upper body swayed, trembled, jerked a few times, seemed about to topple. Then he stopped. Righted himself.

Looked in our direction.

He'd butchered the Ardullos at age nineteen, making him thirty-five. He looked ancient.

'Ardis?' said Swig.

No reaction. Peake was staring in our direction but not making contact. He closed his eyes. Rolled his head. Another two minutes of tardive ballet.

Swig gave a disgusted look and waved his hand, as if to say, 'You asked for it.'

Milo ignored that and stepped closer. Peake began rocking

faster, licking his lips, the tongue emerging, curling, retreating. Several toes on his left foot jumped. His left hand fluttered.

'Ardis, it's Mr Swig. I've got some visitors for you.'

Nothing.

Swig said, 'Go ahead, Detective.'

No response to 'Detective.'

I bent and got down at Peake's eye level. Milo did, too. Peake's eyes had remained closed. Tiny waves seemed to ruffle – eyeballs rolling behind gray skin. His chest was white and hairless, freckled with blackheads. Gray nipples – a pair of tiny ash piles. Up close the burning smell was stronger.

Milo said, 'Hey,' with surprising gentleness.

A few new shoulder tics, tongue calisthenics. Peake rolled his head, lifted his right hand, held it in midair, dropped it heavily.

'Hey,' Milo repeated. 'Ardis.' His face was inches from Peake's. I got closer myself, still smelling the combustion but feeling no heat from Peake's body.

'My name's Milo. I'm here to ask you about Dr Argent.'

Peake's movements continued, autonomic, devoid of intent.

'Claire Argent, Ardis. Your doctor. I'm a homicide detective, Ardis. Homicide.'

Not an errant eyeblink.

Milo said, 'Ardis!' very loud.

Nothing. A full minute passed before the lids lifted. Halfway, then a full view of the eyes.

Black slots. Pinpoints of light at the center, but no definition between iris and white.

'Claire Argent,' Milo repeated. 'Dr Argent. Bad eyes in a box.'

The eyes slammed shut. Peake rolled his head, the tongue explored air. One toe jumped, this time on the right foot.

'Bad eyes,' said Milo, nearly whispering, but his voice had gotten tight, and I knew he was fighting to keep the volume down. 'Bad eyes in a box, Ardis.'

Ten seconds, fifteen . . . half a minute.

'A box, Ardis. Dr Argent in a box.'

Peake's neuropathic ballet continued, unaltered.

'Bad eyes,' Milo soothed.

I was looking into Peake's eyes, plumbing for some shred of soul.

Flat black; lights out.

A cruel phrase for mental disability came to mind: 'No one home.'

Once upon a time, he'd destroyed an entire family, speedily, lustily, a one-man plague.

Taking the eyes.

Now his eyes were twin portholes on a ship to nowhere.

No one home.

As if someone or something had snipped the wires connecting body to soul.

His tongue shot forward again. His mouth opened but produced no sound. I kept staring at him, trying to snag some kind of response. He looked through me – no, that implied too much effort.

He was, I was. No contact.

Neither of us was really there.

His mouth cratered, as if for a yawn. No yawn. Just a

gaping hole. It stayed that way as his head craned. I thought of a blind newborn rodent searching for its mother's nipple.

The music from the ceiling switched to 'Perfidia,' done much too slowly. Ostentatious percussion that seemed to lag behind wah-wah trumpets.

Milo tried again, even softer, more urgent: 'Dr Argent, Ardis. Bad eyes in a box.'

The tardive movements continued, random, arrhythmic. Swig tapped his foot impatiently.

Milo stood, knees cracking. I got to my feet, catching an eyeful of the chain on the wall. Coiled, like a sleeping python.

The room smelled worse.

Peake noticed none of it.

No behav. change.

12

OUTSIDE THE room, Swig said, 'Satisfied?'

Milo said, 'Why don't we give Heidi a try with him?'

'You've got to be kidding.'

'Wish I was, sir.'

Swig shook his head, but he hailed a tech standing across the hall. 'Get Heidi Ott, Kurt.'

Kurt hustled off and we waited among the inmates. Patients. Did it make a difference what you called them? I started to notice lots of tardive symptoms – a tremor here, lip work there – but nothing as severe as Peake's. Some of the men seemed oriented; others could have been on another planet. Shuffling feet in paper slippers. Food stains on clothing.

Swig went into the nursing station, used the phone, glanced at his watch. He was back just as Heidi Ott came through the double doors.

'Hello, Heidi.'

'Sir?'

'Because of the information you provided, Detective Sturgis has been trying unsuccessfully to communicate with Ardis Peake. Since you've got a track record, why don't you give it a shot?'

'Sir, I—'

'Don't worry,' said Swig. 'Your sense of duty is beyond reproach. The main thing is, let's get to the bottom of this.'

'I—'

'One thing before you go in there. You're sure Peake actually spoke to you – real words, not just grunts.'

'Yes, sir.'

'Tell me exactly what he said.'

Heidi repeated the story.

'And this was the day before Dr Argent died?'

'Yes, sir.'

'Had Peake talked to you before?'

'Not about Dr Argent.'

'What did he say?'

'Nothing much. Mostly mumbles. Yeah, no, nods, grunts. When we asked him questions.' Tug on the ponytail. 'Nothing, really. That's why I paid attention to him when he did start—'

'You were monitoring his speech.'

'Yes, sir. Dr Argent was hoping she might be able to increase his verbal output. His behavioral output in general.'

'I see,' said Swig. 'Any particular reason she wanted to do that?'

Heidi glanced at us. 'Like I told these gentlemen, she said he was a challenge.'

A faint, scraping sound grew louder, and we all turned. Paper soles on linoleum. A few of the men in the hall had drifted closer. Swig looked at them and they stopped. Retreated.

He smiled at Heidi. 'Looks like you've got the challenge, now.'

She went in alone, stayed for twenty minutes, emerged, shaking her head. 'How long do you want me to try?'

'That'll be enough,' said Swig. 'It was probably just an isolated incident. Meaningless rambling. For all we know, he does that when he's alone. Thanks, Heidi. You can get back to work. We'd all better get back to work.'

As I drove off the grounds, Milo said, 'What the hell turns a human being into *that*?'

'Answer that and you've got the Nobel,' I said.

'But we've got to be talking biology, right? No amount of stress can do that.' The air-conditioning was on, but sweat dripped off his nose and spotted his trousers.

'Even in concentration camps people rarely went mad from suffering,' I said. 'And schizophrenia has the same prevalence in nearly every society – two to four percent. Cultural factors influence how madness is expressed, but they don't cause it.'

'So what is it – brain damage, genetics?'

'The highest risk factor is having a relative with schizophrenia, but only a very small percentage of schizophrenics' relatives become ill. Slightly more schizophrenics are born during winter and spring, when virus levels are higher. Some studies have implicated prenatal influenza. It's all speculation.'

'Hell,' he said, 'maybe it's just bad luck.'

He wiped his face with a tissue, pulled out a panatela, unwrapped it, and jammed it in his mouth, but didn't light up.

'I had a couple crazy relatives,' he said. 'Two aunts – my mother's cousins. Loony Letitia had this thing for baking, did it nonstop. Cookies every day, hundreds of them. She ended up spending all her money on flour and sugar and eggs, started neglecting herself, trying to steal ingredients from the neighbors. They finally put her away.'

'Sounds more like manic behavior than schizophrenia,' I said. 'Anyone ever try her on lithium?'

'This was years ago, Alex. She died in the asylum – choked on her dinner, how's that for a bad joke? Then there was Aunt Renee, stumbling around the neighborhood, looking like a mess. She lived till she was pretty old, died in some county facility.'

He laughed. 'That's my pedigree.'

'I had a schizophrenic cousin,' I said. Brett, two years my senior, son of my father's older brother. As children we'd played together. Brett had competed fiercely, cheated chronically. During college he metamorphosed from a Young Republican to an SDS honcho. By his senior year he was an unwashed, silent recluse who accumulated narcotics arrests, dropped out of sight for five years, finally ended up in an Iowa board-and-care home. I assumed he was still alive. There'd been no contact between us for over two decades. Our fathers hadn't been close . . .

'There you go,' said Milo. 'Tainted stock. Starkweather, here we come.'

'Starkweather's only for the chosen few,' I said.

'Bad little madmen. So what makes crazy people violent?'

'Another Nobel question. The main ingredients seem to be alcohol and drug use and a strong delusional system.

But not necessarily paranoia. Psychotics who kill usually aren't trying to protect themselves from attack. They're more likely to be acting on some paranormal or religious delusion – waging war against Satan, battling space aliens.'

'Wonder what Peake's mission was.'

'God only knows,' I said. 'Dope and booze were obviously in play. Maybe he thought the Ardullos were mantises from Pluto. Or nineteen years of twisted sexual impulses finally exploded. Or a random circuit in his brain shorted out. We just don't know why some psychotics blow.'

'Great. I'll never be out of work.' His voice drifted off.

'In one sense,' I said, 'Peake's typical. Schizophrenic breaks occur most frequently in young adulthood. And long before Peake fell apart, he'd been showing signs of schizotypy – it's a fancy name for oddness. Low mental skills, social ineptitude, poor grooming, eccentricities. Some eccentrics stay mildly strange, others move on to full-blown schizophrenia.'

'Oddness,' he said. 'Take a walk in the park, walk out of a restaurant, there're some *odd* guys wanting spare change. Which one's gonna start wielding the cleaver?'

I didn't answer.

He said, 'If Peake had any sort of thought system, he must have been in a helluva lot better shape than what we saw today.'

'Probably. Though behind all the tardive symptoms there could still be some thinking going on.'

'What does "tardive" mean, exactly?'

'Late-onset. It's a reaction to Thorazine.'

'Is it reversible?'

'No. At best, he won't get worse.'

'And he's still crazy. So what good's the Thorazine doing him?'

'Neuroleptics are best at controlling delusions, hallucinations, bizarre behavior. What psychiatrists call the positive symptoms of schizophrenia. The negatives – poor speech, flat mood, apathy, attentional problems – don't usually respond. Drugs can't put back what's missing.'

'Well-behaved vegetables,' he said.

'Peake's an extreme case, possibly because he didn't start out with that much intellect. His TD's also very severe. Though he's not getting that much Thorazine. Despite what Dollard told us about high-dosing, Peake's prescription has remained at five hundred milligrams, well within the recommended range. They probably haven't needed to high-dose him because he behaves himself. Behaves very little. Psychologically, he's disappeared.'

Milo removed the cigar, placed it between his index fingers, and sighted over the tobacco bridge. 'If Peake was taken off Thorazine, would he be able to talk more?'

'It's possible. But he could also fall apart, maybe even revert to violence. And don't forget, he was on Thorazine when he talked to Heidi. So he's capable of speech while medicated. Are you still taking this in-a-box stuff seriously?'

'Nah . . . I guess I can't get away from the eye thing – hey, maybe *I'm* delusional and Peake's a true prophet. Maybe Satan *has* dispatched the Pluto Mantises.'

'Maybe,' I said, 'but would he inform Peake?'

He laughed, chewed the cigar some more. '"Bad eyes in a box."'

'For all we know, Claire tried talking to him about his crime and sparked some kind of memory. "In a box" could mean his own incarceration. Or something else. Or nothing at all.'

'OK, OK, enough of this,' he said, pocketing the cigar. 'Back to basics: Check out Claire's finances and Stargill's. Go over Richard's file again, too. For the hundredth time, but maybe there's something I missed. And if you're not jammed, now's as good a time as any to go see Dr Theobold at County. Maybe one of us will come up with something remotely resembling a factoid.'

He grinned. 'Lacking that, I'll settle for some juicy delusions.'

13

I CALLED Dr Myron Theobold's office and got an appointment for ten-fifteen the next morning. By nine-forty-five I was clearing my head in the fast lane of the 10 East, enduring the crawl to the interchange, moving with the smog stream toward San Bernadino. I got off a few exits later, on Soto Street in East LA, drove past the county morgue, and pulled into the main entrance of the dun-colored metropolis that was County General Hospital.

Perennially underfunded and overstressed, County's a wonder: First-rate medicine for the tired and the poor, last stop for the hopeless and the addled. I'd done some clinical training here, taught occasional seminars, but it had been two years since I'd set foot on the hospital campus. Outwardly, little had changed – the same sprawl of bulky, homely buildings, the constant parade of people in uniforms, the halting march of the ill.

One of those hot, overcast days that makes everything look decayed, but after Starkweather, County seemed fresh, almost perky.

Theobold's office was on the third floor of Unit IV, one of the half-dozen no-frills annexes sprouting at the rear of the complex like afterthoughts. Dazed-looking men and women in open-backed pajamas wandered white-tiled halls. Two grim nurses escorted a heavy black woman toward an open door. IV's in both her arms. Tears marked her cheeks like dew on asphalt. In an unseen place, someone retched. The overhead pager recited names emotionlessly.

Theobold's secretary occupied a space not much bigger than Peake's cell, surrounded by gunmetal filing cabinets. A stuffed Garfield clung to the handle of one drawer. Empty chair. A note said, 'Back in 15 min.'

Theobold must have heard me enter because he stuck his head out of the rear doorway. 'Dr Delaware? Come on in.'

I'd met him a few years ago, and he hadn't changed much. Sixtyish, medium height and build, graying fair hair, white beard, large nose, close-set brown eyes behind aviator specs. He wore a wide-lapeled herringbone sport coat the color of iced tea, a beige vest checked with blue, a white shirt, a blue tie.

I followed him into his office. He was a psychiatry vice-chairman and a respected neurochemistry researcher, but his space wasn't much more generous than the secretary's. Haphazardly furnished with what looked like castoffs, it sported another collection of file cases, brown metal furniture, a storm of books. An attempt to freshen things up with a faux-Navajo rug had failed long ago; the rug's threads were unraveling, its color bands fading. The desk supported a turbulent swirl of paperwork.

Theobold squeezed behind the desk and I took one of the two metal chairs wrinkling the fake Navajo.

'So,' he said. 'It's been a while. You're still officially faculty, aren't you?'

'Courtesy faculty,' I said. 'No salary.'

'How long since you've been down here?'

'Couple of years,' I said. His attempts at cordiality were deepening the lines on his face. 'I appreciate your seeing me.'

'No problem.' He cleared the area around the phone. Papers flew. 'I had no idea you led such an interesting life – police consultant. Do they pay well?'

'About the same as Medi-Cal.'

He managed a chuckle. 'So what have you been up to, otherwise? Still at Western Peds?'

'Occasionally. I do some consulting, mostly legal work. A few short-term treatment cases.'

'Able to deal with the HMO's?'

'I avoid them when I can.'

He nodded. 'So . . . you're here about poor Claire. I suppose that detective thought I'd confide secrets to you that I withheld from him, but there's really nothing more to tell.'

'I think he felt it was more a matter of knowing the right questions to ask.'

'I see,' he said. 'Persistent type, Sturgis. Smarter than he lets on. He tried to disarm me by playing to class consciousness – "I'm the humble working-class cop, you're the big smart doctor." Interesting approach. Does it work?'

'He's got a good solve rate.'

'Good for him . . . The problem is, he was wasting his acting talents on me. I wasn't holding back. I have no inside information about Claire. I knew her as a researcher, not as a person.'

'Everyone seems to say that about her.'

'Well, then,' he said, 'at least I'm consistent. So no one has much to offer about her?'

I nodded.

'And here I thought it was me – the way I run my projects.'

'What do you mean?'

'I like to think of myself as a humane administrator. Hire good people, trust them to do their jobs, for the most part keep my hands off. I don't get involved in their personal lives. I'm not out to parent anyone.'

He stopped, as if expecting me to pass judgment on that.

I said, 'Claire worked for you for six years. She must have liked that.'

'I suppose.'

'How'd you find her?'

'I'd put in for my grant and she applied for the neuropsych position. She was completing a postdoc at Case Western, had published two papers as a grad student, sole author. Nothing earth-shattering, but encouraging. Her interest – alcoholism and reaction times – meshed with mine. No shortage of alcoholics here. I thought she'd be able to attract her own funding, and she did.'

All facts I'd read in Claire's résumé.

'So she worked with you and on her own research.'

'Twenty-five percent of her time was her research; the rest she spent on my longitudinal study of neuroleptic outcomes – NIMH grant, three experimental drugs plus placebo, double-blind. She tested the patients, helped organize the data. We just got renewed for five more years. I just hired her replacement – bright kid from Stanford, Walter Yee.'

'Who else worked on the study?' I said.

'Three research fellows besides Claire – two MD's, one PhD pharmacologist.'

'Was she friendly with any of them?'

'I wouldn't know. As I said, I don't meddle. It's not one of those situations where we fraternize after hours.'

'Five-year renewal,' I said. 'So there was no financial reason for her to leave.'

'Not in the least. She probably could've renewed her own study, too. She had substance-abuse money from NIH, completed the final study before she left. Inconclusive results, but well run, very decent chance. But she never applied.' He glanced upward. 'Never even told me she was allowing the grant to lapse.'

'So she must have been intending to leave for some time.'

'Looks that way. I was pretty irritated at her. For not wanting to follow through. For not communicating. Irked at myself, too, for not staying in touch. If she'd come to me, most likely I'd have been able to raise her to full-time, or to find her something else. She was very good at what she did. Dependable, no complaints. I managed to get Dr Yee on full-time. But she never bothered to – I suppose you're right. She wanted to leave. I have no idea why.'

'So she never complained.'

'Not once. Even the way she told me she was leaving

– no personal meeting; she just sent in a summary of her data with a note that the grant was finished and so was she.'

That reminded me of the way she'd divorced Joe Stargill.

'Who'd she work with on her own grant?'

'She got part-time secretarial help from the main pool, ran all her own studies, analyzed her own data. That was also irksome. I'm sure she could've applied for ancillary funding, brought more money into the department, but she always wanted to work by herself. I suppose I should be grateful. She took care of herself, never bothered me for anything. The last thing I need is someone who requires hand-holding. Still . . . I suppose I should've paid more attention.'

'A loner,' I said.

'But all of us are. In my group. I didn't think I'd been hiring antisocial types, but perhaps on some level . . .' Wide smile. 'Did you know I started as an analyst?'

'Really.'

'You bet, classical Freudian, couch and all. This' – he touched the beard – 'used to be a very analytic goatee. I attended the institute right after residency, got halfway through – hundreds of hours cultivating the proper "hmm" – before I realized it wasn't for me. Wasn't for anyone, in my estimation, except possibly Woody Allen. And look at the shape *he's* in. I quit, enrolled in the biochem PhD program at USC. I'm sure those choices mean something psychodynamically, but I'd rather not waste time trying to figure out what. Claire seemed to me the same way – scientific, focused on reality, self-possessed. Still, she must have been terribly unhappy here.'

'Why do you say that?'

'Leaving for a place like *that*. Have you been there?'

'Yesterday.'

'What's it like?'

'Highly structured. Lots of high-dose medication.'

'Brave new world,' he said. 'I can't see why Claire would have wanted that.'

'Maybe she craved clinical work.'

'Nonsense,' he said sharply. Then he smiled apologetically. 'What I mean is, she could've had all the clinical work she wanted right here. No, I must have missed something.'

'Could I talk to the other fellows?' I said.

'Why not? Walt Yee didn't know her, of course, and I don't believe Shashi Lakshman did, either – he's the pharmacologist, has his own lab in a separate building. But maybe she interfaced with the MD's – Mary Hertzlinger and Andy Velman. Let me call Shashi first.'

A few seconds on the phone confirmed that Dr Lakshman had never met Claire. We took the stairs down to a second-floor lab and found Doctors Hertzlinger and Velman typing at personal computers.

Both psychiatric fellows were in their thirties and had on white coats. Mary Hertzlinger wore a short brown dress under hers. She was thin, with cropped platinum-blond hair, ivory skin, well-formed but chapped lips. Andrew Velman's coat was buttoned up high, revealing a black shirt collar and the tight knot of a lemon-yellow tie. He was short, broad, with black wavy hair, a gold stud in his left ear.

I asked them about Claire.

Velman spoke first, in a clipped voice. 'Virtual stranger. I've been here two years and maybe we exchanged twenty sentences. She always seemed too busy to hang out. Also, I do the structured clinical interviews on the study and she did the neuropsych testing, so at any given time, we'd be with different patients.'

'Did she ever say why she was leaving to work at Starkweather?'

'No,' he said. 'I didn't even know about that until Mary told me.' He glanced at Hertzlinger. So did Theobold.

She held her coat closed with one hand and said, 'She told me a few days before she left.' Low, smooth voice. 'I had a really small office on the floor below, and she asked me if I wanted hers. I went to look at it and said yes, helped her carry some boxes to her car. She said her grant had run out and she hadn't tried to renew it. She'd just written a note informing Dr Theobold.'

Theobold said, 'What reason did she give you, Mary?'

'None.'

'What was her mood when she told you?' I said.

'Pretty calm. Not agitated or upset . . . I'd have to describe her as calm and deliberate. As if she'd planned it for a while, was at peace with it.'

'Time to move on,' said Velman.

'Did you socialize with her?' I asked Hertzlinger.

She shook her head. 'Same thing as Andy – we had almost no contact. I've only been here a year. We saw each other in the cafeteria and had coffee. Maybe three, four times. Never lunch. I never saw her *eat* lunch. Sometimes when

I was on my way out to the caf, I'd pass her office and her door would be open and she'd be at her desk working. I remember thinking, *What a work ethic, she must be extremely productive*.'

'The times you did have coffee,' I said, 'what did you talk about?'

'Work, data. After I found out what happened to her, I realized how little I knew about her. It's so grotesque – do the police have any idea who did it?'

'Not yet.'

'Terrible,' she said.

Velman said, 'Had to have something to do with Starkweather. Look at the patient population she got herself involved with.'

I said, 'Only problem is, the patients don't get out.'

'Never?'

'So they claim.'

He frowned.

'Did she tell either of you that she was going to Starkweather?'

Velman shook his head.

Mary Hertzlinger said, 'She told me. The day we moved the boxes. It surprised me, but I didn't question her – she was like that. You didn't get personal with her.'

'Did she give a reason?' I said.

'Not really a reason,' she said. 'But she did say something . . . uncharacteristically flippant. We'd just loaded the car. She thanked me, wished me luck, and then she smiled. Almost *smugly*.'

'What was funny?' said Theobold.

'Exactly,' said Hertzlinger. 'I said something to the effect that "I'm glad you're pleased about your plans." That's when she said it: "It's not a matter of being pleased, Mary. So many madmen, so little time."'

14

SHE WAS in a big damn hurry to work with psychotics?' said Milo.

It was noon. We were standing next to the Seville, on Butler Avenue, across from the West LA station.

'She had plenty of psychotics at County,' I said. 'She wanted *madmen*.'

'Why? To squeeze a few more syllables out of them? To hell with all that, Alex, I'm concentrating on the boring stuff for now. Located a safe-deposit box at her bank, actually managed to finagle my way in with the death certificate. No cash, no dope, no B&D videos, no drooling letters from psycho pen pals. Stone empty. So if she did have some secret life going, she kept it very well wrapped.'

'Maybe we should go back further – grad school, the years before she moved to LA. I can try talking to someone at Case Western.'

'Sure, but tomorrow you'll have a chance at something better. Her parents are arriving on the red-eye tonight. I have a date with them at eight A.M. down at the morgue. No need for them to view the body, tried to talk them out of it, but they insisted. After all that fun, I'll try to sit down with them. I'll give you a call where and when. Probably be late afternoon.'

Several young officers walked by. He watched them for a while, stared at the roof of the Seville, flicked dirt off the vinyl. 'Reviewing Richard's file was sobering. Not as much of a file as I remembered. The only people I spoke to were Richard's landlady and parents and the staff at the restaurant where he worked. No listings in the "Known Associates" column. Sound familiar? I made another try at locating the film outfit that Richard might've auditioned for – Thin Line. Still can't find a trace of them. You'd think even a rinky-dink outfit would make a mark somewhere.'

'Something about the movie bothers you?'

'They've got carpenters on movie sets, right? All sorts of tools, including saws.'

'Plenty of knives in restaurants, too.'

'Maybe I'll go back there.'

'One possible angle on Thin Line,' I said. 'Even fly-by-nights need equipment. A small outfit would be likely to rent rather than own. Why not check some of the leasing companies?'

'Very good,' he said. 'Thank you, sir.' He laughed. 'Any other case I wouldn't consider the film thing half a lead. But these two – you don't wanna blame the victim, Alex, but the least they could've done is *relate* to someone.'

I wanted another look at Claire's résumé, so the two of us crossed over to the station and walked upstairs to the detectives' room. Milo retrieved the box of material he'd taken from Claire's house. He hadn't booked it into the evidence room, meaning he'd planned some review himself. He left to get a cup of coffee while I searched.

I found the résumé near the middle, neatly typed and stapled. The Wite-Out in the 'Marital Status' slot was a chalky lozenge. She'd been born in Pittsburgh, lived there through college before moving to Cleveland to attend Case Western.

Thousands of miles from Richard Dada's Arizona childhood, little chance of a connection there.

I scrounged until I found the first study she'd published – the student research that had impressed Myron Theobold.

Solo author, just as he'd said, but at the bottom of the first page, in very small print, were acknowledgments and thanks: 'To the Case Western Graduate Fund for supplies and data analysis; to my parents, Ernestine and Robert Ray Argent, for their unwavering support throughout my education; and to my dissertation chairman, Professor Harry I. Racano, for his thoughtful guidance.'

One P.M. in LA was four in Cleveland. Using Milo's phone, I dialed 216 Information. None of the other detectives paid notice to a civilian using city equipment. Scrawling the number for Case Western's psychology department, I called and asked for Professor Racano.

The woman at the other end said, 'I'm sorry, but there's no one here by that name.'

'He used to be on the faculty.'

'Let me check our faculty directory.' Several moments passed. 'No, I'm sorry, sir, not in the current directory or the emeritus list.'

'Is there anyone around who worked in the department ten years ago?'

Silence. 'Hold on, please.'

Another five minutes before another woman said, 'May I ask what this is about?'

'I'm calling from the Los Angeles Police Department.' Literally. 'Unfortunately, one of your alumnae, Dr Claire Argent, was murdered, and we're trying to locate anyone who might have known her back in Cleveland.'

'Oh,' she said. 'Murdered . . . My God, that's terrible . . . Argent. No, I've only been here six years, she must have been before my time – how terrible, let me check.' I heard paper shuffling. 'Yes, here she is, on the alumni roster. And she was Professor Racano's student?'

'Yes, ma'am.'

'Well, I'm sorry to tell you Professor Racano's deceased as well. Died right after I came on. Cancer. Nice man. Very supportive of his students.'

Racano's tolerance of Claire's solo launch suggested an easygoing nature.

'Is there anyone who might have known Dr Argent, Ms . . . ?'

'Mrs Bausch. Hmm, I'm afraid there aren't too many people in the building right now. There's a big symposium going on over at the main auditorium, one of our professors just won a prize. I can ask around and get back to you.'

'I'd appreciate that.' I gave her Milo's name. Just as I put the phone down, it rang. Milo was nowhere in sight so I took the call. 'Detective Sturgis's desk.'

A familiar voice said, 'I'd like to leave a message for Detective Sturgis.'

'Heidi? It's Dr Delaware.'

'Oh . . . hi – listen, I'm sorry I couldn't get anything out of Peake today.'

'Don't worry about it.'

'It didn't help my credibility with Swig, either. After you were gone he called me into his office and made me go over the whole thing again: What Peake said, when he said it, was I sure I heard right.'

'Sorry for the hassle.'

'It would've sure been nice to be able to prove it . . . Anyway, I just wanted to call to let Detective Sturgis know I've decided to leave Starkweather in a couple of weeks, but if there's anything else he needs, he can call me.'

'Thanks, Heidi. I'll tell him.'

'So,' she said, 'you actually work there? Right at the police station?'

'No. I just happen to be here today.'

'Sounds interesting. Meanwhile, I'll keep trying with Peake, maybe something will come up.'

'Don't put yourself in any jeopardy.'

'What, from Ardis? You saw his condition. Not exactly dangerous. Not that I let my guard down – do you think Claire did?'

'Don't know,' I said.

'I keep thinking about her. What happened to her. It seems so strange that anything could touch her.'

'What do you mean?'

'She seemed like one of those people – caught up in their own worlds. Like she was happy being alone. Didn't *need* anyone else.'

15

I CALLED home before leaving the station. Robin was out, and all that awaited me was paperwork – final reports on custody cases that had already been decided. I told my own voice on the message machine that I'd be back by five.

Talking to myself.

Put a cell phone in a psychotic's hand and he could fake normalcy.

The encounter with Ardis Peake had stayed with me.

Monster.

Hard to connect that mute, emaciated husk with someone capable of destroying an entire family.

What better endorsement for Mr Swig's highly structured system?

What turns a human being into that?

I'd given Milo the short-version lecture and he'd been gracious enough not to complain. But I had no real answers; no one did.

I wondered what questions had led Claire to Starkweather. And Peake. She'd gravitated to him shortly after taking the job. Why, of all the madmen, had *he* been the one whose pathology had drawn her in?

The other thing that troubled me was Peake's assault on

the eyes of the little Ardullo girl. Had I been too hasty minimizing his gibbering at Heidi?

Or perhaps it was simple: Claire had learned about the eyes and discussed it with him. Had it elicited something in him – guilt, excitement, a horrible nostalgia?

Bad eyes in a box. Was the box a coffin? Peake's imagery of the dead child. Reliving the crime and feeding off the memory, the way lust killers did?

It all hinged on learning more about Claire, and so far her ghost had avoided capture.

No entanglements, no known associates. Not much impact on her world.

Ardis Peake, on the other hand, had been a star in his day.

I drove to Westwood and used the computers at the U's research library to look up the Ardullo massacre. The murders had been covered nationally for one week. The periodicals index offered half a page of citations, and I went looking for microfiche.

Most of the articles were nearly identically worded, lifted intact from wire service reports. An arrest headshot showed a young Peake, stick-faced, hollow-cheeked, sporting a full head of long, stringy, dark hair.

Wild-eyed, startled, a cornered animal. The Edvard Munch screamer on jet fuel.

A large bruise spread beneath his left eye. The left side of his face swelled. Rough arrest? If so, it hadn't been reported.

The facts were as I remembered them. Multiple stab

wounds, crushing skull fractures, extensive mutilation, cannibalism. The articles filled in names and places.

Scott and Theresa Ardullo, thirty-three and twenty-nine, respectively. Married six years, both UC Davis agricultural grads. He, 'the scion of a prosperous farming family,' had developed an interest in winegrowing but concentrated on peaches and walnuts.

Brittany, five years old.

Justin, eight months.

Next came the happier-times family photo: Scott hand in hand with a restless-looking little girl who resembled her mother, Theresa holding the baby. Pacifier in Justin's mouth, fat cheeks ballooning around the nipple. Ferris wheel in the background, some kind of fair.

Scott Ardullo had been muscular, blond, crew-cut, grinning with the full pleasure of one who believes himself blessed. His wife, slender, somewhat plain, with long dark hair held in place by a white band, seemed less certain about happy endings.

I couldn't bear another look at the children's faces.

No picture of Noreen Peake, just an account of the way she'd been found, sitting at the kitchen table. My imagination added the smell of apples, cinnamon, flour.

A ranch superintendent named Teodoro Alarcon had found Noreen's body, then discovered the rest of it. He'd been placed under sedation.

No quote from him.

Treadway's sheriff, Jacob Haas, said: 'I served in Korea and this was worse than anything I ever saw overseas. Scott and Terri took those people in out of the goodness of their hearts and this is how they get repaid. It's beyond belief.'

Anonymous townspeople cited Peake's strange habits – he mumbled to himself, didn't bathe, cruised alleys, pawed through garbage cans, ate trash. Everyone had known of his fondness for sniffing propellants. No one had thought him dangerous.

One other attributed quote:

'"Everyone always knew he was weird, but not that weird," said a local youth, Derrick Crimmins. "He didn't hang out with anyone. No one wanted to hang with him because he smelled bad and he was just too weird, maybe into Satan or something."'

No other mention of satanic rituals, and I wondered if there'd been any follow-up. Probably not, with Peake out of circulation.

Treadway was labeled a 'quiet farming and ranching community.'

'"The worst things we usually have," said Sheriff Haas, "are bar fights, once in a while some equipment theft. Nothing like this, never anything like this."'

And that was it.

No coverage of the Ardullos' funeral, or Noreen Peake's.

I kept spooling, found a three-line paragraph in the LA *Times* two months later reporting Peake's commitment to Starkweather.

Using 'Treadway' as a keyword pulled up nothing since the murders.

Quiet town. Extinct town.

How did an entire community die?

Had Peake somehow killed it, too?

* * *

Milo called in a message while I was out on my morning run:

'Mr and Mrs Argent, the Flight Inn on Century Boulevard, Room 129, one P.M.'

I did some paperwork, set out at twelve-thirty, taking Sepulveda toward the airport. Century's a wide, sad strip that cuts through southern LA. Turn east off the freeway and you might end up in some gang gully, carjacked or worse. West takes you to LAX, past the bleak functionalism of airport hotels, cargo depots, private parking lots, topless joints.

The Flight Inn sat next to a Speedy Express maintenance yard. Too large to be a motel, it hadn't passed through hotel puberty. Three stories of white-painted block, yellow gutters, cowgirl-riding-an-airplane logo, inconspicuous entry off to the right topped by a pink neon VACANCY sign. The bi-level self-park wrapped itself around the main building. No security in the lot that I could see. I left the Seville in a ground-floor space and walked to the front as a 747 roared overhead.

A banner out in front advertised king-size beds, color TV, and discount coupons to happy hour at someplace called the Golden Goose. The lobby was red-carpeted, furnished with vending machines selling combs and maps and keychains with Disney characters on the fobs. The black clerk at the counter ignored me as I strolled down the white-block hall. Fast-food cartons had been left outside several of the red doors that lined the corridor. The air was hot and salty, though we were miles from the ocean. Room 129 was at the back.

Milo answered my knock, looking weary.

No progress, or something else?

The room was small and boxy, the decor surprisingly cheery: Twin beds under blue quilted floral covers that appeared new, floating-mallard prints above the headboard, a fake-colonial writing desk sporting a Bible and a phone book, a pair of hard-padded armchairs, nineteen-inch TV mounted on the wall. Two black nylon suitcases were placed neatly in one corner. Two closed plywood doors, chipped at the bottom, faced the bed. Closet and bathroom.

The woman perched on a corner of the nearer bed had the too-good posture of paralyzing grief. Handsome, early sixties, cold-waved hair the color of weak lemonade, white pearlescent glasses on a gold chain around her neck, conservative makeup. She wore a chocolate-brown dress with a pleated bottom, and white piqué collar and cuffs. Brown shoes and purse. Diamond-chip engagement ring, thin gold wedding band, gold scallop-shell earrings.

She turned toward me. Firm, angular features held their own against gravity. The resemblance to Claire was striking, and I thought of the matron Claire would never become.

Milo made the introductions. Ernestine Argent and I said 'Pleased to meet you' at exactly the same time. One side of her mouth twitched upward; then her lips jammed shut – a smile reflex dying quickly. I shook a cold, dry hand. A toilet flushed behind one of the plywood doors and she returned her hands to her lap. On the bed nearby was a white linen handkerchief folded into a triangle.

The door opened and a man, drying his hands with a hand towel, struggled to emerge.

Working at it because he could barely fit through the doorway.

No more than five-seven, he had to weigh close to four hundred pounds, a pink egg dressed in a long-sleeved white shirt, gray slacks, white athletic shoes. The bathroom was narrow and he had to edge past the sink to get out. Breathing deeply, he winced, took several small steps, finally squeezed through. The effort reddened his face. Folding the towel, he tossed it onto the counter and stepped forward very slowly, rocking from side to side, like a barge in choppy water.

The trousers were spotless poly twill, held up by clip-on suspenders. The athletic shoes appeared crushed. Each step made something in his pocket jingle.

He was around the same age as his wife, had a full head of dark, curly hair, a fine, almost delicate nose, a full-lipped mouth pouched by bladder cheeks. Three chins, shaved close. Brown eyes nearly buried in flesh managed to project a pinpoint intensity. He looked at his wife, studied me, continued to lumber.

Mentally paring away adipose, I was able to visualize handsome structure. He pressed forward, perspiring, breathing hard and raspy. When he reached me, he stopped, swayed, righted himself, stuck out a ham-hock arm.

His hands were smallish, his grip dry and strong.

'Robert Ray Argent.' A deep, wheezy voice, like a bass on reverb, issued from the echo chamber of his enormous body cavity. For a second, I imagined him hollow, inflated. But that fantasy faded as I watched him struggle to get to the nearer bed. Every step sounded on the thin carpeting, each limb seemed to shimmy of its own accord. His forehead was beaded, dripping. I resisted the urge to take his elbow.

His wife got up with the handkerchief and wiped his brow.

He touched her hand for an instant. 'Thanks, honey.'

'Sit down, Rob Ray.'

Both of them with that soft, distinctive Pittsburgh drawl.

Moving slowly, bending deliberately, he lowered himself. The mattress sank down to the box spring and creaked. The box spring nearly touched the carpet. Rob Ray Argent sat, spread-legged, inner thighs touching. The gray fabric of his pants stretched shiny over dimpled knees, pulled up taut over a giant pumpkin of a belly.

He inhaled a few times, cleared his throat, put his hand to his mouth, and coughed. His wife stared off at the open bathroom door before walking over, closing it, sitting back down.

'So,' he said. 'You're a psychologist, like Claire.' Dark circles under his armpits.

'Yes,' I said.

He nodded, as if we'd reached some agreement. Sighed and placed his hands on the apex of his abdomen.

Ernestine Argent reached over and handed him the handkerchief and he dabbed at himself some more. She pulled another white triangle from her purse and pecked at her own eyes.

Milo said, 'I was just telling Mr and Mrs Argent about the course of the investigation.'

Ernestine gave a small, involuntary cry.

'Honey,' Robert Ray said.

She said, 'I'm OK, darling,' almost inaudibly, and turned to me. 'Claire loved psychology.'

I nodded.

'She was all we ever *really* had.'

Rob Ray looked at her. Parts of his face had turned plum-colored; other sections were pink, beige, white – apple-peel mottle caused by the variable blood flow through expanses of skin. He turned to Milo. 'Doesn't sound like you've learned much. What's the chance you find the devil who did it?'

'I'm always optimistic, sir. The more you and Mrs Argent can tell us about Claire, the better our chances.'

'What else can we tell you?' said Ernestine. 'No one disliked Claire; she was the nicest person.'

She cried. Rob Ray touched her shoulder with his hand.

'I'm sorry,' she finally said. 'This isn't helping. What do you need to know?'

'Well,' said Milo, 'let's get a basic time frame, for starters. When was the last time you saw Claire?'

'Christmas,' said Rob Ray. 'She always came home for Christmas. We always had a nice family time, no exception last Christmas. She helped her mother with the cooking. Said in LA she never cooked, too busy, just ate things out of cans, takeout.'

Consistent with the kitchen at Cape Horn Drive.

'Christmas,' said Milo. 'Half a year ago.'

'That's right.' Rob Ray flexed his left foot.

'That would be right around the time Claire left County Hospital and moved to Starkweather Hospital.'

'Guess so.'

Milo said, 'Did she talk about changing jobs?'

Headshakes.

'Nothing at all?'

More silence.

Ernestine said, 'She never talked about her work in specifics. We never wanted to be nosy.'

They hadn't known. I watched Milo hide his amazement. Rob Ray tried to shift his weight on the bed. One leg cooperated.

Milo said, 'Did Claire talk about any sort of problems she might be having? Someone who was giving her difficulty – at work or anywhere else?'

'No,' said Rob Ray. 'She had no enemies. That I can tell you for sure.'

'How did she act during her Christmas visit?'

'Fine. Normal. Christmas was always a happy time for us. She was happy to be home, we enjoyed having her.'

'How long did she stay?'

'Four days, like always. We went to a bunch of movies; she loved her movies. Saw the Pittsburgh Ice Extravaganza, too. When she was a little girl, she skated. The last day, she came into our store, helped us out a bit – we're in giftware, have to stay open somewhat during the holiday season.'

'Movies,' I said. Joseph Stargill had said the same thing.

'That's right – the whole family loves 'em,' said Rob Ray.

'She was happy, had no problems,' said Ernestine. 'The only problem for us was we didn't see her enough. But we understood, what with her career. And travel's hard for us. The business.'

'No buck-passing when it's yours,' said Rob Ray. 'Also, I don't travel well – my size. But so what? This had nothing to do with Claire's trip home or her problems. There'd be no reason for anyone to hate her; this had to be some maniac on the loose – someone from that place she worked.' His skin had deepened to scarlet and his words emerged between rough inhalations. 'I tell you, I find out anyone put her in danger, I'll— Let's just say a lot of lives are going to be made miserable.'

'Darling,' said his wife, patting his knee. To us: 'What my husband's saying is, Claire was kind and generous and sweet. No one could've hated her.'

'Generous to the nth,' Rob Ray agreed. 'Back in high school, she was always the first to volunteer to help others. Old people at the hospital, animals at the shelter – didn't matter, she was there at the head of the line. She loved animals especially. We used to have a dog, a little Scottie. You know how kids never take responsibility with pets, it's always the parents who end up with it. Not our situation. Claire did everything, feeding it, cleaning up after it. She was always trying to fix things – broken wings on bugs, anything. We knew she'd be some kind of doctor, I would've guessed a veterinarian, but psychologist was fine. She always got good grades – it doesn't make sense, Detective Sturgis. At the morgue – what we just saw – I just don't . . . It had to be a maniac – this Starkweather place is nothing but maniacs?'

'Yes, sir,' said Milo. 'It's the first thing we looked at. So far, no leads. Apparently the inmates never get out.'

'Sure,' said Rob Ray. 'Isn't there always some screwup

that lets someone out? Some stupid *mistake*?' Tears began coursing silently down the jelly of his cheeks.

'You're right, sir,' said Milo. 'But so far I haven't come up with anything.'

His tone had gentled; suddenly he seemed like a much younger man.

'Well,' said Rob Ray. 'I can tell you're good people. Where you from originally? Your folks, I mean.'

'Indiana.'

Satisfied nod. 'I know you're trying.'

Suddenly one log-arm moved with astonishing speed, slamming upward to the big man's face, as he ground the handkerchief to his eyes.

'Oh, Rob,' said his wife, and she was crying again, too.

Milo went into the bathroom and brought them water.

Rob Ray Argent said, 'Thanks, I'm supposed to drink a lot, anyway. For my joints, keep them lubricated.' Half a shrug made his sloping shoulders jiggle. He plucked shirt fabric out of a fat fold.

Milo said, 'So Claire visited only on Christmas.'

'Yes, sir.'

'Is that since she moved to Los Angeles or since she went to graduate school in Cleveland?'

'Los Angeles,' said Rob Ray. 'When she was at Case Western she came home for Thanksgiving, Easter, summers. She helped us out in the store, summers.'

'Once she moved to LA, how often did she write?'

Silence.

'We're phoners, not writers,' said Ernestine. 'Long distance is so economical nowadays. We have one of those calling plans.'

I remembered Claire's phone bills. No recent calls to Pittsburgh. Had she dialed her parents from the office? Or had she become a stranger to them? Adding them to the club of strangers we'd encountered at every turn?

'So she called,' said Milo.

'That's right,' said Ernestine. 'Every so often.'

Milo scribbled. 'What about her marriage? And the divorce. Anything I should know about that?'

Ernestine lowered her eyes. Her husband took a long, noisy breath.

'She said she'd gotten married in Reno,' he said. 'Soon after. One of her calls.'

'So she told you over the phone,' said Milo. 'Did she seem happy about it?'

'I'd say yes,' said Ernestine. 'She apologized for not telling us before, said it was one of those sudden things – love at first sight. She said the husband was a nice fellow. A lawyer.'

'But you never met him.'

'I'm sure we would've, but Claire didn't stay married to him very long.'

Two years, no contact.

'So she visited on Christmas while she was married.'

'No,' said Ernestine. 'Not during the marriage. Last Christmas she was divorced already.'

Milo said, 'Did she explain why she got divorced?'

'She called after it happened, said she was fine, everything was friendly.'

'She used that word?' said Milo. '"Friendly."'

'Or something to that effect. She was trying to reassure *me*. That was Claire. Take care of everyone else.'

She glanced at her husband. He said, 'I know this sounds weird to you – our not meeting him. No big white wedding. But Claire always needed her freedom. She— It was— That's just the way she was. Give her her freedom and she got straight A's. She was always a good kid – a great kid. Who were we to argue? You do your best, who knows how your kids are going to turn out? She turned out great. We gave her freedom.'

Focusing on me during most of the speech. I nodded.

'We asked to meet him,' he said. 'The husband. She said she'd bring him by, but she never did. I got the feeling it didn't work too well from the beginning.'

'Why's that?'

'Because she never brought him out.'

'But she never actually complained about the marriage,' said Milo.

'She never said she was unhappy,' said Rob Ray, 'if that's what you're getting at. Why? Do you suspect him of having anything to do with it?'

'No,' said Milo. 'Just trying to learn what I can.'

'You're sure?'

'Absolutely, sir. At this point, he's not a suspect. No one is, unfortunately.'

'Well,' said Rob Ray, 'I know you'd tell us if it was different. The only mention she made of him was sometimes at the end of a conversation, she might say, "Joe sends his regards." She did say he was a lawyer, not a courtroom lawyer, a business lawyer. When she called he was never home. I got the feeling he was always working. She was, too. One of those modern marriages. That's probably what happened, they were too busy for each other.'

Ernestine said, 'She did send us a picture. Of the wedding – the chapel. So we knew what he looked like. A redhead. I remember joking to Rob Ray about little ginger-haired grandchildren.'

She started to cry again, checked it, apologized under her breath.

Rob Ray said, 'You'd have to know the kind of girl she was to understand. Very independent. She always took care of herself.'

'Took care of others, too,' I said.

'Exactly. So you can see why she'd need to unwind. And she unwinds by going off by herself to the movies. Or reading a book. Privacy's a big thing with her, so we try to respect that. Mostly she does things by herself. Except when we go out to the movies together. She likes doing that with me – we're both crazy for the movies.'

The lapse into present tense made my own eyes began to ache.

He might've realized it, too. His shoulders lowered suddenly, as if someone had pushed down upon them, and he stared at the bedcovers.

'Any particular kind of movies?' I said.

'Anything good,' he mumbled. His face stayed down. 'It was something we did together. I never pushed her to do sports. Tell the truth, being large, I wasn't exactly ready to run around, myself, so I was glad she was that kind of kid, could sit still and watch a movie.'

'Even when she was tiny,' said Ernestine, 'she could amuse herself. She was the sweetest little thing. I could leave her in her playpen, go about my housework, and no matter what was happening all around her, she'd just sit there and play with whatever you put in there.'

'Creating her own world,' I said.

Her smile was sudden, unsettling. 'Exactly, Doctor. You put your finger right on it. No matter what was happening all around her, she created her own world.'

No matter what was happening all around her. Second time she'd used the phrase within seconds. Did it imply some kind of family turmoil?

I said, 'Privacy as an escape.'

Rob Ray looked up. Uneasiness in his eyes. I tried to engage him. He turned away. Ernestine watched him, twisted the handkerchief.

'About the way Claire got married,' she said. 'Rob Ray and I *had* a big church wedding, and it put my father in debt for two years. I always thought one of Claire's intentions was to be considerate.'

'What put a light in her eyes,' said Rob Ray, 'was consideration. Helping people.'

'Before Mr Stargill,' said Milo, 'did Claire have any other boyfriends?'

'She dated,' said Ernestine. 'In high school, I mean. She wasn't some social butterfly, but she went out. Local boys, nothing steady. A fellow named Gil Grady took her to the prom. He's a fire lieutenant now.'

'What about later?' said Milo. 'College? Graduate school?'

Silence.

'How about once she moved to LA?'

'I'm sure,' said Ernestine, 'that when she wanted to date, she had her pick. She was always very pretty.'

Something – probably her most recent memory of her daughter, gray, damaged, laid out on a steel table – caused her face to collapse. She hid herself behind both hands.

Her husband said, 'I can't see that this is leading us anywhere.'

Milo looked at me.

'Just one more thing, please,' I said. 'Did Claire ever get involved in arts and crafts? Painting, woodwork, that kind of thing?'

'Crafts?' said Rob Ray. 'She drew, like any other kid, but that's about it.'

'Mostly she liked to read and go to the movies,' said Ernestine. 'No matter what was happening all around her, she could always find some quiet time for herself.'

Rob Ray said, 'Excuse me.' Lifting himself laboriously, he began the trudge to the bathroom. The three of us waited until the door closed. Running water sounded through the wood.

Ernestine began speaking softly, frantically: 'This is so hard on him. When Claire was growing up, children made fun of him. Cruel children. It's glandular; sometimes he eats less than I do.'

She stopped, as if daring us to debate. 'He's a wonderful man. Claire was never ashamed, never treated him any way but respectful. Claire was always proud of her family, no matter what—'

The last word ended too abruptly. I waited for more. Her lips folded inward. As she bit down on them, her chin shuddered. 'He's all I've got now. I'm worried about what this will do to him—'

Another toilet flush. Several moments later, the door opened and Rob Ray's big head appeared. Repeat of the laborious exit, the huffing trek to the bed. When he finally settled, he said, 'I don't want you to think Claire was some strange kid, all locked up in her room. She was a tough kid, took care of herself, wouldn't fall in with anything bad for her. So this had to be an abduction, some kind of maniac.'

Talking louder, more forcefully, as if he'd refueled.

'Claire was no fool,' he went on. 'Claire knew how to take care of herself – had to know.'

'Because she lived alone?' I said.

'Because— Yes, exactly. My little girl was independent.'

Later, sitting in a coffee shop on La Tijera with Milo, I said, 'So much pain.'

'Oh, man,' he said. 'They seem like good people, but talk about delusions. Making like it's one happy family, yet Claire never bothers to bring the husband around, never calls. She cut them off, Alex. Why?'

'Something the mother said made me wonder about family chaos. She used the phrase "no matter what was happening all around her" three times. Emphasizing that Claire coped well. Maybe there was turmoil. But they're sure not going to tell you now. Pretty memories are all they've got. And why would it matter?'

He smiled. 'All of a sudden the past isn't relevant?'

'It's always relevant to someone's life,' I said. 'But it may not have had a thing to do with Claire's death. At least, I don't see it.'

'A maniac, like the old man said.'

'He and his wife might be holding back family secrets, but I don't think they'd obstruct you,' I said. 'Claire's been out here for years. I think LA's more relevant than Pittsburgh or Cleveland.'

He gazed past me, toward the cash register, waved for service. Other than two red-eyed truckers at separate booths, we were the only customers.

A waitress came over, young, nasal, eager to please. When she left with our sandwich order, I said, 'If she grew up with disruption, wanted her adult life quiet, that empty living room makes a bit more sense. But how it helped make her a victim, I don't know.'

Milo tapped a front incisor. 'Dad's size alone would've been disruptive. Kids making fun of him, Claire having to deal with it.' He drank coffee, peered through the coffee shop's front window. An unseen jetliner's overhead pass shook the building.

'Maybe that's it,' I said. 'Growing up with him could also've made her comfortable with folks who were different. But when it came to her personal life, she drew a clear line: No fuss, no mess. Escaping to solitude, just as she had as a child.'

The waitress brought the sandwiches. She looked disappointed when Milo said there'd be nothing else. He took a bite of soggy ham as I assessed my burger. Thin, shiny, the color of dry mud. I put it aside. One of the truckers tossed cash on the table and hobbled out the front door.

Milo took two more gulps of his sandwich. 'Nice how you worked the arts-and-crafts question in. Hoping for some wood-shop memories?'

'Wouldn't that have been nice.'

He bit down on something disagreeable and held the bread at arm's length before returning it to the plate. 'Some scene at the morgue. The coroner did his best to put her back together, but it was far from pretty. I tried to discourage them again from viewing. They insisted. Mom actually handled it OK; it was Dad who started breathing real hard, turned beet red, braced himself against the wall. I thought we'd end up with another corpse. The morgue attendant's been staring at the poor guy like he's some freak-of-the-week, now he's really gawking. I got them out of there. Thank God he didn't collapse.'

Neither of us talked for a while. Ever the prisoner of my training, I lapsed into thoughts of Claire's childhood. Escape from . . . something . . . finding refuge in solitude . . . because solitude spun layers of fantasy . . . theater of the mind. Real theaters.

I said, 'Claire's love of movies. That's something both the parents and Stargill mentioned. What if it led beyond just watching? Caused her to have acting aspirations? What if she answered a casting call – the same one Richard Dada answered?'

'She likes flicks, so all of a sudden she wants to be a star?'

'Why not?' I said. 'It's LA. Maybe Claire did a bit on *Blood Walk*, too. There's your link with Richard. The killer met both of them on the set.'

'Everything we've learned about this woman tells us she's a privacy nut. You think she'd put herself in front of a camera?'

'I've known actors who were extremely shy. Taking on someone else's identity allowed them to cut loose.'

'I guess,' he said doubtfully. 'So they both meet some loon on the set and he decides to pick them off for God knows what motive . . . Then why the time lapse between the murders?'

'Maybe there are other murders in between that we don't know about.'

'I looked for similars. Anything in car trunk, anything with eye wounds or saw marks. Nothing.'

'OK,' I said. 'Just a theory.'

The waitress came over and asked if we wanted dessert. Milo's barked 'No thanks' made her step backward and hurry away.

'I understand about role-playing, Alex, but we're talking Ms Empty Room, her big thrill was being alone. I can see her taking in a matinee by herself, pretending to be Sharon Starlet, whatever. But going to the movies isn't *being* in the movies. Hell, I still can't believe there's no link to *Starkweather*. The woman worked with homicidal *murderers*, for God's sake, and I'm expected to take it on faith that none of them got out and hunted her down. Meanwhile, we sit here wondering about some hypothetical *acting* gig.'

He pressed both temples, and I knew a headache had come on.

The waitress brought the check and held it out at arm's length. Milo shoved a twenty at her, asked for aspirin, ordered her to keep the change. She smiled and hustled away looking frightened.

When she brought the tablets, he swallowed them dry. 'To hell with Swig and his court orders. Time to get with

State Parole, see what they can tell me about Starkweather creeps flewing the coop since Claire went to work there. After that, sure, the movie thing, why not? Equipment rentals, like you suggested.'

Crumpling the aspirin packet, he dropped it into an ashtray. 'Like you said, it's LA. Since when has logic ever meant a damn thing here?'

16

IN THE coffee-shop parking lot, he cell-phoned Sacramento, billing through LAPD. Authorization took a while. So did being shunted from clerk to supervisor to clerk. Every few seconds a plane swooped down to land. I stood around as he burned up calories keeping his voice even. Finally, his patience earned him the promise of a priority records search from State Parole.

'Which means days instead of weeks,' he said, walking over to a nearby phone booth and lifting a chained Yellow Pages from its shelf. Dried gum crusted the covers. 'One thing the supervisor did confirm: Starkweather guys do get out. Not often, but it happens. She knows for a fact because there was a case five years ago – some guy supposed to be on close supervision returned to his hometown and shot himself in the local barbershop.'

'So much for the system,' I said. 'Maybe that's why Swig was nervous.'

'The system is bullshit. People aren't machines. Places like Quentin and Pelican Bay, there's all kinds of trouble. Either you cage them completely or they do whatever the hell they please.' He began paging through the phone directory. 'OK, let's find some rental outfits, play cinema sleuth.'

Most of the film equipment companies were in Hollywood and Burbank, the rest scattered around the Valley and Culver City.

'Hollywood first,' he said. 'Where else?'

It was just after three P.M. when I followed Milo's unmarked onto the 405 and over to the 101. We got off at Sunset. Traffic was mean.

The Hollywood outfits were in warehouse buildings and large storefronts on the west end of the district, between Fairfax and Gower. A concentration on Santa Monica Boulevard allowed us to park and cover half a dozen businesses quickly. The mention of Thin Line Productions and *Blood Walk* evoked baffled stares from the rental clerks, most of whom looked like thrash-metal band castoffs.

On the seventh try, at a place on Wilcox called Flick Stuff, a bony, simian-looking young man with a massive black hair extension and a pierced lip slouched behind a nipple-high counter. Massively unimpressed by Milo's badge. Maybe twenty-one; too young for that level of world-weariness. Behind him were double doors with an EMPLOYEES ONLY sign. In the background, a female vocalist shouted over power chords. Joan Jett or someone trying to be her. Big Hair wore a tight black T-shirt and red jeans. A slogan on the shirt: *No Sex Unless It Leads to Dancing*. His arms were white and hairless, more vein than muscle. Lumpy fibroid dope scars in the crooks said he'd probably had police experience.

Milo said, 'Were you working here twenty months ago, sir?'

'Sir' made the kid smirk. 'Off and on.' He managed to slouch lower.

Price lists were tacked to the surrounding walls. Day rates for sandbags, Western dollies, sidewalls, Magliners, wardrobe racks, Cardellini lamps, Greenscreens. Surprisingly cheap; a snow machine could be had for fifty-five bucks.

'Remember renting to an outfit called Thin Line Productions?'

I expected a yawn, but Big Hair said, 'Maybe.'

Milo waited.

'Sounds familiar. Yeah, maybe. Yeah.'

'Could you check your files, please?'

'Yeah, hold on.' Hair opened the double doors and disappeared, returned waving an index card, looking ready to spit. 'Yeah, now I remember them.'

'Problems?' said Milo.

'Big problems.' Hair wiped his hands on the black T-shirt. The grubby steel ring through his upper lip robbed his expression of some of the injured dignity he was trying to project.

'What'd they do?' said Milo.

'Stiffed us fourteen grand worth.'

I said, 'That's a lot of equipment.'

'Not for Spielberg, but for assholes like that, yeah. We gave 'em everything. Mikes, props, fake blood, filters, misters, eye chamois, coffee makers, cups, tables, the fuckin' works. The big items were a dolly and a couple of cameras – old gear, no studio would touch 'em, but still they cost. Supposed to be a ten-day rental. They had no history with us and it was obviously like a virgin voyage, so we demanded double deposit and they gave us a check that we verified was covered. I got ID, everything by the book. Not only didn't they pay up, they fucking split with the equipment. When we tried to cash the deposit check, guess what?'

He bared his teeth. Surprisingly white. Behind them, something glinted. Pierced tongue. No click when he talked – the voice of experience. Were pain thresholds rising among the new generation? Would it make for a better Marine Corps?

I said, 'What made you think it was a virgin voyage?'

'They putzed around, didn't know what they were doing. What pisses me off is I guided them, man, told them how to get the most for their money. Then they go and screw me.'

'You got blamed?'

'Boss said I did the transaction, I was assigned to find 'em, try to recover. I couldn't find shit.'

'You say "they,"' said Milo. 'How many people are we talking about?'

'Two. Guy and a girl.'

'What'd they look like?'

'Twenties, thirties. She was OK-looking, blond hair – light blond, like Marilyn Monroe, Madonna, when she was like that. But long and straight. Nice body, but nothing special. OK face. He was tall, older than her, trying to play hip.'

'How old?' said Milo.

'Probably in his thirties. She was maybe younger. I wasn't really paying attention. She didn't say much, it was mostly him.'

'How tall was he?' said Milo.

'About your size, but skinny. Not as skinny as me, but nothing like you either.' Smirk.

'Hair color?' said Milo.

'Dark. Black. Long.'

'Like yours?'

'He wished, man. His was curly, like a perm, maybe went to here.' He touched his shoulders.

'Platinum blond for her,' said Milo, writing. 'Long and curly for him. Maybe wigs?'

'Sure they were,' said Hair. 'It's not exactly hard to tell, man.'

'What kind of clothing did they wear?'

'Regular. Nothing special.'

'Any other distinguishing marks?'

Hair laughed. 'Like "666" on their foreheads? Nope, unh-uh.'

'Could you identify them if you saw them again?'

'I dunno.' The pierced tongue slid between his upper and lower teeth. The mannerism formed his mouth into a tragedy-mask frown. 'Probably not. I wasn't really paying attention to their faces. I was concentrating on getting them the most for their money.'

'But maybe you could recognize them?'

'Why, you have a picture?'

'Not yet.'

'Well, bring one if you get it. Maybe, no promises.'

'The fact they were wearing wigs,' said Milo. 'That didn't bother you?'

'Why should it?'

'Maybe they were hiding something.'

Hair laughed. 'Everyone in the industry hides something. You never see a chick with a natural rack anymore, and half the guys are wearing wigs and eye shadow. Big fucking deal – maybe they were acting in their own flick, doing it all. That's the way it is with a lot of these indie things.'

'They tell you anything about the flick?'

'Didn't ask, they didn't say.'

'*Blood Walk*,' said Milo. 'Sounds like a slasher flick.'

'Could be.' Boredom had returned.

'They rented fake blood.'

'Couple gallons. I picked out the best we had, nice and thick. Then they butt-ream me like that. Boss *loved* that.'

'Any hint it might've been porn?'

'Anything's possible,' said Hair. 'I know most of the porn people, but there's always new assholes trying to break in. I don't think so, though. They didn't have that virgin porn feel.'

'What's the virgin porn feel?'

'Stoned-happy on Ecstasy, big fucking adventure. They didn't say much – thinking about it, they didn't say hardly nothing at all.'

'Boss take it any further than having you look for them?' said Milo.

'What do you mean?'

'Did he run a trace on them? Hire a collection agency?'

'He put 'em out to collection and when that didn't work, he wrote it off. We had a good year, I guess he can piss away fourteen grand.'

'Does this kind of thing happen all the time?'

'Getting ripped off? Not all the time, but yeah, it happens. But not usually for this much. And usually we collect something.'

'Do you still have their file?'

'I didn't throw it out.'

'Could we please see it, Mr . . . ?'

'Bonner. Vito Bonner.' He wiped his hands again. 'Let me go back and check. They rip someone else off? That why you're here?'

'Something like that.'

'Man,' said Bonner. 'Talk about stupid. We warned the other companies in the neighborhood. Burbank and Culver, too.' A black sprig of false hair tickled his chin and he slapped it away. 'I think we warned the Valley, too. So anyone who rented to them after that deserves to get cornholed.'

We sat in the unmarked and studied the file. The tab read THIN LINE: BLOOD WALK, *BAD DEBT*. The first page was a letter from an Encino collection agency reporting an extensive search, no results. Next came the rental application. Thin Line's address was listed on Abbot Kinney Boulevard in Venice. Venice phone exchange with the notation that it traced to a pay phone.

'Bit of a drive to Hollywood,' I said. 'Especially with rental outfits close by in Santa Monica. They didn't want to foul their own nest.'

Milo pored over the form, nodding. The signature at the bottom was hard to read, but a black business card stapled to the file folder said:

Griffith D. Wark
PRODUCER AND PRESIDENT
THIN LINE PRODS

The pay-phone number in the lower left corner. White printing on black. Old-fashioned camera logo in the lower right-hand corner.

'Bogus phone,' he said. 'Scam from the get-go . . . Wark. Sounds like a phony moniker.'

'Griffith D. W.,' I said. 'Ten to one it's an inversion of D. W. Griffith. I'll also bet the W in "D. W." was Wark. Not very subtle, but old Vito didn't catch it.'

'Old Vito probably knows more about Maglites than film history.' He flipped to the next page. 'Here's the bank verification on the deposit check – B. of A. branch out in Panorama City. These guys were all over the place.'

He studied his Timex. 'Too late to call the manager. I'll drive by the Venice address, see if they really did have a place there; then I'll get the file over to the lab just in case some old latents from known bad guys show up. Tomorrow, it's on the horn to every other prop house in the county, see if Mr Wark talked anyone else out of gear.'

'You like the film thing now,' I said.

'Work with what you've got,' he said. 'I'm an old stinkhound: When something smells bad, I go nosing.'

'The casting ad could have been another scam – get wannabes to pay for auditioning.'

'Wouldn't surprise me. Hollywood's one big scam, anyway – image *über alles*. Even when it's supposedly legit. One of my first cases, back when I was doing Robbery, was—' He named a well-known actor. 'Got his start as a student, doing artsy stuff using gear he stole from the university's theater arts department. When I caught up with him he was a real fresh-mouth, no remorse. Finally, he agreed to return everything and the U decided not to take it any further. A few years later, I'm watching TV and this asshole's up for an Oscar, some social-issues film about prison reform, making a holier-than-thou speech. And what about—' He named a major director. 'I know for a fact he got *his* foot in the door by selling coke to studio execs. Yeah, this Wark found the right business for a psychopath. The only question is how relevant his mischief is to *my* cases.'

I got home just after six. Robin's truck was in the carport. The house smelled wonderful – the salty bouquet of chicken soup.

She was at the stove, stirring a pot. Her hair was loose, tumbling down her back; black sweats accentuated the auburn. Her sleeves were pushed up to her elbows and her face looked scrubbed. Steam from the soup had brought up some sweat. Down by her feet, Spike squatted, panting, ready to pounce for a scrap. The table was set for two.

When I kissed her, Spike grumbled. 'Be a good sharer,' I said.

He grumbled some more and waddled over to his water bowl.

'Winning through intimidation,' I said.

Robin laughed. 'Thought we'd eat in. Haven't seen enough of you lately.'

'Sounds great to me. Want me to prepare something?'

'Not unless there's something else you want.'

I looked into the pot. Golden broth formed a bubbling home for carrots, celery, onions, slivers of white meat, wide noodles.

'Nothing,' I said, moving behind her, cupping her waist, lowering my hands to her hips. I felt her go loose.

'This,' I said, 'is one of those great fantasies – he chances upon her as she cooks and, lusty stallion that he is . . .'

She laughed, let out two soft breaths, leaned back against me. My hands rose to her breasts, loose and soft, unfettered by the thin fleece of the sweats. Her nipples hardened against my palms. My fingers slipped under the waistband of her pants. She inhaled sharply.

'You shrinks,' she said, placing her hand over mine. Guiding it down. 'Spending too much time on fantasy, not enough on reality.'

17

I WOKE up the next morning thinking about Mr and Mrs Argent's claim that Claire had chosen psychology because she wanted to nurture people. Yet she'd opted for neuropsychology as a specialty, concentrating on diagnostics, avoiding treatment. On research diagnostics, charts and graphs, the hieroglyphics of science. She'd rarely ventured out of her lab. On the face of it, she'd nurtured nothing but data at County.

Until six months ago and the shift to Starkweather. Maybe Robin was right, and the move represented getting in touch with her altruism.

But why *now*? Why *there*?

Something didn't fit. My head felt like a box full of random index cards. I circled the office, trying to collate. Robin and Spike were out, and the silence chewed at me. There had been a time, long ago, when I was content living alone. The knots and liberties of love had changed me. What had Claire experienced of love?

The phone ring was glass shattering on stone.

'Small stuff first,' said Milo. 'Joseph Stargill's not quite as rich as he claimed, because some of his properties are mortgaged, but he still comes out over four mil in the black.

His law practice brings in around a hundred and eighty K a year. If he's a greedy psychopath or he hated Claire's guts, I suppose three hundred K might motivate him, but I can't find evidence of either, and a probate lawyer tells me Stargill would have a hell of a time getting hold of that property. With no will, the state takes most of it and Claire's parents get the rest. Stargill's not off the suspect list completely; I still have to nose around about any bad investments he might have. But he's been kicked down several notches.

'Item Two: No other prop company reports being bilked by Mr Wark or Thin Line, so maybe he wasn't out for a big-time equipment rip-off, just wanted to supply his own shoot, decided to keep the gear when they were through. No progress finding Wark. The *Blood Walk* script has definitely not been registered with any of the guilds, no one's heard of Thin Line, and there's no evidence the film was ever released. I contacted film-developing labs, because if there was ever footage it might've been processed somewhere. Nada. At the B. of A. in Panorama City, no dice over the phone, I have to come in, present a warrant to get a look at the Thin Line account.'

'Busy day,' I said.

'With zippo to show for it. I'm thinking this whole movie angle is a distraction. Especially with Item Three: The clerk from State Parole called me, God bless her. Turns out a Starkweather inmate *was* released, seven months ago. A guy named Wendell Pelley. Three weeks before Claire went to work there. It's a narrow window, but Pelley could've learned about Claire from some buddy still in there.

Or Claire actually had contact with him. Think about it: Her official start date was three weeks after Pelley got released, but what's to say she didn't go to Starkweather before then? To take a look, see if it was right for her. Let's say she runs into Pelley by accident – he's about to be sprung, so they make him a trusty – a tour guide, like Hatterson. She's coming there to help people, and here's a success story. It could be appealing to her, right?'

'Sure,' I said, 'but seven months ago means Pelley was released one month *after* Richard Dada's murder.'

'So someone else did Dada. That's always been a possibility.'

His tone said not to push it. 'What's Pelley's background?' I said.

'White male, forty-six, got committed twenty-one years ago for shooting his girlfriend and her three little kids up in the Sierras – gold country. Apparently Pelley was trying to do some mining, brought the rest of them along to be one happy family, got drunk, convinced himself they were trying to rob his claim, and went berserk. Diagnosis of paranoid schizophrenia, drug and booze history, too wacky for trial.'

'Why'd they let him out?'

'Staff recommendation from Starkweather is all State Parole had.'

'Swig approved the release,' I said. 'So he held back plenty.'

'Shmuck. Never liked him. Gonna look into *his* background, but right now Pelley's whereabouts are my main concern.'

'He's on the run?' I said. 'Released inmates are supposed to get counseling and random drug tests.'

'Funny thing 'bout that, isn't it? Pelley was bunking in a halfway house near MacArthur Park. The operators haven't seen him for a *month*. They claim they notified his parole officer right away. I tried to reach the PO, no callback yet.'

'Whom would the parole officer be obligated to notify?'

'The local police. Ramparts Division. They can't find any record of notification. The system, huh?'

'Would Swig be notified?'

'Maybe. If so, it's something else he held back on. Not that he's any use to us at this point. Pelley wouldn't be likely to run back to Starkweather.'

'So what's next?' I said. 'A statewide alert?'

'Nah,' he said. 'That's for TV. Officially, Pelley hasn't done anything bad yet, so no way does State Parole or anyone else want to get the press on it, panic the public. If Ramparts does get notified, all it means is Pelley's face and stats go up on a bulletin board in the station, maybe if the desk's feeling real cooperative they issue photo memos for the squad car dashboards. Meaning if Pelley acts up publicly and a uniform gets there in time, he's busted. But if he doesn't cause problems, he can probably fade into the woodwork.'

'Out on the streets three weeks before Claire joins the staff at Starkweather,' I said. 'You could be right. She met Pelley and he became her outpatient project.'

'Hey,' he said, 'she told that psychiatrist she was ripe for it. "So many madmen, so little time."'

'And maybe Pelley and Peake maintained some sort of

communication. Maybe Peake talked to him because they had some kind of rapport. They had one important thing in common: They both murdered families.'

'As good a basis for friendship as I've ever heard.' He cursed.

'Heidi never mentioned Pelley's release. But she came on staff after Claire, might not have heard about it.'

'I want to talk to Heidi again, anyway,' he said. 'So far she's the only one in that place showing any desire to help. She's due on shift at three. I'm gonna be out on the road all day, trying to trace Pelley, so I left a message with your number as backup. OK?'

'OK. I can also try that head psychiatrist at Starkweather – Aldrich – see what he knows about Pelley.'

'No, not yet – I need to be discreet. If it turns out Pelley's our bad guy, whoever okayed his release is gonna be up the creek. No reason to warn them, give them time to get their defenses up. Give Swig a chance to get on the horn with Uncle Senator and unleash a paper barrier.'

He sounded angry but exhilarated.

'You have a good feeling about this,' I said.

'Don't know about that, but I will tell you one thing: This is a helluva lot more to my liking than movies and all that hocus-pocus about Peake's gibberish. This is the world as I know it: Bad guy gets out on the street, bad things happen . . . Guess my faith in crappy endings has been validated once again.'

I heated up some of the leftover soup and chewed on a hard roll as I thought about Milo's enthusiasm for Wendell Pelley.

In addition to his being clear for the Dada murder, Pelley had used a gun, not a knife. But maybe twenty-one years had changed his killing style. And he *had* bolted the halfway house.

Still, Milo was relying on what he hated most: Theory. If he'd looked at it coldly, he might've tempered his enthusiasm. I hadn't said a thing. I'd continue to keep my doubts to myself. One thing doing therapy had taught me: Timing is all.

My service rang at three-twenty-three. I'd been expecting a call from Heidi Ott, but the operator said, 'It's a Dr Hertzlinger, from County General Hospital. She says it's about Dr Argent.'

'Put her on.'

Click. 'Dr Delaware? Mary Hertzlinger. I was calling Detective Sturgis, but someone at the station gave me this number.'

'He's out, asked me to take some messages. What's up?'

'After you and he left, I found myself thinking more about Claire. And I began to wonder if I'd misspoken. About that strange parting shot – "So many madmen, so little time." You asked me if Claire seemed upset when she said it, and I said no, she was actually smiling. But the more I considered it, the more I realized how unlike Claire the remark was. Because she'd never joked before. Never displayed any sense of humor, really. I don't mean that unkindly – she was just a very serious person. Off the job, I try not to analyze people, but you know how it is. Anomalies attract me.'

'Me, too. Occupational hazard.'

She laughed softly. 'Anomalies also make me wonder about anxiety.'

'You think Claire was anxious about switching jobs?'

'It's just speculation,' she said, 'but she just rattled off that line as if she'd rehearsed it. Had been reciting it to herself. Because, let's face it, it *was* a strange thing to do. Claire's job was secure, Dr Theobold liked her. To just pick up and leave for a place like Starkweather? She'd never worked with patients, let alone homicidal psychotics. It really doesn't make sense.'

'Maybe after doing all that research, she wanted to help people directly.'

'Then why Starkweather? Who gets help there?'

'So you're saying the decision scared her but she went ahead, anyway,' I said.

'Yes, but that doesn't make sense, either, does it? If she was nervous, why do it? I'll bet if she'd marched into Dr Theobold's office and announced she'd changed her mind, he'd have taken her back in a flash, no questions asked. So it's confusing. I tried to think back, what her demeanor had been as we cleaned out those boxes. What we'd been talking about. I couldn't remember much, but I *did* recall something: She mentioned leaving some material behind in the office closet, said she'd be back for it later in the afternoon. But I was in the office all day and she never returned. Ever. After I met you, I went to check, and sure enough, there it was, back in a corner. Two cartons with her name on them. The flaps were closed but not sealed, so I opened one up – I hope I didn't ruin anything by doing that?'

'No,' I said. 'Find anything interesting?'

'Mostly they were journal reprints. Claire's own publications and some articles related to her alcoholism research. But there was also a plastic bag full of newspaper clippings. Photocopies, actually, and when I read them, I knew I had to call Detective Sturgis. They were all about a mass murder that took place sixteen years ago—'

'The Ardullo family,' I said. 'Ardis Peake.'

Silence. 'So you already know.'

'Peake's at Starkweather. He was one of Claire's patients.'

'Oh, my . . . So Claire was interested in him before she went there – maybe he was one of the reasons she took the job. But why would that be?'

'Good question,' I said. 'Where are the clippings now?'

'Right here in front of me – I won't touch another thing, haven't even gone near the second box. Someone can pick them up any time before eight tonight, and I'll be back in around seven A.M.'

'Thanks,' I said. 'And thank you for calling. Soon as I can reach Detective Sturgis, I'll let him know.'

'This Peake,' she said. 'He's still in there – incarcerated?'

'Yes.'

'So it couldn't have been him,' she said, sounding relieved. 'I started to read the clippings. The things he did . . . Anyway, that's it.'

'One more thing,' I said. 'Did Claire ever mention loving the movies?'

'Not to me. Why?'

'We've been told it was a main form of recreation for her.'

'I suppose that wouldn't surprise me,' she said. 'Sure. I could see that – losing herself in fantasy.'

'You saw her as someone with an active fantasy life?'

'I saw her as someone who might've *depended* upon an active fantasy life. Because she didn't – I don't want to be cruel, but the truth is, she just didn't seem to have much of a *real* life.'

Interested in Peake before she'd taken the job.

Her project. Trying to increase his verbal output.

Or so she'd claimed. What about him had really caught her interest?

Stashed the clippings along with her research data.

Because she considered the *clippings* data?

Why would an alcoholism researcher raised in Pittsburgh and schooled in Cleveland be concerned with a sixteen-year-old atrocity in a California farm town?

A town that no longer existed.

I thought about the abolition of Treadway. An entire community obliterated. What role had been played by Ardis Peake's savage night?

Peake's blood walk . . . I wrestled with it some more. Claire, a researcher, coming upon something . . .

It was three-forty, and Heidi Ott still hadn't called. I checked out with my service and drove back to the library.

18

FIRST I photocopied and reviewed the murder articles I'd pulled up yesterday. No new insights. Using 'Ardullo' and 'Ardis Peake' as keywords, I went back twenty years before the crimes and pulled up five references, all from the LA *Times*.

November 24, 1929:

ARDULLO LEADS INDIANS
TO GRIDIRON VICTORY
Red Schoen, *Times* sportswriter

Two fourth-quarter record-breaking runs by star quarterback Henry 'Butch' Ardullo led the Stanford Indians to a 21–7 victory over the UC Bears in last Sunday's cliffhanger game.

Ardullo, already renowned for his passing, showed his leg-stuff, accomplishing a pair of unimpeded Mercury imitations to the touchdown line, 70 and 82 yards respectively. The capacity crowd showed its appreciation with a standing ovation, and professional scouts, alerted to Ardullo's stellar performance all season, were reputed to be eyeing the husky junior. No one will be surprised when Butch is tapped on the shoulder for stardom, maybe even while still in his cap and gown. More important to assembled Palo Alto stalwarts and alums, a Rose Bowl place for the Redskins is all but assured.

December 8, 1929:

INJURY SIDELINES GRIDIRON STAR
Red Schoen, *Times* sportswriter

A broken femur suffered during practice yesterday led to Stanford great Henry 'Butch' Ardullo being carried from the field on a stretcher.

Ardullo, the Pacific College League's high-scoring quarterback, had been expected to lead the Indians in their upcoming Rose Bowl game with USC. Doctors treating the injured junior have pronounced his football career over.

August 12, 1946:

FARMERS GROUP SAYS IMMIGRANT LABOR NECESSARY TO FEED STATE
John M. D'Arcy, *Times* staff writer

A consortium of California fruit growers met with Deputy Agriculture Secretary Clement W. Chase in Washington this week to request relaxation of immigration laws in order to permit increased numbers of 'wetback' laborers from Mexico.

The Affiliated Agricultural Network claims that tighter

immigration laws will raise labor costs to the point of 'severe abuse of the domestic consumer,' according to AAN president Henry Ardullo, a peach and walnut grower from Treadway, California.

'These people,' said Ardullo, 'can come up here and earn ten times what they can down in Mexico and still give us excellent labor value. They do jobs no one else wants, so American workers don't get hurt. Meanwhile, Mrs Housewife gets to go to the grocery store and stock up on the finest, most nutritious produce ever grown on this planet at a price that makes healthful eating the only logical choice.'

Anti-immigration groups oppose the variance. Secretary Chase said he will consider the petition and issue a ruling.

January 14, 1966:

RESIST LAND BOOM LURE, SAYS GROWER
Stephen Bannister, *Times* business writer

Farmers need to resist the temptation to sell their land at high market prices, says a prominent Kern County fruit grower, because the future of the family farm is at stake.

'Quick profits pose a difficult temptation, and Lord knows farming can be difficult, what with all the government restrictions,' said Henry Ardullo, a walnut and peach farmer from Treadway, California, and past president of the Affiliated Agricultural Network, a group representing the interests of independent growers. 'But the farm is the soul of California. This state is America's breadbasket,

and if we cut off the hand that feeds us in the name of easy money, what are we leaving to our children? Golf courses and country clubs are pretty, but try feeding your family with turf grass.'

Ardullo's comments were made at a GOP fundraiser at the Fairmont Hotel in San Francisco, where he shared the dais with State Senators William Greben and Rudy Torres, and real estate developer Sheridan Krafft.

March 5, 1975:

OBITUARIES

Henry Ardullo, college gridiron star and agricultural exec

Henry 'Butch' Ardullo died at his ranch in Treadway, California, this past Wednesday. Renowned as a quarterback at Stanford University, where he broke several records for running and passing, Ardullo received a BA in business in 1930. He had been widely expected to enter professional football until an injury ended his athletic career.

Upon graduation, he joined the family enterprise, a large walnut and peach plantation begun by his father, Joseph (Giuseppe) Ardullo, an immigrant from Naples who came to California in 1883, found work as a fruit vendor in San Francisco and invested his profits in real estate in and around the Kern County community of Treadway, where he planted hundreds of fruit trees from stock acquired in England, Italy and Portugal.

Upon Joseph Ardullo's death in 1941, Henry Ardullo took over the business, Ardullo AA Fruit, which he renamed and incorporated as BestBuy Produce, and continued to purchase land, amassing large private real estate holdings in the lower central valley region. Elected as president of Affiliated Agricultural Network, a post-World War II consortium of independent growers, in 1946, Ardullo represented grower interests in Washington, including a successful petition for relaxation of immigration laws to allow increased numbers of farm laborers into California. He was a member of Kiwanis, the Treadway Chamber of Commerce, and the Farm League and a contributor to the Republican party; he served as central valley chairman of United Way from 1953 to 1956.

He married Stanford classmate Katherine Ann Stethson, daughter of a Palo Alto department store owner, in 1933. She died in 1969. A son, Henry Ardullo, Jr, died in a mountain climbing accident in Nepal, in 1960. The senior Ardullo is survived by his other son, Scott Stethson Ardullo of Treadway, vice president of BestBuy Produce.

The farm is the soul of California.

It had taken the rampage of a madman to bring Henry Ardullo's nightmare home.

A family obliterated. An entire town wiped off the map. Once sentimentality had been taken care of, high real estate values had done the rest.

Sad, but I couldn't see any connection to Claire or the demons hissing in Ardis Peake's head.

Could she have had a family connection to the Ardullos? Her parents hadn't mentioned it. There seemed no reason for them to conceal history. Still, people often hid their reasons. I found a pay phone just outside the reading room, phoned the Flight Inn, and asked for the Argents' room. Rob Ray's familiar rumble said, 'Yes?'

'Mr Argent? Dr Delaware.'

'Oh. Hello.'

'Sorry to bother you again, sir, but I had one more question.'

'Lucky you caught us,' he said. 'We're on our way out the door and back home.'

'I'll be quick, Mr Argent. Do you have any relatives in California? Specifically, in the farming business?'

'Farming? Nope.'

'Does the name Ardullo mean anything to you?'

'No again. I thought you might be calling about some progress – what's this all about?'

'The Ardullos were a family Claire showed some interest in – she'd read up on them, held on to some newspaper clippings.'

'*Were* a family?' he said. 'Something happened to them?'

'Unfortunately, they were murdered. Fifteen years ago, and Claire seemed to be interested in the case.'

'Murdered. The whole family?' He nearly choked on the last two words. 'So what— I don't mean, so what they were murdered. So what about Claire? No, I don't know them, never did. It was probably just something . . . professional. Doing her work. Have to go, goodbye.'

'Have a good flight,' I said.

'Oh, yeah,' he said. 'It's going to be a great flight – at least I'm getting out of your lousy city.'

His anger rang in my head and I hung up feeling foolish and intrusive. What had I hoped to accomplish? What did big money and land deals have to do with Claire's murder?

Now that I was thinking straight, I realized there was a simple explanation for the clippings: Knowing she was transferring to Starkweather, Claire had plugged the hospital's name into some data banks, come across the description of Peake's bloody night. Once she got there, she looked him up, found him near vegetative. A challenge.

So many madmen, so little time.

After all those years in the lab, she was hungry for clinical raw meat – for a firsthand look at astounding criminal madness. Maybe she'd even intended to write Peake up, if she made some kind of progress.

She'd entered the world of madness, but – Milo's enthusiasm for Wendell Pelley aside – I wondered if that had anything to do with her death. Right at the beginning, my gut had told me someone organized – twisted but sane – had cut her throat, stashed her in the car trunk, made off with the bit of cash in the as yet undiscovered purse. Left no clues.

Maybe the same person who'd bisected Richard Dada, maybe not. Any similarities between the two cases could be explained by abnormal psychology: Psychopaths weren't that original. Confront enough evil and you smell the same garbage over and over.

No voices in the head here. Maybe Pelley was now sane

enough to pull it off, maybe not. In any case, I couldn't help thinking we were up against something coldhearted, orchestrated.

Murder for fun. A production.

There was nothing more I could do, so I drove home, spent some time outdoors, weeding, pruning, feeding the fish, netting leaves out of the pond.

Just before five, my service patched Heidi Ott through.

'Doctor?' She sounded buoyant. 'I can't believe it, but Peake's talking again, and this time Swig can't accuse me of being hysterical. I got it on tape!'

19

'TUH.'

'What's that, Ardis?'

Tape buzz. I clocked it. Twenty-two seconds—

'What did you say, Ardis . . . ? You just said something . . . because you want to talk to me, right, Ardis . . . ?'

Thirty-two seconds.

'Ardis? Could you open your eyes . . . please?'

A minute. Ninety seconds, a hundred . . . Heidi Ott held up her finger, signaling us to be patient.

It was just before midnight, but her eyes were bright. She and Milo and I were in an interrogation room at the station – a hot, Lysol-smelling yellow closet barely large enough for the three of us. Heidi's hair was tied back and styled with a shark clip. She'd come straight from Starkweather and the clip of her ID badge protruded from a breast pocket. The recorder was a tiny black Sony.

'Just a bit more,' she said, tapping her fingers on the steel table.

Her voice on the tape said, '*OK, Ardis. Maybe tomorrow.*'

Thirty-three seconds. Footsteps.

'Tuh.'

'Tuh, Ardis? Two? Two what?'

Twenty-eight seconds.

'Ardis?'

'Tuh guh.'

'To go?'

'Tuh guh choo choo bang bang.'

'To go choo choo bang bang? What does that mean, Ardis?'

Fifteen seconds.

'Choo choo bang bang, Ardis? Is that some sort of game?'

Eighteen seconds.

'Ardis? What's choo choo bang bang?'

Thirty seconds, forty, fifty.

'What does it mean, Ardis?'

Eighty-three seconds. Click.

She said, 'At that point, he turned away from me, wouldn't open his eyes. I waited awhile longer, but I knew it was all I was going to get out of him.'

'"Choo choo bang bang,"' said Milo.

She colored. 'I know. It's pretty stupid, isn't it? I guess I shouldn't have gotten so jazzed. But at least it's something, right? He's talking to me. Maybe he'll keep talking.'

'Where'd you keep the recorder?' I said.

'In my pocket.' She pointed to the navy photographer's vest she'd draped over her chair. 'I tried yesterday, too, but nothing happened.'

'"Choo choo bang bang,"' said Milo. '"Bad eyes in a box."'

'I've been trying to figure out some connection,' said Heidi. Suddenly, she looked very tired. 'Probably wasting your time. Sorry.'

'No, no,' said Milo. 'I appreciate your help. I'd like to keep the tape.'

'Sure.' She popped it out of the machine, gave it to him, placed the recorder back in the vest pocket, collected her purse, and stood.

Milo held out a hand and they shook. 'Thanks,' he said. 'Really. Any information is helpful.'

She shrugged. 'I guess . . . Want me to keep taping?'

'I don't want you to do anything that violates regulations.'

'Never heard of any regulation against taping.'

'It's generally illegal to tape anyone without their knowledge, Heidi. Jail prisoners lose the presumption of privacy, but whether or not that applies to the men at Starkweather, I don't know.'

'OK,' she said. 'So I won't do it anymore.' Shrugging, she moved toward the door. 'Kind of strange, isn't it? Protecting *them*. That's another reason I don't want to stick around.'

'What's that?'

'Swig talks all the time about humane care, how they're human beings, too. But I just can't find much sympathy for them, and I'd rather work with people I care about. At least they can't leave. I guess that's the main thing.'

'Speaking of which,' said Milo. 'One of them did get out.'

Her knuckles whitened around the purse handle. 'I never heard that. When?'

'Before you came on staff.'

'Who? What was his name?'

'Wendell Pelley.'

'No,' she said. 'Never heard of him – why, is he some sort of suspect in Claire's murder?'

'No,' said Milo. 'Not yet. I'm just trying to cover all bases. Anything you could find out about Pelley would be useful. Like, did he and Peake associate with each other.'

'I can try . . . long as I stay at Starkweather.'

'Two more weeks.'

'Yes, but if there's something you think I can . . . Are you saying this Pelley is what Peake's little speeches are all about? Pelley's been communicating with Peake? Sending him messages, and Peake's babbling them back at me?'

'I wish I knew enough to theorize, Heidi. Right now I'm simply looking into everything.'

'OK . . . I'll do what I can.' Sharp tug of the ponytail. Looking troubled, she opened the door. Milo and I walked her downstairs to the street. Her car was parked at the curb, half-lit by a streetlamp. Old, dented Chrysler minivan. A bumper sticker read, 'Climbers Get High Naturally.'

Milo said, 'What's the highest mountain you ever tackled?'

'I'm more of a wall person than a mountain person. Sheer surfaces, the more vertical the better.' She smiled. 'Promise you won't tell? The best one wasn't exactly legal. Power station near the Nevada border. We did it at three A.M., then parachuted down.'

'Adrenaline high,' said Milo.

'Oh, yeah.' She laughed, got in the van, and drove away.

'Got your junior G-woman on the job,' I said. 'I think she's found a new source of adrenaline.'

'Yeah, she's a little hyper, isn't she? But at least someone's cooperating . . . So, what do you think about Peake's latest soliloquy?'

'If there's some deep psychological meaning, it's eluding me.'

'"Choo choo bang bang."' He laughed. 'Talk about loco motives.'

We returned to the Robbery-Homicide room. A Dunkin' Donuts takeout box dominated Milo's desk. He said, 'Shouldn't you be getting home to Robin?'

'I told her it might take a while.'

He studied the notes he'd scrawled in the interrogation room. 'Heidi,' he said. 'Our little mountain girl. Too bad everything she's come up with is probably worth a warm bucket of spit . . . "Choo choo bang bang." What's next? Peake reads selections from Dr Seuss?'

He rubbed his eyes, stacked some papers, squared the corners with his thumbs.

'You think it was poor judgment?' he said. 'Asking her to check on Pelley?'

'Not if she's discreet.'

'Worse comes to worst, Swig finds out, gets all huffy. He can't afford to make too big a deal of it – bad publicity.'

'Anything new on Pelley's whereabouts?' I said.

'Zilch. Ramparts *was* notified by the PO, so there's something positive. Other than that, the PO wasn't very helpful. Caseload in the hundreds; to him, Pelley was just another number. I doubt he could point him out in a crowd.'

He pulled a folded sheet out of his jacket pocket and handed it to me. LAPD Suspect Alert. Pelley's vital statistics and a photo so dark and blurry I couldn't see it being useful for anything. All I could make out was a round, clean-shaven Caucasian face smudged with indeterminate features. Thin, light-colored hair. Serious mouth. The crime was failure to report.

'This is what they're using?' I said, placing the paper on the desk.

'Yeah, I know – not exactly Cartier-Bresson. But at least they're looking. I did some looking, too. Driving around the neighborhood, checking out MacArthur Park, Lafayette Park, alleys, con bars, some other bad-guy spots I know. Visited the halfway house, too. Old apartment building, cons out in front, some Korean guy running the place – sincere enough, told me he'd been a social worker in Seoul. But he barely speaks English, and basically all he does is warehouse the residents, do random drug tests maybe four times a year. Counseling consists of asking the cons how they're doing. The ones I saw hanging around didn't look at all insightful. As for Pelley, all the Korean could say was that he'd been quiet, hadn't caused problems. None of the cons remembered a damn thing about him. Of course.'

He reached for a piece of stale cinnamon roll. 'He could be a thousand miles away by now. I didn't do much better with Stargill's investment records. The Newport money managers wouldn't talk to me, and they informed him I'd been asking around. He calls me, all irate. I tell him I'm just trying to clear him, how about he voluntarily gives me a look at his stock portfolio. If everything checks out, we call it a day. He says he'll think about it, but I could tell he won't.'

'Hiding something?' I said.

'Or just guarding his privacy – everyone gets privacy,

right? Even guys who cook and eat babies. Everyone except citizens who get laid out on steel tables, some white-coat peeling off their face, doing the Y-cut, playing peekaboo with their internal organs. No privacy there.'

20

Robin didn't stir when I slipped into bed beside her at one A.M. Visions of Peake's crimes and the knowledge that I hadn't helped Milo much kept me up for a while, heart beating too fast, muscles tight. Deep-breathing myself into an uneasy torpor, I finally slipped off. If dreams intruded, I had no memory of them in the morning, but my legs ached, as if I'd been running from something.

By nine A.M., I was drinking coffee and catching what passes for TV news in LA: Capped-toothed jesters hawking showbiz gossip, the latest bumblings of the moronic city council, the current health scare. Today, it was strawberries from Mexico: Everyone was going to die from an intestinal scourge. Back when I'd treated children, the news had frightened more kids than any horror flick.

I was about to switch off the set when the grinning blonde gushed, 'And now more on that train accident.'

The story merited thirty seconds. An unidentified man had lain across the MetroRail tracks just east of the city limits, squarely in the path of an empty passenger train. The engineer spotted him and put on the emergency brake, but not in time.

Choo choo.

I called Milo.

He picked up right away. 'Yeah, yeah, the little train that couldn't. Probably nothing. Or maybe Peake really is a prophet and we should be worshiping him instead of keeping him locked up. Nothing much else on my plate, so I called the coroner. The deceased is one Ellroy Lincoln Beatty, male black, fifty-two. Petty criminal record – mostly possession and drunk and disorderly. The only thing that intrigued me was that Beatty spent some time in a mental hospital. Camarillo, thirteen years ago, back when they were still open for that kind of business. No mention of Starkweather, but you never know. The accident happened in Newton Division. I wish Manny Alvarado had the case, but he retired and the new guy isn't great about returning calls. I figured I'd head over to the morgue before lunch. Feel free to join me. If it gets you hungry, we can have lunch later. Like a big rare steak.'

'Basically, the head and the lower extremities,' said the attendant. He was a short, solidly built Hispanic named Albert Martinez, with a crew cut and goatee and thick-lensed glasses that enlarged and brightened his eyes. The crucifix around his neck was gold and hand-tooled, vaguely Byzantine.

The coroner's office was two stories of square, smooth, cream stucco, meticulously maintained. Back in East LA. Back at County Hospital. Claire's old office was a few blocks away. I hadn't realized it before, but she'd come full circle.

'The rest of him is pretty much goulash,' said Martinez. 'Personally, I think it's amazing we got what we did. The train must have hit him at what – forty, fifty miles per?'

The room was cool, immaculate, odorless. Empty steel tables equipped with drain basins, overhead microphones, a wall of steel lockers. A junior high student would recognize all of it; too many TV shows had dimmed the shock. But television rarely offered a glimpse at the contents of the lockers. Dead people on TV were intact, clean, bloodless props resting peacefully.

I hadn't been down here since internship, wasn't enjoying the experience.

'How'd you identify him?' said Milo.

'Welfare card in his pocket,' said Martinez. 'The lower extremities still had pieces of pants on and the pocket was in one piece. All he had on him was the card and a couple of bucks. The interesting thing is, you could still smell the booze on him. Even with all the other fluids. I mean, it was really strong. Only other time I smelled it that strong was this woman, died in childbirth, must have drunk two bottles of wine that night and she arrested on the delivery table. Her amniotic fluid was red – wine-red, you know? Almost purple. She must have been saturated with Thunderbird or whatever. The baby was dead, obviously. Probably lucky.'

Martinez touched his crucifix.

'When's Beatty's autopsy scheduled?' said Milo.

'Hard to say. It's the usual backlog. Why?'

'It might be related to something. So you're saying Beatty must have been pretty juiced.'

'To smell that strong? Sure. My guess would be way over the limit. He probably got blasted, wandered onto the tracks, lay down for a nap, and boom.' Martinez smiled. 'So, could I be a detective?'

'Why bother?' said Milo. 'Your job's more fun.'

Martinez chuckled. 'Those tracks – they really should do something about them, no fence, no guardrail when they get close to the train yard. I grew up around there, used to play on the tracks, but they weren't running trains back then. You remember last month? The little kid who wandered on, walking home from school? Not far from where Beatty got hit. That kid, we didn't get anything recognizable on him. They should put a fence up, or something . . . So, anything else?'

'I'd like to look at Beatty.'

'Really? How come?'

'I want to think of him as a person.'

Martinez's thumb and forefinger closed around the bottom of the crucifix. 'A person, huh? Well, maybe looking at him isn't the right way to do that, you know?'

Milo said, 'Humor me.'

Martinez walked over to a locker, slid the drawer out silently, drew back white sheeting.

The face was gray, surprisingly intact except for a thatch of lacerations on the left cheek. Ash gray, because in life Ellroy Beatty had been black. White lint of kinky beard stubble, maybe four, five days' worth. Untrimmed mass of gray hair. The eyes were open, dull, dry, the lips caked with pinkish crust. That vacant look common to all dead faces. No matter what your IQ in life, when the soul flies, you look stupid.

Below the neck was empty space. Clean decapitation except for a few fringes of trachea and jugular, meaty muscle fibers protruding. Two feet down the table was a white-wrapped package that Martinez needlessly explained was 'the lower extremities.'

Milo stared at the ashen chunk that had once borne the consciousness of Ellroy Beatty. Not blinking, not moving. I wondered how many times he'd been down here.

Just as Martinez said, 'OK?' the door opened and a man strode in. He wore scrubs, a hairnet, paper slippers, a loose mask around his neck. About Beatty's age, tall, stoop-shouldered with a deeply tanned face and a thick black beard.

He glanced at us, read the index card in his right hand, and headed for one of the steel lockers, two rows away.

Then he saw Ellroy Beatty's head and flushed with anger. 'What the hell's going on here?'

Martinez said. 'Some kind of problem, Dr Friedman?'

'I'd sure as hell say so. Who cut up my DB?'

'Your DB?' said Martinez.

'That's what I said. Are you *deaf*, Albert?' Friedman turned to Milo. 'And who the hell are you?'

'LAPD.'

'I thought Willis Hooks was on this one.'

'No,' said Milo. 'Hooks is Central. This is a Newton case, the detective's Robert Aguilar.'

'*What?*' said Friedman, jabbing the card. 'The paperwork says Central, Hooks. How long have you been doing this, Mr Aguilar?'

Milo said, 'I'm Sturgis, Doctor. West LA.'

Friedman blinked. 'What the hell—' He stepped closer to Ellroy Beatty's head. 'Let me tell you, Detective, someone's in deep dirt. I had this DB scheduled for a post and someone cut his goddamn head off! And what's he doing in *that* drawer when he's supposed to be over here?' Friedman waved the card.

'No one moved him, Dr Friedman,' said Martinez. 'He got put here right away. And no one cut him, this is the—'

'*Bullshit*, Albert! Bullshit on *toast* – bullets don't sever your damn head! Bullets don't—'

'This is DB Beatty,' said Martinez. 'The one who was hit by a—'

'I know who he *is*, Albert!' Another wave of the card. 'Beatty, Leroy. Gunshot wound to the head, brought in last night—'

'Beatty, Ellroy,' said Martinez.

'*Leroy*, Albert. Says so right here.' The card was thrust at Martinez's face. 'Case number 971132; Time of Delivery: Three-sixteen A.M.'

Martinez rolled up some of the sheeting covering Beatty's legs. Pulling out a toe tag, he read, 'Ellroy Beatty, hit by a train. TOD three-forty-two A.M., case number 971135.'

Friedman looked down at the head. Then the card. Then the numbers on the steel drawers. He yanked one open.

Inside was an intact body, naked, gray.

Exact same gray as Ellroy Beatty.

Same face.

All four of us stared.

I looked from corpse to corpse. Minor discrepancies materialized: Leroy Beatty had slightly less hair on top than

Ellroy, but more on the bottom. A full white beard. No scratches on his face, but a keloid scar puckered the right jawline, probably an old knife wound.

The neat, blackened hole in his forehead looked too innocuous to have killed him. The impact had caused facial distortion – swelling around the nose, puffiness under the eyes. Bloodred eyeballs, as if he'd stared too long into the fires of hell.

Friedman's head was swiveling now, too.

'Twins,' said Martinez. 'Brother Ellroy, meet Brother Leroy.'

Friedman turned on him. 'Don't joke, Albert. What the hell's going on?'

'Good question,' said Milo.

It took two hours to put it all together. Dr Friedman left long before then, muttering about having to work with incompetents.

I sat with Milo in a morgue conference room. Detective Robert Aguilar from Newton showed up first. Young, good-looking, with a sleek black pompadour, he wore a gray pin-striped suit tailored to his trim frame. Manicured nails. He spoke very crisply, a little too fast, tried to come across lighthearted but couldn't pull it off. Milo'd told me he was new to the division, a Detective I. For all I knew, this was his first case.

Last to arrive was Willis Hooks from Central. I'd met him when he worked Southwest. A series of killings of handicapped people that had given me a glimpse of a cowardly new world.

Hooks was in his early forties, black, five-nine, heavy, with a clean head, bulldog jowls, and a thick, drooping mustache. His navy blazer had that baggy, too-long look you sometimes see with big-chested men. His shoes were dusty.

'Milo,' he said, sitting down. 'Dr Delaware. Fate keeps putting us in the same room.'

Aguilar watched and listened, trying, I guessed, to gauge Hooks's mood. To know with whom to align himself.

'Fate or just plain bad luck, Willis,' said Milo.

Hooks laughed hoarsely and spread pudgy fingers on the table.

Milo said, 'Willis, this is Robert Aguilar.'

'Newton Division,' said Aguilar.

'Charmed,' said Hooks. 'Yours is the train?'

'Yup,' said Aguilar. 'Ellroy Lincoln Beatty, male black, fifty-two.'

'Mine's Leroy Washington Beatty, male black, fifty-two. Think they could be distantly related?'

Before Aguilar could answer, Hooks winked and said, 'Mine went down around three A.M., give or take.'

'Mine, too,' said Aguilar.

'How 'bout that?' Hooks turned to Milo. 'It appears someone's got it in for the Beatty family. Maybe we should find out if they've got any other siblings. Maybe there's some more Beatty 187's all over town – hell, this could be a Beatty Holocaust. If not, least we should do is warn them.'

Aguilar frowned. Taking out a gold Cross pen, he began writing in his pad.

Hooks said, 'Got some ideas, Detective?'

Aguilar looked up. His lips were tight. 'Just charting the data flow.'

Hooks pursed his lips and his mustache bristled. 'Well, that's good. So tell me, Detective Sturgis. What's your connection to the Bobbsey twins?'

'You're not going to believe this,' said Milo.

We left the morgue at twelve-thirty P.M. Mission Road was alive with pedestrians. The air smelled like fried chicken.

'Grease,' said Milo. 'Yum. Lunch?'

'Not in the mood,' I said.

'Such strength of character.'

He'd left the unmarked in the red zone turnaround in front of the building along with other police vehicles. I'd used a nearby lot. A white-and-blue coroner's van circled past us and cruised out to the street.

Milo said, '"Choo choo bang bang." A train and a gun.' He rested a foot on the unmarked's front bumper. '"Bad eyes in a box." Both times Peake spouts off the day before. So when does the bastard go on the Psychic Hotline and start raking in serious money?'

'If the news got out, I'm sure agents would be doing lunch with him at Spago.'

He huffed. 'So what the hell does it mean, Alex?'

'Two homeless men, a psychologist, a waiter,' I said. 'Wide range of ages, both sexes, blacks, whites. If there's a connection, I don't see it. Maybe Wendell Pelley's behind some of it. But he didn't do Dada. So if Dada's part of the mix, it means more than one killer. Same if the Beatty brothers really were killed simultaneously.'

'Fine, fine, there's a psycho army out there. For all we know, Peake spouted off about Richard, too, but till Claire showed up, no one was around to listen. The question is how the hell does Peake know?'

'The only logical possibility,' I said, 'is that he has some link to the outside.'

'Got to be Pelley,' he said. 'Or another Starkweather alum. Guys like that would know all the boozehound places like the train tracks, the alley where Leroy was shot. Booze and mental illness, you said so yourself: Bad combination. And Pelley's history fits: He was blind drunk when he shot his girlfriend and her kids. Now he's living on the streets again. The Beattys are just the kind of people he'd run into.'

'Why use the train?' I said. 'Why not shoot both of them?'

'The guy's crazy. Maybe a voice told him to do it that way. Choo choo goddamn bang bang. The main thing is, there's some pattern here.'

I didn't reply.

He said, 'You have a problem with Pelley?'

'No,' I said. 'I just can't see any conceptual link, even eliminating Richard Dada from the mix, between Claire and the Beattys.'

'The Beattys were alcoholics,' he said. 'Claire worked with alcoholics. Maybe they were her patients.'

'They'd fit the County profile,' I said, 'but that still doesn't offer any motive to kill them. It had to have something to do with Peake. His crimes – those clippings Claire held on to. She targeted him because there was something she wanted to learn about him. Or *from* him. I went back into the newspaper files and got some background on the Ardullo family. Scott's father was a major agricultural figure, adamant about not selling farmland to developers – he'd been wooed for years, but refused. Then he died, Scott and his family got murdered, and all the Ardullo land was sold. Be interesting to know who inherited.'

'What?' he said. 'We're running off in a whole other direction? The Ardullos were eliminated for *profit*, and Peake's some corporate *hit* man? C'mon, Alex, I'm more likely to believe Peake can flow through walls at will, off people, and return to his beddy-bye at the Loon Farm.'

'I know Peake's disorganized, but big money always adds another dimension. Maybe you should at least visit Treadway – Fairway Ranch. Maybe someone will be around who remembers.'

'Remembers what?'

'The crime. Something. Just to be thorough.'

'Right now being thorough means finding Wendell Pelley.'

He placed both hands on the hood of the unmarked and gazed over at the coroner's building, then up at the milky sky. Behind us were Dumpsters, water pumps, the rears of two antique hospital buildings. Sculpted cornices and ornate moldings topped crumbling brick. More Victorian London than East LA. Jack the Ripper would've found it cozy.

'OK,' I said. 'Let's stick with here-and-now. I can even

give you a motive. The Beatty twins died at around the same time. That has a ritual flavor to it – a game. My vote is slaughter for fun. That also fits with the second-killer scenario. Plenty of precedent: Leopold and Loeb, Bianchi and Buono, Bittaker and Norris. It could return Richard Dada to the victim list. Pelley's buddy killed Dada before Pelley was released. But only a month before – the crime would still be psychologically fresh. Maybe the buddy's descriptions of how he did it turned Pelley on, got him back in the murder game.'

'And the other bastard could be some nutcase Pelley hooked up with at the halfway house, Alex. I saw the guys living there. Not the Kiwanis Club. OK, I'm going back, gonna be a little more assertive. Gonna continue patrolling Ramparts on my own, too. Keep checking the bum haunts. Play more phone tag with other divisions, neighboring cities, in case Pelley and/or Nut Buddy has been a bad boy somewhere else. Though the site of the Beattys' murders says they're still local. Which makes sense. They probably have no wheels, can't hit the freeway.'

That reminded me of something. 'The first time we discussed Richard, we talked about someone without a car. Maybe a bus rider. Same for Claire's phantom boyfriend.'

'There you go,' he said. 'Bus-riding lunatics. You said he wouldn't look crazy. How do you feel about that, now?'

'Pretty much the same,' I said. 'All four murders were planned and meticulous. Whoever killed Richard and Claire had the sense not to steal their cars. And murdering the Beattys on the same night adds another level of calculation.

Choreography. So if Pelley is involved, he's probably not actively psychotic. At least not externally. Don't forget, they let him out. He must've appeared coherent.'

'When he kills, he's neat. That makes me feel a whole lot better.' Shaking his head, Milo reached for the car door.

I said, 'So the Treadway thing's off the table, completely?'

'You don't want to let go of it?'

'Those clippings bother me, Milo. Whatever Pelley's role in all this, something went on between Claire and Peake. She sought him out, made him a project. He predicted her murder. Sixteen years ago, he took out Brittany Ardullo's eyes. Claire's eyes were also targeted. It's almost as if he'd been trying to connect the two crimes – somehow relive his past, using a surrogate.'

'The Beattys' eyes weren't messed with.'

'But Richard's eyes *were* taken. Too much variation, too much that doesn't fit. Peake's the only link. If we understand more about him – his history – it may get us closer to Pelley. And whoever else is involved.'

He swung the door open. 'I just don't have the time, Alex. But if you want to go out there, fine. I appreciate the effort – I'll even phone Bunker Protection, see if I can get them to be cooperative. Meanwhile, I go nut-hunting right here on the streets.'

'Good luck,' I said.

'Luck doesn't seem to be cutting it.' He withdrew his hand from the door and placed it on my shoulder. 'I'm being a cranky bastard, aren't I? Sorry. Not enough sleep, too much futility.'

'Don't sweat it.'

'Let me apologize anyway. Contrition's good for the soul. And thanks for all your time on this. I mean it.'

'My thanks will be your getting good grades and cleaning your room.'

He laughed. Much too loudly. But maybe it helped.

21

TWENTY MILES north of LA, everything empties.

I'd stopped at home long enough to pick up and scan the articles I'd photocopied at the library, gulp down some coffee, and get back on the freeway. The 405 took me to the 101 and finally Interstate 5, this time headed north. The last fast-food signs had been five miles back and I shared the freeway with flatbeds hauling hay, long-distance movers, the odd car, a few Winnebagos lumbering in the slow lane.

I had a heavy foot, speeding past brown, rumpled-blanket mountains, groves of scrub oak and pine and California pepper trees, the occasional grazing horse. The heat hadn't let up, but the sky was awash with pretty clouds – lavender-gray swirls, satin-shiny, as if an old wedding dress had been draped over the world.

The clippings had given me three possible contacts: Teodoro Alarcon, the ranch superintendent who'd found the bodies; Sheriff Jacob Haas; and the only other person to comment on Ardis Peake's strange behavior without protection of anonymity, a kid named Derrick Crimmins. No listings on Alarcon or Crimmins, but a Jacob B. Haas had an address at Fairway Ranch. I called his number and a hearty male voice on a machine told me Jake and Marvelle were unavailable, but feel free to leave a message. I said I'd be in town on LAPD business and would appreciate it if Sheriff Haas could spare me some time.

The highway forked, the truck route sprouting to the right and draining the traffic from three lanes. Radar surveillance warnings were all around, but the eternity of open road before me was too seductive and I kept the Seville at 85, zipping past Saugus and Castaic, the western ridge of Angeles Crest National Forest, the Tejon Pass, then the Kern County border.

Shortly after eleven, I exited at Grapevine and bought some gas. My freeway map showed me how to get to Fairway Ranch, but I confirmed directions with the sleepy-looking attendant.

'That's for old people,' he said. He was around nineteen, crew-cut, tan, and pimpled, with four earrings in his left lobe.

'Visiting Grandma,' I said.

He looked up and down the Seville. 'It's pretty nice there. Rich people, mostly. They play a lot of golf.' The mini-truck with the huge wheels and the Radiohead bumper sticker parked near the garbage cans was probably his. Freshly waxed. His eyes narrowed as he continued to stare at the Seville. I try to keep the car in good shape, but it's a '79 and there are limits.

'Used to be another town around here,' I said.

His stare was dull.

'Treadway,' I said. 'Farms, ranches, peaches, and walnut groves.'

'Oh, yeah?' Profound indifference. 'Cool car.'

I thanked him and left, taking a narrow northeastern road

toward the Tehachapi Mountains. The range was gorgeous – high and sharp, peaks of varying height laid against one another masterfully, more perfectly arranged than any artist's composition could ever be. The lower hills were dun, the upper ridges the precise ash-gray of the Beatty brothers' dead faces. Some of the more distant crests had faded to a misty purple. Wintry colors even at this time of year, but the heat was more intense than in LA, burning through the clouds as if they were tissue paper.

The road rose sharply. This was subalpine terrain. I couldn't imagine it as farmland. Then ten miles in, a sign reading FAIRWAY RANCH: A PLANNED COMMUNITY directed me down a left-hand pass that cut sharply through walls of granite. Another sign – STEEP GRADE: REDUCE SPEED – came too late; I was already hurtling down a roller-coaster chute.

A good two miles of chute. At the bottom was flat green patchwork centered by a diamond-bright aquamarine lake. The lake was amorphous – too perfectly shapeless, it shouted man-made. Two golf courses hugged the water, one on each side, fringed by lime-colored trees with feathery tops – California peppers. Red-topped houses were grouped in premeditated plots. Spanish tile on cream stucco, interspersed with trapezoids of green. The entire layout – maybe five miles wide – was outlined in white, as if drawn by a child too fearful to go outside the lines.

As I got closer I saw that the white was waist-high beam-and-post fencing. An exact duplicate of the 'planned community' sign appeared a hundred yards later, over a smaller plaque that said Bunker Protection patrolled the premises.

No gates, just a flat, clean road into the development. Fifteen MPH speed limit and warnings to watch for slow-moving golf carts. I obliged and crawled past stretches of perfect rye grass. Lots more pepper trees, shaggy and undulating, subplanted with beds of multicolored impatiens.

A thousand feet in, another dozen signs on a stout, dark tree trunk that might have been walnut offered a crash course in the layout of Fairway Ranch.

Balmoral Golf Course to the north, White Oak to the south, Reflection Lake straight ahead. The Pinnacle Recreation Center and Spa to the north, Walnut Grove Fitness Center to the south. In the middle, Piccadilly Arcade.

Other arrows pointed to what I assumed were six different housing subdivisions: Chatham, Cotswold, Sussex, Essex, Yorkshire, Jersey.

The mountains were two or three miles away but seemed to be closer. Sparkling color and knife-edge detail said the air was pure.

Beyond the tree post was a small single cube of a building. The rounded edges and blatant texture of pseudo-adobe. More Spanish tile.

Letting the Seville idle, I looked around. Acres of grass and scores more California peppers, a few clumps of peach trees with curling leaves. A handful of larger trunks with bark that matched the color and texture of the signpost and had to be walnuts. No fruit or blossoms. Dead branches and truncated tops.

Imagining the stink of fertilizer, the grind of machinery, pickers moving through sun-dappled rows, I thought of Henry Ardullo's resolve never to sell out.

In the distance I could see assortments of houses – sugar cubes with red tile roofs. Not a hint of half-timber, brick, slate, or wood shingle.

Sussex, Essex . . . English monikers, Southwest architecture. In California, escape from logic was sometimes construed as freedom.

I heard an engine start. A pale blue Ford sedan with blackwall tires was parked next to the cube. Now it drove forward very slowly and stopped right next to me. Understated shield logo on the driver's door. Crossed rifles above 'BP, Inc. A Security Corporation.' No cherry on top, no conspicuous display of firearms.

At the wheel was a mustachioed young man wearing a pale blue uniform and mirrored shades.

'Morning, sir.' Tight smile.

'Morning, Officer. I'm here to visit Jacob Haas on Charing Cross Road.'

'Charing Cross,' he said, stretching it out so he could appraise me. 'That's all the way over in Jersey.'

I resisted the temptation to say, 'Atlantic City or Newark?'

'Thanks.'

He cleared his throat. 'New around here?'

'First time,' I said.

'Relative of Mr Haas?'

'Acquaintance. He used to be the sheriff. Back when it was Treadway.'

He hesitated a moment before saying, 'Sure.' The same dullness I'd seen on the gas jockey's face. Treadway meant nothing to him, either. He knew nothing of the area's history. How many people did? I looked past him at the peach and walnut trees, now just woody memorials. Nothing else from the ranching days remained. Certainly not a hint of the bloodbath at the Ardullo ranch. If Jacob Haas wasn't in, or if he refused to see me, I'd wasted my time. Even if he talked, what could I hope to learn?

The security guard's car phone buzzed and he picked up, nodded, told me, 'Jersey's way at the end – go straight through to the lake, turn right. You'll see a sign pointing to the White Oak golf course. Just keep on and it'll be there.'

I drove away, watched him through my rearview mirror as he performed a three-point turn and headed toward Balmoral.

Piccadilly Arcade was a small shopping center due east of the security office. Grocery with a post office and ATM, dry cleaner, two clothing shops leaning toward golf togs and velour jogging suits. A sign outside the second said the movie tonight was *Top Gun*.

My drive to Jersey took me past perfectly appointed public buildings – the clubhouse, the spa – tennis courts, swimming pools. The houses looked better from a distance.

They varied in size by development. Essex was the high-rent district – detached split-levels and two-story haciendaitas on postage-stamp lots, some landscaping, lots of Cadillacs and Lincolns, a few satellite dishes. Clear views of the lake. Fit-looking white-haired people in activewear. Further inland, Yorkshire was mock-adobe town houses clumped in fours and fives. A little skimpier in the flower-and-shrub department, but still immaculate.

The lake was obscured, now, by peppers. The trees were

hardy, drought resistant, clean. They'd been brought into the San Fernando Valley years ago by the truckload, taking over the chaparral and contributing to the death of the native oaks. A quarter-mile of shaded road before Jersey appeared.

Mobile homes in an open lot. The units were uniformly white and spotless, with plenty of greenery camouflage at the base, but clearly prefab. Just a few trees on the periphery and no direct access to the lake, but majestic views of the mountains.

The few people I saw also looked in good shape, perhaps a bit more countrified. Parked in front of the mobiles were Chevys, Fords, Japanese compacts, the occasional RV. The road that split the subdivision was freshly asphalted. No-frills, but the overall feel was still cleanliness, good maintenance, seniors settled in contentment.

I parked in one of the ten public spaces at the end and found Charing Cross Road easily enough – first street to the right.

Jacob and Marvelle Haas announced ownership of their Happy Traveler with a wood-burned sign over the front door. Two vehicles – a Buick Skylark and a Datsun pickup – so maybe someone was home. Some improvements had been added to the unit: Green canvas window awnings, an oak door that looked hand-carved, a cement porch stacked up to the entrance. Potted geranium and cactus at the top, along with an empty fishbowl still housing a carbon filter. The door knocker was a brass cocker spaniel. Around its neck hung a garland of tiny cowries.

I lifted the dog and let it concuss against the door.

A voice called out, 'One minute.'

The man who opened was younger than I'd expected – younger than any of the residents I'd seen, so far. Sixty, if that, with iron-gray hair brushed straight back, and very acute eyes the same color. He wore a short-sleeved white knit shirt, blue jeans, black loafers. His shoulders were broad, but so were his hips. A lip of fat curled over his belt buckle. His arms were long, hairless, thin except at the wrists, where they picked up some heft. His face was narrow, sun-spotted in places, cinched around the eyes, and sagging around the bone lines, but his skin had a sheen, as if someone had buffed him lovingly.

'Dr Delaware,' he said in that same hearty voice. But his expression didn't match – cautious, tentative. 'Got your message. Jacob Haas.'

When we shook hands, his grip seemed reluctant – bare contact, then quick pressure around my fingers before he pulled away and stepped back inside.

'C'mon in.'

I entered a narrow front room that opened to a kitchenette. A window air conditioner hummed. The interior wasn't cool, but the worst of the heat had been kept at bay. No knotty pine, no framed homilies, no trailer-park clichés. Deep gray berber carpeting floored the mobile. White cotton sofa and two matching easy chairs, glass-and-brass coffee table, blue-and-white Chinese garden bench serving as a perch for daffodils in a deep blue vase.

Picasso prints hung on panel walls painted pale salmon. Black lacquer bookshelves held paperbacks and magazines, a thirty-five-inch TV with VCR and stereo setup, and a skinny black vertical rack full of CD's. The Four Seasons,

Duane Eddy, the Everly Brothers, Tom Jones, Petula Clark.

Rock and roll was old enough to retire.

The room smelled of cinnamon buns. The woman on the sofa got up and said, 'Marvelle Haas, so pleased to meet you.' She wore a navy polo shirt, white slacks, white sandals, looked to be her husband's age. More wrinkled than he, but a trim figure. Short, wavy hair dyed mahogany.

Her grip was strong. 'Have a nice drive up from LA?'

'Very nice. Beautiful scenery.'

'It's even more beautiful when you live here. Something to drink?'

'No, thanks.'

'Well, then, I'll be shoving off.' She kissed her husband's cheek and put her arm around his shoulder – protectively, I thought. 'You boys be good, now.'

'Now, that's no fun,' Haas said. 'Drive carefully, hon.'

She hurried to the door. Her hips rotated. Years ago, she'd been beautiful. She still was.

When the door closed after her, Haas seemed to get smaller. He motioned toward the chairs. We both sat.

'She decided to visit her sister in Bakersfield,' he said, 'because she didn't want to be here when you were.'

'Sorry—'

'No, not your fault. She doesn't like unpleasantness.' Crossing his legs, he plowed his hair with one hand and studied me. 'I'm not sure I want to be doing this, myself, but I guess I feel obligated to help the police.'

'I appreciate that, Sheriff. Hopefully it won't be unpleasant.'

Haas smiled. 'Haven't been "Sheriff" for a while. Quit right after the Ardullos, started selling insurance for my father-in-law. Two years later, there was no need for a sheriff – no more town.'

'Who closed it down?'

'Group called BCA Leisure bought all the land. One of those multinational deals – Japanese, Indonesian, British. The American partners are a development group out in Denver. Back then they were buying up land right and left.'

'Was there any resistance from the residents?'

'Not a peep,' he said. 'Farming's always been a tough life, and in Treadway only two families made a serious living from it, the Ardullos and the Crimminses. Between them, they owned ninety percent of the land. The rest of us were just here to keep their businesses going – like share-croppers. So once they sold out, it wasn't much of a brainer. The sheriff job was only part-time, anyway. I was already living up in Bakersfield, near my in-laws. Doing bookkeeping for my father-in-law.'

'When did you move back here?'

'Five years ago.' He smiled again. 'Like I said, it was near my in-laws. Seriously, I decided to pack it in when I figured I had enough policies tucked away to be comfortable. And Bakersfield was starting to look like LA. We were thinking out of state, maybe Nevada, then this unit came up – a lucky deal, because Fairway units don't stay vacant very long. We said, why not. The air's great, terrific fishing, they show movies, you can do all your shopping right here. We travel half the year, a small place is perfect.

We don't go mobiling, this thing's as rooted as any regular house. We fly. Vegas, when there's a show we want to see. Alaska, Canada. This year, we did a big one. London, England. Saw the Chelsea Flower Show because Marvelle likes flowers. Beautiful country. When they say green, they mean it.'

His tone had relaxed. I hated what I had to do, decided to approach the task indirectly. 'The Ardullos and the Crimminses. A boy named Derrick Crimmins was quoted in an article I read about the crime.'

'Carson Crimmins's son. The younger one – he had two boys, Derrick and Carson Junior, Cliff. Yeah, I remember both of them hanging around the crime scene, along with a bunch of other kids. I don't remember Derrick talking to the press, but sure, I can see him shooting off his mouth, he always had a mouth on him. So, tell me, why do the police send a psychologist to talk about the Monster? Don't tell me it's some kind of evaluation, they're thinking of letting him out.'

'No,' I said. 'He's locked up tight, no release in sight. I just saw him. He's pretty deteriorated.'

'Deteriorated,' he said. 'Like what, a vegetable?'

'Close to.'

'Well that's good. He shouldn't be alive . . . *Deteriorated* – the village idiot, that's how everyone saw him. Myself included. He was treated with kindness, pity, it's a big-city lie that small-town people are prejudiced and intolerant, like those morons you see on *Jerry Springer*. The Monster received more kindness in Treadway than he ever would've in LA. Him *and* his mother. A couple of drifters, not a penny in their pockets, they just showed up one day and got taken in.'

Haas stopped, waited for comment. I just nodded.

He said, 'She was no charm-school gal, Noreen. And *he* was certainly no prize. But no one let 'em starve.'

'Was she a difficult person?'

'Not difficult, but not exactly pleasant, either. She was sloppy-looking, kind of puffy in the face, like she cried all night. You'd try talking to her and she'd hang her head and mutter. Not as crazy as Ardis, but if you ask me they were both retarded. Him more than her, but she was no genius. It was nothing but kindness on the Ardullos' part, taking her and Ardis in. She could cook, but Terri Ardullo was a fine cook herself. It was charity, pure and simple. Done in a way to give them some dignity.'

'Scott and Terri were charitable people.'

'Salt of the earth. Scott was a nice fellow, but it was Terri had the ideals. Religious, involved in all the church activities. The church was on land donated by Butch Ardullo – Scott's dad. Presbyterian. Butch was born a Catholic, but Kathy – his wife – was Presbyterian, so Butch converted and built the church for her. *That* was a sad thing. Demolishing that church. Butch and his crew built it themselves – beautiful little white-board thing with carved moldings and a steeple they had made by some Danish fellow over in Solvang. Butch's house was something, too. Three stories, also white board, with a big stone porch, land stretching out in all directions. They grew walnuts and peaches commercially but kept a small citrus grove out in back. You could smell the blossoms all the way out to the main road. They gave most of the oranges and lemons away. The Crimmins place was almost as big, but not as tasteful. Two mansions, opposite sides of the valley.'

His eyes clouded. 'I remember Scott when he was a kid. Running around the groves, always cheerful. The house was happy. They were rich folks, but down-to-earth.'

He got up, filled a glass with bottled water from the fridge. 'Sure you don't want a drink?'

'Thanks, I will.'

He brought both tumblers to the coffee table. Two gulps and his was empty.

'Refill time,' he said. 'Don't want to parch up like a raisin. Need more BTU's on the AC.'

Another trip to the kitchenette. He drained the glass, ran his finger around the rim, set off a high-pitched note. 'You still haven't told me why you're here.'

I began with Claire's murder. Her name drew no look of recognition. When I recounted Peake's babbling, he said, 'I can't believe you came all the way up here because of that.'

'Right now, there's very little else to go on, Mr Haas.'

'You just said he's deteriorated, so who cares what he says? Now, what is it exactly you think I can help you with?'

'Anything you can tell me about Peake. That night.'

His hands flew together and laced. Fingertips reddened as they pressed into knuckles. Nails blanched the color of clotted cream.

'I've spent a long time trying to forget that night, and it doesn't sound like you've got any good reason to make me go through it again.'

'I'm sorry,' I said. 'If it's too difficult—'

'Damn thirst,' he said, springing up. 'Must be going diabetic or something.'

22

HAAS RETURNED looking no happier, but resigned.

'It happened at night,' he said, 'but no one found out till the morning. I was the second to know. Ted Alarcon called me – he was one of Scott's field supervisors. Scott and Ted were supposed to drive up early to Fresno, take a look at some equipment. Scott was going to pick up Ted, and when he didn't, Ted called the house. No answer, so he drove over, went in.'

'The door was open?' I said.

'No one locked their doors. Ted figured Scott had overslept, maybe he should go upstairs and knock on the bedroom door. That shows you the kind of guy Scott was – a Mexican supervisor felt comfortable going upstairs. But on the way, Ted passed through the kitchen and saw it. Her.' He licked his lips. 'After that, God only knows how he had the strength to go upstairs.'

'The papers said he followed the bloody sneaker prints.'

'Ted was a gutsy guy, Vietnam vet, saw combat.'

'Any idea where I can locate him?'

'Forest Lawn,' he said. 'He died a couple years later. Cancer.' He patted his sternum. 'Fifty years old. He smoked, but nothing will convince me the shock didn't break down his health.'

He sat up straighter, as if affirming his own robustness.

I said, 'So Ted went upstairs, saw the rest of it, and called you.'

'I was still in bed, the sun had just come up. The phone rings and someone's breathing hard, gasping, sounding crazy, I can't make head nor tail out of it, Marvelle's saying, "What's going on?" Finally, I recognize Ted's voice, but he's still not making any sense, I hear "Mr Scott! Miss Terri!"' He shook his head. 'I just knew something bad had happened. When I got there, Ted was on the front porch with a big pool of vomit in front of him. He was a dark-skinned fellow, but that morning he was white as a sheet. He had blood on his jeans and shoes, at first I thought *he'd* done something crazy. Then he started throwing up some more, managed to stand up, just about collapsed. I had to catch him. All the while he's crying and pointing back at the house.'

Putting his knees together, Haas hunched and sank lower on the couch. 'I took my gun out and went in. I didn't want to mess anything up, so I was careful where I stepped. The light was on in the kitchen. I saw Noreen Peake sitting on a chair – I mean you couldn't really tell it was her, but I knew. Maybe it was the way she was dressed—' His hand waved stiffly. 'Ted's boot prints were in the blood – he wore Westerns – but so were others. Sneakers. I still didn't know if anyone was up there, so I moved really quietly. The lights were on wherever he'd – like he was showing off what he'd done. Scott and Terri were next to each other – hugging each other. I ran across the hall . . . found the little girl . . .'

He emitted a low-pitched noise, like poorly oiled gears

grinding. 'The FBI interviewed me, wrote it up for their research. Get your bosses at LAPD to find you a copy.'

I nodded. 'What led you to Peake's shack?'

'The damn blood, it was obvious. The trail had thinned but it ran down the back stairs and out the back door. Specks and spots but you could still see bits of sneaker prints. It kept going maybe twenty yards on the pathway; then it died completely. At that point, I didn't know I was looking for Peake, only that I should head back to the shack. The sneakers were right inside Peake's door. Clerk over at the five-and-dime said Peake had tried to shoplift 'em a few weeks before and when she caught him, he mumbled and paid something and she let him keep the damn things.'

Haas glared. 'That was the trouble. Everyone was too nice to him. He stumbled around town looking dumb and spooky; we didn't have any real crime in Treadway, didn't recognize him for what he was. It was a peaceful place, that's why a part-timer like me could be the law. Mostly what I did was help people fix stuff, check on shut-ins, make sure someone didn't get in his car when he was blind drunk. More of a damn social worker. But Peake . . . he was always strange. We were all too damn trusting.'

His hands were working furiously. Time to give him some breathing room. I said, 'When Treadway closed down, what happened to all the town records?'

'Boxed and shipped up to Bakersfield. But forget about finding anything there. We're talking maps, plot plans, and not much of it, at that. Sounds to me like you're digging a dry hole, Doctor. Why don't you go back to LA and tell your bosses to forget all this psychological stuff. Peake's locked up, that's the main thing.'

He looked at his wrist. No watch. He got up and found it on one of the bookshelves, put it on, checked the dial.

I said, 'I appreciate your spending the time. Just a few more things. The article I read said you found Peake sleeping.'

'Like a—' His mouth trembled. 'I was going to say like a baby. Christ – yeah, he was asleep. Lying on his back, hands folded over his chest, snoring, face all smeared with blood. At first I thought he'd been killed too, but when I looked closer I could see it was just stains, and that made me jam the cuffs on him.'

He wiped sweat from his cheeks. 'That place. I'd seen it from the outside but never been inside before. A sty – smelled worse than a dog run. What little stuff Peake owned was all jumbled and thrown around. Spoiled food, armies of bugs, empty bottles of booze, cans of spray paint, glue tubes, porno magazines he must've gotten somewhere else, 'cause that garbage wasn't sold in Treadway. No one recalls Peake traveling, but he must've. For the dope, too. He had all kinds of pills – speed, downers, phenobarbital. The prescription pharmacist was over in Tehachapi, and they had no record of any prescriptions. So it must have been street stuff. Scum like Peake can get any sort of thing.'

'Was he stoned that night?'

'Had to be. Even after I cuffed him and screamed in his face, stuck my gun right under his nose, I could barely rouse him. He kept fading in and out, got this real dumb smile on his face, and then he'd close his eyes and be in Never-Never

Land again. It was all I could do not to shoot him right there. Because of what he did – what I found in his shack.' He turned away. 'On his hot plate. He'd taken the knife with him, the one he used on the little girl, grabbed that baby boy out of the crib, and—'

He sprang up again. 'Hell, no, I won't go there. Took me too damn long to erase those pictures from my head. Goodbye, Doctor – don't say another word, just goodbye.'

He hurried to the door, held it open. I thanked him for his time again.

'Yeah, sure.'

'Just one more thing,' I said. 'Who inherited Scott and Terri's estate?'

'Bunch of relatives all over the state. Her folks were from Modesto, and Scott still had family up in San Francisco, on his mother's side. The lawyer in charge said there were two dozen or so heirs, but no one was fighting. None of them gave a damn about inheriting, they were all broken up about how the money came to them.'

'Do you remember the lawyer's name?'

'No. Why the hell would it matter?'

'I'm sure it doesn't,' I said. 'And Scott's mother was already deceased.'

'Years before. Heart condition. *Why?*'

'Just being thorough.'

'Well, you're sure being that.' He started to close the door.

I said, 'Mr Haas, is there anyone else around here who might be willing to talk to me?'

'What?' he said, furiously. 'This wasn't enough?'

'As long as I'm up here, I might as well cover all bases – you were a lawman, you know what it's like.'

'No, I don't. And I don't want to. Forget it. There's no one from the old days. Fairway's for old city folk looking for peace and quiet. I'm the only Treadway hick in the place. Which is why they stuck me out with the trailers.' His laugh was cold.

I said, 'Any idea where Derrick Crimmins—'

'The Crimminses are as gone as anyone else. After Carson Senior and his wife got their money out of the land, they moved to Florida. I heard they bought a boat, did all this sailing, but that's *all* I know. If they're alive, they'd be old. At least he would.'

'His wife was younger?'

'She was a second wife.'

'What was her name?'

'I don't remember,' he answered too quickly. His voice had hardened and he had closed the door till only a five-inch crack remained. The half-face I saw was grim. 'Cliff Crimmins is also gone. Motorcycle accident in Vegas – it made the papers. He was into that motocross stuff, stunt driving, parachuting, surfing, anything with speed and danger. Both of them were like that. Spoiled kids, always had to be the center of attention. Carson bought them all the toys they wanted.'

The door closed.

I'd raised someone else's stress level. Some psychologist.

No end to justify the means, either.

Had he reacted with special vehemence when the topic

was the second Mrs Crimmins, or had I already primed his emotional pump so that anything I said raised his blood pressure?

Walking back to the car, I decided upon the former: How likely would he be to forget the name of one of the richest women in town? So something about Mrs Crimmins bothered him . . . but big deal. Maybe he'd hated her. Or loved her. Or lusted for her without satisfaction.

No reason to think it related to anything I was after.

I didn't even know what I was after.

Dry hole.

It was still before noon, and I felt useless. Haas claimed no Treadway residents were around, and maybe he was telling the truth. But I felt unsettled – something about his demeanor – why had he agreed to see me, started off amiable, then turned?

Probably just horror flashbacks.

Still, as long as I was up here . . . I'd already exhausted the major news sources on the Ardullo murders, but small towns had local papers, and Treadway's might've covered the carnage in detail. The records had all been shipped to Bakersfield. Not much of it, Haas claimed. But city libraries appreciated the value of old news.

As I reached the Seville, a baby blue security sedan nosed through the trailer park. Different guard at the wheel, also young and mustachioed. Maybe that was the Bunker Protection image.

He cruised alongside me, stopped the way the first man had.

Staring. No surprise. He'd been told about me.

I said, 'Have a nice day.'

'You too, sir.'

On my way out, I tripled the speed limit.

Back at the Grapevine gas station, I made a few calls and learned that the main reference library for Kern County was Beale Memorial, in Bakersfield.

Another forty-five minutes of driving. I found Beale easily enough, a ten-year-old, modernistic, sand-colored structure in a nice part of town, backed by a two-hundred-vehicle parking lot. Inside was a fresh-smelling atrium and the feel of efficiency. I told the smiling librarian at the reference desk what I was after and she directed me to the Jack Maguire Local History Room, where another pleasant woman checked a computer database and said, 'We've got twenty years of something called the *Treadway Intelligencer*. Hard copy, not microfiche.'

'Could I see it, please?'

'All of it?'

'Unless that's a problem.'

'Let me check.'

She disappeared behind a door and emerged five minutes later pushing a dolly bearing two medium-sized cardboard boxes.

'You're in luck,' she said. 'It was a weekly, and a small one, so this is twenty years. You can't take it out of the room, but we're open till six. Happy reading.'

No raised eyebrows, no intrusive questions. God bless librarians. I wheeled the dolly to a table.

* * *

A small one, indeed. The *Intelligencer* was a seven-page green sheet and the second carton was half empty. Copies, beginning with January 1962, were bound by the dozen and bagged in plastic. The publisher and editor-in-chief was someone named Orton Hatzler, the managing editor Wanda Hatzler. I copied down both names and started to read.

Wide-spaced text and a few photos with surprisingly good clarity. Weather reports on the front page, because even in California weather mattered to farmers. High school dances, bumper crops, science projects, 4-H Club, scouting expeditions, gleeful descriptions of the Kern County Fair ('Once again, Lars Carlson has shown himself to be the peach-pie-eating champion of all time!'). Page two was much the same, and three was reserved for wire-service snips abstracting the international events of the day and for editorials. Orton Hatzler had been a strong hawk on Vietnam.

Butch Ardullo's name cropped up frequently, mostly in stories related to his leadership in the farm organization. A photo of him and his wife at a Fresno charity ball showed a big man with a bulldog face and a gray crew cut hovering over a willowy, refined-looking, dark-haired woman. Luck-of-the-draw genetics had favored Scott with his father's build and his mother's facial features.

Scott had inherited athletic skills, as well. The first time I found his name was under one of those football-hero group shots – players selected for the Kern County all-star game kneeling and beaming in front of a goalpost. Scott had played halfback for Tehachapi High, acquitted himself honorably.

No pictures of Terri Ardullo, which made sense. She wasn't a Treadway native, had grown up in Modesto.

Carson Crimmins's name showed up regularly, too. The other rich man in town. From what I could make out, Crimmins had started out as Butch Ardullo's ally in the fight for the family farm, but had switched course by the early seventies, expressing his frustration with low walnut prices and the rising cost of doing business, and advertising his willingness to sell 'to the highest serious bidder.'

No pictures of him. No comments from Butch Ardullo. The *Intelligencer* avoided taking sides.

March 1969. An entire issue devoted to Katherine Stethson Ardullo's funeral. References to a 'lingering illness,' and to the hiking death, years before, of the oldest son, Henry Junior. The article was augmented by old family snapshots and pictures of Butch and Scott at graveside, heads hung low.

August 10, 1974. Orton Hatzler mourned Nixon's resignation.

The following December, a hard frost damaged both the Ardullo and the Crimmins crops. Butch Ardullo said, 'You've got to be philosophical, ride out the bad times with the good.' No comment from Carson Crimmins.

March 1975. The death of Butch Ardullo. Two extra pages in a memorial issue. This time, Scott stood alone in the cemetery. Carson Crimmins said, 'We had our differences, but he was a man's man.'

June 1976. Announcement of Crimmins's marriage to 'the former Sybil Noonan, of Los Angeles. As we all know, Miss Noonan, a thespian who has acted under the name Cheryl

Norman, met Mr C. on a cruise to the Bahamas. The nuptials took place at the Beverly Wilshire Hotel in Beverly Hills. Maid of honor was the bride's sister, Charity Hernandez, and co-best men were Mr C.'s sons, Carson Jr and Derrick. The newlyweds are honeymooning in the Cayman Islands.'

Two photos. Finally a look at Carson Crimmins. Black tie. In the first shot, he and his new wife cut a five-tiered cake. He looked to be around sixty, tall, stooped, bald, with a too-small face completely overpowered by a beak of a nose. The nose bore down upon a fleshless upper lip. A pencil mustache added movie-villain overtones. Tiny, dark eyes glanced somewhere to the left – away from the bride. His smile was painful. A wary owl in a tuxedo.

The second Mrs Crimmins – she who'd narrowed Jacob Haas's eyes and hardened his voice – was in her late thirties, short, with full arms and a lush body packed into a tight silk sheath of a sleeveless wedding dress. What looked to be a deep tan. Spiky tiara perched upon a pile of platinum hair. Lots of teeth, lipstick, and eye shadow, a generous offering of cleavage. No ambivalence in her thousand-watt smile. Maybe it was true love, or perhaps the rock on her finger had something to do with it.

The second picture showed the Crimmins boys flanking the newlyweds. On the left was Carson Junior, around seventeen. Haas had said Derrick was younger, but that was hard to tell. Both boys were thin, rangy, with prominent noses and a touch of their father's avian look. Better-looking than their father – stronger chins, broader shoulders. The same thin lips. Carson Junior was already his father's height, Derrick slightly taller. Junior's hair was wild, blond, curly,

Derrick's dark and straight, hanging past his shoulders. Neither boy seemed to share the joy of the day. Both projected that immovable sullenness unique to teenagers and mug-shot criminals.

April 1978. The front-page story was a visit to Treadway by representatives of a company called Leisure Time Development. Carson Crimmins's invitation. Scott Ardullo said, 'It's a free country. People can sell what's theirs. But they can also show some guts and hold fast to the farming tradition.' No follow-up progress reports.

July 1978. The wedding of Scott Ardullo and Theresa McIntyre. The bridal gown, a 'flowing affair complete with 10-foot train and hand embroidery, including Belgian lace and freshwater pearls, was imported from San Francisco.' No cleavage here; Theresa Ardullo had favored long sleeves and full cover.

I moved on to the next batch of papers.

A half-year after the developers' visit, there was still no mention of land sales or negotiation, offers from other companies.

Crimmins's overtures rejected because Scott Ardullo had refused to sell out and no one wanted to deal for half a loaf?

If so, Crimmins wasn't commenting on the record. In July 1978, he and Sybil took a cruise to the Bahamas. Snapshots of her on deck, doing justice to a flowered bikini, a tall, iced drink in one hand. The text said she'd 'entertained the other guests with lilting renditions of show tunes and Broadway classics.'

Nothing of interest till January 5, 1980, when I came

across an account of 'The Farm League New Year's Ball and Fund-raiser' at the Silver Saddle Lodge in Fresno.

Mostly pictures of people I didn't recognize. Till the bottom of page four.

Scott Ardullo dancing, but not with his wife.

In his arms was Sybil Crimmins, white-blond hair long and flowing over bare tan shoulders. Her gown was black and strapless; her breasts were barely tucked into its skimpy bodice as they pressed against Scott's starched white chest. Her fingers were laced with his and her big diamond ring sparkled between his digits. He looked down at her, she gazed up at him. Something different in his eyes – at odds with the solid-young-businessman image – too much heat and light, a hint of stupidity.

Dopey surrender.

Maybe it was too many drinks, or the novelty of holding someone who wasn't your wife, feeling her warm breath against your face. Or maybe a big party had offered the two of them the chance to flaunt something they'd been savoring in dark, musky rooms.

It could be why Jacob Haas had tightened up when talking about Sybil Crimmins. Scott, a boy he'd long admired, straying with a platinum-haired strumpet from LA?

As I stared at the picture, it seemed to give off waves of heat. Worth well more than a thousand words. I was surprised the *Intelligencer* had published it.

I found an editorial three weeks later that might've explained that:

After much soul-searching, as well as witnessing, first-hand, the triumphs and the travails of those noble enough – and some would say sufficiently quixotically inclined – to brave the elements of Nature as well as the much more malignant Forces of Big Government, this newspaper must weigh in on the side of rationality and self-preservation.

It's all fine and well for those born with silver spoons in their mouths to pronounce righteously about abstract ideals such as the Sanctity of the Family Farm. But to the bulk of the populace, those hardy but bowed men entrusted with the day-to-day, backbreaking labor that keeps the ground fertile, the branches laden, and the trucks loaded with Bounty, the story is quite another one.

Joe Average in Treadway – and, we'd venture to wager, any agricultural community – toils day after day for fixed wages, with no promise of security or profit, or long-term investment. In most cases, his meager plot of backyard and his domicile are all he owns, and sometimes even that is tethered to some Financial Institution. Joe Average would love to plan for the Future, but he's usually too overwhelmed by the Present. So when Good Fortune smiles in the form of rising land values, offering said Mr Average the chance of Real Gain, he cannot be condemned for seizing the opportunity to afford his family the same safety and comfort that the more fortunate regard as their birthright.

Sometimes good sense and the rights of individuals must prevail.

At our last Kiwanis luncheon, Mr Carson Crimmins said it best: 'Progress is like a jet plane. Fly with it or stand on the runway and you risk getting blown away.'

Those of more fortunate lineage but less vision would do well to realize this.

Times change, and change they must. The history of this great country is based upon Free Will, Private Property, and Self-reliance.

Those who resist the voice of the future may find themselves in that Godless state known as Stagnation.

Times change. Brave and smart men change along with them.

Humbly,
O. Hatzler

Scott Ardullo, fallen out of editorial good graces. Still, wouldn't the picture have embarrassed Carson Crimmins as well?

I read through subsequent issues, waiting for Scott's written response to the editorial. Nothing. Either he hadn't bothered, or the *Intelligencer* had refused to print his letter.

Five weeks later, Orton and Wanda Hatzler's names were gone from the paper's masthead. In their place, in ornate, curlicued typescript:

Sybil Crimmins
PUBLISHER, EDITOR AND CHIEF WRITER

A pink sheet now, and cut back to three pages, flimsy as a supermarket mailer. No more wire-photo material. In its place, gushing movie reviews that seemed copied from press releases, barely literate accounts of local events, and amateurishly drawn cartoons with no apparent point. The too-large signature: 'Derrick C.'

Three barely filled pages, even twenty months later, when the headline screamed:

SLAUGHTER AT THE ARDULLO RANCH!
RATCATCHER PEEKE ARRESTED!
by Sybil Noonan Crimmins
Publisher, Editor and Chief Writer

Treadways darkest hour has arrived, or so it seemed when Sheriff Jacob Haas was called by Best Buy Produce Supervisor Teodoro 'Ted' Alarcon to the ranch and found a horrible massacre of unbelievable proportion. Their in the house, Sheriff Jacob Haas found several dead bodies, namely the ranch cook, Miss Noreen Peeke who was subjected to unbelievable and unhumane treatment at the hand of a dark fiend. Upstairs, were the other bodies, the ranch owner Scott Ardullo who got the place from his dad, Butch Ardullo, Scott's wife Terri and their daughter little Brittany who was around five years old. It was all horrible. But no sign of one other member of the family. The baby – Justin. All of us remember how Terri had such a hard labor with him and it would've been great for him to be OK.

But the terror continued. Sheriff Haas followed the blood and walked all the way to the back of the house where Noreen Peeke's son Ardith was living at the time and their he found Justin. Good taste says we won't go into detail but let's just say whoever did that to a tiny little infant is a fiend of unbelievable satan-like proportion. We are sick over this.

Ardith Peeke was drunk and stoned on all sorts of drugs. He was the ratcatcher on the ranch, going after all sorts of rodents and other pests, as well. So he probably had all sorts of weapons and poisons but we don't know yet what he used on those poor people.

Its really terrible and unbelievable, that something like this could happen in a small, peaceful place like ours but that seems to be the way the world is going, look at the Manson Family and how they attacked people who thought they were safe because they had money and lived behind gates. And the music of today, no one sings about love and romance, it's all nasty stuff and getting worse.

So the message, I guess is, trust in God, only He can protect you.

Sheriff Haas called in the FBI and the Bakersfield police to consult on this because its way out of what he usually deals with. He told me he was in Korea but never saw anything like this.

My sources tell me Ardith Peeke has always been weird. Sometimes people tried to help him – I know my sons Cliff and Derrick sure did, trying to get him involved in some athletic activities and whatnot, theater projects, you name it. Anything to bring him out of his shell, because they figured he was lonely. But he wouldn't hear of it. He just stayed by himself snorting paint and glue and whatnot. My sources tell me he was too into himself to relate to other people, some sort of severe mental illness.

Why did he suddenly do such a terrible thing?

Will we ever know?

Everyone loved the Ardullos, they were here so long, working hard even when it wasn't sure that would help because crop prices were so low. But working hard because that's what they believed in, they were salt of the earth people, they just loved to work.

HOW COULD THIS HAPPEN HERE – IN TREADWAY!?

IN AMERICA!!!!???

But that's what happens when the mind goes I guess.

I wish I had the answers but I'm only a journalist not an oracle.

I wish God worked in ways that we could understand – why should babies and children suffer like that? What makes a guy just go crazy like that?

Questions, questions, question.

When I get some answers, I'll keep you posted.

S.N.C.

She never did.

Last edition of the *Intelligencer*.

23

RETURNING TO the main reference room, I pulled up San Francisco, Bakersfield, and Fresno microfiche on the Ardullo slayings. Nothing that hadn't been covered down in LA.

In the Modesto *Bee* I found an obituary for Terri McIntyre Ardullo. Her death was described as 'untimely,' no mention of homicide. The bio was brief: Girl Scout, volunteer for the Red Cross, honor student at Modesto High, member of the Spanish Club and the Shakespeare Society, BA from UC Davis.

She'd been survived by her parents, Wayne and Felice McIntyre, and sisters Barbara McIntyre and Lynn Blount. A Wayne McIntyre was listed in Modesto. Feeling like a creep, I dialed and told the elderly woman who answered that I was conducting a search for relatives of the Argent family of Pennsylvania, in anticipation of the first Argent reunion, to be held in Scranton.

'Argent?' she said. 'Then why us?'

'Your name came up on our computer list.'

'Did it? Well, I'm afraid your computer got it wrong. We're not related to any Argents. Sorry.'

No anger, no defensiveness.

No idea what had interested Claire about Peake.

I pictured him in his room, grimacing, twitching, rocking autistically. Nerve endings firing randomly as Lord knew what impulses coalesced and scrambled among the folds of beclouded frontal lobes.

The door opens, a woman enters, smiling, eager to help.

A new doctor. The first person to show any interest in him in sixteen years.

She kneels down beside him, talks soothingly. Wanting to help him . . . help he doesn't want. Help that makes him angry.

Put her in a box. Bad eyes.

I went searching in Miami newspapers for items about the Crimminses. Obituaries were the daily special: The *Herald* informed me that Carson and Sybil Crimmins had died together twelve years ago, in a yacht explosion off the coast of south Florida. An unnamed crew member had perished as well. Carson was listed as a 'real estate developer,' Sybil as a 'former entertainer.' No pictures.

Next came a *Las Vegas Sun* reference to Carson Crimmins, Jr's, death in a motocross accident, two years later, near Pimm, Nevada. Nothing on the younger brother, Derrick. Too bad; he'd talked on record once. Maybe he'd be willing to reminisce, if I found him.

Former *Intelligencer* publisher Orton Hatzler was memorialized in a back-page paragraph of the *Santa Monica Evening Outlook*. He'd died in that beach town of 'natural causes' at the age of eighty-seven. Just a few miles from my house. Memorial services at the Seaside Presbyterian

Church, donations to the American Heart Association, in lieu of flowers. The surviving widow: Wanda Hatzler.

Maybe she still lived in Santa Monica. But if I found her, what would I ask about? I'd uncovered a financial battle between the Ardullo and Crimmins clans, had played Sherlock with a single photograph that suggested another type of competition. But nothing suggested that the slaughter of the Ardullos had resulted from anything other than one madman's blood feast.

I thought of the suddenness of the attack. Asian cultures had a word for that kind of unprovoked savagery: '*Amok*.'

Something about Peake's amok had caught Claire Argent's interest, and now she was dead. Along with three other men . . . and Peake had predicted the murders of two of them. Prophet of doom in a locked cell. There had to be a common thread.

I abandoned the periodicals indexes and searched computer databases for Wanda Hatzler and Derrick Crimmins. Find-A-Person coughed up a single approximation: Derek Albert Crimmins on West 154th Street in New York City. I used a library pay phone, called, and participated in a confused ninety-second conversation with a man who sounded very old, very gentle, and, from his patois, probably black.

W. Hatzler was listed in Santa Monica, no address. The woman's voice on the tape machine was also elderly, but hearty. I gave her machine the same spiel I'd offered Jacob Haas, told her I'd stop by later today.

Before I left Bakersfield, I phoned Milo. He was away from his desk and not answering his cell phone. Route 5 clogged up just past Newhall. An accident had closed the northbound lanes and caused rubberneck spillover in the opposite direction. A dozen flashing red lights, cop cars from several jurisdictions and ambulances parked diagonally across the freeway, news copters whirring overhead. An overturned truck blocked the mouth of the nearest on-ramp. Inches from its front wheels was a snarled mass of red and chrome.

A highway patrolman waved us on, but inertia slowed us to a snail slide. I turned on KFWB. The accident was a big story: Some sort of altercation between two motorists, a chase off the ramp, then an abrupt U-turn that took the pursuing vehicle the wrong way. Road rage, they were calling it. As if labeling changed anything.

It took over two hours to get back to LA, and by the time I reached the Westside the skies had darkened to charcoal splotches underlaid with vermilion. Too late to drop in on an old woman. I bought gas at Sunset and La Brea and called Wanda Hatzler again.

This time, she answered. 'Come on over, I'm expecting you.'

'You're sure it's not too late?'

'Don't tell me you're one of those morning people.'

'As a matter of fact, I'm not.'

'Good,' she said. 'Morning people should be forced to milk cows.'

I called home to say I'd be late. Robin's message said she'd be in Studio City till eight, doing some on-site repairs at a recording session. Synchrony of the hyperactive. I drove to Santa Monica.

Wanda Hatzler's address was on Yale Street, south of Wilshire, a stucco bungalow behind a lawn of lavender, wild onions, thyme, and several species of cactus. An alarm company sign protruded from the herbs, but no fence surrounded the property.

She was at the curb by the time I finished parking, a big woman – nearly six feet, with healthy shoulders and heavy limbs. Her hair was cut short. The color was hard to make out in the darkness.

'Dr Delaware? Wanda Hatzler.' Brisk shake, rough hands. 'I like your car – used to have a Fleetwood until Orton couldn't drive anymore and I got tired of supporting the oil companies. Show me some identification just to play it safe, then come inside.'

Inside, her house was cramped, warm, bright, ash-paneled and filled with chairs covered in at least three variations of brown paisley cotton. Georgia O'Keeffe prints hung on the walls, along with some muddy-looking California plein-air oils. An open doorway peeked into the kitchen, where soft dolls were arranged on the counter – children in all sorts of native costumes propped up sitting, a tiny stuffed kindergarten. Old white two-burner stove. A saucepan sat above dancing blue flames, and a childhood memory hit me: The cold-afternoon fragrance of canned vegetable soup. I tried not to think of Peake's culinary forays.

Wanda Hatzler closed the door and said, 'Go on, make yourself comfortable.'

I sat in a paisley armchair and she stood there. She wore a deep green V-neck pullover over a white turtleneck, loose gray pants, brown slip-on shoes. The hair was black well salted with silver. She could've been anywhere from seventy to eighty-five. Her face was broad, basset-hound droopy, crumpled as used wrapping paper. Moist blue-green eyes seemed to have suction power over mine. She wasn't smiling but I sensed some sort of amusement.

'Something to drink? Coke, Diet Coke, hundred-proof rum?'

'I'm fine, thanks.'

'What about soup? I'm going to have some.'

'No, thanks.'

'Tough customer.' She went into the kitchen, filled a mug, came back and sat down, blew into the soup, and drank. 'Treadway, what a hole. Why on earth would you want to know anything about it?'

I told her about Claire and Peake, emphasizing a therapeutic relationship gone bad, keeping prophecy out of it, omitting the other murders.

She put the mug down. 'Peake? I always thought he was retarded. Wouldn't have pegged him for violence, so what do I know? The only psychology I ever studied was an introductory course at Sarah Lawrence back in another century.'

'I'll bet you know plenty.'

She smiled. 'Why? Because I'm old? Don't blush, I *am* old.' She touched one seamed cheek. 'The truth is in the flesh. Didn't Samuel Butler say that? Or maybe I made it up. Anyway, I'm afraid I can't give you any ideas on Peake. Never had a feel for him. Now you're going to leave. Too bad. You're good-looking and I was looking forward to this.'

'To talking about Treadway?'

'To maligning Treadway.'

'How long did you live there?'

'Too long. Never could stand the place. At the time of the murders, I was working in Bakersfield. Chamber of Commerce. Not exactly a cosmopolis but at least there was some semblance of civilization. Like sidewalks. At night I helped my husband put the paper to bed. Such as it was.'

She lifted the mug and drank. 'Have you read the rag?'

'Twenty years' worth.'

'Lord. Where'd you get hold of it?'

'Beale Memorial Library.'

'You *are* motivated.' She shook her head. 'Twenty years' worth. Orton would be shocked. He knew what he'd come down to.'

'He didn't like publishing?'

'He liked publishing fine. He would've preferred running *The New York Times*. He was a Dartmouth boy. The *Intelligencer* – doesn't that reek of East Coast sensibilities? Unfortunately his politics were somewhere to the right of Joe McCarthy, and after the war that wasn't very fashionable. Also, he had a little problem.' She pantomimed tossing back a drink. 'Hundred-proof rum – developed a taste for it when serving in the Pacific. Lived to eighty-seven, anyway. Developed palate cancer, recovered, then leukemia, went into remission, then cirrhosis, and even that took years to kill him. His doctor saw an X-ray of his liver, called him a medical miracle – he was oodles older than me.'

Laughing, she finished the soup, got up, poured a refill, came back. 'The *Intelligencer* was Orton hitting bottom.

He began his career at *The Philadelphia Inquirer* and proceeded to embark on a downward slide for the rest of his life. Treadway was our last stop – we bought the rag for next to nothing and settled into a life of crushing tedium and genteel poverty. Gawd, I hated that place. Stupid people everywhere you looked. Social Darwinism, I suppose: The smart ones leave for the big city, only the idiots remain to breed.' Another laugh. 'Orton used to call it the power of positive backpedaling. He and I decided not to breed.'

I made sure not to look at the dolls in the kitchen.

She said, 'The only reason I stayed there was because I loved the guy – very good-looking. Even handsomer than you. Virile, too.'

She crossed her legs. Were those eyelashes batting?

I said, 'The Ardullos don't sound stupid.'

She gave a dismissive wave. 'Yes, I know: Butch went to Stanford – he told anyone who'd listen. But he got in because of football. Everyone else liked him, but I didn't. Pleasant enough, superficially. One of those fellows who's convinced he's a magnet for females, puts on the Galahad act. Too much confidence in a man is not an endearing trait, particularly when it's unjustified. Butch had no fire – stolid, straight-ahead as a horse with blinders. Point him in a direction and he went. And that wife of his. An oh-so-delicate Victorian relic. Taking to her bed all the time. I used to think it was phony baloney, called her Little Miss Vapors. But then she surprised me and actually died of something.'

She shrugged. 'That's the trouble with being malicious

– occasionally one is wrong, and a nasty little urge to repent seeps in.'

'What about Scott?'

'Smarter than Butch, but no luminary. He inherited land, grew fruit when the weather obliged. Not exactly Einstein, eh? Which isn't to say I wasn't shocked and sickened by what happened to him. And his poor wife – sweet thing, liked to read, I always suspected there might be an intellectual streak hidden somewhere.'

Her lip trembled. 'The worst thing was those babies . . . By the time it happened, Orton and I had just sold the paper and moved down here. When Orton read about the murder in the *Times*, he vomited, sat down at his desk, and wrote a story – as if he were still a journalist. Then he ripped it up, vomited again, drank daiquiris all night, and passed out for two days. When he woke up, he couldn't feel his legs. Took another day to convince him he wasn't dying. Great disappointment for him. He cherished the idea of drinking himself to death, sensitive soul. His big mistake was taking the world seriously – though I guess in a case like that you'd have to. Even I cried. For the babies. I wasn't good with children – found them frightening, too much vulnerability, a big girl like me never seemed suited to those little twig bones. Hearing what Peake had done confirmed all that. I didn't sleep well for a long time.'

She brandished the mug. 'I haven't thought about it in years, wondered if raking it up might bother me, but apart from thinking about the babies, this is rather fun. For twenty years we lived above the newspaper office, scrounged for advertising, took extra jobs to get by. Orton did people's bookkeeping, I tutored incredibly stupid children in English and wrote press releases for the yahoos at the C. of C.'

'So you never had much contact with Peake.'

'I knew who he was – rather conspicuous fellow, lurching around in the alleys, going through the garbage – but no, we never exchanged a single sentence.' She recrossed her legs. 'This is good. Knowing I can still remember a few things – some juice in the old machine. What else would you like to know?'

'The Crimmins family—'

'Morons.' She sipped more soup. 'Worse than the Ardullos. Vulgarians. Carson was like Butch – uncreative, obsessed by the dollar – but minus the charm. In addition to walnuts, he grew lemons. Orton used to say he looked as if he'd been weaned on them. Never seemed to take pleasure in anything – I'm sure you have a word for it.'

'Anhedonia.'

'There you go,' she said. 'I should've taken Intermediate Psychology.'

'What about Sybil?'

'Slut. Gold digger. Dumb blonde. Right out of a bad movie.'

'Out for Crimmins's money,' I said.

'It sure wasn't his looks. They met on a cruise line, fawgawdsakes, what a horrid cliché. If Carson had had a brain in his head he'd have jumped overboard.'

'She caused him problems?'

Pause. Eyeblink. 'She was a vulgar woman.'

'She claimed to be an actress.'

'And I'm the Sultan of Brunei.'

'What kind of difficulties did she cause?' I said.

'Oh, you know,' she said. 'Stirring things up – wanting to run everything the moment she hit town. Transform herself into a *star*. She actually tried to get a theater group going. Got Carson to build a stage in one of his barns, bought all sorts of equipment. Orton laughed so hard telling me about it, he nearly lost his bridgework. "Guess who moved in, Wanda? Jean Harlow. Harlow in Horseshit."'

'Who did Sybil plan on acting with?'

'The local yokels. She also tried to rope in Carson's boys. One of them, I forget which, had a minor knack for drawing, so she put him to work painting sets. She told Orton they both had "star quality." I remember her coming into the office with her ad for the casting call.'

Leaning toward me, she spoke in a chirpy, little-girl voice: '"I tell you, Wanda, there's hidden talent all over the place. Everyone's creative, you just have to bring it out." She even thought she'd rope Carson in, and just being civil was a performance for him. Guess what play she had planned? *Our Town*. If she'd had a brain, you could have credited her with some irony. *Our Dump*, she should've called it. The whole thing fell apart. No one showed up at the audition. Carson helped that along. The day before the ad was supposed to run, he paid Orton double not to print it.'

'Stage fright?'

She laughed. 'He said it was a waste of time and money. He also said he wanted the barn back for hay.'

'Was that pretty typical?' I said. 'Crimmins buying what he wanted?'

'What you're really asking is, Was Orton corrupt when he dealt with wealth and power?, and the answer is, Absolutely.' She smoothed her sweater. 'No apologies. Carson and Butch ran that town. If you wanted to survive, you played along. When Butch died, Scott took over his half. It wasn't even a town. It was a joint fiefdom with the rest of us serfs balancing on a wire between them. Orton was caught right in the middle. By the late seventies, we decided we were getting the heck out, one way or the other. Orton had qualified for Social Security and mine was about to kick in, plus I'd inherited a small annuity from an aunt. All we wanted was to sell the printing equipment and get something for ownership of the paper. Orton approached Scott first, because he thought Scott would be easier to deal with, but Scott wouldn't even listen.'

Beating her chest, she put on a gorilla face. '"Me farmer, me do nothing else." Straight ahead and pigheaded, just like his father. So Orton went to Carson, and to his surprise, Carson said he'd consider it.'

'Surprise because Carson was uncreative?'

'And because everyone knew Carson wanted to get out of Treadway himself. Each year there'd be talk of some new real estate deal.'

'How long had that been going on?'

'Years. The main problem was Scott wouldn't hear of it, and half the land wasn't very attractive to the developers. The approach Orton used with Carson was to suggest the paper might be a good activity for Sybil, to keep her out of trouble.' She snapped her fingers. 'That did the trick.'

Now I understood the *Intelligencer*'s sudden editorial shift toward Crimmins.

'What other kind of trouble was Sybil getting into?' I said.

She smiled archly. 'What do you think?'

'I saw a picture of her and Scott at a dance.'

The smile faltered, then changed course, growing wider, fuller, ripe with glee.

'Oh, that picture,' she sang. 'We might as well have published them naked. Orton wasn't going to print it, a gentleman to the last. But that night, he was sloshed to the gills, so I put the paper to bed.'

Breathing in deeply, she savored the exhalation.

I said, 'What was the fallout?'

'Nothing public. I suppose there was tension among those directly concerned. Terri Ardullo always impressed me as tightly wound, but she didn't run around after Sybil with a hatchet. The Ardullos were never the type to air their laundry in public. Same for Carson.'

'What did the serfs have to say about it?'

'Nothing that I heard. Doesn't pay to antagonize the nobility if you want to eat. And it wasn't as if everyone didn't already know about Scott and Sybil.'

'The affair was public knowledge?' I said.

'For months. Certainly since Sybil's production fell apart. I suppose she needed another role.' She shook her head. 'The two of them adopted a flimsy cover: First, Scott's truck would speed out of town. An hour later, the slut's little Thunderbird would zoom away. She'd always return first, usually with shopping bags. Sometimes she'd visit the peasants in the local stores, showing off what she'd acquired. Then, sure enough, Scott's truck would zip past. Ludicrous. How could they possibly think they were getting away with it?'

'So Carson had to know.'

'I don't see how he couldn't have.'

'And no reaction at all? He never tried to stop it?'

'Carson was much older than Sybil. Maybe he couldn't cut the mustard, didn't mind someone else keeping her busy from time to time. Perhaps that's why he bought Orton's line about finding Sybil recreation. We were certainly trying to exploit him – did you read the rag after she took over?'

'Borderline coherent.'

'You're a charitable young man.' She stretched. 'My, this *is* great fun.'

'What can you tell me about Jacob Haas?' I said.

'Well-meaning but a boob. Before he became sheriff, he'd been working as a bookkeeper in Bakersfield. He got the job because he'd served in Korea, took some law enforcement courses in junior college, didn't offend anyone.'

'Meaning he wasn't aligned with either Butch or Carson.'

'Meaning he never put their kids in jail.'

'Was that ever a possibility?' I said.

'Not with Scott, but with the Crimmins boys, sure. Two obnoxious little buggers – spoiled rotten. Carson gave them fast cars, which they proceeded to race down Main

Street. It was common knowledge that they drank and took drugs, so it was only luck they never killed anyone. One of them paid for his recklessness a few years later – died motorcycling.'

'Any other offenses besides drunk driving?'

'General bad character. They treated the migrants like dirt. Chased the migrant girls. When the picking season was over, they switched gears and bothered the local girls. I remember one night, very late, I'd just finished with the paper, walked outside to get some air, when I saw a car screech to a stop down the block. One of those souped-up things with stripes on the side, I knew right away whose it was. The back door opened, someone fell out, and the car sped away. The person lay there for a second, then got up and started walking down the middle of Main Street very slowly. I went over. It was a little Mexican girl – couldn't have been older than fifteen, and she spoke no English. Her face was all puffy from crying and her hair and clothes were messed and torn. I tried to talk to her but she just shook her head, burst into tears, and ran away. The street ended a block later and she disappeared in the fields.'

'Whose fields?' I said.

Her eyes narrowed, then closed. 'Let me think about that . . . North. That would have been Scott's alfalfa field.'

'So no consequences for Cliff and Derrick?'

'None.'

'How did they get along with their stepmother?'

'Are you asking if they slept with her?' she said.

'Actually, my imagination hadn't carried me that far.'

'Why not? Don't you watch talk shows?'

'You're saying Sybil—'

'No,' she said. 'I'm not saying anything of the sort. Merely musing. Because she was a slut and they were healthy big boys. To be fair – something I generally detest – I never picked up an inkling of anything quite so repellent, but . . . How'd they get along? Who loves a stepmother? And Sybil wasn't exactly the maternal type.'

'But she managed to get them involved in her theatrical production.'

'Only one of them – the one who drew.'

'Derrick,' I said. 'She wrote about it in the *Intelligencer*. Still, spoiled adolescents don't do things they hate.'

She turned quiet. 'Yes . . . I suppose he must have enjoyed it. Why all these questions about the Crimmins clan?'

'Derrick Crimmins's name came up in newspaper accounts of the murders. Commenting about Peake's oddness. Other than Haas, he was the only person to speak on the record, so I thought I'd track him down.'

'If you find him, don't send regards. Of course he'd jump at the chance to ridicule Peake. He and his brother delighted in tormenting Peake – another bit of their delinquency.'

'Tormenting how?' I said.

'What you'd expect from rotten kids – teasing, poking. More than once I saw the two of them and a gang of others they ran with collecting in the alley that ran behind our office. Peake used to hang around there, too. Inspecting garbage cans, looking for paint cans and God knows what. The Crimmins brats and their friends must have been bored, gone after some sport. They circled him, laughed, cuffed him around a bit, stuck a cigarette in his mouth but refused to light it. The last time, I'd had enough, so I stepped out into the alley using some blue language and they dispersed. Not that Peake was grateful. Didn't even look at me, just turned his back and walked away from me. I never bothered again.'

'How'd Peake react to the ridicule?' I said.

'Just stood there like this.' Her facial muscles slackened and her eyes went blank. 'The boy was never all there.'

'No anger?'

'Nope. Like a zombie.'

'Were you surprised when he exploded into violence?'

'I suppose,' she said. 'It wouldn't surprise me, today, though. What do they always say – "It's the quiet ones"? Can you ever tell about anyone?'

'Any theories about why he killed the Ardullos?'

'He was crazy. You're the psychologist, why do crazy people act crazy?'

I started to thank her and moved to stand but she waved me still. 'You want a theory? How about bad luck, wrong time, wrong place. Like walking off a curb, getting hit by a bus.'

Her lips worked. She looked ready to cry. 'It's not easy – surviving. I keep waiting for something to happen to me, but my luck keeps running in the black. Sometimes it's infuriating – yet another day, the same old routine.' Another wave. 'All right then, be off. Abandon me. I haven't helped you, anyway.'

'You've been very helpful—'

'Oh, please, none of that.' But she reached over and took my hand. Her skin was cold, dry, so smooth it seemed inorganic. 'Bear that in mind, Doctor: Longevity can be hell, too. Knowing things will inevitably go bad, but not knowing when.'

24

WHEN I left, just after eight P.M., Wilshire was a pretty stream of headlights under a black-pearl sky. My head hurt – stuffed with history and hints. More hatred and intrigue in Treadway than I'd counted on. But still no connection to Claire Argent. Ready to end the workday, I called my service from the pay booth in the parking lot.

An earful: Robin would be delayed till ten, and a particularly obnoxious Encino attorney wanted my help on a festering custody case. He knew I worked only for the court, not as a hired gun, and he hadn't paid his bill for a consultation I'd done last year. Delusions were everywhere.

The fifth message was from Milo: 'I'll be at my desk by seven-thirty, get in touch.'

The operator said, 'He sounded pretty irritated, your detective friend.'

I drove to the station, announced myself at the desk, waited as the clerk called up to the Robbery-Homicide room. Uniforms passed in and out. No one paid me any attention as I scanned the Wanted posters. A few minutes later the stairwell door opened and Milo bounded out, brushing hair off his forehead.

'Let's go outside, I need air,' he said, not bothering to

stop. His suit was the color of curdled oatmeal, the right lapel stained with something green. His tie was tight, his neck was suffering, and he looked like a poster boy for National Hypertension Week.

We reached the sidewalk and started walking up Butler. Dry, acidic heat hung in the air and I wished I'd stopped for a cold drink.

'Nothing on Pelley, yet,' he said, 'so don't ask. It's the Beatty twins who've been occupying my day. Brother Leroy told people he had an acting gig.'

'Which people?'

'His fellow juiceheads. Willis Hooks and I were down at the murder scene this evening. Not far from a liquor store where Leroy used to hang, along with some other grape-suckers. Couple of them said Leroy had bragged about becoming a movie star.'

'How long ago was this?' I said.

'Time isn't a strong concept with these guys, but they figure three, four months. Leroy also told his drinking buds he was gonna get his brother involved with the movie – said once the director found out he had a twin, he offered to pay more. The winos thought he was just running his mouth, 'cause Leroy tended to do that when he got sufficiently drunk. They didn't even believe Leroy *had* a twin. He'd never mentioned Ellroy.'

'Did Leroy report back after the filming?'

'No. He returned a week later, cranky, refusing to talk about it. If he'd gotten hold of any cash, no one saw it. His buddies figured he'd gone on a bender, flushed it all down his gullet.'

'Or Mr Griffith D. Wark stiffed someone else,' I said. Now my mind was racing. Fragments of history coming together . . . pieces fitting . . .

'I thought of that,' he said. 'None of them saw any tall white guy chatting up Leroy.'

'Did Ellroy's drinking pals have anything to say about the movie?'

'Aguilar hasn't found any pals for Ellroy yet. He seems to have been the loner twin, lived by himself near the train tracks. One of the conductors remembers seeing him from time to time, stumbling around. Figured he was crazy because he was always talking to himself.'

He scratched the side of his nose. 'So here I am, stuck with the movie angle again. Maybe it's a link between Dada and the twins, but still no tie-in with Claire. Except for the fact that she *went* to the movies. Hell, can't you see me explaining *that* to her parents? I showed her picture to the bums and they didn't recognize her. No surprise, why would she have gone down to some South Central wino kip? I'm gonna head back tonight to that place in Toluca Lake where Richard used to wait tables – the Oak Barrel. It's a long shot, but maybe Claire dined there. For all we know, Mr Wark picked up both of 'em there – and incidentally, you were right about Wark being D. W. Griffith's middle name. I looked it up. So this asshole sees himself as a cinema hotshot.'

He scratched his head. 'This is exactly the kind of flaky bullshit I hate dealing with. Why would Wark – or anyone else – bump off his cast?'

'Keeping the budget low?' I said.

'Better not give the studios any ideas. Seriously, what's going on here? And how – and *why* – would a robot like *Peake* be clued in?'

'Maybe Wark's filming murder.'

'A snuff thing?'

'That, or a variant – not necessarily a sexual angle. A chronology of unnatural death – a literal blood walk. For the underground market. That would explain why the script's never been registered and why Wark used a fake name to rent his equipment and cut out on the bill. It could also explain the diversity of victims and methods. And the ritualism. We could be dealing with someone who sees himself as a splatter auteur. Playing God by setting up characters – real people – then bumping them off. Psychopaths depersonalize their victims. Wark could be accomplishing the ultimate degradation: Reducing his "cast" to prototypes: The Twins, The Actor, that kind of thing. It's cruel, primitive thinking – exactly the way kids play out their anger. Some angry kids never grow up. As far as Peake is concerned, he could be involved because Wark wants him involved. Because Wark's someone out of Peake's past. Wark's mightily affected by Peake's crimes. Now he's creating his own production, wants to integrate Peake into the process. And I've got a possible candidate for Wark: A fellow named Derrick Crimmins.'

I told him everything I'd learned about Treadway. The longtime conflict between the Ardullos and the Crimminses, Scott's affair with Sybil, the Crimmins boys' antisocial behavior, Derrick's involvement with Sybil's abortive theater group.

'He had no special love for his stepmother, Milo, but he stayed involved with her. Because the whole notion of theater – of production – grabbed him personally. He also matches the physical description Vito Bonner gave us of Wark – tall, thin – and his age fits. Derrick would be in his mid-thirties now.'

Milo took a long time to think about that. We were walking dark residential streets, shoes slapping the pavement. 'So all the Crimminses except this Derrick are dead?'

'Father, stepmother, brother, all by accidental death. Interesting, isn't it?'

'Now he's a family murderer, too?'

'Rigging accidents can also be seen as a form of production – setting up scenes. Derrick was far from a model citizen. Wanda Hatzler described him and his brother as spoiled bullies and possible rapists.'

I stopped.

'What?' he said.

'Something else just occurred to me. Sheriff Haas told me that after the murder Peake was found with lots of different drugs in his shack, including some illegal prescription pills, phenobarbital. None was missing from the pharmacy in Treadway and no one in the Ardullo household had obtained a prescription for it. So Haas was certain it had to have been obtained out of town. But no one ever saw Peake leave Treadway. So maybe he had a dope source in town. Wanda saw Derrick and his friends hanging around with Peake, mostly to harass him. Peake offered no resistance, was extremely passive. What if the Crimmins boys were the ones who supplied him with drugs – having fun with the village idiot? The night of the massacre, Peake got massively stoned, his psyche broke down, and he slaughtered the Ardullos. And Derrick and his brother realized they'd played an indirect role in it. Someone else might be horrified by that, but the Crimmins boys had plenty of reason to hate Scott Ardullo. His refusal to sell his land had obstructed their father's big development deal for years. And Scott was sleeping with their stepmother. What if they were *pleased* with what Peake had done? Took some vicarious *credit* for it? And, in a sick sense, it was a successful production: The land deal went through, the family became rich again. That kind of high could've been powerful stuff for a kid who'd already shown some serious antisocial tendencies. A few years later, Derrick tries his hand at something more direct: Blowing up Daddy and Stepmom's boat. And, once again, he gets away with it.'

'Or,' he said, 'the boat thing really was an accident, someone else gave Peake his dope, Wark's not Derrick, and Derrick's just some playboy drinking piña coladas in Palm Beach while working on his melanoma.'

'All that, too,' I said. 'But as long as we're being contentious, I'll go you one further: Derrick and Cliff's involvement was more than vicarious. They fed Peake dope and played on his delusions intentionally. *Prodded* him to kill the Ardullos. They were dominant, aggressive; Peake was passive, impressionable. Maybe they learned that Peake harbored some resentment of his own toward the Ardullos, and they used that. Perhaps they never really expected it to happen – idle teenage dope talk – and when Peake ran amok, they were frightened, initially. Then amazed. Then pleased.'

He knuckled his eyes. 'What happened during your childhood to make you think this way?'

'Too much spare time.' *Alcoholic father, depressed mother, dark hours alone in the basement fighting to escape the noise upstairs, struggling to create my own world . . .*

'My, my, my.'

'At the very least,' I said, 'wouldn't it be good to find out where Derrick lives, what his financial situation is, does he have some sort of police record?'

'Fine,' he said. 'Fine.'

Back in Robbery-Homicide, he played with the computer. No wants or warrants out on Derrick Crimmins, no listings on the sex offender rosters or the FBI's VICAP file, and as far as we could tell, he wasn't occupying space in any California jail.

A call to the Department of Motor Vehicles police info line revealed zero current registrations under that name.

Same for Griffith D. Wark. Find-A-Person yielded several D. Crimminses but no Derricks. No G. D. Wark.

Milo said, 'I'll follow up with Social Security tomorrow. I'll even check out the death certificates for the Crimmins family, just to show you I care. Where exactly did the boat thing go down?'

'All I know is, out on the water off the coast of south Florida,' I said. 'Brother Cliff crashed on a motocross run in Pimm, Nevada.'

He scribbled, closed his pad, got up heavily. 'Whoever this Wark is, how's he contacting Peake?'

'Maybe with ease,' I said. 'Maybe he works at Starkweather.'

He grimaced. 'Meaning I need to get a look at personnel records. My old pal Mr Swig . . . If this *Blood Walk is* a mega-snuff, you think Wark's actually hoping to sell it?'

'Or he just wants to keep it around for his own amusement. If he's Derrick and he inherited a bundle and doesn't need money, it could be one big, sick diversion.'

'A game.'

'I always thought the murders had a gamelike quality to them.'

'If only,' he said, 'you were a stupid guy and I could kiss off your fantasies . . . OK, back to Planet Earth. The Oak Barrel.'

'I'll come with, if you want.'

He checked his Timex. 'What about hearth and home?'

'Too hot to light a fire in the hearth, and the home's empty for a couple more hours.'

'Suit yourself,' he said. 'You drive.'

Toluca Lake's a pretty secret sandwiched between North Hollywood and Burbank. The main drag is a curving eastern stretch of Riverside Drive lined with low-profile shops, many with their original forties and fifties facades. The housing ranges from garden apartments to major estates. Bob Hope used to live there. Other stars still do, mostly those leaning toward the GOP. Lots of the great Western flicks were shot nearby, at Burbank Studios and up in the surrounding foothills. The Equestrian Complex is just a short drive away, as is NBC headquarters.

A quick turn on either side of Riverside takes you onto quiet streets emptied at night by permit-only parking and an attentive police force. Toluca Lake restaurants tend to be dim and spacious, leaning toward that unclassifiable fare known as continental cuisine, once an LA staple, now nearly extinct west of Laurel Canyon. White hair doesn't elicit sneers from the wait staff, martinis aren't the retro craze of the minute, piano bars endure.

From time to time I testify in a Burbank court and find myself down here, thinking about the perfect suburbia of black-and-white TV shows: Moderne furniture, fat sedans, dark lipstick. Jack Webb tippling steely-eyed at a vinyl-padded bumper, winding down after a long day on the set. Nearby might be the guy who played Ward Cleaver, whatever his name was.

I'd been to a few of the Riverside Drive restaurants, but not the Oak Barrel. It turned out to be a modest stack of bricks and stucco squatting on a southeastern corner, half-lit by streetlamps, the cask-and-tankard logo discreetly outlined in green neon above the porte-cochère. A parking lot twice the size of the restaurant put the construction date at late forties, early fifties. No valet, just a well-lit asphalt skillet with scores of spaces, a quarter of them occupied. Lincolns, Cadillacs, Buicks, more Lincolns.

The front door was oak inlaid with a panel of bubbled glass. We walked in, confronted a lattice screen, stepped around it into a small reception area backed by the cocktail lounge. Four drinkers flashing elbow. TV news winking above a wall full of bottles. No sound on the set. The air was icy, seasoned with too-delicate piano music, the lighting barely strong enough to let us make out colors. But the maître d's bright green jacket managed to work its way through the gloom.

He was tall, at least seventy, with slicked white hair, Roman features, and black-rimmed eyeglasses. A reservation book was spread out before him on the oak lectern. Plenty of open slots. The lattice blocked a view of the main dining room to his left, but I could hear silverware clatter, conversational thrum. The pianist was turning 'Lady Be Good' into a minuet.

The maître d' said, 'Good evening, gentlemen.' Capped smile, clear diction peppered by an Italian accent. As we came closer, he said, 'Ah, Detective. Nice to see you again.' A small gold rectangle on his jacket was engraved LEW.

'Hey, you remember,' said Milo, with joviality that might've been real.

'I still got a memory. And we don't get too many police, not here. So this time you come to eat?'

'To drink,' said Milo.

'This way.' A green sleeve flourished. 'You making any progress on Richard?'

'Wish I could say I was,' said Milo. 'Speaking of which, has this woman ever been here?' A photo of Claire had snapped into his hand like a magician's dove.

Lew smiled. '"Speaking of which," huh? You here to drink anything but information?'

'Sure. Beer, if you carry that.'

Lew laughed and peered at the picture. 'No, sorry, never saw her. Why? She know Richard?'

'That's what I'd like to know,' said Milo. 'Tell me, is there anything else that came to mind since the last time I was here?'

The maître d' handed back the photo. 'Nah. Richard was

a good boy, quiet. Good worker. We don't usually hire the so-calleds, but he was OK.'

'The so-calleds,' I said.

'So-called actors, so-called directors – mostly they're punks, think they're overqualified for everything, doin' you a big favor to show up. Nine times outta ten they can't handle carrying a bread plate or they end up mouthing off to some regular and I gotta untangle everybody's shorts.'

He reached behind his back and tugged upward.

'We prefer old guys,' he said. 'Classy pros. Like me. But Richard was OK for a kid. Polite – "madam" and "sir," not that goddamn "you guys." Nice boy, very nice boy, that's why even though he wanted to be an actor I hired him. Also, he begged me. Said he really needed the money. And I was right about him. Good worker, got the orders right, no complaints – c'mon, let's go over, get you gents a nice drink.'

The bar was an enormous lacquered walnut parabola rimmed with red leather. Brass bar, red stools with brass legs. The four drinkers were all glassy-eyed middle-aged men wearing sport coats. One necktie, three sport shirts with open collars spread over wide lapels. Plenty of space between them. They stared into tall glasses on paper coasters, dipped thick hands into dishes of nuts, olives, roast peppers, sausage chunks, pink curls of boiled shrimp pierced by red plastic toothpicks. The bartender was pushing sixty, dark-skinned, with luxuriant hair and the face of a carved tiki god. He and a couple of the drinkers looked up as Lew showed us to the end of the bar, but a second later, everyone had settled back into booze hypnosis.

Lew said, 'Hernando, bring these gents . . .'

'Grolsch,' said Milo. I asked for the same and Lew said, 'Some of that sauterne for me, the reserve stuff, but just a little.'

Hernando's hands moved like a chop-sockey hero. After he'd delivered the drinks and returned to the center of the bar, Milo said, 'You ever get a customer named Wark?'

'Work?'

'Wark.' Milo spelled it. 'Mid to late thirties, tall, thin, dark hair, could be curly. Claims to be a film producer.'

The maître d's eyes were merry. 'Plenty of claims-to-be's, but no, I don't recall any Wark.'

Milo sipped his beer. 'What about Crimmins? Derrick Crimmins. He might have come in with a woman, younger, long blond hair.'

'"Might," "maybe" – this is still about Richard?'

'Maybe,' said Milo.

'Sorry, no Crimmins either, but people come in without reservations, we don't know their names.'

'We're talking eight, nine months ago. Would you remember every name – even with an excellent memory?'

Lew looked hurt. 'You want me to check the reservation books, I'm happy to do it, but I can tell you right now, weird names like that I'd definitely remember.' He closed his eyes. 'Tall and skinny, huh? Richard's customer?'

'Could be.'

'I am thinking of one guy, never gave me a name, just waltzed in expecting to be seated – but no girl, just him. I remember him clearly because he caused problems. Monopolized Richard's time to the point where the other customers weren't getting their food. They start complaining to the busboys, the busboys gripe to me, I have to deal with it. Another reason I remember is it was the only time I had any kind of problem with Richard. Not that he gave me any lip – it wasn't *his* problem, it was the guy's, just kept gabbing to Richard and Richard didn't know what to do. He'd just been working here for a few weeks. We drum into 'em, The customer's always right, so this musta put Richard in a situation, know what I mean? So I have to deal with it, doing my best to be polite, but the guy is not polite about it. Gives me the look, like who am *I* to tell *him*, know what I mean?'

'Did Richard say what the guy was talking to him about?'

'No, but the guy did. Something like, "Hey, I could be his meal ticket, you think he wants to work here for the rest of his life?" Richard's off at another table, looking at me out of the corner of his eye, letting me know this isn't his idea. I offered the guy some comp wine, but he just said something nasty, threw down money, and left. Barely covered the check, not much left over for Richard. Caesar salad, veal parmigiana, German chocolate cake.'

'So tell me,' said Milo, 'what song was the piano playing?'

Lew grinned. 'Probably "You Talk Too Much."' He shrugged. 'I'm just lucky, always had a memory, never bother with that elderberry stuff, Ginkgo biloba, any a that. Tell the truth, sometimes it's not fun. I got two ex-wives I wouldn't mind forgetting.' His laugh was phlegmy. 'You got pictures of this Wark guy, I can tell you right away if it's the same one.'

'Not yet,' said Milo. 'Can you describe him?'

'Six-two, maybe -three, skinny, those all-black clothes like they do now, the so-calleds. My day, that was going to a funeral.'

'Hair?'

'Long, dark. Not curly, though. Straight down – like a wig. Come to think of it, it probably *was* a wig. Big nose, little eyes, skinny little mouth. Not a good-looking guy. Hungry like, know what I mean? And tan – like he baked himself under a lamp.'

'How many times did he come in here?'

'Just that once. One thing that might help, I saw his car. Corvette. Not a new one – the style with the big swoop in front? Bright yellow. Like a taxicab. I saw it because after he left, I cracked the door, made sure he was really leaving. You're saying he had something to do with Richard getting killed? Sonofabitch.'

'Don't know,' said Milo, finishing his drink. 'You've been very helpful. I appreciate it. Is there anyone else working tonight who might remember the guy?'

Lew ran his finger around his wineglass. The sauterne was brassy gold. He hadn't touched it. 'Maybe Angelo – I'll check. Want a refill?'

'No, thanks. You didn't happen to get a look at the Corvette's license plate? Even a few numbers.'

'Ha,' said the maitre d'. 'You're one a those cockeyed optimists, huh? Like in the song – think I'll go tell Doris to play that.'

25

ANGELO WAS a short, bald waiter of the same vintage as Lew, rushing flush-faced between two large tables. When the maître d' beckoned him away, his frown turned a pencil mustache into an inverted V and he approached us, muttering under his breath. Milo had talked to him, too, months ago, but he recalled the interview only vaguely. The trouble-maker in black evoked nothing from him but a shrug.

'This is concerning Richard,' said Lew.

'Richard was a nice kid,' said Angelo.

Milo said, 'Is there anything else you can tell us about him?'

'Nice kid,' Angelo repeated. 'Said he was gonna be a movie star – gotta get back, everyone's bitching about not enough mushrooms in the sauce.'

'I'll talk to the kitchen,' said Lew.

'Good idea.' Angelo left.

Lew said, 'Sorry 'bout that, his wife's sick. Give me your card and I'll call you when I have a chance to look at those books.'

Driving back to the city, I said, 'Maybe the meeting at the Oak Barrel was Richard's audition. Richard answers the casting ad, Wark says let me meet you where you work. See you in your natural habitat. Like a hunter sighting prey. It would also eliminate the need for Wark to have a formal casting location.'

'Pretty gullible of Richard.'

'He wanted to be a star.'

He sighed. 'Curly wig, straight wig – this is starting to feel nasty. Now all we have to do is find Mr W., have a nice little chat.'

'You've got a car now. A yellow Corvette isn't exactly inconspicuous.'

'DMV doesn't list colors, only make, model, and year. Still, it's a start, if the 'Vette wasn't stolen. Or never registered . . . Big fenders – probably a seventies model.' He sat up a bit. 'A 'Vette could also explain why Richard was stashed in his own car. 'Vettes don't have trunks.'

'Someone else to think about,' I said. 'The blond girlfriend. She fits the second-driver theory. She waits nearby until Wark's ditched Richard's VW, picks Wark up, they drive away. Untraceable. No reason to connect the two of them with Richard.'

'Every producer needs a bimbo, right? Her I don't even have a *fake* name for.' Taking out a cigar, he opened the window, coughed, and thought better of it. He closed his eyes, and his fleshy features settled into what might have passed for stupor. I stayed on Riverside, going west. By Coldwater Canyon, he still hadn't spoken. But his eyes opened and he looked troubled.

'Something doesn't fit?' I said.

'It's not that,' he said. 'It's the movie angle. All these years sweeping the stables and I finally break into showbiz.'

* * *

I didn't hear from him in the morning and Robin and I went for breakfast down by the beach in Santa Monica. By eleven, she was back in the shop with Spike and I was taking a call from the obnoxious Encino attorney. I listened to one paragraph of oily spiel, then told him I wasn't interested in working with him. He sounded hurt, then he turned nasty, finally slammed down the phone, which provided a bit of good cheer.

Two seconds later, my service phoned. 'While you were on the line, Doctor, a Mrs Racano called from Fort Myers Beach, Florida.'

Florida made me think of the Crimmins boating accident. Then the name clicked in: Dr Harry Racano, Claire's major professor. I'd called Case Western two days ago, asking about him. I copied down the number and phoned. A crisp-voiced woman answered.

'Mrs Racano?'

'This is Eileen.'

'It's Dr Alex Delaware from Los Angeles. Thanks for calling.'

'Yes,' she said guardedly. 'Mary Ellen at Case told me you called about Claire Argent. What in God's name happened to her?'

'She was abducted and murdered,' I said. 'So far, no one knows why. I was asked to consult on the case.'

'Why did you think Harry could help you?'

'We're trying to learn whatever we can about Claire. Your husband's name showed up on one of her papers. Faculty advisers can get to know their students pretty well.'

'Harry was Claire's dissertation chairman. They were

both interested in alcoholism. We had Claire at the house from time to time. Sweet girl. Very quiet. I can't believe she's been murdered.'

Talking faster. Anxious about something?

'Claire worked on alcoholism here,' I said, 'but a few months before she was killed, she quit her job somewhat abruptly and took a position at Starkweather Hospital. It's a state facility for the criminally insane.'

Silence.

'Mrs Racano?'

'I wouldn't know about any of that. Claire and I hadn't been in contact since she left Cleveland.'

'Did she ever show an interest in homicidal psychotics?' I said.

Her sigh blew through the phone like static. 'Have you met her parents?'

'Yes.'

'And . . . But of course they wouldn't say anything. Oh, Dr Delaware, I suppose you'd better know.'

She gave me the basic facts. I got the details back at the research library newspaper files.

The Pittsburgh *Post-Gazette*, twenty-seven years ago, but it could've been any major paper. The story had been covered nationally.

FAMILY SLAIN IN YOUTH'S RAMPAGE

Responding to calls from concerned neighbors, police entered a west Pittsburgh home this morning and discovered the bodies of an entire family, and, hiding in the basement, the youth who is alleged to have murdered them.

James and Margaret Brownlee, and their children, Carla, 5, and Cooper, 2, had been stabbed and beaten to death with a knife and a tenderizing mallet obtained from the kitchen of their Oakland home. Brownlee, 35, was a delivery supervisor for Purity Bottled Water, and his wife, 29, was a homemaker. Both were described as early risers with regular habits, and by noon yesterday, when Mr Brownlee hadn't left for work and none of the other family members had appeared, neighbors called the police.

The suspect, Denton Ray Argent, 19, was found crouching near the furnace, still clutching the murder weapons and drenched with blood. Argent, who lived with his parents and a younger sister three doors down from the Brownlees, was termed odd and reclusive, a high school dropout whose personality had changed several years before.

'He was around fourteen when it started,' said a woman who declined to be identified. 'Even before then, he wasn't very social – quiet, but the whole family was, they kept to themselves. But when he got to be a teenager he stopped taking care of himself, real sloppy. You'd see him walking around, talking to himself, waving his hands around. We all knew he was strange, but no one thought it would ever come to this.'

Reports that Denton Argent had worked briefly as a gardener for the Brownlees have not been confirmed. Argent was taken into custody at central jail, pending booking and further investigation.

Plugging Denton Argent's name into the computer pulled up several more stories that reiterated the crime. Then nothing for a month until a page-three item appeared:

FAMILY KILLER COMMITTED TO HOSPITAL

Alleged mass murderer Denton Argent has been judged legally insane and incapable of assisting in his own defense by three court-appointed psychiatrists. Argent, accused of slaying Mr and Mrs James Brownlee and their two small children in a homicidal spree that shocked the quiet Oakland neighborhood and the entire city, was evaluated by doctors hired by both the prosecution and the defense.

'It was pretty clear,' said Assistant District Attorney Stanley Rosenfield, assigned to prosecute the case. 'Argent is severely schizophrenic and completely out of touch with reality. No purpose would be served by going to trial.'

Rosenfield went on to say that Argent would be committed to a state hospital for an indefinite term. 'Should he ever regain competence, we'll haul him into court.'

One week after that:

MURDERER'S FAMILY STAYS PUT – AND MUM

The parents of family killer Denton Argent have no plans to move from the Chestnut Street address where, three doors from their well-kept house, their son slew all four members of a neighboring family.

Argent, 19, was judged criminally insane and incapable

of assisting in his own defense against the charges of murdering James and Margaret Brownlee and their two young children, Carla, 5, and Cooper, 2. His parents, Robert Ray and Ernestine Argent, owners of a local gift shop, have refused to talk to the press, but neighbors report they have stated an unwillingness to 'run from what Denton did.' Their shop was closed for three weeks but later reopened, reportedly with a substantial drop in business. But the general attitude of the neighborhood was charitable.

'These are decent people,' said another neighbor, Roland Danniger. 'Everyone knew Denton was strange, and maybe they should've tried to help him more, but how could they know he'd turn violent? If I feel sorry for anyone, it's the little sister; she's always kept to herself, now you don't see her at all.'

The reference was to Argent's younger sister, Claire, 12, who was removed from her public junior high school and is reportedly being tutored at home.

Five years later:

FAMILY SLAYER DIES IN ASYLUM

Mass murderer Denton Argent has died of a brain seizure in his cell at Farview State Hospital, authorities reported today.

Argent, 24, murdered an entire family during a bloody early-morning spree five years ago. Judged mentally incompetent, he was committed to the state facility, where he has resided without incident. The seizure, possibly due to a previously undiagnosed epileptic condition, or to psychiatric medication, caused Argent to pass out in his locked cell and to choke on his own vomit in the middle of the night. His body was discovered the following morning. Hospital authorities report no suspicions of foul play.

'Harry never found out until Claire's last year in grad school,' Eileen Racano had said. 'It was a shock. The poor thing, carrying around that burden.'

'How did she bring it up?'

'It was during the time she was working on the final draft of her dissertation. That's always a stressful period, but Claire seemed to be having an especially hard time. Writing didn't come easily to her, and she was a perfectionist, drafting and redrafting. She told Harry she was worried she wouldn't pass her orals.'

'Was that a possibility?' I said.

'Her grades were excellent and her research was solid.'

I let the unspoken 'but' hang in the air.

'Back then, personality issues couldn't be considered,' she said.

'So your husband had reservations about Claire's temperament.'

'He thought she was a sweet young woman, but . . . too closed off. And to grow up under a shadow like that . . . Harry felt she hadn't dealt with it. That it might cause her problems later on.'

'How exactly did he find out?' I said.

'One morning he came into the lab and found Claire there. She looked awful; it was obvious she'd been working all night. Harry asked her why she was driving herself so hard and she said she had no choice, she just *had* to pass, it was everything she'd lived for. Harry said something to the effect that there was life beyond grad school, and Claire fell apart – sobbing, telling Harry he didn't understand, that becoming a psychologist was all that mattered, she *had* to do it, she wasn't like other students. Harry asked in what way, and that's when it all came out. Afterward, Claire just curled up on the chair, shivering. Harry gave her his jacket and stayed with her until she calmed down. After that, we reached out more to Claire, invited her over for dinner. Harry was a wonderful man. His students all loved him. Years after he went emeritus, we'd still get letters and cards and visits. Not from Claire, though. After that one episode, she closed up, refused to talk about it. Harry couldn't demand that she receive therapy, but he suggested it strongly. Claire promised she would, but she never confirmed that she had.'

'So she passed her exams, received her doctorate, and went her own way.'

'Believe me,' she said, 'it troubled Harry. He even debated holding her up – he was in real conflict, Dr Delaware. But ethically, he knew he couldn't. Claire had fulfilled all the requirements for graduation, and he felt she'd never trust anyone again if he went public with her story. The funny thing was, at her orals, she was the picture of confidence. Charming, in control, as if nothing had ever happened. Harry chose to take that as a sign that she'd gotten help. But once she had her degree in hand, she shut us out completely. Even after she received the fellowship right here at Case Medical School we never heard from her. A year later, we heard she got a job in Los Angeles. Harry said, "Claire's going off to the Wild West." The whole incident bothered him. He wondered if he should've been more forceful in getting her to deal with the guilt.'

'She felt guilty about what her brother had done?'

'Unjustified guilt, but yes, that's the way Harry saw it, and his insights were almost always correct. He saw neuropsychology as an escape for Claire. Testing, numbers, lab work, no need to get into feelings. He wondered if she'd ever leave the field, and now you tell me she did.'

'Her brother died of a seizure,' I said. 'Did your husband wonder if Claire's career choice might have been related to her seeking an organic basis for Denton's crimes?'

'That, too. But he worried that someday that defense would crumble. Because she wouldn't find any simple answers, might grow disillusioned. Harry was a neuropsychologist himself, but he was also a master psychotherapist. Along with his alcoholism research, he worked with MADD, treating the families of drunk-driving victims. He tried to teach his students the value of maintaining emotional balance.'

'Claire didn't get the message.'

'The Claire we knew didn't. She was such a . . . distant girl. Seemed to be punishing herself.'

'In what way?'

'All work, no play, never attending department functions,

no friendships with the other students. I'd bet the dinners at our home were her main social contacts. Even the way she furnished her room, Dr Delaware. Student housing's never gorgeous, but most students try to do something with what the university gives them. One night it was especially cold, and Harry and I drove her home. The way she lived shocked us. All she had was a bed, a desk, and a chair. I told Harry it looked like a jail cell. He wondered if she might be trying, symbolically, to share her brother's fate.'

Now I knew why Claire had refused to talk about her family to Joe Stargill.

Now I understood Rob Ray and Ernestine's willingness to let Claire shut them out of her life: Monumental shame.

No matter what was happening around her . . .

I'd wondered about family chaos, but my imagination hadn't stretched far enough.

Like so many people who enter the helping fields, Claire had been trying to heal herself. Approaching it from a distance, at first, as she hid behind hard data and lab work. Working for Myron Theobold, a man who'd abandoned psychoanalysis for a PhD in biochemistry. *I like to think of myself as a humane administrator . . . I don't get involved in their personal lives. I'm not out to parent anyone.*

Staying with Theobold all those years because he allowed her to remain a stranger.

Then something changed.

Professor Racano had suspected professional escape wouldn't work forever, and he'd been right. Last year, Claire had gone looking for answers – going about it with characteristic academic detachment, scanning library files for rampages similar to her brother's.

Why at that point in her life? Perhaps something had weakened her defenses . . . The only thing that came to mind was the divorce. Because marrying Joe Stargill had been another sad stab at normalcy, and it had failed.

I thought of how she and Stargill had met. That afternoon in the Marriott bar, impulsive, just like the Reno wedding. Yet ultimately, Claire's motivation for pairing up with Stargill had been anything but hasty, most probably unconscious. She'd preserved the secrecy with which she'd encrusted herself since adolescence by selecting a self-absorbed child of alcoholics who could be counted upon to concentrate on his own problems and keep his nose out of hers.

Casual pickup, incredible sex. The semblance of physical intimacy, unencumbered by exploration. Stargill had described the marriage as the parallel movement of two busy roommates.

Claire had made a brief stab at decorating her home and her life. After Stargill moved out, she stripped the house bare. Not for serenity. Back to the cell.

Punishing herself, just as Professor Racano had suspected. Trying, once again without consciously realizing it, to replicate Denton Argent's bleak fate in order to bond, somehow, with the brother who'd polluted her formative years.

She'd been twelve when Denton slaughtered the Brownlees. But maybe much younger when she realized there was something different – maybe dangerously different – about her only sibling. Did she blame herself for not telling someone?

Or was she simply ashamed to be linked genetically to a monster?

I thought of how the Argents had refused to move. Remaining on the same block had to have been wrenching for them. For the entire neighborhood. Had Claire been shunned for the rest of her childhood?

When Denton seized fatally, she'd been seventeen, still living at home. An upbringing capped at both ends by trauma, shame, and loss. Adolescence was hallmarked by the quest for identity. What had happened to Claire's sense of self?

Had she ever visited Denton at the asylum, or had her parents forbidden contact? Had she planned, at some point, to talk to her brother about his crimes? Tried to make sense of events that defied explanation?

If so, Denton's death had killed any hope.

Years later, she decided to look for answers anyway. Learning about the Ardullo murders must have seemed like salvation.

The parallels between the two cases chilled my blood. I could only imagine how Claire had felt, spooling microfiche, only to come upon Denton's doppelgänger in Ardis Peake.

First, shock. Then sickening, spreading familiarity, empathy in its worst incarnation.

Finally, a glimmer of reprieve: One last chance to tackle the Big Why.

Now that I knew what I did, Claire's move to Starkweather, her zeroing in on Ardis Peake, wasn't puzzling at all.

So many madmen, so little time.

Not a choice, really. A psychologically preordained dance backed by the choreography of pain.

A dead certainty.

26

'NO LUCK,' said Milo.

'On what?'

'Anything. The Corvette, any sort of locale on either Wark or Derrick Crimmins. No Social Security on Wark, and Crimmins's last tax filing was ten years ago. In Florida. Didn't get to take it any further 'cause I was tied up in the courthouse. Trying to get three separate judges to OK warrants on Peake's mail and his phone calls. No go. Prophecy didn't impress them. The third one laughed me out of chambers and told me to consult a palm reader.'

It was nearly five. He'd pulled up in my driveway a few minutes ago. Now he was scrounging in the fridge, bent sharply as he eyed a lower shelf, the ridges and bulges of his service revolver protruding through his too-tight tweed jacket.

'Claire's relationship to Peake didn't matter?' I said.

He shook his head, pulled out mayonnaise, mustard, a packet of corned beef I'd forgotten about, got some corn rye of similar vintage from the bread box. Slapping together a limp-looking sandwich, he sat down, chomped out a semicircle.

'"Gobbledygook" was the operative word,' he said. 'And

"psychotic meanderings." They all said Peake was, at most, a material witness. If that. Also, his mental state rendered him unlikely to provide significant materiality, so the entire rationale falls apart.'

Another chunk of sandwich disappeared. 'I didn't do any better on getting into Wark's B. of A. account. A fictitious person only remotely and theoretically associated with an eight-month-old homicide doesn't cut the evidentiary mustard.'

'Mommy,' I said, 'I wanna be a policeman when I grow up.'

His grin was savage. 'Now for the happy news: Wendell Pelley is no longer a suspect. At least not for the Beatty brothers. Wendell Pelley is deceased. For well over a week – before choo choo bang bang. His body showed up in a county garbage dump in Lennox six days ago. Sheriff's deputy happened to read the wire I put out and called. The dump's organized, so they were able to pinpoint what load Pelley came in on. Commercial container behind an industrial laundry. It was collected three days before he was found, but the maggot feast indicates Pelley could have been in there a while before that. No sign of violence to the corpse. Looks like he fell asleep in the Dumpster and got shipped out with the trash.'

'Crushed to death?'

'No, they spotted him before compaction – what was left of him. Cause of death was extreme dehydration and malnutrition. The sonofabitch starved himself. I called the Korean who runs the halfway house. He said yeah, Pelley hadn't been eating much before he split. Probably weighed a hundred and twenty back then. No, he didn't see that as reason for alarm, Pelley wasn't causing problems.'

'Talk about self-punishment,' I said. 'Pelley made it all the way from Ramparts to Lennox on foot?'

'He probably walked through alleys in some not-nice neighborhoods, found his final resting place, curled up, and died.'

'Not a trace of foul play?'

'Nothing, Alex. They filed it as a definite suicide. I read the report and it's pretty clear. Desiccation, cachexia, low hemoglobin count, something about his liver chemistry that said he hadn't received adequate nutrition for a long time. No wounds, no broken bones; his neck bones were intact, and so was his skull. The only damage was what the maggots had done.'

Staring at what was left of the sandwich, he hesitated, gulped it down, wiped his face, got himself a beer.

'Think about that, Alex. Feeling so low that you throw yourself out in the garbage.'

'He could still be good for Claire,' I said.

'If I could show that he and Claire ever met, maybe. But now that he's dead? Also, given the fact that he's *not* good for Dada or the Beattys, my enthusiasm for him has faded considerably. I got carried away. Like Mr Dylan said, too much of nothing.'

He returned to the fridge, got an apple, bit down noisily.

'Maybe I can throw you a little cheer,' I said. 'For what it's worth, I know why Claire sought out Peake.'

I told him about Denton Argent's rampage. His chewing slowed. When I finished, he put the apple down. 'Her brother. Never heard of the case.'

'Me, neither. It happened twenty-seven years ago.'

'I was in Vietnam . . . So what was she hoping to learn by glomming on to Peake?'

'Her conscious motive was probably wanting to understand psychotic violence. Being a psychologist – and a researcher – legitimized it. But I think she was really trying to understand why her family – her childhood – had been shattered.'

'And Peake could've told her that?'

'No,' I said. 'But she would've denied her motives.'

'So she attaches herself to Peake, tries to get him to open up about what he did.'

'Maybe she did more than try,' I said. 'If anyone could pry him open, it would've been Claire. Because she was the only person to spend any significant time with him during his commitment. She *cared*. What if she succeeded, and Peake told her something that put her in danger?'

'Such as?'

'He hadn't acted alone. He'd been prodded by the Crimmins brothers. Or believed he had. Alternatively, Peake's still in contact with Crimmins and told him Claire was getting too nosy. Crimmins decided to fix the problem. That's how Peake knew about Claire's murder the day before it happened.'

'*If* he knew,' he said. '"Bad eyes in a box" ain't exactly evidence. As I was reminded three times today.' He picked up the apple, twirled it by the stem. 'Very creative, Alex, but I don't know. It all hinges on Peake having conversations. Faking out being a veg.'

'What if his mental dullness isn't all due to psychosis?'

I said. 'What if the bulk *is* caused by his medication? The severity of his tardive symptoms and the fact that he's never had his dosage altered from five hundred milligrams show he reacts strongly to moderate amounts of Thorazine. Let's say Claire decided to experiment, withdrawing pills in order to restore some clarity. And it worked.'

'She tampered on the sly?'

'We're talking intense motivation. A woman who gave up her job just to get next to Peake. If she thought easing up on his Thorazine would open him up, why not? She could've rationalized that it was for his own good – the meds were increasing his neurological problems, he could get by on less. The obvious risk would have been an increase in his violent impulses, but she might've felt confident she could deal with that.'

'Heidi was working with him, too,' he said. 'She wouldn't suspect?'

'Heidi's medically and psychologically unsophisticated. Claire told her what she wanted her to know. Any changes may have been subtle – a few sentences here and there. And they may have occurred only in response to Claire's prodding. Claire was spending intense one-on-one time with Peake, probing very deliberately. She knew what she wanted: A window into Peake's violence. And, by extension, Denton's. Even if Peake did say something to Heidi, there'd be no reason for her to comprehend. Or care. She'd dismiss it as gibberish, just as she did with the "bad eyes" recitation until Claire turned up dead.'

'And with Claire gone, Peake gets his full dosage again.'

'And lapses into incoherence.'

'OK,' he said. 'Let me take this all in . . . Peake blabs, Claire finds out someone else was involved . . . and Wark enters the picture because he and Peake are somehow in contact—'

'Because Wark works at Starkweather—'

'Yeah, yeah, let me put this in order . . . Peake wakes up – maybe he does get more violent. Or at least belligerent with Wark. He makes threats – "I've got this doctor who's really interested in me. I told her you turned me into a monster, she believes me, she's gonna get me out of here." Even if Claire never said that, Peake could believe it – delusional. He's still crazy, right?'

I nodded.

'Still,' he said, 'that's an awful lot of gabbing for old Monster.'

'Unless he's been faking.'

'I brought that up at the beginning. You said it was unlikely.'

'The context has changed.'

He shot out of his chair, paced the room, buttoned and unbuttoned his coat. 'If Wark was threatened, why not kill Peake?'

'Why bother?' I said. 'Back on a full dose – or a higher one, if someone's tinkering in the opposite direction – Peake's no threat. He'll live out his life in his S&R room, the tardive symptoms will intensify until he's neurologically cooked, one day someone will walk in and find him dead. Just like Denton.'

'Claire could just do that?' he said. 'Pull pills with nobody noticing?'

'Starkweather gives its staff plenty of latitude. Dr Aldrich was Claire's nominal supervisor, and he didn't seem to know much about her cases. Neither did Swig. In that respect, working at Starkweather was similar to her job with Theobold – plenty of solitude. The style to which she'd become accustomed since childhood.'

'So,' he said, 'I waltz in there again and ask to look at the personnel files. Swig's gonna roll out the carpet.'

'You can use the publicity threat – filing for warrants, the media getting hold of it. No reason for him to know the judges haven't cooperated. Ask to meet with the men in Claire's group. That's certainly reasonable. While you're there, try to work in the personnel records.'

He circled some more. 'One more thing. The Beatty brothers. Why would Crimmins/Wark tell Peake about killing them? On the contrary, if Peake's hassling him, the last thing he'd want would be for Peake to know anything.'

'Good point,' I said. 'So maybe it's Column A: Peake and Crimmins still *are* colluding. Carrying on the alliance that led to Peake's original blood walk. Having fun with it – recording it on film.' My gut tightened. 'I just thought of something. The eye wounds. What's a camera lens?'

He stopped pacing. 'An eye.'

'An all-seeing eye. Invisible, omniscient, director as god. These crimes are about power and control. Actors as subjects. *Subjected*. Camera observation goes only one way. I see, you don't. No eyes for *you*.'

'Then why weren't the Beattys' eyes messed with?'

'Maybe because they were already impaired. Drunk – blind drunk?'

'Nutso,' he said. 'Back to the booby hatch. Maybe while I'm there I'll rent a room . . . OK, I'll set it up for tomorrow. I'd like you there, see what else you can pick up. Meanwhile, I'll do more tracing on Crimmins, see if I can find out the last time he surfaced under his own name, learn more about those family accidents.'

A big finger poked the expanse of wash-and-wear that covered his heart. He winced.

'You OK?' I said.

Laboriously, he stood up. 'Just gas – serve me something healthier next time.'

27

GLOSSY WALLS painted a peach pink that managed to be unpleasant. A dozen blond fake-wood school desks lined up in two rows of six. The facing wall was nearly spanned by a spotless blackboard. Rounded edges blunted the plastic frame; no chalk, two soft erasers.

Directly in front of the board was an oak desk, bolted to the floor. Nothing atop the surface. The right-hand wall bore two maps of the world, equal-area and Mercator projection. Posters taped to the walls offered treatises on table manners, nutrition, the basics of democracy, the alphabet in block and cursive, a chronology of US presidents.

Duct tape fastened the posters: No thumbtacks.

The American flag in the corner was plastic sheeting atop a plastic rod, also bolted.

Outward trappings of a classroom. The students wore khaki uniforms and barely fit behind the blond desks.

Six of them.

Up front sat an old man with beautiful golden-white hair. Kindly granddad on a laxative commercial. Behind him were two black men in their thirties, one mocha-toned, freckled, and heavy, with Coke-bottle glasses and a rashlike beard, the other lean, with a hewn-onyx face and the glint-eyed vigilance of a hunter surveying the plains.

At the head of the next row was a very thin creature in his twenties with hollow cheeks, haunted eyes, and blanched lips. Gray fists knuckled his temples. He sat so low his chin nearly touched the desktop. Stringy brown hair streamed from under a gray stocking cap. The hat was pulled down to his eyebrows and made his head appear undersized.

Behind him was giant Chet, yawning, flexing, sniffing, exploring the interior of his mouth with his fingers. So big he had to sit sideways, giraffe legs stretched into the aisle. No hint of the bony horror concealed by khaki trousers. He recognized Milo and me right away, winked, waved, blew a raspberry, said, 'Yo bro my man whus shakin and bakin baked Alaska Juneau you know hot cold tightass don't sneeze on me homey you too homely homo fuck me up the ass.' The lean black man glared.

When we'd seen Chet the first day, Frank Dollard hadn't mentioned he'd been part of Claire's group. Today, Dollard wasn't saying much of anything; he stood in a corner and glared at the inmates.

The last man was a small, sallow Hispanic with a shaved head and a grease-stain mustache. The room was air-conditioned to meat-locker chill, but he sweated. Rubbed his hands together, craned his neck, licked his lips.

More tardive symptoms. I scanned the room for other signs of neurological damage. Grandpa's hands trembled a bit, but that could've been age. Probably the freckled black man's gaping mouth, though that might have been psychotic stupor or a twisted daydream . . .

Frank Dollard swaggered to the front of the room and positioned himself behind the oak desk. 'Morning, gentlemen.'

No more warmth in his voice than fifteen minutes ago, when he'd met us at the inner gate, arms folded across his chest.

'Here again,' he'd finally said, making no move to free the lock.

Milo said, 'Just couldn't stay away, Frank.'

Dollard huffed. 'What exactly are you trying to accomplish?'

'Solve a murder, Frank.' Milo's hand grazed the lock.

Dollard took a long time pulling out his key ring, locating the right key, inserting it in the lock, giving one sharp turn. The bolt released. Several more seconds were taken up in pocketing the key. Finally, Dollard shoved the gate open.

Once we were in, he smiled sourly. 'Like I said, what exactly are you trying to accomplish?' Not waiting for an answer, he smoothed his mustache and began walking across the yard. The dirt stretched ahead of us, brown and smooth as butcher's paper.

Milo and I started to follow. Dollard increased the distance between us. The heat and the light were punishing. Inmates stared. If one of them had come from behind, Dollard would have been no use at all.

Three techs stood watch on the yard. Two Hispanics and a blocky white man, nothing close to Derrick Crimmins's physical description.

Dollard unlocked the rear gate and we approached the main building. Instead of entering, he stopped several feet from the door and rattled his key ring.

'You can't see Mr Swig. Not here.'

'Where is he?' said Milo.

'Hospital business. He said to give you fifteen minutes' access to the Skills for Daily Living group. That's it.'

'Thanks for your time, Frank,' said Milo, too mildly. 'Sorry to be such a bother.'

Dollard blinked, pocketed the keys. Gazing back at the yard, he clicked his teeth together. 'These guys are like trained animals, you can't vary the stimulus-response too much. Your coming in here is disruptive. Top of that, it's pointless. No one here had anything to do with Dr Argent.'

'Because no one gets out.'

'Among other things.'

'Wendell Pelley got out.'

Dollard blinked again. His tongue rolled under his lower lip. 'What does that have to do with the price of eggs?'

'A nutcase gets out, a few weeks later one of his shrinks is dead?'

'Dr Argent was never one of Pelley's shrinks. I doubt she ever ran into him.'

'Why was Pelley released?'

'You'd have to ask one of the doctors.'

'You have no idea, Frank?'

'I don't get paid to have ideas,' said Dollard.

'So you said the first time,' said Milo. 'But we both know that's crap. What'd Pelley do to get out?'

Dollard's leathery skin reddened and his shoulders rose. Suddenly, he chuckled. 'More like what he didn't do. Act crazy. He hadn't been crazy for a long time.'

'Medical miracle?' said Milo.

'My opinion, the guy was never really psychotic in the first place, just a drunk. I'm not saying he faked anyone out. People who knew him when he was first committed said he was all over the place – hallucinating, acting wild, at one point they had to put him in restraints. But then a month or two later, that all stopped, even without meds. So, my opinion, it was severe alcohol poisoning and he got detoxed.'

'Then why wasn't he sent back to trial?'

'Because when he got arrested we were still doing not guilty by reason. He was off the hook.'

'Lucky him,' said Milo.

'Not so lucky – he still got cooped up here for twenty-odd years. Longer than he would've been in prison. Maybe it wasn't just alcohol. Pelley'd been mining for years; he could've got some kind of heavy-metal poisoning in his system. Or he was just a short-term crazy, freaked out and got better. Whatever, he never needed any neuroleptics, just some antidepressants. Year after year, he's hanging around, no symptoms, guess they thought it didn't make sense.'

'Antidepressants,' said Milo. 'Sad sack?'

'Why all the interest? He cause problems on the outside?'

'Only for himself, Frank. Starved himself to death.'

Dollard's mouth twitched. 'He never liked to eat . . . So where'd they find him?'

'In a garbage dump.'

'Garbage dump,' said Dollard, as if visualizing it. 'This is gonna sound bleeding-heart, but he wasn't really that bad of a guy. At least when I talked to him, he really felt remorse for what he'd done to his girlfriend and those kids. Didn't even wanna get out. Which don't excuse what he did, but . . .' He shrugged. 'What the hell, we all have to go sometime.'

'Who was his doctor?' I said.

'Aldrich. Not Argent.'

'You're sure he had no contact with Dr Argent?'

Dollard laughed. 'Can't be sure of anything but death and taxes. And to answer your next question, he wouldn't a known Peake, either. Pelley was on B Ward, Peake's always been on C.'

'What about out on the yard?' I said.

'Neither of them ever went out onto the yard that I saw. Peake never leaves his damn *room*.'

'So who did Peake have contact with?'

Dollard's eyes got cold. 'I answered that last time you were here, Doc. No one. He's a damn zombo.' He looked at his watch. 'And you're wasting my time. Let's get this over with.'

Turning, he stomped past the big gray building, bull neck pitched forward. A well-trodden dirt path veered to the right. When we reached the west side of the building, the dirt kept snaking to a group of three low, single-story beige structures cooking in the full sun.

A sign said ANNEXES A, B, AND C. Behind the smaller buildings sprawled another brown yard, as wide as the one in front, locked and empty. Then more chain link and a bulk of forest. Not eucalyptus, like at the entrance. Denser, green-black, some kind of pine or cedar.

'Where does that lead?' said Milo.

'Nowhere.'

'Thought there was only one building.'

'These aren't buildings, they're annexes,' said Dollard, smiling. He hurried us past A. Double-locked door, plastic windows. Darkness on the other side of the panes, no signs of habitation. Outside were a few plastic picnic benches and a cement patio swept clean. The silence was punctured by occasional shouts from the main yard. No birdsongs, no insect chitters, not even the faintest stutter of traffic.

Annex B was empty, too. I sensed something behind me, glanced over my shoulder. The main building, shielded from the morning sun, had darkened to charcoal.

Then the illusion of movement danced in a corner of my right eye, and my head buzzed, seized by split-second vertigo that passed just as quickly.

I looked back without stopping. Nothing. But for that brief interval, the entire structure had seemed to tilt forward, as if straining on its foundation. Now it was immobile as a building had to be, rows of windows dull and black, blank as a series of empty scorecards.

Dollard hurried to Annex C, stopped at the door, nodded at the pair of techs standing guard. Two black men. No Wark. They checked us out before stepping back. Dollard used his key, opened the door wide, peeked in, let the steel-reinforced panel swing back in Milo's face as he charged in.

'Morning, gentlemen,' Dollard repeated.

None of the men returned the greeting. He said, 'Let's do the pledge,' and began reciting. No one stood. Dollard's tone was bored. Chet and Grandpa and the lean black man joined in.

'Hey, all you patriots,' said Dollard when it was over.

'Born in the USA,' said Chet. To us: 'Top of the morning to ya morning becomes Elektra electrified all those ions ioning boards gotta keep everything smooth, pressed, even the French cuffs, fisticuffs cuffing up Rodney King yo bro.'

The lean black man angled his head toward Chet and shook it disgustedly. No one else seemed to pay attention to the giant's ramblings, though the old man's hands were shaking more conspicuously.

'OK,' said Dollard, perching on the edge of the oak desk. 'It's been a while since you guys got together because Dr Argent no longer works here but—'

'Fuck her,' said the sweating Hispanic. 'Fuck her in the ass.'

'Paz,' said Dollard in a tight voice. 'Keep it clean.'

'Fuck her,' said Paz. 'Giving us her pretty-face attention and then cutting out on us.'

'Paz, I explained to you that she didn't quit, she was—'

'Fuck her,' Paz insisted. Sweat dripped from his chin. He appeared on the verge of tears. 'Fucking fucked *up*, man . . . no fair.' He looked at his classmates. None of them paid attention.

'Fuck her,' he said weakly. 'Can't mother*fucking* treat *people* like that.'

'Fuck you,' said Chet, cheerfully. 'Fuck everyone everything the old Kama Sutra pretzel bake about time we had some fun around here oral love oral roberts oral hygiene.'

'Fuck her,' said Paz sadly. He closed his eyes. His chest vibrated with every exhalation. The vibrations slowed. Within seconds, he appeared to be sleeping.

'Nighty-night,' Chet said. 'Fuck everyone equality for all

rights and responsibilities and participatory democracy with liberty under God livery too riding a pale horse—'

'Enough,' said the lean black man. Weary voice, but clear, calm, almost parental.

'Good point, Jackson,' said Dollard. To Chet: 'Enough, big man.'

Chet remained cheerful. His yellow beard was littered with crumbs and his eyes were bloodshot. He gave a throaty, equine laugh. 'Enough is too much enough is never enough unless which is a paradox so enough can be anything depending on the dimension of—'

'Hey, man,' said Jackson, sitting up straighter, 'we all know you went to school, you're a genius, but hey. *OK?*' Baring his teeth at Chet.

Chet said, 'I'm no genius I'm the genus and the species and the—'

'Yeah, yeah, yeah, the mama, the son, and the Holy Roller Ghost,' said Jackson. 'Hey, OK. Chill out, OK?' His grin was pantherish.

Chet said, 'Hey hey hey bro muhfuh you know whu hey hey hey I be OK you be—'

Jackson moved forward in his chair.

'*Chet*,' said Dollard.

'*Chet*,' said Jackson.

'*Chet*,' giggled Chet. Slapping his desk, he reached down, bared his ruined leg, ran his hand along the pole of skin-sheathed bone.

Dollard said, 'Cover that up.'

Jackson had disengaged, was staring at the ceiling. Kindly Grandpa twiddled his thumbs and smiled sweetly.

Paz let out a loud belching snore.

Chet continued to finger-walk up and down his own leg. A smile spread slowly, bristling the yellow beard.

Another snore from Paz.

'Cover it,' said Dollard.

Chet laughed and complied.

The heavy, freckled black man's head lolled; he seemed to be sleeping, too. Grandpa caught my eye and favored me with a smile. His cheeks were fresh apples. The comb tracks in his hair were drafting-table precise.

The only one who hadn't moved was the pale, thin man in the stocking cap. His fists remained glued to his temples.

Dollard said, 'Gentlemen, these guys are from the police. And speaking of Dr Argent, they want to ask you some *questions* about her.'

Only Grandpa and Chet observed Milo's walk to the desk. Dollard remained in place for a moment, as if unwilling to cede ground; then he stepped aside.

'Po-lice,' said Chet. 'Good man gendarme right to bear two arms got to guard society from the dregs and the dross and the eggs and the boss born in the USA! I was po-lice myself po-lite Poe Edgar Allan lite trained with Special Forces me and Chuck Yeager and Annabel Lee and Bobby McGee—'

'Good,' said Milo. 'We need all the help we can get. About Dr Argent—'

A harsh whisper cut through the introduction: '*The Jews did it.*'

Stocking Cap. He hadn't moved. His face had all the life of bleached driftwood.

'Got a point, there,' said Chet. 'Karl Marx violent overthrow all those other semites semiotics antibiotics no that was Fleming no Jew a Scot—'

'The Jews did it,' Stocking Cap repeated.

Dollard said, 'Enough of that, Randall.'

Chet said, 'Maybe valid Jack the Ripper writing on the wall the Jews are the men who didn't not do it or somesuch doubletriplenegative which in the alternate universe parallel systems parallelograms dodecahedrons you never know anything's possible—'

'Randall's a racist asshole,' said Jackson. 'He don't know shit and neither do you.' He showed teeth again, began picking at his cuticles.

Dollard glared at us. *Look what you've done*.

'Randall's a racist motherfucker,' said Jackson matter-of-factly.

Randall didn't react. Paz and the freckled black man remained asleep.

'One more word out of you, Jackson,' said Dollard, 'and it's S&R.'

Jackson fidgeted wildly for several seconds, but he kept silent.

Dollard turned to Milo: 'Finish up.'

Milo looked at me. I moved next to him. 'So, Dr Argent was working with you guys.'

Kindly Grandpa said, 'Would you be so kind as to inform us exactly what exactly happened to the poor woman?'

Dollard said, 'We've already been through that, Holtzmann.'

'I realize that, Mr Dollard,' said Holtzmann. 'She was

murdered. How tragic. But perhaps if we knew the details we could assist these police officers.'

Gentle voice. Twinkly blue eyes. Coherent. What had gotten him in here?

'I gave you all the details you need to know,' said Dollard.

Paz's eyes opened. And closed. Someone passed wind and the stink floated through the room, then dissipated.

Randall's head raised an inch. His fists began grinding into his skull. The stocking cap was filthy. The hand slipped down a bit and I saw that the skin around his temples was red and raw, scabbed in places.

I said, 'If there's anything—'

'How did it happen?' said Grandpa Holtzmann. 'Was she shot? If so, was it a handgun or a long gun?'

'She wasn't shot,' said Dollard. 'And that's all you need to—'

'Stabbed, then?' said Holtzmann.

'What does it matter, Holtzmann?'

'Well,' said the old man, 'if we're to be of assist—'

Chet said, 'The modus is always a clue signature profile-wise psychological penmanship so to speak to squeak—'

'*Was* she stabbed?' said Holtzmann, pressing forward so that the desk bit into his trunk.

'Holtzmann,' said Dollard, 'there's no reason for—'

'She *was* stabbed!' the old man exclaimed. 'Fileted to the bone, hallelujah!' Working at his zipper with both hands, he exposed himself, began masturbating frantically. Singing out in a fine rich baritone: 'Stabbed, stabbed, stabbed, glory be! Gut the bitch in pieces three!'

Dollard took him roughly by the shoulders and shoved him toward the door.

To us, 'You, too. Out. Meeting over.'

As we exited, Chet shouted, 'Wait I've solved it cherchez la femme cherchez la femme—!'

Outside, Dollard locked the door to the annex and handed Holtzmann over to the other two techs. The old man simpered but looked thrilled.

The taller tech said, 'Tuck yourself in. *Now*.'

Holtzmann obeyed, dropped his hands to his side.

'Nice to meet you.' Kindly Grandpa again. 'Mr Dollard, if I've offended—'

'Don't say another damn word,' Dollard ordered him. To the techs: 'Keep them in there while I deal with *these* two. I'll send Mills back to help you.'

The techs moved Holtzmann to the wall, had him face the stucco. 'Don't budge, old man.' Pointing at the door, one of them said, 'They OK in there, Frank?'

'Chet Bodine's running his mouth like a broken toilet and Jackson's ticked at him. At Randall, too – he's doing the Aryan crap.'

'Really?' said the tech lightly. 'Haven't heard that in a while, thought we had it under control.'

'Yeah,' said Dollard. 'Something must have tensed them all up.'

When we were back at the main building, he said, 'Now, that was a good expenditure of taxpayers' money.'

Milo said, 'I want to see Peake.'

'And I want to fuck Sharon Stone—'

'Take me to Peake, Frank.'

'Oh, sure, just like that. Who the hell do you think—' Again, Dollard checked his anger. Chuckled. 'That requires authorization, Detective. Meaning Mr Swig, and, like I said, he's not—'

'Call him,' said Milo.

Dollard bent one leg. 'Because you order me to do it?'

'Because I can be back here in an hour with serious backup and a warrant on you for obstruction of justice. My bosses are antsy about this one, Dollard. Maybe Swig will eventually be able to protect you, but seeing as he's not here, he won't stop you from going through the process. I'm talking Central Booking. You were a cop, you know the drill.'

Dollard's face was the color of rare steak. His words came out slow and clipped. 'You have no idea what kind of deep shit you're getting yourself into.'

'I have a real good idea, Frank. Let's play the media game. Bunch of TV idiots with sound trucks and cameras. The slant I'll give them is the police were saddled with a stroke-inducing whodunit homicide and you did everything in your power to impede. I'll also throw in a nice little sidebar about how you geniuses judged a mass murderer sane and qualified for release and then he proves how sane he is by turning himself into garbage. When all that hits the fan, Frank, think Uncle Senator's gonna help Swig, let alone you?'

Dollard's jaw jutted. He toed the dirt. 'Why the hell are you doing this?'

'Just what I was going to ask you, Frank. Because this change of attitude on your part puzzles me. Ex-cop, you'd expect something different. Makes me wonder, Frank. Maybe I should be looking closer at you.'

'Look all you want,' said Dollard, but his head drew back and his voice lacked conviction. Squinty eyes examined the sky. 'Do your thing, man.'

'Why the change, Frank?'

'No change,' said Dollard. 'The first time you were here was courtesy, the second time tolerance. Now you're a disruption – look at what you just did to those guys.'

'Murder's a disruption,' said Milo.

'I keep telling you, *this* murder had nothing to— Forget it. What the *hell* do you want from me?'

'Take me to Peake. After that, we'll see.'

Dollard's toe stirred up more dirt. 'Mr Swig's in a serious budget meeting and can't be—'

'Who's second in command?'

'No one. Only Mr Swig authorizes visits.'

'Then leave him a message,' said Milo. 'I'll give you five minutes; after that, I'm outta here and it's a whole different game. When's the last time you had your fingers rolled for prints?'

Dollard looked up at the sky again. Someone on the yard howled.

Milo said, 'OK, Doc, we're outta here.'

Dollard let us walk ten paces before saying, 'Screw it. You get ten minutes with Peake, in and out.'

'No, Frank,' said Milo. 'I get what I want.'

28

WE ENTERED the main building. Milo got to the door first, throwing off Dollard's rhythm. Lindeen Schmitz was at the front desk, talking on the phone. She began to smile up at Milo, but a glance from Dollard stopped her.

We rode up to C Ward in silence. On the other side of the double doors, four inmates idled. I could see the nurses in the station chatting cheerfully. Laughter, shallow and grating, spilled from the TV room.

Dollard stomped to Peake's room, unlocked the peep hatch, flipped the light switch, frowned. He released both bolts and opened the door cautiously. A brief look inside. 'Not here.' Trying to sound annoyed, but puzzlement took over.

'How about that,' said Milo. 'He never leaves his room.'

'I'm telling you,' said Dollard, 'he never does.'

'Maybe he's watching TV,' I said.

We went over to the big room, scanned the faces. Two dozen men in khaki stared at the screen. Canned yuks poured out of the box – a sitcom. No one in the room was laughing. Peake wasn't in the audience.

Back in the corridor, Dollard had flushed again. The rage of a dogmatist proven wrong. 'I'll get to the bottom of this.'

He was heading for the nursing station when a sluggish, abrasive sound stopped him.

Swish swish . . . swish swish . . . swish swish . . . Like a snare drum bottoming a slow dance. Seconds later, Peake stepped out from around the left side of the station.

Swish . . . Paper slippers shuffling on linoleum.

Heidi Ott held his elbow as he stumbled forward, eyelids half-shut, each step causing his triangular head to bob like that of a rear-window stuffed dog. In the merciless fluorescence of the hallway, the bits of stubble on his head and face looked like random blackheads. The furrows on his skull seemed painfully deep. He was bent over sharply, as if his spine had given way. As if gravity would have pulled him down but for Heidi's grip.

Neither of them noticed us as she propelled him whispering encouragement.

Dollard said, 'Hey,' and she looked up. Her hair was drawn back in a tight bun, her expression bland. Peake could've been any kind of invalid, she his long-suffering daughter.

She held him back. Peake swayed, opened his eyes, but still didn't seem to be aware of our presence. He rolled his head. His purple-slug tongue oozed out, curled, remained suspended for several seconds before retreating.

'What's going on?' said Dollard.

'Taking a walk,' said Heidi. 'I thought some exercise might help.'

'Help with what?' said Dollard. His thick arms snapped across his chest, fingers digging into stout biceps.

'Is something wrong, Frank?'

'No, everything's great, terrific – *they* want to see him again. Be nice if he was where he's supposed to be.'

'Sorry,' said Heidi, glancing my way. 'Is he on room restriction? I didn't hear about it.'

'Not yet he isn't,' said Dollard. 'Go on, put him back.' To Milo: 'Do your thing, I'll be back in fifteen.'

Arms still folded, he walked off.

Heidi smiled uneasily – a teenager embarrassed by Dad's outburst. 'OK, Ardis, exercise time's over.' One of Peake's eyes opened wider. Bleary, unfocused. He licked his lips, extended his tongue again, rolled his shoulders.

'No one bothers to get him out,' said Heidi. 'I thought it might help with . . . you know.'

'Verbal output,' I said.

She shrugged. 'It didn't seem like a bad idea. C'mon, Ardis, let's get you back.'

She guided him across the hall to his room, led him to his bed, sat him down. He stayed exactly where she put him. For several seconds, no one said anything. Peake didn't budge for a while. Then the tongue-thrusts renewed. Both eyes fluttered, struggled to stay open, couldn't.

Heidi said, 'Could one of you please turn off the light? I think it bothers him.'

I flipped the switch and the room turned gray. Peake sat there, licking and rolling his head. The same reek of intestinal gas and charred wood seemed to press forward, a putrid greeting triggered by our entry.

Heidi turned to Milo. 'Why was Frank so bugged? Is something wrong?'

'Frank's not in a good mood. So tell me, has Peake been talking at all since you taped him?'

She shook her head. 'No, sorry. I've been trying, but nothing. That's why I thought some exercise . . .'

Peake rolled his head. Rocked.

Milo motioned us away from the bed. We moved toward the doorway.

Milo said, 'So no elaboration on "choo choo bang bang."'

Heidi's eyes widened. 'Does that actually mean something?'

Milo shrugged. 'Let me ask you, did Peake ever mention anything else – like a name?'

'What name?' she said.

'Wark.'

She repeated it very slowly. 'Doesn't really sound like a name . . . more like a bark.'

'So he might've blurted it and you would've thought it was just gibberish?'

'Maybe . . . But no, he never said that.' She reached to tug her ponytail. Nothing there. Her hand rose to the tight bun. 'Wark . . . No, he never said that. Why? Who is it?'

'Maybe a friend of Peake's.'

'He doesn't have any friends.'

'Old friend,' said Milo. 'Are you still taping?'

'I tried . . . when I could. Why's Frank so uptight?'

'Frank doesn't like being told what to do.'

'Oh,' she said. 'And you've got him actually working.'

'Frank doesn't like to work?'

She hesitated. Moved closer to the door, looked out through the hatch. 'This may not be true, but I heard he got fired from some police department for sleeping on the job. Or something like that.'

'Who'd you hear it from?' said Milo.

'Just talk on the wards. He's also a sexist – treats me like I don't belong. You saw his attitude – I mean, what's wrong with taking someone who never gets out for a walk? All the other patients are watching TV, it's not like anyone's getting neglected.'

I said, 'Has Frank been giving you other problems?'

'Basically what you just saw – attitude. Swig likes him, so he doesn't have to do too much scut.'

She glanced back at Peake. He continued to sit and rock and lick air. 'You're saying Peake actually has a friend? From his past?'

'Hard to believe?' I said.

'Sure is. I've never seen him make contact with anyone.'

Milo said, 'No mail?'

'Not that I know about. Same with phone calls. He never leaves his room.'

'Till today,' I said.

'Well, yeah. I was trying to help out. What's this Wark done? What's going on?'

'Probably nothing,' said Milo. 'Just working all the angles. You drill a bunch of wells, hope for a trickle every now and then.'

'Sounds too slow for me,' said Heidi. 'No offense.'

'Not like jumping off power stations.'

She smiled. 'Very few things are.'

We left Peake's room and she locked the door.

Milo said, 'Any idea where I could get a personnel list?'

'I guess in the front office. Why?'

'To see who else I should talk to.'

'If it's about Peake,' she said, 'I'm the only one worth talking to. No one else pays attention to him, now that Claire's gone.'

'How much time exactly did she spend?' I said.

'Hmm. Hard to say. There were times when I was on shift when she'd be in there as long as an hour. Sometimes every day. Usually every day. She was like that – involved.'

'With everyone?'

'No,' she said. 'Not really. I mean she spent more time with her patients, in general, than the other docs. But Peake was . . . she seemed to be especially interested in him.'

'Speaking of her patients,' I said, 'we just met the men in the Living Skills group. Low-functioning, just like you said. Any idea what criteria she used to pick them?'

'We never discussed that. I was just the tech. Mostly I stood guard, got supplies. To be honest, the group never really went anywhere. Claire seemed to be . . . observing them more than training. The group only met seven times before she was . . .' Shaking her head. Stroking the bun. 'Sometimes it just hits me. What actually *happened* to her.'

'Do you have any background information on the men? What they did to get here?'

'Let's see . . . there's Ezzard Jackson – skinny black guy. He killed his wife. Tied her up in their house and burned it down. Same with Holtzmann – the old man you'd never think could do anything criminal. He cut his wife up, stored the pieces in the freezer, marked them the way a butcher would – flank, loin. Randall shot his parents – he was into some Nazi stuff, had some delusion they were part of a Zionist plot . . . Who else . . . The other black guy. Pretty. That's his name – Monroe Pretty. Killed his kids, four of them, little ones. Drowned them in the bathtub, one by one. Sam Paz – the Mexican guy – went bonkers at his brother's wedding. Shot his brother and his mother and a bunch of bystanders. All told, I think six people died. The giant, Chet Bodine, was living like a hermit. Killed some hikers.'

So many madmen, so little time . . .

I said, 'All except Chet victimized family members.'

'Actually, Chet wasn't picked for the group,' she said. 'He found out about it, asked Claire if he could join. He was so verbal, she thought it might stimulate the others, so she agreed. Yeah, you're right. I never thought about it, but she must've been interested in family killers.'

Milo said, 'Any idea why?'

She pulled a bobby pin from the bun, slipped it back in. 'To be honest, it probably doesn't mean that much. Lots of the guys in here have murdered family members. Isn't that what crazy people usually do when they freak? Like Peake, he started with his mother, right? At least, that's what Claire told me.'

'What else did she tell you about Peake's crimes?'

She touched the tip of her nose. 'Just what he did. His mom and an entire family. What does any of that have to do with Claire being killed?'

'Maybe nothing,' said Milo. 'So are you gonna keep working with Peake?'

'I guess. If you want me to. Not that I'm accomplishing much.'

'Don't get yourself in trouble, Heidi. I appreciate whatever you do.'

'Sure,' she said, gnawing her lip.

'Is there a problem?'

'Like I told you before, I was figuring it was time to move on. Was kind of waiting until you got to the bottom of Claire's murder.'

'Wish I could tell you it would be soon, Heidi,' he said. 'Meanwhile, as long as Dr Delaware's here, he might as well give Peake a try.'

'Oh, sure,' she said. 'Whatever.'

The door closed after me with a pneumatic hiss.

I stood halfway between the door and the bed, watching Peake. If he was aware of my presence, he didn't show it.

I watched. He did tongue calisthenics. Rocked, rolled, fluttered his eyes.

Standing there immobile, suspended in gray light, I began to feel formless, weightless. My nose habituated to the stink. Keeping my eyes on Peake's hands, I edged closer. A few more minutes of observation and I thought I'd detected a cadence to his movements.

Tongue-thrust, curl and hover, lingual retreat, neck roll clockwise, then counterclockwise.

Approximately ten-second sequences, six repetitions per minute, played out against the constant rocking of his torso.

I took in other details.

His bed wasn't made. Looked as if it was never made. The hands rested on rumpled, sweat-stained covers. The fingers of the left hand were hooked in the sheeting, half-hidden.

Hands that had wreaked so much ruin . . . I moved to within inches of the bed, standing over him for a while.

No change in the routine. I kneeled. Bringing myself down to Peake's eye level. His eyes were glued shut. Strain-marks at the corners said he was pressing the lids together tightly. A few moments ago, with Heidi, they'd been half-open. Responding to that bit of stimulation? Withdrawing further, once returned to isolation?

I heard a tapping from below. Looked down. His feet. Bare – the paper slippers had come off without my noticing.

Two thin white feet. Oversized feet. Unnaturally long toes. Drumming the floor, faster than the upper-body movements, out of rhythm with the tardive dance.

So much motion, but no flavor of intent – the inanimate dangle of a puppet.

All through it, his eyes remained sealed. This close I could see dry, greenish crust flecking the lashes.

'Ardis,' I said.

The beat went on.

I tried again. Nothing.

A few minutes later: 'Ardis, this is Dr Delaware. I want to talk to you about Dr Argent.'

Nothing.

'Claire Argent.'

No response. I repeated myself. Peake's eyelids remained shut, but started to tic – lids contracting and releasing, lateral movement visible under the skin. A few green specks dropped onto his lap.

Reaction? Or random movement?

I sidled closer. Had he wanted to kiss me or claw out my eyes, he could've.

'Ardis, I'm here about Dr Argent.'

Another eyelid tic – a jerky wave traveling beneath the papery skin.

Definite response. On some level, he was able to focus.

I said, 'You were important to Dr Argent.'

Tic tic tic.

'She was important to you, Ardis. Tell me why.'

His eyelids quivered like a frog in a galvanic experiment. I counted the time in tardive sequences: One TD, two TD's . . . ten TD's.

Twelve. Two minutes. He stopped.

Subjectively, it seemed longer than a hundred and twenty seconds. I was far from bored, but time was dragging. I started wondering how many minutes Peake's rampage had consumed. Had the Ardullos been fully awake or asleep? Or somewhere in between – a murky semiconsciousness as they died, thinking it was all a bad dream?

I mentioned Claire's name again. Peake's eyes ticced. But nothing more.

I thought back to his arrest photo, the look of terror in *his* eyes. It reminded me of something – a vicious dog from my boyhood. It had drawn lots of blood but, when finally cornered by the dog catcher, had curled up and whimpered like a starving pup . . .

How much violence was fear catapulted back at the world? Was all viciousness cowardice at the root?

No, I didn't think so, was still convinced Claire's murderer had acted from a position of power and dominance.

Fun.

Had Peake enjoyed his blood walk? Looking at him now, I found it hard to imagine him extracting enjoyment out of anything.

As I watched him now, the notion of this husk decapitating his own mother, stalking up the stairs, bloody knife in hand, running from room to room inflicting agony and death, seemed impossibly remote . . .

As unlikely as kindly Mr Holtzmann sectioning and freezing his wife.

In this place, logic meant nothing.

I said, 'Bad eyes in a box.'

No flutter beneath the lids.

'Choo choo bang bang.'

Nothing.

I tried it again. Same lack of response.

Back to basics. Claire's name.

'Dr Argent,' I said.

Nothing. Had I turned him off?

'Dr Argent cared about you, Ardis.'

Five TD's, six . . . the eyes ticced.

'Why did Dr Argent die, Ardis?'

Eleven, twelve . . . tic, tic, tic.

'What about Wark?' Fourteen . . . 'Griffith D. Wark.'

Sixteen, seventeen. Nothing.

'*Blood Walk.*'

Static eyelids.

Maybe the tics meant nothing, and I'd fooled myself into allowing a random neurological spark to take on meaning.

Delusions were everywhere . . .

Knowing this might be my last shot with Peake, I decided to keep going. Keep it simple.

Moving close enough to whisper in his ear. 'Dr Argent. Claire Argent.'

The eyelids jumped spasmodically and I retreated with a pounding heart.

He froze. No more TD for several seconds.

The eyes opened, revealing a sliver of gray white.

Looking at me. Seeing me? I wasn't sure.

They closed.

'Dr Argent cared,' I said.

No eye movement – but the cords of his neck tightened; he craned toward me. Again, I drew back involuntarily.

Unable to see me but turning toward me, and I couldn't help feeling he was . . . engaging me. His mouth gaped wider. No tongue visible, and now he was making a gagging sound, as if choking on it. Suddenly, his head thrust forward, a snake darting, the eyelids fluttering once again, wildly.

I stared in fascinated horror as he tilted his head upward, neck stretched so tight it seemed to elongate impossibly. What little mandible he had pointed up at the ceiling.

I took another step backward. His arms began climbing. Slowly. Painfully.

His eyes opened. Remained open. Wide, very wide. Fixed on the ceiling.

As if heaven resided in the plaster . . . as if he were *praying* to something.

He gurgled, gagged some more. How far had he retracted the slug of muscle into his gullet?

His arms rose higher. Supplication . . .

He coughed, made no sound. The neck rolls resumed, more frantic than ever, epileptically rapid. More gagging. His sunken chest heaved. I thought of Denton Argent, dead in his cell, brain burned out from seizing, and wondered if I should do something.

But Peake seemed to be breathing fine. Not a seizure. New pattern of movement.

He began rocking faster. His scrawny buttocks lifted from the mattress as he thrust his chest upward.

Offering himself.

His right hand sank to his mouth. Four fingers jammed inside.

He withdrew them and the tongue appeared – yanked free – flapped like a fish on deck, curled, hovered . . .

Return of the initial TD sequence: Thrust, curl, hover, retract. But his rear remained inches above the bed, feet barely touching the ground. Unnatural – it had to strain – did he even *feel* pain?

Then, suddenly, it was over, and his head had lowered to its usual slump, his arms were back in the bedcovers, and the beat went on . . .

One TD, two TD's . . .

I sat there with him for five more minutes, whispering, coaxing, to no effect.

Now Claire's name left him silent as paint. Maybe a new approach would startle him into another outburst.

'The Beatty brothers,' I said. 'Ellroy. Leroy.'

Zero.

'Choo choo bang bang.'

Nothing.

'One with a gun, one run over by a train.'

Deaf, blind, mute.

Still, Claire's name had stimulated him. I needed more time with him, knew I wouldn't get much.

Keep going.

One TD, two . . .

I whispered: 'The Ardullos.'

No change.

'The Ardullos – Scott Ardullo, Terri—' Yes, yes, yes there it was: The eyelid tic, faster than before, much faster, a churning of the lids as if the eyeballs were rotating at jet speed.

'Terri and Scott Ardullo,' I said.

The eyes opened. Alive now.

Fixed on mine.

Awake.

Clear intent. To do what?

He stared at me. Didn't move at all.

Paying close attention? To me.

Success, but I felt as if a scorpion were cakewalking along my spine.

I checked his hands. *Those* hands. Both knotted in the sheets.

Keep a look out for sudden movement.

'Scott and Terri Ardullo,' I said.

The stare.

'Scott and Terri. Brittany and Justin.'

The stare.

'Brittany and Justin.'

He blinked. Once, twice, six times, twenty, forty – eyelid convulsions, which wouldn't – or couldn't – cease.

Metronomic, hypnotic. I felt myself being drawn in. *Avoid that, watch his hands . . .*

His arms rose again. Fear stabbed me and I stood up quickly, backed away.

He didn't seem to notice.

Stood, himself.

Unsteadily, but managing to remain upright. Stronger than he'd appeared out in the hallway, in Heidi's grasp.

Still staring. Hot stare. Hands curling slowly into fists.

Straightening his spine.

Stepping toward me.

OK, you've done it, Delaware. Success!

He moved another step closer. I braced myself, plotted my defense. How much damage could he do, unarmed, so thin, so feeble?

Another step. His arms reached out, inviting embrace.

I retreated toward the door.

His mouth opened, contorted – no tongue-thrusts, just the excruciating labor of the lipless orifice struggling to change form, fighting to talk or scream . . . working so hard, working working—

Suddenly, a shrill, dry sound escaped. Soft, wispy, echoing – soft, but it pounded my ears—

His arms began to climb again, very slowly. When they were parallel with his shoulders, they flapped. Birdlike. Not a bird of prey, something thin, deliberate, delicate – a crane.

Without warning, he turned his back on me and hobbled – still flapping, miming flight – to the far corner of the room.

Pressing his back to the wall, keeping the arms stretched. Head tilted to the right.

Above him, the metal restraint hooks embedded in the wall hovered like warnings.

Eyes still open – wide open – *stretched* open; I could see wet pink borders all around. *Wet* eyes. Tears welling, overflowing, streaming down sunken cheeks.

His left leg crossed over its mate so that he was standing on one leg.

More avian posturing – no, no, something else—

Posing.

Unmistakable pose.

His body had formed a cross.

Crucifixion on an unseen scaffold.

Tears flooded his face. Uncontrollable, silent sobs, brutally paroxysmic, each gush seizing ownership of his fragile body and shaking it like a wet kitten.

Weeping Jesus.

29

HE STAYED that way, just stayed that way.

How long had I been in there? Surely Dollard, hostile and impatient, would be returning soon and ordering me out.

Five minutes later, it hadn't happened.

Peake remained against the wall. The tears had slowed, but they hadn't stopped.

The stink had returned. My skin itched. Senses returning, heightening. I wanted out.

Knocking on the brown steel door produced only a feeble thump. Could it be heard out in the hall? No sounds from the outside made their way inside the cell. I tried the hatch. Locked. Released only from the outside. The door hatch opened from the outside. Sensory deprivation. What did that do to already damaged minds?

Another knock, louder. Nothing.

Peake stayed frozen in the cruciform pose, pinioned by invisible spikes.

The names of his victims had loosened his tears. Remorse or self-pity?

Or something I could never hope to understand?

I thought of him entering the Ardullo kitchen, spotting his

mother, the strength it had taken to saw through the cervical spine . . . Upstairs, swinging Scott Ardullo's baseball bat.

The children . . .

Their names had triggered the Jesus pose.

Martyr pose.

No remorse at all?

Seeing himself as a *victim*?

Suddenly, the absurdity and futility of what I was doing hit me – trying to pry information from a diseased mind that smoothly morphed sin and salvation. What use could this be to anyone?

Had Claire prodded Peake the same way? Died, somehow, because of her curiosity?

The narrow room started to close in on me. I was up against the door, couldn't get far enough away from the white, dangling creature.

Just a trickle of tears, now.

Crying for himself.

Monster.

Serene in his suffering.

His head rotated very slowly. Lifted a bit. Faced me. Something surfaced in his eyes that I hadn't seen before.

Sharpness. Clarity of purpose.

He nodded. Knowingly. As if the two of us shared something.

I pressed my back against the door.

The space opened behind me and I tumbled back.

Heidi said, 'Sorry! I should've opened the hatch and warned you, first.'

I regained my balance, took a breath, smiled, tried to look composed. Milo watched me, along with Dollard and the trio of doctors – Aldrich, Steenburg, and Swenson. All in sport shirts, as if they'd just gotten in from the golf course. Nothing playful on their faces.

Heidi started to close the door, looked into the room, went pale. 'What's he doing? What's going on?'

The others rushed over and stared. Peake had returned to the full Jesus pose, head cocked to the right. But no tears.

I said, 'He got up a few minutes ago, positioned himself that way.'

Aldrich said, 'My, my . . . Has he done this before, Heidi?'

'No. Never. He never gets off the bed.' She sounded scared. 'Dr Delaware, you're saying he actually moved on his own?'

'Yes.'

Steenburg and Swenson looked at each other. Aldrich said, 'Interesting.' The gravity of his tone bordered on comical. Trying to assume authority on a case he knew nothing about.

Frank Dollard said, 'What'd you say to him to get him that way?'

'Nothing,' I said.

'You didn't talk to him?'

Milo said, 'What's the big deal? He used to think he was a vegetable, now he's evolved into Jesus.'

Dollard and doctors glared at him.

'Psychosis is a disease,' said Aldrich. 'It's unseemly to ridicule.'

'Sorry,' said Milo.

Swenson said, 'Has he ever talked about religious themes, Heidi?'

'No. That's what I'm trying to tell you. He doesn't talk much, period.'

Swenson turned contemplative, laced his hands over his belt buckle. 'I see . . . So it's something altogether new.'

Dollard jutted his head in my direction. 'You'd better tell us what you were talking to him about. We need to know, in case he starts acting out.'

Aldrich said, 'Is there some problem, Frank?'

'These people are a problem, Dr Aldrich. They keep coming in here, disrupting, going at Peake. Mr Swig authorized only fifteen minutes with the SDL group, no time with Peake.' He pointed through the door. 'Look at that. Guy like that, who knows what could happen? And for what? He couldn'ta had anything to do with Dr Argent. I told 'em that, you told 'em that, Mr Swig told 'em that—'

Aldrich turned to Milo. 'What *is* your purpose here, Officer?'

'Investigating Dr Argent's murder.'

Aldrich shook his head. 'That's not an answer. Why are you questioning *Peake*?'

'He said something that might have predicted Dr Argent's murder, Doctor.'

'Predicted? What in the world are you talking about?'

Milo told him.

'"In a box,"' said Aldrich. He faced Heidi. Steenburg and Swenson did the same. 'When did he *say* this to you?'

'The day before it happened.'

'An oracle?' said Steenburg. 'Oh, please. And now he's Jesus – am I the only one who sees a trend toward irrelevance?'

Swenson said, 'At least it's original. Relatively, that is. We don't get a lot of Jesuses anymore.' He smiled. 'Plenty of Elvises but not that many Jesuses. Maybe it's the godless state of our culture.'

No one else seemed amused.

Swenson wouldn't give up. 'We can always do what Milton Erickson did with his Jesuses – give him carpenter's tools and have him fix something.'

Aldrich scowled and Swenson looked the other way.

'Officer,' said Aldrich, 'let me get this clear: On the basis of this supposed . . . utterance, you're back here?'

'It's an unsolved homicide, Dr Aldrich.'

'Even so . . .' Aldrich moved closer to the doorway and peered inside. Peake hadn't budged. He closed the door.

Dollard said, 'They caused a ruckus in SDL, too. Herman Randall's all worked up, shouting Nazi stuff in his room. We might think of upping his meds.'

'Might we?' said Aldrich. He turned to Heidi. 'How about you and I meeting after lunch to review Mr Peake's file. Make sure what we're seeing in there isn't some kind of regression.'

'I'd think just the opposite,' I said. 'He's showing more mobility and affective response.'

'Affective response?'

'He was crying, Dr Aldrich.'

Aldrich took another look inside. 'Well, he's not crying

now. Just hanging there looking pretty regressed. Looks like catalepsy to me.'

I said, 'Is there any chance of reducing his meds?'

Aldrich's eyes bugged. 'Why in the world would we do *that*?'

'It might loosen him up verbally.'

'Loosen him up,' said Swenson. 'Just what we need, a loose Jesus.'

A couple of figures in khaki had drifted out of the TV room. The inmates stared at us, began heading our way. Swenson and Steenburg stepped forward. The men turned, reversed direction, collected near the door to the TV room, returned inside.

Aldrich said, 'Thank you for your opinion, Doctor. However, you and Officer Sturgis must leave immediately. No further contact with Mr Peake or any other patients until cleared by myself or Mr Swig.' To Steenburg and Swenson: 'We'd better get moving. The reservation's at one.'

Crossing the yard, Dollard walked even farther ahead. Big Chet was on the yard and he started to come over, gesticulating and laughing, tugging at his hair like a toddler.

Dollard's palm shot out. 'Stay back!'

The giant halted, pouted, yanked a clump of hair out of his head. The yellow filaments floated to the ground like dandelion petals.

His expression said, *Look what you made me do*.

'Idiot,' Dollard growled.

Chet's eyes slitted.

Dollard waved and two techs jogged over from across the yard. Chet saw them, froze, finally skulked away. Four steps later, he stopped, looked at us over his shoulder.

'Mark my words,' he bellowed. 'Cherchez la femme Champs Elysées!'

Dollard threw the gate open, slammed it after us, left without a word.

As we waited to get Milo's gun and my knife, I said, 'Something sure yanked his shorts.'

'Makes you wonder, doesn't it?' he said. The moment we got in the Seville, he was on the cell phone, asking for the number of the Hemet police department. I let the car idle as he talked. The car seat was a griddle and I cranked the air-conditioning to an arctic blast. Milo got transferred half a dozen times, maintained collegial cheer through every step, but he looked as if he'd swallowed something slimy. The air inside the car cooled, hit my face, turned my sweat icy. Milo was drenched.

He hung up. 'Finally got a supervisor who'd talk. Heidi was right. Dollard was a major-league goldbrick: Ignored calls in his zone, took unauthorized leaves, put in for unjustified overtime. They couldn't prove anything serious enough to prosecute him – probably didn't want to. Easier just to ask him to leave.'

'How long ago was this?'

'Four years ago. He went straight to Starkweather. Supervisor made a crack about nutcases being perfect for Frank, no one to complain when he slacked off.'

'Swig likes him,' I said. 'Tells you something about Swig.'

'High standards, all around.'

I drove out of the parking lot. Convection waves rose from the asphalt.

'What *did* you do to get Peake to play Jesus in the school play?'

'Mentioned the Ardullos' names. After I got a response to Claire's name – eye tics, tensing up. When I whispered Brittany's and Justin's names into his ear he stood up, went to the wall, assumed the pose. I'd been thinking of him as lethargic, stuporous, but he can move fast when he wants to. If he'd jumped me, I'd have been unprepared.'

'So he's *not* a total veg. Maybe he's a sneaky bastard, playing all of us. Makes sense when you think about how he walked in on his mother. She's sitting there coring apples, he gets behind her, she has no idea what he's going to do.'

'He surprised the Ardullos, too,' I said. 'Sheriff Haas said they left their doors unlocked.'

'Everyone's nightmare. Right out of a splatter flick.'

The eucalyptus forest appeared, a big gray bear split by a yawning mouth of road.

'So,' he said, 'was he crying real tears?'

'Copiously. But I'm not sure it was remorse. When he turned and stared at me, I started to feel something else: Self-pity. The Jesus pose fits that, too. As if he sees himself as a martyr.'

'Sick bastard,' he said.

'Or maybe,' I said, 'hearing the kids' names evoked an overpowering memory. Recall of not acting alone. Of taking the rap for something the Crimmins brothers put him up to. Maybe he communicated that to Claire. I didn't see anything close to speech, but with a lowered dosage . . .'

He cooled his hands on the air-conditioning vent. 'Why do you think Dollard turned so hostile?'

'Antsy about our return visit. Something to hide.'

Milo didn't answer. We exited the forest and summer light whitened the windshield. The trees shimmered as they broiled. I could sense the heat trying to claw its way in.

'What about some kind of hospital scam?' I said. 'Financial mismanagement. Or trafficking in prescription drugs. Claire found out about it and that's what put her in jeopardy. Maybe Peake knew, too. Learned someone was going to hurt Claire and the "prophecy" was his way of warning her.'

We were free of the hospital grounds, heading toward the sludge yards and the freight barns. I wondered where the rear forest behind the annexes led, was unable to see the tall dark trees from here.

'How would Peake find out?' he said.

'Loose lips. Everyone assumes he's vegetative, can't process. I saw enough today to convince me that's not true. If Dollard was involved in something illegal, he might've said or done something that Peake noticed.'

'That careless?'

'How many cases have you closed because someone was careless?'

'Peake warns Claire,' he said. 'Now he's a hero?'

'Maybe on some level, he bonded with Claire. Appreciated the attention Claire was giving him.'

'Then why warn Heidi?'

'Claire wasn't at work that day, so Peake did the next best thing: Told her assistant. Not a clear message, because he was struggling to talk through the Thorazine haze and his neurological problems.'

'Everyone treats Peake like he's wallpaper, but he's sucking up information.'

'He's *functioned* like wallpaper for sixteen years. It wouldn't be hard to get complacent. That could be why Dollard was so upset when he saw Peake playing Jesus. Now *he* realizes Peake's capable of more. He's nervous, doesn't want us back there. Look how he bad-mouthed us to Aldrich. And Aldrich played into it. Or Aldrich is part of it.'

'Big-time staff racketeering?'

'Like you said, it's not a tight ship. Either way, Dollard just got what he wanted. We won't get through those gates again without a court order.'

'"Bad eyes in a box,"' he said. 'That has Peake knowing someone is gonna gouge Claire's eyes and stash her somewhere closed. I might be able to buy Dollard blabbing to some compadre in general terms about getting Claire, but I *can't* see him laying it out in detail.'

I had no answer for that. He pulled out his pad, made some notes, closed his eyes, seemed to doze. We reached the freeway. I floored the Seville, crossed over to the fast lane, sped to the interchange, headed west on the 10, past the old brick buildings on the fringes of downtown, surprise survivors of the big quake. A huge blowup of a movie poster had been painted on one of them. Some hypertrophied bionic cop flashing fire from gun-barrel knuckles. If only it were that easy.

Milo said, 'Dollard a scamster . . . our Mr Wark, his partner. But what about Richard, the Beatty twins? How do they connect to any hospital racket?'

'Don't know,' I said. 'But if Wark *is* Derrick Crimmins, his working there makes sense on another level: He was drawn by Peake's presence, just as Claire was. Because Peake's rampage made a major impression on him. And if my guess about his being Peake's drug source sixteen years ago is right, that would fit with the racket being a dope thing. Dollard smuggles out pharmaceuticals, hands them over to Wark, who sells them on the street. Wark had enough money in that Bank of America account to cover the gear rental when Vito Bonner called to validate the check. So he's got some sort of cash source. Being the outside man would also make Wark the perfect choice for ambushing and murdering Claire. Dollard alerts Wark, gives Wark Claire's address from personnel files; Wark stalks her, kills her in West LA, dumps her in her own car. No reason for anyone ever to connect it to Starkweather. What's the mantra everyone there keeps reciting? "It couldn't be related to her work." I looked around the hospital today to see if anyone fit Wark's physical description. The only one tall and thin enough is Aldrich, but he's too old, and I doubt Wark would masquerade as a doctor – too risky. But there are over a hundred people on staff and we've run into maybe twenty.'

'And we get no access to the personnel records.' Milo

punched the dashboard lightly. Keeping his arm stiff; I knew he wanted to hit much harder.

'How about approaching it another way?' I said. 'Let's assume Peake's presence is what attracted Wark to Starkweather initially. But he also needed money, and the job had to be something he could qualify for quickly. That would eliminate anything with extensive training – doctor, psychologist, nurse, pharmacist – and leaves lower-level positions: Cooks, custodians, gardeners, psych techs. A would-be producer down on his luck might see the first three as beneath him. Psychiatric technician, on the other hand, has some cachet, could be construed as almost-a-doctor. And psych techs are licensed by the state. The medical board keeps a roster.'

Milo's smile spread very slowly. 'Worth a try.'

The movie-poster mural flashed in my head. 'Another reason for Wark to take the job: If he sees himself as some dark-side cinema auteur, what better place to dredge up bloody plots than Starkweather? *That* could explain Richard and the Beatty twins: They're part of Wark's film game.'

'The snuff extravaganza, again – we're all over the place with this.'

'Like you said, drill a few wells . . .'

He massaged his temples. 'OK, OK, enough talk, I need to *do* something. I put calls in to Miami and Pimm, Nevada, this morning. When we get back, I'll see if anyone called. And the psych board for that tech list. Though for it to be of any use, Wark would've had to register under that name or Crimmins, or something close.' He rubbed his face. 'Long shots.'

'Better than nothing,' I said.

'Sometimes I wonder.'

30

WE WERE back in the detectives' room by two P.M. Friday. Most of the desks were empty. Del Hardy's was next to Milo's, and Milo waved me to Del's chair. Del had partnered with Milo years ago – an early alliance cemented by mutual respect and shared alienation. Del had been one of the first black D's to get an assignment west of La Brea. Now he had plenty of black colleagues, but Milo remained a one-man show. Maybe that had wedged them apart, or perhaps it was Del's second wife, a woman with strong views on just about everything. Milo never talked about it.

I used Del's phone to call the state psychiatric board, got put on hold electronically. Milo's desktop was clear except for a message slip taped to the metal. He peeled it loose and read it, and his eyebrows arched.

'Callback from Orlando, Florida. Some guy named Castro "happy to talk about Derrick Crimmins."'

He punched numbers, loosened his tie, sat down. A recorded voice of indeterminate gender told me my call would be accepted as soon as an operator was free. I watched Milo's shoulders bunch as his call came through.

'Detective Sturgis for Detective Castro,' he said. 'Oh, hi. Thanks for calling back . . . Really? Well that's interesting

– listen, could I put someone else on the line? Our psychological consultant . . . Yeah, occasionally we do . . . Yeah, it's been helpful.'

Placing a hand over the mouthpiece, he said, 'Hang up and punch my extension number.'

The recorded voice broke in, thanking me for my patience. I cut it off, made the conference adjustment, introduced myself.

'George Castro,' said a thick voice on the other end. 'We all set now?'

'Yeah,' said Milo. 'Dr Delaware, Detective Castro was just saying he's been waiting for someone to call him about Derrick Crimmins.'

'Waiting a long time,' said Castro. 'This is like Christmas in the summer. Tell the truth, I gave up, figured he might be dead.'

'Why's that?'

'Because his name never showed up in any crime list I could find, but bad guys don't just give up. And that kid was real bad. Got away with multiple murder.'

'His parents,' said Milo.

'You got it,' said Castro. 'Him and his brother – Cliff. Cliff was older, but Derrick was smarter. What a pair. Kind of a pre-Menendez Menendez, only the Crimminses didn't even come close to getting arrested. It was my curse. It's been jammed in my craw ever since. Tell me what you have him on, the little bastard.'

'Nothing definite,' said Milo. 'Can't even find him. So far it looks like scamming and homicide.'

'Well, that's our boy, to a T. I got to tell you, this really takes me back. I was new to Miami Beach. Did a year on Bunco, then Homicide. Moved down the year before from Brooklyn for the sun, never thought about what being named Castro would mean in Miami.' He stopped, as if waiting for laughter. 'And I'm Puerto Rican, not Cuban. Anyway, I worked some pretty ugly stuff up north. Bed-Stuy, Crown Heights, East New York. But none of the scum I met ever bothered me as much as those brothers. Killing your own folks for dough – dad and stepmother, actually. It was a Coast Guard case, because the boat blew up in the water – half a mile offshore – but we did the land work. No doubt at all about it being dirty. Someone rigged a pipe bomb to the fuel tank, and the whole thing turned into sawdust. Three people died, actually. Old man Crimmins, his wife, and some Cuban kid they'd hired to captain. They were out marlin fishing. Boom. Shreds of bone, and that's about it.'

'Did the Crimmins boys build the bombs?'

'Doubtful. We had some theories about that – down here there's quite a few characters with explosives experience floating around. Mobbed-up types, druggies, Marielitos. Alibis narrowed it down to half a dozen scrotes; we hauled 'em all in, but no one talked. And no one's bank account had suddenly gotten fat. I had my eye on two of them in specific – pair of Dominicans with a dry-cleaning joint as cover. They'd been busted before on a nearly identical explosion in a clothing warehouse, weaseled out on lack of evidence. We pulled in every informant we had, couldn't shake a rumor loose. That tells me the payoff was big bucks.'

'The boys had money?'

'Big allowances – fifty grand a year, each. Back then you

could have someone taken out for a hundred bucks. One to five thousand would get you someone competent, fifteen a stone pro. We scoured the brothers' bank accounts, found some nice-sized cash withdrawals during the weeks before the explosion, but we couldn't make anything outta that because that's the way they lived in general: The old man gave 'em the fifty at the beginning of the year, they took out play money as they needed it – four, five a month. Spent every penny. So there was no change in pattern. They used a smart-mouthed lawyer, he didn't give us an extra syllable.'

'You focused on them right away 'cause of the inheritance angle?'

'You bet,' said Castro. 'First commandment, right? Follow the honey trail. With the stepmother gone, they were the old man's sole heirs, figured to get millions. Also, their alibis were too damn perfect: Both out of town, they made sure to let us know that first thing. It was like one minute of phony grief, then, "Oh, by the way, we were in Tampa, riding motorcycles." Showing us some admission ticket to a race they'd been in – all ready with it. And smirking – rubbing my face in it. Because we'd had contact before. Back when I was on Bunco. Which is the third thing that nailed them in my mind: They'd been bad boys before. Fraud. Like I said, murder and cons, perfect fit.'

'What was the con?' said Milo.

'Nothing brilliant. They cruised the beach, picked up senile old people, drove them out to some swampland that they pitched as vacation lots. Then they'd head over to the marks' bank, wait while the marks withdrew cash for a down payment, hand them some bullshit deed of trust, and split.

They preyed on real deteriorated old folk. Most of the time, the marks didn't even know they'd been fleeced. And the withdrawals weren't huge – five, six hundred bucks – so the banks didn't notice. It ended when some old lady's son got wind of it – local surgeon. He waited with his mom on the beach until she pointed out Derrick.'

'They serve time?'

'Nah,' said Castro angrily. 'Never even got charged. Because Daddy hired a lawyer – the same smart-mouth who shielded them on the boat thing. The weakness was the identification angle. The lawyer said he'd have fun with the old people on the stand – show they were too demented to be reliable witnesses. The DA didn't want to risk it. A couple of bank tellers thought they could make an ID but they weren't sure. Because Derrick and Cliff wore disguises – wigs, fake mustaches, glasses. Stupid stuff, amateurish, they coulda dressed up like Fidel for all the marks noticed. We couldn't trace the phony deeds back to them, either – primitive shit, mimeographed jobs. The whole thing was so low-level it woulda been funny if it hadn't been so cruel. In the end, the old man made restitution, case closed.'

'How much restitution?'

'I think it was six, seven thou. Not a major con, but remember, we're talking a one-month period and two kids in their early twenties. That's what I found scary: So young and so cold. My experience was you got plenty violent kids at any age, but it usually takes a few years to season a frosty con like that. It wasn't like they were so bright – neither of them went to college, both just bummed around on the beach. Cliff was actually kind of a cabbage-head. But they had that con edge. They were lucky, too. One good ID and they mighta gone down – at least probation.'

He laughed again. 'Lucky bastards. The excuse they gave was the stupidest thing of all: Big misunderstanding, the old folk were too mentally disturbed to know the difference between reality and fantasy, the land thing was never supposed to be taken seriously. It was all part of some movie they were doing on con games. They even showed us the outline of a script. One page of bullshit – scam games and hot cars – something like *The Sting* meets *Cannonball Run*. They claimed they were gonna sell it to Hollywood.' He laughed again. 'So they actually got out there, huh?'

'Derrick made it,' said Milo. 'Cliff died a few years after Daddy and Stepmom. Motocross accident near Reno.'

'Oh boy,' said Castro. 'Interesting.'

'Very.'

'Like I told you, cold. I always saw Derrick as the idea guy. Cliff was a party dude. Better-looking than Derrick, nice tan, expert water-skier, pussy hound. And, yeah, motorcycles, too. He had a bunch of them. A collection. They both did. So Derrick might very well know how to rig one . . . I figured if anyone cracked, it'd be Cliff, my plan was to split them apart, see if I could play one against the other. But the lawyer wouldn't let me get close. I'll never forget the last time I talked to them. I'm asking questions, faking being civil, and those two are looking at their lawyer and he's telling me they don't have to answer and they're smirking. Finally, I leave, and Derrick makes a point of walking me to the door. Big old house, tons of furniture, and he and his brother are gonna get it all. Then he smiles at me, again. Like, "*I* know, *you* know, fuck you, Charlie." The only comfort I got out of it was they didn't get as rich as they thought they would.'

'How much they get?' said Milo.

'Eighty grand each, mostly from the sale of the house. The place was heavily mortgaged, and by the time they paid estate taxes, commission, all that good stuff, there wasn't much left. They were figuring the old man was sitting on big-time cash, but turns out he'd made some bad investments – land deals, as a matter of fact – which is funny, don't you think? Leveraged up the YY. He'd even cashed in his insurance policies as collateral for some loans. The only other assets were the furniture, pair of three-year-old Caddies, golf clubs and a golf cart, and the stepmom's jewelry, half of which turned out to be costume and the rest new stuff, which doesn't maintain its value once you take it out of the store. The other funny thing was, the boat *hadn't* been borrowed on. Apparently the old man loved it, kept up with his slip fees and maintenance. Nice-looking thing, from the pictures. The old man had stuffed fish all over the house.' He laughed louder. 'Fifty grand worth of boat, minimum, free and clear, and that they blew up. So tell me more about what Derrick did out there.'

Milo kept it sketchy.

'Whoa,' said Castro. 'Creepy murder, that's a whole new level . . . Makes sense, I guess. Keep getting away with it, you start thinking you're God.'

'The thing that interests me,' said Milo, 'is from what we can tell, Derrick isn't living well. No car registrations, no address in any swank neighborhood that we can find, and he may have taken a low-paying job under an alias. So he must not have invested that eighty grand.'

'He wouldn't. He'd plow right through it, just like any other sociopath.'

'I can't find any Social Security for him except when he lived in Miami,' said Milo. 'So no jobs under his own name. Any idea what he's been doing all these years?'

'Nah,' said Castro. 'He left town nine or ten months after the murder, they both did, left no trail. The case was officially open, but no one was really working on it. In my spare time, I kept following the money, drove by some clubs they hung out at. Then one day a source at County Records called me – I'd asked to be told when the estate was settled. That's when I learned how little they were gonna get. The address on the transfer was in Utah. Park City. I traced it. POB. It was winter by then. I figured the little fucks went skiing with the death money.'

'Scams, murder, movies,' I said. 'No known address. Need a closer fit?'

Milo shook his head. I felt sparked by what we'd just learned but he seemed dejected.

'What is it?'

'First Derrick offs his parents, then his brother, probably for Cliff's share of the eighty grand. This is professional evil.'

'What was left of Cliff's share,' I said. 'Like Castro said, they probably chewed right through it. Maybe Derrick chewed faster.'

'Derrick the dominator . . . arrogant, just like you've been saying.'

'Good criminal self-esteem,' I said. 'And why not? He does bad things and gets away clean. And maybe he had practice with family elimination.'

'The Ardullos,' he said. 'Spurring Peake on – well, your guesses have been pretty right on, haven't they?'

'Aw shucks,' I said. 'Now all we need to do is find Derrick. Let me get back on the line with the psychiatric board.'

'Sure. I'll hit Pimm again. And Park City. Maybe Derrick tried a land scam there, too.'

'If you want, I'll give you some other possibilities.'

'What?'

'Aspen, Telluride, Vegas, Tahoe. This is a party boy. He goes where the fun is.'

The dejected look returned. 'Those kinds of record checks could take weeks,' he said. 'The guy's right here, polluting *my* city, and I can't put a finger on him.'

It took several calls to learn that psychiatric tech licenses were granted for periods ranging from thirteen to twenty-four months. Individual names could be verified, but sending the entire list was unheard-of. Finally, I found a supervisor willing to fax the roster. Another twenty minutes passed before paper began spooling out of the sorry-looking machine across the room.

I read as it unraveled. Page after page of names, no Crimmins, no Wark.

Another alias?

Griffith D. Wark. Scrambling a film maestro. Manipulative, pretentious, arrogant. And strangely child-like – playing pretend games.

Seeing himself as a major Hollywood player. The fact that he'd never produced anything was a nasty bit of potential dissonance, but the same could be said of so many coutured reptiles occupying tables at Spago.

Psychopaths could deal with dissonance.

Psychopaths had low levels of anxiety.

Besides, there were other types of productions.

Blood Walk.

Bad eyes in a box.

Something else about human snakes: They lacked emotional depth, faked humanity. Craved repetition. *Patterns.*

So maybe Wark had co-opted other major directors. I was no film expert but several names came to mind: Alfred Hitchcock, Orson Welles, John Huston, John Ford, Frank Capra . . . I scanned the tech list. None of the above.

But Wark was D. W. Griffith's *middle* name. What was Hitchcock's?

I called the research library at the U, asked for the reference desk, and explained what I needed. The librarian must have been puzzled, but odd requests are their business and, God bless her, she didn't argue.

Five minutes later I had what I needed: Alfred Joseph Hitchcock. John no middle name Huston. Frank NMN Capra. George Orson Welles. John NMN Ford; real name, Sean Aloysius O'Feeney.

Thanking her, I turned back to the tech list. No Capras, four Fords, one Hitchcock, no Hustons, no O'Feeneys . . .

no obviously cute manipulations of Hitchcock or Ford . . . Then I saw it.

G. W. Orson.

Co-opting a genius.

Delusions were *everywhere*.

31

'CITIZEN CREEP,' said Milo, looking at the circled name.

'G. W. Orson got licensed,' I said. 'That's about all I could get except for the address he put on his application form.'

He studied the address slip. 'South Shenandoah Street . . . around Eighteenth. West LA territory . . . only a few blocks from the shopping center where Claire was dumped.'

'The center's far from Claire's house, so why would she shop there? Unless she went with someone else.'

'Crimmins? They had a relationship?'

'Why not?' I said. 'Let's assume Orson – and Wark – are both Crimmins aliases. We have no employment records yet, but Crimmins is a psych tech, so it's not much of a leap to assume he works at Starkweather, or did in the past. He ran into Claire. Something developed. Because they had two common interests: The movies and Ardis Peake. When Claire told Crimmins she'd picked Peake as a project, he decided to find out more. When Crimmins learned Claire was uncovering information potentially threatening to him, he decided to cast her in *Blood Walk*.'

'Kills her, films her, dumps her,' he said. 'It holds together logically; now all I have to do is prove it. I canvassed the shopping center, showed her picture to every clerk who'd been working the day she was killed. No one remembered seeing her, alone or with anyone else. That doesn't mean much, it's a huge place, and if I can get a picture of Crimmins, I'll go back. But maybe we can get a look at him in person.' He waved the address slip. 'This helps big-time. First let's see if he registered his 'Vette.'

The call to DMV left him shaking his head. 'No G. W. Orson cars anywhere in the state.'

'Lives in LA, but no legal car,' I said. 'That alone tells us he's dirty. Try another scrambled director's name.'

'Later,' he said, pocketing the address. 'This is something real. Let's go for it.'

The block was quiet, intermittently treed, filled with plain-wrap, single-story houses set on vest-pocket lots that ranged from compulsively tended to ragged. Birds chirped, dogs barked. A man in an undershirt pushed a lawn mower in slo-mo. A dark-skinned woman strolling a baby looked up as we passed. Apprehension, then relief; the unmarked was anything but inconspicuous.

Years ago, the neighborhood had been ravaged by crime and white flight. Rising real estate prices had reversed some of that, and the result was a mixed-race district that resonated with tense, tentative pride.

The place G. W. Orson had called home was a pale green Spanish bungalow with a neatly edged lawn and no other landscaping. A FOR LEASE sign was staked dead center in the grass. In the driveway was a late-model Oldsmobile Cutlass. Milo drove halfway down the block and ran the plates. 'TBL Properties, address on Wilshire near La Brea.'

He U-turned, parked in front of the green house. A stunted old magnolia tree planted in the parkway next door cast some shade upon the Olds. Nailed to the trunk was a poster. Cloudy picture of a dog with some Rottweiler in it. Eager canine grin. 'Have You Seen Buddy?' over a phone number and a typed message: Buddy had been missing for a week and needed daily thyroid medication. Finding him would bring a hundred-dollar reward. For no reason I could think of, Buddy looked strangely familiar. Everything was starting to remind me of something.

We walked to the front of the green house, stepping around a low, chipped stucco wall that created a small patio. The front door was glossy and sharp-smelling – fresh varnish. White curtains blocked the front window. Shiny brass door knocker. Milo lifted it and let it drop.

Footsteps. An Asian man opened the door. Sixties, angular, and tanned, he wore a beige work shirt, sleeves rolled to the elbows, matching cotton pants, white sneakers. Creepily close to Starkweather inmate duds. I felt my hands ball and forced them to loosen.

'Yes?' His hair was sparse and white, his eyes a pair of surgical incisions. In one hand was a crumpled gray rag.

Milo flashed the badge. 'We're here about George Orson.'

'Him.' Weary smile. 'No surprise. Come on in.'

We followed him into a small, empty living room. Next door was a kitchen, also empty, except for a six-pack of paper towel rolls on the brown tile counter. A mop and a broom were propped in a corner, looking like exhausted marathon dancers. The house echoed of vacancy, but stale odors – cooked meat, must, tobacco – lingered, battling for dominance with soap, ammonia, varnish from the door.

Vacant, but more lived-in than Claire's place. The man held out his hand. 'Len Itatani.'

'You work for the owner, sir?' said Milo.

Itatani smiled. 'I am the owner.' He produced a couple of business cards.

TBL Properties, Inc.
LEONARD J. ITATANI, PRES.

'Named it after my kids. Tom, Beverly, Linda. So what did Orson do?'

'Sounds like you had problems with him, sir,' said Milo.

'Nothing but,' said Itatani. He glanced around the room. 'Sorry there's no place to sit. There's some bottled water, if you're thirsty. Too hot to be cleaning up, but summer's prime rental time and I want to get this place squared away.'

'No thanks,' said Milo. 'What did Orson do?'

Itatani pulled a square of tissue paper from his shirt pocket and dabbed a clear, broad forehead. No moisture on the bronze skin that I'd noticed. 'Orson was a bum. Always late with his rent; then he stopped paying at all. Neighbor complained he was selling drugs, but I don't know about that, there was nothing I could do. She said all kinds of cars would show up at night, be here a short time, and leave. I told her to call the police.'

'Did she?'

'You'd have to ask her.'

'Which neighbor?'

'Right next door.' Itatani pointed south.

Milo's pad was out. 'So you never talked to Orson about selling drugs?'

'I was going to, eventually,' said Itatani. 'What I did try to talk to him about was the rent. Left messages under the door – he never gave me a phone listing, said he hadn't bothered to get one. That should've warned me.' Another swipe at the dry brow. 'Didn't want to scare him off with any drug talk until he paid the rent he owed me. Was this close to posting notice. But he moved out, middle of the night. Stole furniture. I had his first and last and damage deposit in cash, but he trashed more than was covered by the deposit – cigarette burns on the nightstands, cracked tiles in the bathroom, gouges in the wood floors, probably from dragging cameras around.'

'Cameras?'

'Movie cameras – big, heavy stuff. All sorts of stuff in boxes, too. I warned him about the floors; he said he'd be careful.' He grimaced. 'Had to refinish a hundred square feet of oak board, replace some of it totally. I told him no filming in the house, didn't want any funny business.'

'Like what?'

'You know,' said Itatani. 'A guy like that, says he's making movies but he's living here. My first thought was something X-rated. I didn't want that going on here, so I made it clear: This was a residence, not a budget studio. Orson said he had no intention of working here, had some kind of arrangement with one of the studios, he just needed to store some equipment. I never really believed that – you get a studio contract, you don't live here. I had a bad feeling about him from the beginning – no references, he said he'd been freelancing for a while, working on his own projects. When I asked him what kind of projects, he just said short films, changed the subject. But he showed me cash. It was the middle of the year, the place had been vacant for a long time, I figured a bird in the hand.'

'When did he start renting, sir?'

'Eleven months ago,' said Itatani. 'He stayed for six months, stiffed me for the last two.'

'So it's been five months since he left,' said Milo. 'Have you had other tenants since?'

'Sure,' said Itatani. 'First two students, then a hairdresser. Not much better, had to evict them both.'

'Did Orson live alone?'

'Far as I know. I saw him with a couple of women; whether or not he moved them in, I don't know. So what'd he do to get you down here?'

'A few things,' said Milo. 'What did the women look like?'

'One was one of those rock-and-roll types – blond hair, all spiky, lots of makeup. She was here when I showed up to ask about the overdue rent. Said she was a friend of Orson's, he was out on location, she'd give him the message.'

'How old?'

'Twenties, thirties, hard to tell with all that makeup. She wasn't tough or anything – kind of polite, actually. Promised to tell Orson. Nothing happened for a week, I stopped by again but no one was here. I left a note, another week passed, Orson sent me a check. It bounced.'

'Remember what bank it was from?'

'Santa Monica Bank, Pico Boulevard,' said Itatani. 'Closed account, he'd only had it for a week. I came over a third time, looked through the window, saw he still had his stuff here. I could've posted right there, but all that does is cost money for filing. Even if you win in Small Claims, try collecting. So I left more messages. He'd call back, but always late at night when he knew I wasn't in.' He ticked his fingers. '"Sorry, been traveling." "There must be a bank mixup." "I'll get you a cashier's check." By the next month, I'd had it, but he was gone.'

'What about the second woman?' said Milo.

'Her I didn't meet, I just saw her with him. Getting into his car – that's another thing. His car. Yellow Corvette. Flashy. *That* he had money for. The time I saw the second woman was around the same time – five, six months ago. I'd come by to get the rent, no one was home. I left a note, drove away, got halfway up the block, saw Orson's car, turned around. Orson parked and got out. But then he must've seen me, because he got back in and drove off. Fast, we passed each other. I waved but he kept going. She was on the passenger side. Brunette. I'd already met the blonde, remember thinking *He can't pay the rent but he can afford two girlfriends*.'

'You figured the brunette was his girlfriend.'

'She was with him, middle of the day. They were about to go into the house.'

'What else can you tell me about her?'

'I didn't get much of a look at her. Older than the blonde, I think. Nothing unusual. When she passed me, she was looking out the window. Right at me. Not smiling or anything. I remember thinking she looked confused – like why was Orson making a getaway, but . . . I really can't say much about her. Brunette, that's about it.'

'How about a description of Orson?'

'Tall, skinny. Every time I saw him he wore nothing but black. He had these black boots with big heels that made him even taller. And that shaved head – real Hollywood.'

'Shaved head,' said Milo.

'Clean as a cueball,' said Itatani.

'How old?'

'Thirties, maybe forty.'

'Eye color?'

'That I couldn't tell you. He always reminded me of a vulture. Big nose, little eyes – I think they were brown, but I wouldn't swear to it.'

'How old was the brunette in the car?'

Itatani shrugged. 'Like I said, we passed for two seconds.'

'But probably older than the blonde,' said Milo.

'I guess.'

Milo produced Claire's County Hospital staff photo.

Itatani studied the picture, returned it, shaking his head. 'No reason it *couldn't* be her, but that's as much as I can say. Who is she?'

'Possibly an associate of Orson. So you saw the brunette with Orson five, six months ago.'

'Let me think . . . I'd say closer to five. Not long before he moved out.' Itatani dabbed his face again. 'All these questions, he must've done something really bad.'

'Why's that, sir?'

'For you to be spending all this time. I get burglaries at

some of my other properties, robberies, it's all I can do to get the police to come out and write a report. I knew that guy was wrong.'

Milo pressed Itatani for more details without success; then we walked through the house. Two bedrooms, one bath, everything redolent of soap. Fresh paint; new carpeting in the hallway. The replaced floorboards were in the smaller bedroom. Milo rubbed his face. Any physical evidence of Wark's presence had long vanished.

He said, 'Did Orson keep any tools here – power tools?'

'In the garage,' said Itatani. 'He set up a whole shop. He kept more movie stuff in there, too. Lights, cables, all kinds of things.'

'What kind of tools did he have in the shop?'

'The usual,' said Itatani. 'Power drill, hand tools, power saws. He said he sometimes built his own sets.'

The garage was flat-roofed and double-width, taking up a third of the tiny backyard. Outsized for the house.

I remarked on that.

Itatani unlocked the sliding metal door and shoved it up. 'I enlarged it years ago, figured it would make the place easier to rent.'

Inside were walls paneled in cheap fake oak, a cement floor, an open-beam ceiling with a fluorescent fixture dangling from a header. The smell of disinfectant burned my nose.

'You've cleaned this, too,' said Milo.

'First thing I cleaned,' said Itatani. 'The hairdresser

brought cats in. Against the rules – he had a no-pets lease. Litter boxes and those scratch things all over the place. Took days to air out the stink.' He sniffed. 'Finally.'

Milo paced the garage, examined the walls, then the floor. He stopped at the rear left-hand corner, beckoned me over. Itatani came, too.

Faint mocha-colored splotch, amoebic, eight or nine inches square.

Milo knelt and put his face close to the wall, pointed. Specks of the same hue dotted the paneling. Brown on brown, barely visible.

Itatani said, 'Cat pee. I was able to scrub some of it off.'

'What did it look like before you cleaned it?'

'A little darker.'

Milo got up and walked along the back wall very slowly. Stopped a few feet down, wrote in his pad. Another splotch, smaller.

'What?' said Itatani.

Milo didn't answer.

'What?' Itatani repeated. 'Oh – you don't— Oh, no . . .' For the first time, he was sweating.

Milo cell-phoned the crime-scene team, apologized to Itatani for the impending disruption, and asked him to stay clear of the garage. Then he got some yellow tape from the unmarked and stretched it across the driveway.

Itatani said, 'Still looks like cat dirt to me,' and went to sit in his Oldsmobile.

Milo and I walked over to the south-side neighbor. Another Spanish house, bright white. The mat in front of the door said GO AWAY. Very loud classical music pounded through the walls. No response to the doorbell. Several hard knocks finally opened the door two inches, revealing one bright blue eye, a slice of white skin, a smudge of red mouth.

'What?' a cracked voice screeched.

Milo shouted back, 'Police, ma'am!'

'Show me some ID.'

Milo held out the badge. The blue eye moved closer, pupil contracting as it confronted daylight.

'Closer,' the voice demanded.

Milo put the badge right up against the crack. The blue eye blinked. Several seconds passed. The door opened.

The woman was short, skinny, at least eighty, with hair dyed crow-feather black and curled in Marie Antoinette ringlets that reminded me of blood sausages. A face powdered chalky added to the aging-courtesan look. She wore a black silk dressing gown spattered with gold stars, three strings of heavy amber beads around her neck, giant pearl drop earrings. The music in the background was assertive and heavy – Wagner or Bruckner or someone else a goose-stepper would've enjoyed. Cymbals crashed. The woman glared. Behind her was a huge white grand piano piled high with books.

'What do you want?' she screamed over a crescendo. Her voice was as pleasing as grit on glass.

'George Orson,' said Milo. 'Is it possible to turn the music down?'

Cursing under her breath, the woman slammed the door, opened it a minute later. The music was several notches lower, but still loud.

'Orson,' she said. 'Scumbag. What'd he do, kill someone?' Glancing to the left. Itatani had come out of his car and was standing on the lawn of the green house.

'Goddamn absentee landlords. Don't care who they rent to. So what'd that scumbag do?'

'That's what we're trying to find out, ma'am.'

'That's a load of double-talk crap. What'd he *do*?' She slapped her hands against her hips. Silk whistled and the dressing gown parted at her neckline, revealing powdered wattle, a few inches of scrawny white chest, shiny sternal knobs protruding like ivory handles. Her lipstick was the color of arterial blood. 'You want info from me, don't hand me any crap.'

'Mr Orson's suspected in some drug thefts, Mrs—'

'*Ms*,' she said. 'Sinclair. *Ms* Marie Sinclair. Drugs. Big boo-hoo surprise. It's about time you guys caught on. The whole time that lowlife was here there'd be cars in and out, in and out, all hours of the night.'

'Did you ever call the police?'

Marie Sinclair looked ready to hit him. 'Jesus Almighty – only six times. Your so-called officers said they'd drive by. If they did, lot of good it accomplished.'

Milo wrote. 'What else did Orson do to disturb you, Ms Sinclair?'

'Cars in and out, in and out wasn't enough. I'm trying to practice, and the headlights keep shining through the drapes. Right there.' She pointed to her front window, covered with lace.

'Practice what, ma'am?' said Milo.

'Piano. I teach, give recitals.' She flexed ten spidery

white fingers. The nails were a matching red, but clipped short.

'I used to do radio work,' she said. 'Live radio – the old RKO studios. I knew Oscar Levant, what a lunatic – another dope fiend, but a genius. I was the first girl pianist for the Cocoanut Grove, played the Mocambo, did a party at Ira Gershwin's up on Roxbury Drive. Talk about stage fright – George *and* Ira listening. There were giants back then; now it's only mental midgets and—'

'Orson told Mr Itatani he was a film director.'

'Mr Ita*whosis*' – she sneered – 'doesn't give a damn *who* he rents to. After the scumbag moved out, I got stuck with two sloppy kids – real pigs – then a fag cosmetologist. Back when I bought this house—'

'When Orson lived here, did you ever see any filming next door?' said Milo.

'Yeah, he was Cecil B. DeMille – no, never. Just cars, in and out. I'm trying to practice and the damn headlights are glaring through like some kind of—'

'You practice at night, ma'am?'

'So what?' said Marie Sinclair. 'That's against the law?'

'No, ma'am, I was just—'

'Look,' she said. Her hands separated from her hips, clamped down again. 'I'm a night person, as if it's any of your business. Just woke *up*, if it's any of your *business*. Comes from all those years of clubbing.' She stepped onto the porch, advanced on Milo. 'Nighttime's when it comes alive. Morning's for suckers. Morning people should be lined up and shot.'

'So your basic complaint against Orson was all the traffic.'

'*Dope* traffic. Those kinds of lowlifes, what was to stop

someone from pulling out a gun? None of those idiots can shoot straight, you hear about all those colored and Mexican kids getting shot in drive-bys by accident. I could've been sitting in there playing Chopin, and *pow!*'

She squeezed her eyes shut, punched her forehead, jerked her head back. Black ringlets danced. When her eyes opened, they were hotter, brighter.

Milo said, 'Did you ever get a good look at any of Orson's visitors?'

'Visitors. Hah. No, I didn't look. Didn't want to see, didn't want to know. The headlights were bad enough. You guys never did a damn thing about them. And don't tell me to turn the piano around, because it's a seven-foot-long Steinway and it won't fit in the room any other way.'

'How many cars would there be on an average night, Ms Sinclair?'

'Five, six, ten, who knows, I never counted. At least he was gone a lot.'

'How often, ma'am?'

'A lot. Half the time. Maybe more. Thank God for small blessings.'

'Did you ever talk to him directly about the headlights?'

'What?' she screeched. 'And have him pull out a gun? We're talking *scumbag*. That's *your* job. I *called* you. Lot of good it did.'

'Mr Itatani said Orson had a machine shop out in the garage. Did you ever hear sawing or drilling?'

'No,' she said. 'Why? You think he was manufacturing the dope back there? Or cutting it, whatever it is they do to that crap?'

'Anything's possible, ma'am.'

'No, it's not,' she snapped. 'Very *few* things are possible. Oscar Levant will not rise from the dead. That cancer in George Gershwin's genius brain will not— Never mind, why am I wasting my time. No, I never heard *drilling* or *sawing*. I never heard a damn thing, because during the day, when I sleep, I keep the music on – got one of those programmable CD players, six discs that keep repeating. It's the only way I can go to sleep, block out the damn birds, cars, all that daytime crap. It was when I was up that he bothered me. The lights. Trying to get through my scales and the damn headlights are shining right on the keyboard.'

Milo nodded. 'I understand, ma'am.'

'Sure you do,' she said. 'Too late, too little.'

'Anything else you can tell us?'

'That's it. Didn't know I was going to be tested.'

Milo showed her Claire's picture. 'Ever see her with Orson?'

'Nope,' she said. 'She looks like a schoolteacher. Is she the one he killed?

The crime-scene crew arrived ten minutes later. Itatani sat in his Oldsmobile, looking miserable. Marie Sinclair had gone back inside her house, but a few other neighbors had emerged. Milo asked them questions. I followed as he walked up and down the block, knocking on doors. No new revelations. If George Orson had been running a dope house, Marie Sinclair had been the only one to notice.

A pleasant old woman named Mrs Leiber turned out to be the owner of Buddy, the missing dog. She seemed addled, disappointed that we weren't here to investigate the theft. Convinced Buddy had been dognapped, though an open gate at the side of her house indicated other possibilities.

Milo told her he'd keep his eyes open.

'He's such a sweetie,' Mrs Leiber said. 'Got the courage but not any meanness.'

We returned to the green house. The criminalists were still unpacking their gear. Milo showed the stains in the garage to the head tech, a black man named Merriweather, who got down and put his nose to it.

'Could be,' he said. 'If it is, it's pretty degraded. We'll scrape. If it *is* blood, should be able to get a basic HLA typing, but DNA's a whole other thing.'

'Just tell me if it's blood.'

'I can try that now.'

We watched him work, wielding solvents and reagents, swabs and test tubes.

The answer came within minutes:

'O-positive.'

'Richard Dada's type,' said Milo.

'Forty-three percent of the population,' said Merriweather. 'Let me scrape around here and inside the house, it'll take us the best part of the day, but maybe we can find you something interesting.'

Back in the unmarked, Milo phoned DMV again, cross-referencing vehicle registrations with the Shenandoah address. No match.

Gunning the engine, he pulled away from the curb, tires squealing. Less urgency than frustration. By the time we were back on Pico, he'd slowed down.

At Doheny, we stopped for a red light and he said, 'Richard's blood type. Orson's cutting out on the rent could explain why Richard was cut in half and Claire wasn't. By the time he did her, he'd lost his machine shop, didn't have the time – or the place – to set up . . . All that stolen movie junk. He has to keep it somewhere. Time to check out storage outfits . . . Be nice if Itatani could've ID'd Claire as the woman in the car.'

'If she was, Itatani saw her shortly before she was murdered. Maybe she and Orson did go shopping at the center, and that's why he dumped her there. What stores are there?'

'Montgomery Ward, Toys "R" Us, food joints, the Stereos Galore she was found behind.'

'Stereos Galore,' I said. 'Might they sell cameras?'

He looked in his rearview mirror, hung an illegal U-turn.

The front lot was jammed and we had to park on the far end, near La Cienega. Stereos Galore was two vast stories of gray rubber flooring and maroon plastic partitions. Scores of TV's projected soundlessly; blinking, throbbing entertainment centers spewed conflicting backbeats; salespeople in emerald-green vests pointed out the latest feature to stunned-looking customers. The camera section was at the rear of the second floor.

The manager was a small, dark-skinned, harried-looking man named Albert Mustafa with a precise black mustache and eyeglasses so thick his mild brown irises seemed miles away. He shepherded us into a relatively quiet corner, behind tall displays of film in colorful boxes. The cacophony from below filtered through the rubber tiles. Marie Sinclair would have felt at home.

Claire Argent's picture evoked a blank stare. Milo asked him about substantial video purchases.

'Six months ago?' he said.

'Five or six months ago,' said Milo. 'The name could be Wark or Crimmins or Orson. We're looking for a substantial purchase of video equipment or cameras.'

'How much is substantial?' said Mustafa.

'What's your typical sale?'

'Nothing's typical. Still cameras range from fifty dollars to nearly a thousand. We can get you set up with basic video for under three hundred, but you can go high-tech and then you're talking serious money.'

'Every sale is in the computer, right?'

'Supposed to be.'

'Do you categorize your customers based upon how much they spend?'

'No, sir.'

'OK,' said Milo. 'How about checking video purchases over one thousand dollars, four to six months ago. Start with this date.' He recited the day of Claire's murder.

Mustafa said, 'I'm not sure this is legal, sir. I'd have to check with the home office.'

'Where's that?'

'Minneapolis.'

'And they're closed by now,' said Milo.

'I'm afraid so, sir.'

'How about just spooling back to that one day, Mr Mustafa, see what comes up.'

'I'd really rather not.'

Milo stared at him.

'I don't want to lose my job,' said Mustafa. 'But the police help us . . . Just that day.'

Eight credit-card purchases of video equipment that day, two of them over a thousand dollars. No Crimmins, Wark, or Orson, or Argent. Nothing that brought to mind a scrambled director's name. Milo copied down the names and the credit card numbers as Mustafa looked on nervously.

'What about cash sales? Would you have records of those?'

'If the customer purchased the extended warranty. If he gave us his address so we could put him on the mailing list.'

Milo tapped the computer. 'How about scrolling back a few days.'

Mustafa said, 'This isn't good,' but he complied.

Nothing for the entire week.

Mustafa pushed a button and the screen went blank. By the time Milo thanked him, he'd walked away.

32

A FEW more detectives had returned to the Robbery-Homicide room. I pulled a chair up next to Milo's desk and listened as he called Social Security and the Franchise Tax Board. Two hits: Tax refunds had been sent to George Orson. Place of employment: Starkweather State Hospital.

'The checks were sent to an address on Pico – ten thousand five hundred. Commercial zone, ten to one a mail drop. Also, close to Richard's dump site . . . OK, OK, something's happening here. I need to get more specific, find out if he still works at Starkweather.'

'What about Lindeen the receptionist?' I said. 'She likes you. Must be that masculine cop musk.'

He grimaced. 'Yeah, I'm a musk ox . . . OK, why not?' He jabbed the phone. 'Hello, Lindeen? Hi, it's Milo Sturgis. Right . . . Oh, muddling along, how 'bout you . . . Well, that's terrific, yeah I've heard about those, sounds like fun, at least you get to solve something . . . Uh, well, I'm not sure I have anything to . . . Think so? Well, OK, if I can get some free time – after I clear Dr Argent's case . . . No, wish I could say I was . . . Speaking of which, does a psych tech named George Orson still work there?' He spelled the surname. 'Nothing major, but I heard he might've been a friend of Dr Argent's . . . I know she didn't, but his name came up from another party, they said he worked at Starkweather and knew her . . . No?' He frowned. 'Could you? That'd be great.'

He lowered the mouthpiece. 'The name's a little familiar, but she can't connect it to a face.'

'Hundred employees,' I said. 'What's the barter?'

He started to answer, moved the phone back under his mouth. 'Yup, still here . . . Did he? When was that? Any forwarding address?' His pen was poised, but he didn't write. 'So how long was he actually on staff?' Scribble. 'Any idea why he left? No, I wouldn't call him *that*, just checking every lead . . . What's that? That soon? I wish I could say yes, but unless the case clears, I'm pretty— Pardon? Yeah, OK, I promise . . . Yeah, it should be fun. Me, too. Thanks, Lindeen. And listen, you don't need to bother Mr Swig about this. I've got everything I need. Thanks again.'

He hung up. 'The barter is I come give a talk to some murder-mystery club she belongs to. They stage phony crimes, give out prizes for solving them, eat nachos. She wanted me next month but I deferred to their big bash at Christmas.'

'Playing Santa?'

'Ho ho fucking ho.'

'I tell you it's the musk.'

'Yeah, next time I'll shower first . . . The deal on Orson is, he joined Starkweather fifteen months ago, left after ten months of full-time employment.'

'Five months ago,' I said. 'A month after Claire got there. So they had plenty of time to get acquainted.'

'The brunette in the car,' he said. 'Itatani's three-second

observation isn't much, but with this . . . maybe. Orson's file says he worked primarily on the fifth floor, with the criminal fakers – how's that for a match made in hell? But he did do some overtime down on the regular wards, so that gives him access to Peake. No infractions, no problems, he quit voluntarily. His photo's missing from the file, but Lindeen thinks she *might* remember him – maybe he had light brown hair. Probably being overly helpful. Or the guy's got a wig collection.'

'Little dip into the costume box,' I said. 'He produces, directs, *and* acts. Five months ago is also shortly after Richard Dada's murder. Right when Orson closed up shop at Shenandoah, packed up the machine shop. He keeps himself a moving target. Saves money on rent and gets off on the thrill of the con.'

'His relationship with Claire. You think it could've gone beyond an interest in Peake?'

'Who knows? Castro said he wasn't very smooth in Miami, but he's had time to polish his act. For all her love of privacy, Claire might've been lonely and vulnerable. And we know she could be sexually aggressive. Maybe her interest in pathology went beyond the workday. Or Orson promised to put her in pictures.'

He knuckled his eyes, let out air very slowly. 'OK, let's check out that Pico address.'

As we left the building, I said, 'One thing in our favor, he may trip himself up. Because there's rigidity and childishness to his technique. The way he scripted his Miami con. I'll bet he's done the same here. The way he stays in comfort zones, dumping Claire near one of his addresses, Richard near another. He sees himself as some creative wizard, but he always returns to the familiar.'

'Sounds about right,' he said, 'for a showbiz guy.'

Mailbox Heaven. Northeast corner of a scruffy strip mall just west of Barrington, a stuffy closet lined with brass boxes and smelling of wet paper. A young woman came out from the back room, redheaded, bright-eyed, brightening as Milo showed her his badge. Opining that police work was 'cool.'

George Orson's box had been rented to someone else for over a year and she had no records of the original transaction.

'No way,' she said. 'We don't keep stuff. People come and go. That's who uses us.'

We got back in the unmarked. On the way to the station, we passed the spot where Richard Dada's VW had been abandoned. Small factories, auto mechanics, spare-parts yards. Just another industrial park – a cleaner, more compact version of the desolate stretch presaging Starkweather.

Comfort zones . . .

We sat, parked at the curb, not talking, watching men with rolled-up sleeves hauling and driving, loafing and smoking. No gates around the enclosure. Easy entry after hours. Empty, dark acres: The perfect dump site. A flatbed full of aluminum pipe rumbled past. A catering truck with rust-specked white sides sounded a clarion and men marched forward for burritos of dubious composition.

The noise had never abated, but now I heard it for the

first time. Compressors snapping and popping, metal clanging against cement, whining triumph as saw blades devoured wood . . .

I accompanied Milo as he visited shop after shop, asking questions, encountering boredom, confusion, distrust, occasional overt hostility.

Asking about a tall, thin, bald man with a bird face who did woodwork. Maybe a wig, black or brown, curly or straight. A yellow Corvette or an old VW. Two hours, and all the effort bought were lungfuls of chemical air.

Milo drove me back to the station and I headed home, thinking, suddenly and inexplicably, of a missing dog with a nice smile.

Nighttime can be so many things.

Shortly after eight P.M., Robin and I were eating pizza on the deck, tented by a starless purple sky. Just enough dry heat had lingered to be soothing. The quiet was merciful.

Robin had driven up an hour before. Feeling guilty about returning to Starkweather without informing her, I'd filled her in.

'No need for confession. You're here in one piece.'

She'd looked tired, soaked in the tub while I drove into Westwood to get the pizza. I took the truck, playing Joe Satriani very loud. Not minding the traffic, not minding much of anything at all. A couple of beers when I got back didn't raise my anxiety. The bath had refreshed Robin, and staring at her across the table as she worked on a second slice seemed a great way to pass the time.

I'd allowed myself to feel pretty good by the time the unmarked zoomed up in front of the house.

The headlights made my head hurt. Tonight, Marie Sinclair and I were kindred spirits.

The car stopped. Spike barked. Robin waved. I didn't budge.

Milo stuck his head out the passenger's window. 'Oh. Sorry. Nothing earth-shattering. Call me tomorrow, Alex.'

Spike had cranked up the volume, and now he was baying like an insulted hound. Robin got up and leaned over the railing. 'Don't be silly. Come up and eat something.'

'Nah,' he said. 'You lovebirds deserve some quality time.'

'Up, young man. *Now*.'

Spike hurled himself down the stairs, sped to the car, stationed himself at Milo's door and began jumping up and down.

'How do I interpret this?' said Milo. 'Friend or foe?'

'Friend,' I said.

'You're sure?'

'Psychologists are never sure,' I said. 'We just make probability judgments.'

'Meaning?'

'If he pees on your shoes, I was wrong.'

He claimed to have grabbed a sandwich, but one and a half beers later, he started to observe the pizza with interest. I slid it over to him. He got down four slices, said, 'Maybe it's good for me – the spice, cleanses the body.'

'Sure,' I said. 'It's health food. Detoxify yourself.'

He got to work on a fifth slice, Spike curled at his feet, lapping the scraps that fell from his dangling left hand, Milo maintaining a poker face, thinking Robin and I weren't noticing the covert donations.

Robin said, 'Dessert?'

'Don't put yourself out—'

She patted his head and went into the house.

I said, 'So what's not earth-shattering?'

'Found four more George Orson bank accounts. Glendale, Sylmar, Northridge, downtown. All the same pattern: He plants cash for a week, withdraws right after writing checks.'

'Checks for what?'

'Haven't been able to look at them yet. After a certain amount of time – no one seems to know how long – bad paper's destroyed and the data's sent to some computer in the home office.'

'In Minnesota,' I said.

'No doubt. These guys are addicted to paperwork, don't seem to wanna help themselves.'

'Glendale, Sylmar, Northridge, downtown,' I said. 'Orson's spreading himself all over the city. It might also mean he's a restless driver. Consistent with a fun-killer. Anyone remember him?'

'Not a one. The crimes were duly documented, police reports were filed, but no one bothered to check for similars, no one spent much energy following up. Next item: The lab has complete HLA typing from the stains in the garage. I sent over samples of Richard's blood for comparison. Nothing showed up in the rest of the house. Too many cleanings by Mr Itatani – where are negligent slumlords when you need them?'

Spike emitted a pulsating, froglike croak. Milo's left hand slid across the table. Slurp, munch.

'Finally: The lovely and outgoing Ms Sinclair did indeed report the nighttime traffic at the house. A dozen complaints, cruisers were sent out seven times, but all the blues saw were some cars in the driveway, no dope transactions. I spoke to one of the sergeants. He considers Sinclair a crank. I have cleaned up his language. Apparently, bitching's her main hobby. One time she called in at two A.M. about a mockingbird in a tree she claimed was singing off-key intentionally – some bird plot to throw off her piano playing. In the warrant application I thought it best not to describe her psychological status in too much detail, called her a "neighborhood observer." But what a whack job; you guys will never be out of work.'

'Too bad Mrs Leiber didn't notice anything,' I said.

'Who's Mrs Leiber?'

'The lady with the lost dog.'

'Oh, her. All she cared about was the dog.'

'I keep thinking about the dog.'

'What do you mean?'

'His face stays with me. Don't know why. It's as if I've seen him before.'

'In a past life?'

I laughed because it was the right thing to do. Milo slipped Spike a long strip of mozzarella.

Robin came out with iced coffee and chocolate ice cream. Milo finished the pizza and joined us sipping and spooning.

Soon, he'd slid down in his chair, nearly supine, eyes closed, head hanging over the back of the chair.

'Ah,' he said, 'the good life.'

Then his beeper went off.

33

'SWIG,' HE said, returning from the kitchen.

'Someone told him about Peake's Jesus pose,' I said, 'and he's going to make your life a living hell if you don't stay away.'

'On the contrary. He offered a personal invitation to come over. Now.'

'Why?'

'He wouldn't say, just "Now." Not an order, though. A polite request. He actually said please.'

I looked at Robin. 'Have fun.'

She said, 'Oh, please. You'll be pacing the house, end up having one of your sleepless nights.' To Milo: 'Take care of him, or no more beer.'

He crossed his heart. I kissed her and we hurried down to the car.

As he sped down to the Glen and headed south, I said, 'Were you shielding Robin, or did he really not say?'

'The latter. One thing I *didn't* say in front of her. He sounded scared.'

Ten P.M. The night was kind to the industrial wasteland. A hospital security guard was waiting on the road just outside the turnoff, idly aiming a flashlight beam at the ground. As we drove up, he illuminated the unmarked's license plate and waved us forward hurriedly.

'Straight through,' he told Milo. 'They're waiting for you.'

'Who's they?'

'Everyone.'

The guard in the booth flipped the barrier arm as we approached. We drove through without being questioned.

'No surrendering the gun?' I said. 'When do they unfurl the red rug?'

'Too easy,' said Milo. 'I hate it when things go too easy.'

At the parking lot, a black tech with salt-and-pepper hair pointed out the closest parking space. Milo muttered, 'Now I have to tip him.'

When we got out of the car, the tech said, 'Hal Cleveland. I'll take you to Mr Swig.'

Hurrying toward the inner fence without waiting. Running ahead the way Dollard had done, he kept checking to see if we were with him.

'What's the story?' Milo asked him.

Cleveland shook his head. 'I'll leave that to Mr Swig.'

At night, the yard was empty. And different, the dirt frosty and blue-gray under high-voltage lights, scooped in places like ice cream. Cleveland half-jogged. It was nice being able to cross without fear of some psychotic jumping me. Still, I found myself checking my back.

We reached the far gate and Cleveland unlocked it with a quick twist. The main building *didn't* look much different – still ashen and ugly, the clouded plastic windows gaping like an endless series of beseeching mouths. Another guard blocked the door. Armed with baton and gun. First time I'd seen a uniform – or weapons – inside the grounds. He stepped aside for us, and Cleveland hurried us past Lindeen's cleared desk, past the brassy flash of bowling trophies, through the silent hallway. Past Swig's office, all the other administrative doors, straight to the elevator. A quick, uninterrupted ride up to C Ward. Cleveland wedged himself in a corner, played with his keys.

When the elevator door opened, another tech, big and thick and bearded, was positioned right in front of us. He stepped back to let us exit. Cleveland stayed in the lift and rode it back down.

The bearded tech took us through the double doors. William Swig stood midway up the corridor. In front of Peake's room. Peake's door was closed. Another pair of uniformed guards was positioned a few feet away. The bearded man left us to join two other techs, their backs against the facing wall.

No men in khaki. But for the hum of the air conditioner, the ward was silent.

Swig saw us and shook his head very hard, as if denying a harsh reality. He had on a navy polo shirt, jeans, running shoes. The filmy strands atop his head puffed at odd angles. Overhead fluorescents heightened the contrast between his facial moles and the pallid skin that hosted them. Dark dots, like braille, punctuating the message on his face.

Nothing ambiguous about the communication: Pure fear.

He opened Peake's door, winced, gave a ringmaster's flourish.

Not that much blood.

A single scarlet python.

Winding its way toward us from the far right-hand corner of the cell. About three feet from the spot where Peake had played Jesus.

Otherwise the room looked the same. Messy bed. Wall restraints bolted in place. That same burning smell mixed with something coppery-sweet.

No sign of Peake.

The blood trail stopped halfway across the floor, its point of origin below the body.

Stocky body, lying facedown. Plaid shirt, blue jeans, sneakers. A head full of coarse gray hair. Arms outstretched, almost relaxed-looking. Thick forearms. The skin had already gone grayish-green.

'Dollard,' said Milo. 'When?'

'We don't know,' said Swig. 'Someone discovered him two hours ago.'

'And you called me forty-five minutes ago?'

'We had to conduct our own search first,' said Swig. He picked at a mole, brought a rosy flush to its borders.

'And?'

Swig looked away. 'We haven't found him.'

Milo was silent.

'Look,' said Swig, 'we *had* to do our own search first. I'm not even sure I should've called you. It's sheriff's jurisdiction – actually, it's our jurisdiction.'

'So you did me a favor,' said Milo.

'You had an interest in Peake. I'm trying to cooperate.'

Milo stepped closer to the body, kneeled, looked under Dollard's chin.

'Looks like one transverse cut,' he said. 'Has anyone moved him?'

'No,' said Swig. 'Nothing's been touched.'

'Who found him?'

Swig pointed to one of the three techs. 'Bart did.' The man stepped forward. Young, Chinese, delicately built, but with the oversized arms of a bodybuilder. His badge photo was that of a stunned child. B. L. Quan, Tech II.

'Tell me about it,' Milo told him.

'We were in lockdown,' said Quan. 'Not because of any problems; we do it during staff meetings.'

'How frequent are staff meetings?'

'Twice a week for each shift.'

'What days?'

'It depends on the shift,' said Quan. 'Tonight was for the eleven-to-seven. Six-thirty. Friday night, the weekly summary. The patients go in lockdown and the staff goes in there.' He pointed to the TV room.

'No staff on the ward?' said Milo.

'One tech stays outside. We rotate. There's never been any problem, the patients are all locked up tight.'

Milo looked at the body.

Quan shrugged.

'And Dollard was scheduled to be the outside guy tonight.'

Quan nodded.

'But your beeper never went off.'

'Right.'

'So what made you look for him?' said Milo.

'The meeting was over, I was doing a double, and Frank was supposed to talk to me about some patients. Give me the transfer data – meds, things to watch out for, that kind of thing. He didn't show up, I thought he forgot.'

'Was that typical?' said Milo. 'Frank forgetting?'

Quan looked uncomfortable. He glanced at Swig.

'Don't worry,' said Milo. 'You can't embarrass him anymore.'

Quan said, 'Sometimes.'

'Sometimes what?'

Quan shifted his feet. Milo turned to Swig.

'Tell him anything you know,' said Swig. His voice had turned hoarse. He rolled his fingers, rubbed another mole.

'Sometimes Frank forgot things,' said Quan. 'That's why I didn't make any big deal out of it. But then, when I went to get the charts I couldn't find one of them – Peake's. So I checked out Peake's room.'

'You ever find the chart?'

'No.'

'What else?' said Milo.

'That's it. I saw Frank, Peake was gone, I locked the door, put out a Code Three alert. Easy, we were already in lockdown. Mr Swig came in, we brought outside guards onto the wards, and a bunch of us searched everywhere. He's got to be somewhere, it makes no sense.'

'What doesn't?' said Milo.

'Peake disappearing like that. You don't just disappear at Starkweather.'

Milo asked for a key to Peake's room, got Swig's, closed the door and locked it, then moved out of earshot and used his cell phone to call the sheriff. He talked for a long time. None of the guards or techs budged.

The silence seemed to amplify. Then it began to falter – with sporadic knocks from behind some of the brown doors; muffled scuffs, faint as mouse steps. Cries, moans, escalating gradually but steadily into ragged shards of noise that could only be human voices in distress.

A chorus of cries. The guards and techs eyed one another. Swig seemed oblivious.

'Shit,' said the bearded tech. 'Shut the hell up.'

Swig moved farther up the hall. No one attempted to stop the noise.

Louder and louder, frantic pounding from within the cells.

The inmates knew. Somehow, they knew.

Milo pocketed the phone and returned. 'Sheriff's crime-scene team should be here shortly. Squad cars will be searching a five-mile radius outside the hospital grounds. Tell your men in front not to hold anyone up at the gate.'

Swig said, 'We need to keep this under wraps until— What I mean is, let's find out exactly what happened before we jump to—'

'What do *you* think happened, Mr Swig?'

'Peake surprised Frank and cut his throat. Frank's a strong man. So it had to be a sneak attack.'

'What did Peake use to cut him?'

No answer.

'No guesses?' said Milo. 'What about Dollard's own knife?'

'None of the techs are armed,' said Swig.

'Theoretically.'

'Theoretically and factually, Detective. For obvious reasons we have strict—'

Milo cut him off: 'You have rules, an ironclad system. So tell me, are techs and doctors required to check in weapons at the guardhouse the way we were?'

Swig didn't answer.

'Sir?'

'That would be cumbersome. The sheer number of . . .'

Milo looked over at the three techs. No telltale evasive gestures. The big bearded man stared back defiantly.

'So everyone *but* staff is required to surrender weapons?'

'Staff knows not to *bring* weapons,' said Swig.

Milo reached into his jacket, pulled out his service revolver, dangled it from his index finger. 'Dr Delaware?'

I produced my Swiss Army knife. Both guards tensed.

'No one checked us tonight. I guess the system breaks down from time to time,' said Milo.

'Look,' said Swig, raising his voice. He exhaled. 'Tonight is different. I told them to facilitate your entry. I had full knowledge—'

'So you're willing to bet Dollard wasn't carrying the blade that killed him?'

'Frank was very trustworthy.'

'Even though he tended to *forget* things?'

'I've never heard that,' said Swig.

'You just did,' said Milo. 'Let me tell you about Frank. Hemet PD fired him for malfeasance. Ignoring calls, false overtime—'

'I had absolutely *no* knowledge of—'

'So maybe there are other things you have no knowledge of.'

'Look,' Swig repeated. But he added nothing, just shook his head and tried to smooth down his filmy hair. His Adam's apple rose and fell. He said, 'Why bother? You've already got your mind made up.'

Milo turned to the techs. 'If I frisk any of you guys, am I going to turn up something?'

Silence.

He walked across the hall. Bart Quan's feet spread, as if ready for combat, and the other two men folded their arms across their chests – the same resistant stance Dollard had adopted yesterday.

'Tell them to cooperate,' said Milo.

'Do what he says,' said Swig.

Quickly, efficiently, Milo patted down the techs. Nothing on Quan or the tech who hadn't spoken – an older man with droopy eyes – but the jeans of the heavy, bearded man produced a bone-handled pocketknife.

Milo unfolded the blade. Four inches of gracefully honed steel. Milo turned it admiringly.

'Steve,' said Swig.

The heavy man's face quivered. 'So what?' he said. 'Work with these *animals*, you take *care* of yourself.'

Milo kept examining the blade. 'Where'd you get it, Home Shopping Network?'

'Knife show,' said Steve. 'And don't worry, man, I haven't used it since I went hunting last winter.'

'Kill anything?'

'Skinned some elk. Tasty.'

Folding the knife, Milo dropped it in his jacket pocket.

'That's mine, man,' said Steve.

'If it's clean, you'll get it back.'

'When? I want a receipt.'

'Quiet, Steve,' ordered Swig. 'You and I will talk later.'

The bearded man's nostrils opened wide. 'Yeah, right. If I even want to stay in this dump.'

'That's up to you, Steve. Meanwhile, the state's still paying your salary, so listen up: Go down to A and B Wards, make sure everything's in order. Complete foot circuits, constant surveillance including door checks. No breaks till you're notified.'

The bearded man gave Milo one last glare and stomped around the left side of the nursing station.

'Where's he heading?' said Milo.

'Staff elevator.'

'We didn't see any elevator when we toured.'

'The door's unmarked, staff only,' said Swig. 'We need to keep searching. Can I free these guards?'

'Sure,' said Milo.

'Go,' Swig told the uniformed men.

'Where?' said one of them.

'Every damn where! Start with the outer grounds, north and south perimeters. Make sure he's not hiding somewhere in the trees.' Swig turned to the two remaining techs. 'Bart, you and Jim search the basement again. Kitchen, laundry, every storage room. Make sure everything's as tight as it was the first time we looked.'

Barking orders like a general. When everyone had dispersed, Swig turned to Milo. 'I know what you're thinking. We're a bunch of civil-service bumblers. But this is absolutely the first time since I've run this place that we've had anything close to an escape. As a rule, nothing ever—'

'Some people,' said Milo, 'live for the rules. Me, I deal with the exceptions.'

We walked up and down C Ward as Milo inspected doors. Several times, he had Swig unlock hatches. As he peered inside, the noise from within subsided.

'Can't see the entire room through these,' he said, fingering a hatch door.

'We've gone over every room,' said Swig. 'First thing. Everything checks out.'

I said, 'That unmarked staff elevator door. I assume the inmates know about it.'

'We don't make a point of explaining it,' said Swig. 'But I suppose—'

'Reason I mention it is that yesterday Peake and Heidi came from that direction. It was the first time anyone remembers Peake leaving his room for any length of time. I'm wondering if he saw someone enter the elevator, got an idea. Does it stop on every floor?'

'It can,' said Swig.

'Has anyone checked it?'

'I assume.'

Milo bore down on him. 'You assume?'

'My orders were to check everywhere.'

'Your orders were not to carry weapons.'

'I'm sure,' said Swig, 'that— Fine, to hell with it, I'll show you.'

Brown door, slightly wider than those that sealed the inmates' cells. Double key locks, no intercom speaker. Swig keyed the upper bolt and a latch clicked. The door swung open, revealing yet another brown rectangle. Inner door. No handle. Single lock in the center of the panel. The same key operated it, and a flick of Swig's wrist brought forth rumbling gear noise that vibrated through the walls. A few feet away was a smaller door, maybe two feet wide and twice as high.

'Where's the car coming from?' said Milo.

'No way to tell,' said Swig. 'It's a little slow, should be here soon.'

'The first time we were here,' I said, 'Phil Hatterson called upstairs, spoke to someone, and got the elevator sent down. You can't do that with this one.'

'Right,' said Swig. 'The call box for the main elevator is in the nursing station. A tech's in there at all times to monitor meds. Part of station duty's also monitoring inter-floor transport.'

'Did Frank Dollard ever have that duty?'

'I'm sure he did. The staff circulates. Everyone does a bit of everything.'

'When the elevators are keyed remotely, what determines where they stop?'

'You leave the key in until the elevator arrives. When an approved person – someone with a key – rides up, he can release the lock mechanism and punch buttons in the elevator.'

'So once the lock's been released, this operates like any other elevator.'

'Yes,' said Swig, 'but you can't release anything without a key, and only the staff has keys.'

'Do you ever remaster the locks?'

'If there's a problem,' said Swig.

'Which never happens,' said Milo.

Swig flinched. 'It doesn't take something of *this* magnitude to remaster, Detective. Anything out of the ordinary – a key reported stolen – and we change the tumblers immediately.'

'Must be a hassle,' said Milo. 'All those keys to replace.'

'We don't have many hassles.'

'When's the last time the tumblers were changed, Mr Swig?'

'I'd have to check.'

'But not recently, that you can recall.'

'What are you getting at?' said Swig.

'One more thing,' said Milo. 'Each ward is sectioned by those double doors. Every time you walk through, you have to unlock each one.'

'Exactly,' said Swig. 'It's a maze. That's the point.'

'How many keys do the techs need to carry to negotiate the maze?'

'Several,' said Swig. 'I never counted.'

'Is there a master key?'

'I have a master.'

Milo pointed to the key protruding from the inner elevator door. The rumbling continued, louder, as the lift approached. 'That it?'

'Yes. There's also a copy in the safe in one of the data rooms on the first floor. And yes, I checked it. Still there, no tampering.'

The door groaned open. The compartment was small, harshly lit, empty. Milo looked in. 'What's that?'

Pointing to a scrap on the floor.

'Looks like paper,' said Swig.

'Same paper as the sandals the inmates wear?'

Swig took a closer look. 'I suppose it could be – I don't see any blood.'

'Why would there be blood?'

'He cut Frank's throat—'

'There were no bloody footprints in Peake's room,' said Milo. 'Meaning Peake did a nice clean job of it, stepped away as he cut. Not bad for a crazy man.'

'Hard to believe,' said Swig.

'What is?'

'Just what you said. Peake mobilizing that much skill.'

'Close this elevator,' said Milo. 'Keep it locked, don't let anyone in. When the crime-scene people come, I want them to remove that paper first thing.'

Swig complied. Milo pointed to the smaller door. 'What's that?'

'Disposal chute for garbage,' said Swig. 'It goes straight down to the basement.'

'Like a dumbwaiter.'

'Exactly.'

'I don't see any latches or key locks,' said Milo. 'How does it open?'

'There's a lever. In the nursing station.'

'Show me.'

Swig unlocked the station. Three walls of glass, a fourth filled with locked steel compartments. The room felt like a big telephone booth. Swig pointed to the metal wall. 'Meds and supplies, always locked.'

I looked around. No desks, just built-in plastic counters housing a multiline phone, a small switchboard, and an intercom microphone. Set into the front glass was a six-inch slot equipped with a sliding steel tray.

'Too narrow to get their hands through,' said Swig, with defensive pride. 'They line up, get their pills, nothing's left to chance.'

'Where's the lever?' said Milo.

Reaching under the desk, Swig groped. A snapping sound filled the booth. We left the station and returned to the hall. The garbage chute had unhinged at the top, creating a small metal canopy.

'Big enough for a skinny man.' Milo stuck his head in and emerged sniffing. 'Peake wasn't exactly obese.'

Swig said, 'Oh, come on—'

'What else is in the basement?'

'The service areas – kitchen, laundry, pantry, storage. Believe me, it's all been checked thoroughly.'

'Deliveries come through the basement level?'

'Yes.'

'So there's a loading dock.'

'Yes, but—'

'How can you be sure Peake's not hiding out in a bin of dirty laundry?'

'Because we've checked and double-checked. Go see for yourself.'

Milo tapped the elevator door. 'Does this go up to the fifth floor, too – where the fakers are kept?'

Swig looked offended. 'The 1368's. Yes.'

'Does the main elevator go there, too?'

'No. The fifth floor has its own elevator. Express from ground level to the top.'

'A third elevator,' said Milo.

'For Five only. Security reasons,' said Swig. 'The 1368's come in and out. Using the main elevator for all that traffic would create obvious logistical problems. The jail bus lets them off around the back, at the 1368 reception center. They get processed and go straight up to Five. No stops – they have no access to the rest of the hospital.'

'Except for the staff elevator.'

'They don't use the staff elevator.'

'Theoretically.'

'Factually,' said Swig.

'If you want to segregate the fifth floor completely, why even have the staff elevator go there?'

'It's the way the hospital was built,' said Swig. 'Logical, don't you think? If something happens on Five and the staff needs backup, we're ready for them.'

'Ready,' said Milo, 'by way of a slow elevator. How often does something happen on Five?'

'Rarely.'

'Give me a number.'

Swig rubbed a mole. 'Once, twice a year – what does it matter? We're talking temporary disruption, not a riot. Some 1368 trying too hard to impress us with how crazy he is. Or a fight. Don't forget, plenty of the evaluees are gang members.' Swig sniffed contemptuously. Every society had its castes.

'Let's have a look at Five,' said Milo. 'Through the reception center. I don't want anyone to touch that piece of paper.'

'Even if it is an inmate slipper,' said Swig, 'that wouldn't make it Peake's. All the inmates are issued—' He stopped. 'Sure, sure, staff only – what was I thinking?'

On the way down, he said, 'You think I'm some bureaucrat who doesn't give a damn. I took this job because I care about people. I adopted two orphans.'

We got out on the first floor, exited the way we'd come in, followed Swig around the left side of the building. The side we'd never seen. Or been told about.

Identical concrete pathway. Bright lights from the roof yellowed five stories, creating a giant waffle of clouded windows.

Another door, identical to the main entrance.

The structure was two-faced.

A painted sign said INTAKE AND EVALUATION. A guard blocked the entry. Ten yards away, to the left, was a small parking lot, empty, separated from the yard by a chain-link-bordered path that reminded me of a giant dog run. The walkway veered, bled into darkness. Not visible as you crossed the main yard. Not accessible from the main entry. So there was another way onto the grounds, an entirely different entry.

Off to the right I saw the firefly bounce of searchlights, the outer borders of the uninhabited yard we'd seen yesterday, hints of the annex buildings. Unlit, too far to make out details. The search seemed to be carrying on beyond the annexes, fireflies clustering near what had to be the pine forest.

'How many roads enter the hospital grounds?' I said.

'Two,' said Swig. 'One, really. The one you've taken.'

'What about there?' I pointed to the small parking lot.

'For jail buses only. Special access path clear around the eastern perimeter. The drivers have coded car keys. Even staff can't access the gates without my permission.'

I indicated the distant searchlights. 'And that side? Those pine trees. How do you get in there?'

'You don't,' said Swig. 'No access from the western perimeter, it's all fenced.' He walked ahead and nodded at the guard, who stepped aside.

The intake center's front room was proportioned identically to that of the hospital entrance. Front desk, same size as Lindeen's, gunboat gray, bare except for a phone. No bowling trophies, no cute slogans. Lindeen's counterpart was a bullet-headed tech perched behind the rectangle of county-issue steel. Reading a newspaper, but when he saw Swig, he snapped the paper down and stood.

Swig said, 'Anything unusual?'

'Just the lockdown, sir, per your orders.'

'I'm taking these people up.' Swig rushed us past a bare

hall, into yet another elevator and up. Fast ride to Five, during which he used his walkie-talkie to check on the search's progress.

The door slid open.

'Keep on it,' he barked, before jamming the intercom into his pocket. His armpits were soaked. A vein behind his left ear throbbed.

Two sets of double doors, over each a painted sign: I AND E, RESTRICTED ACCESS. As opposed to what?

Where the nursing station would have been was empty space. The ward was a single hall lined with bright blue doors. Higher tech-inmate ratio: A dozen especially large men patrolled.

Milo asked to look inside a cell.

Swig said, 'We went room-to-room here, too.'

'Let me see one, anyway.'

Swig called out, 'Inspection!' and three techs jogged over.

'Detective Sturgis wants to see what a 1368 looks like. Open a door.'

'Which one?' said the largest of the men, a Samoan with an unpronounceable name on his tag and a soft, boyish voice.

'Pick one.'

The Samoan stepped to the closest door, popped the hatch, looked inside, unlocked the blue panel, and held it open six inches. Sticking his head in, he opened the door fully and said, 'This is Mr Liverwright.'

The room high and constricted, same dimensions as Peake's. Same bolted restraints. A muscular young black man sat naked on the bed. The sheets had been torn off a thin, striped mattress. Torn into shreds. Royal blue pajamas lay rumpled on the floor next to a pair of blue paper slippers. One of the slippers was nothing but confetti.

I stepped closer and was hit by a terrible stench. A mound of feces sat in a drying clot near the prisoner's feet. Several pools of urine glistened. The walls behind the bed were stained brown.

He saw us, grinned, cackled.

'Clean this up,' said Swig.

'We do,' said the Samoan calmly. 'Twice a day. He keeps trying to prove himself.'

He flashed Liverwright a victory V and laughed. 'Keep it up, bro.'

Liverwright cackled again and rubbed himself.

'Shake it but don't break it off, bro,' said the Samoan.

'Close the door,' said Swig. 'Clean him up *now*.'

The Samoan closed the door, shrugging. To us: 'These guys think they know what crazy is, but they overdo it. Too many movies.' He turned to leave.

Milo asked him, 'When's the last time you saw George Orson?'

'Him?' said the Samoan. 'I dunno, not in a while.'

'Not tonight?'

'Nope. Why would I? He hasn't worked here in months.'

'Who are we talking about?' said Swig.

'Has he visited since he quit?' Milo asked the Samoan.

'Hmm,' said the Samoan. 'Don't think so.'

'What kind of guy was he?' said Milo.

'Just a guy.' The Samoan favored Swig with a smile. 'Love to chat, but got to clean up some shit.' He lumbered off.

'Who's George Orson?' said Swig.

'One of your former employees,' said Milo. Watching Swig's face.

'I can't know everyone. Why're you asking about him?'

'He knew Mr Peake,' said Milo. 'Back in the good old days.'

Swig had plenty of questions, but Milo held him off. We rode the fifth-floor elevator down to the basement, took a tense, deliberate tour of the kitchen, pantry, laundry, and storage rooms. Everything smelled of slightly rotted produce. Techs and guards were everywhere. Helping them search were orange-jumpsuited janitors. White-garbed cooks in the kitchen stared as we passed through. Racks of knives were in full view. I thought of Peake passing through, deciding to sample. The good old days.

Milo found four out-of-the-way closet doors and checked each of them. Key-locked.

'Who gets keys besides clinical staff?' he asked Swig.

'No one.'

'Not these guys?' Indicating a pair of janitors.

'Not them or anyone else not engaged in patient care. And to answer your next question, nonclinical staff enter through the front like anyone else. ID's are checked.'

'Even familiar faces are checked?' said Milo.

'That's our system.'

'Do clinical staffers take their keys home?'

Swig didn't answer.

'Do they?' said Milo.

'Yes, they take them home. Checking in scores of keys a day would be cumbersome. As I said, we change the locks.

Even in the absence of a specific problem, we remaster every year.'

'Every year,' said Milo. I knew what he was thinking: George Orson had left five months ago. 'What date did that fall on?'

'I'll have to check,' said Swig. 'What exactly are you getting at?'

Milo walked ahead of him. 'Let's see the loading dock.'

Sixty-foot-wide empty cement space doored with six panels of corrugated metal.

Milo asked a janitor, 'How do you get them open?'

The janitor pointed to a circuit box at the rear.

'Is there an outside switch, too?'

'Yup.'

Milo loped to the box and punched a button. The second door from the left swung upward and we walked to the edge of the dock. Six or seven feet above ground. Space for three or four large trucks to unload simultaneously. Milo climbed down. Five steps took him into darkness and he disappeared, but I heard him walking around. A moment later, he hoisted himself up.

'The delivery road,' he asked Swig, 'where does it go?'

'Subsidiary access. Same place the jail bus enters.'

'I thought only the jail buses came in that way.'

'I was referring to people,' said Swig. 'Only jail bus transportees come in that way.'

'So there's plenty of traffic in and out.'

'Everything's scheduled and preapproved. Every driver is preapproved and required to show ID upon demand.

The road is sectioned every fifty feet with gates. Card keys are changed every thirty days.'

'Card keys,' said Milo. 'So if they show ID, they can open the gates on their own.'

'That's a big if,' said Swig. 'Look, we're not here to critique our system, we want to find Peake. I suggest you pay more attention to—'

'What about techs?' said Milo. 'Can they use the access road?'

'Absolutely not. Why are you harping on this? And what does this Orson character have to do with it?'

Shouts from the west turned our heads. Several fireflies enlarged.

Searchers approaching. Milo hopped down off the deck again and I did the same. Swig contemplated a jump but remained in place. By the time I was at Milo's side, I could make out figures behind the flashlights. Two men, running.

One of them was Bart Quan, the other a uniformed guard.

Suddenly, Swig was with us, breathing audibly. 'What, Bart?'

'We found a breach,' said Quan. 'Western perimeter. The fence has been cut.'

Half-mile walk to the spot. The flap was man-sized, snipped neatly and put back in place, wires twisted with precision. It had taken a careful eye to spot it in the darkness. Milo said, 'Who found it?'

The uniform with Quan raised his hand. Young, thin, swarthy.

Milo peered at his badge. 'What led you to it, Officer Dalfen?'

'I was scoping the western perimeter.'

'Find anything else?'

'Not so far.'

Milo borrowed Dalfen's flashlight and ran it over the fence. 'What's on the other side?'

'Dirt road,' said Swig. 'Not much of one.'

'Where does it lead?'

'Into the foothills.'

Milo untwisted the wires, pulled down the flap, crouched, and passed through. 'Tire tracks,' he said. 'Any gates or guards on this side?'

'It's not hospital territory,' said Swig. 'There has to be a border, somewhere.'

'What's in the foothills?'

'Nothing. That's the point. There's no place to go for a good three, four miles. The county clears trees and brush every year to make sure there's no cover. Anyone up there would be visible by helicopter.'

'Speaking of which,' said Milo.

By the time the choppers had begun circling, nine sheriff's cars and the crime-scene vans had arrived. Khaki uniforms on the deputies; I saw Swig tense up further, but he said nothing, had started to isolate himself in a corner, muttering from time to time into his walkie-talkie.

Two plainclothes detectives arrived last. The coroner had just finished examining Dollard, searching his pockets. Empty. Milo conferred with the doctor. The paper scrap in the staff elevator had been retrieved and bagged. As a criminalist carried it past, Swig said, 'Looks like a piece of slipper.'

'What kind of slipper?' said one of the detectives, a fair-haired man in his thirties named Ron Banks.

Milo told him.

Banks's partner said, 'So all we have to do is find Cinderella.' He was a stout man named Hector De la Torre, older than Banks, with flaring mustaches. Banks was serious, but De la Torre grinned. Unintimidated by the setting, he'd greeted Milo with a reminder that they'd met. 'Party over at Musso and Frank's – after the Lisa Ramsey case got closed. My buddy here is good pals with the D who closed it.'

'Petra Connor?' said Milo.

'She's the one.'

Banks looked embarrassed. 'I'm sure he cares, Hector.' To Milo: 'So maybe he rode down in that elevator.'

'No inmates allowed,' said Milo. 'So there's no good reason for there to be a slipper in there. And Dollard's key ring is missing, meaning Peake lifted it. The rest of the techs were in a meeting, so Peake could've easily ridden down to the basement, found a door out, and hightailed it. On the other hand, maybe it's just a scrap that got stuck on the bottom of someone's shoe.'

'No blood in the elevator?' said Banks.

'Not a drop; the only blood's what you just saw in the room.'

'Clean, for a throat cut.'

'Coroner says it wasn't much of a cut. Peake nicked the carotid rather than cut it, more trickle than spurt. Came close to not being fatal; if Dollard had been able to seek help right away, he might've survived. Looks like he went into shock, collapsed, lay there bleeding out. No spatter – most of the blood pooled under him.'

'Low-pressure bleedout,' said Banks.

'A nick,' said De la Torre. 'Talk about bad luck.'

'Peake didn't have much muscle on him,' said Milo.

'Enough to do the trick,' said De la Torre. 'So who cut the fence? Where'd Peake get tools for that?'

'Good question,' said Milo. 'Maybe Dollard carried the blade he was cut with. Maybe one of those Swiss Army deals with tools. Though there'd be no way for Peake to know that, unless Dollard had gotten *really* sloppy and let him see it. The alternative's obvious. A partner.'

Banks said, 'This is some big-time premeditated deal? I thought the guy was a lunatic.'

'Even lunatics can have pals,' said Milo.

'You got that right,' said De la Torre. 'Check out the next city council meeting.'

Banks said, 'Any ideas about who the buddy might be?'

Milo eyed Swig. 'Please go down to your office and wait there, sir.'

'Forget it,' said Swig. 'As director of this facility, I have jurisdiction and I need to know what's going on.'

'You will,' said Milo. 'Soon as we know something, you'll be the first to find out, but in the meantime—'

'In the meantime, I need to be—' Swig's protest was cut short by a beeper. He and all three detectives reached for their belts.

Banks said, 'Mine,' and scanned the readout. A cell phone materialized and Banks identified himself, listened, said 'When? Where?,' wiggled his fingers at De la Torre, and was handed a notepad. Tucking the phone under his chin, he wrote.

The rest of us watched him nod. Emotionless. Clicking off the phone, he said, 'When we got your call I told our desk to keep an eye out for any psycho crimes in the vicinity. This isn't exactly in the vicinity, but it's pretty psycho: Woman found on the Five near Valencia.' He examined his notes. 'White female, approximately twenty-five to thirty-five, multiple stab wounds to torso and face, really messy. Coroner says within the last two hours, which could fit if your boy has wheels. Tire tracks nearby said someone did. She wasn't just dumped there – lots of blood: It's almost certain that's where she got done.'

'What kind of facial wounds?' said Milo.

'Lips, nose, eyes – the guy at the scene said it was really brutal. That fits, right?'

'Eyes,' said Milo.

'My God,' said Swig.

'Was she found on the northbound Five?' I said.

'Yes,' said Banks.

Everyone stared at me.

'The road to Treadway,' I said. 'He's going home.'

34

THE LAST bit of news deflated Swig. He looked small, crushed, a kid with a man's job.

Milo paid him no attention, spent his time on the phone. Talking to the Highway Patrol, informing the sheriffs of the towns neighboring Treadway, warning Bunker Protection. The private firm must have given him problems, because when he got off, he snapped the phone shut so hard I thought he'd break it.

'OK, let's see what shakes up,' he told Banks and De la Torre. To Swig: 'Get me George Orson's personnel file.'

'It's downstairs in the records room.'

'Then that's where we're going.'

The records-room treasures were concealed by one of the unmarked doors bordering Swig's office. Tight space, hemmed by black file cabinets. The folder was right where it should have been. Milo examined it as the sheriff's men looked over his shoulder.

Missing photo, but George Orson's physical statistics fit Derrick Crimmins perfectly: Six-three, 170, thirty-six years old. The address was the mail drop on Pico near Barrington. No phone number.

'What else exactly did this guy do?' said Banks.

'Series of cons, and he probably killed his dad and mom and brother.'

Swig said, 'I can't believe this. If we hired him, his credentials had to be in order. The state fingerprints them—'

'He has no arrest record we know of, so prints don't mean much,' said Milo, taking the file and flipping pages. 'Says here he completed the psych tech course at Orange Coast College . . . No point following that up, who cares if he bogused his education.' To Swig: 'Would there be any record if he actually returned his keys?'

'His file's in order. That means he did. Any irregularity—'

'Is picked up by the system. I know. Of course, even if he did return them, seeing as he got to take them home every day, he had plenty of chances to make copies.'

'Each key is clearly imprinted "Do Not Duplicate."'

'Gee,' said De la Torre. 'That would scare *me*.'

Swig braced himself against the nearest file. 'There was no reason to worry about that. The risk wasn't someone breaking *in*. Why don't you look for him, instead of *harping*? Why would he come *back*?'

'Must be the ambience,' said Milo. 'Or maybe the new air-conditioning.' He looked up at a small grilled grate in the center of the ceiling. 'What about the ductwork? Wide enough for someone to fit?'

'No, no, no,' said Swig, with sudden conviction. 'Absolutely *not*. We considered that when we installed, used narrow ducts – six inches in diameter. It caused technical problems, that's why the work took so long to—' He stopped. 'Peake's my only concern. Should we keep searching?'

'Any reason to stop?' said Milo.

'If he killed that woman on the freeway, he's miles away.'

'And if he didn't?'

'Fine – exactly – got to go, need to supervise.'

'Sure,' said Milo. 'Do your thing.'

Outside the main building, the fireflies continued to dance, fragmented sporadically by the downslanting beams of circling helicopters. Milo yelled at a guard to get us out of there.

He and I and the sheriff's detectives reconvened in the parking lot, next to the unmarked. The white coroner's van was still in place, as were the squad cars and a pea-green sedan that had to be Banks and De la Torre's wheels.

Banks said, 'So what's the theory here? This Orson, or whatever his real name is, snuck in somehow and got Peake loose? What's his motive?'

Milo flourished an open palm in my direction.

'Unclear,' I said. 'It may have had something to do with Peake's original rampage. Crimmins and Peake go way back. It's possible – now I'd say probable – that Crimmins was involved somehow. Either by directly urging Peake to kill the Ardullos or by doing something more subtle.' I described the long-term conflict between the Crimminses and the Ardullos, described Peake's prophecies.

'Money,' said De la Torre.

'That's part of it, but there's more. The root of all this

is power and domination – criminal production. Orson – Derrick Crimmins – sees himself as an artist. I think he views the massacre as his first major creative accomplishment. He's been working on something called *Blood Walk*. At least three people associated with the film are dead; there may very well be others. I think Crimmins has reserved a role for Peake, but I can't say what it is. Now he's decided it's time to put Peake in the spotlight.'

'Sounds nuts,' said De la Torre.

Banks looked back at the yard. 'Funny 'bout that, Hector.' To me: 'So Crimmins is crazy, too? They hired a psychotic to work here?'

'Crimmins comes across as a classic psychopath,' I said. 'Sane but evil. Sometimes psychopaths fall apart, but not usually. Fundamentally, he's a loser – can't hold on to money, can't stick with anything, has had to take jobs that he considers below him. On some level, that enrages him. He takes out his anger on others. But he's fully aware of what he's doing – has been careful enough to shift identities, addresses, pull off one scam after another. All that spells rationality.'

'Rational,' said De la Torre, 'except he likes to kill people.' He stretched both wings of his mustache, distorting the lower half of his face. Releasing the hair, he allowed his lips to settle into a frown. 'OK, now Peake. Basically, you're saying he was a head-case blood freak who turned into a vegetable here because they overdosed him. But for him to cooperate in the escape, he'd have to be significantly better put together than a summer squash. You think he could've been faking how crazy he is?'

'The guys on Five do it all the time,' said Milo.

'And rarely succeed,' I said. 'But Peake's a genuine schizophrenic. For him, it wouldn't be a matter of either/or, it'd be the intensity of his psychosis. At an optimal level, it's possible Thorazine made him more lucid. Clear enough to be able to cooperate in the escape. Crimmins could have played a role, too. He was a significant figure in Peake's life. Who knows *what* fantasies his showing up on the ward could have stimulated.'

'The good old days,' said Milo. 'Like some damn reunion. And once Crimmins got here, he'd have seen right away how rinky-dink the system was. Pure fun. Betcha he had keys to every door within weeks. We know he floated overtime on Peake's ward. Meaning he could wear his badge, drop in whenever he wanted, arouse no suspicion.' He shook his head. 'Peake must've seen it as *salvation*.'

'Crimmins dominated him before, knows he's passive,' I said. 'Slips him a knife. No one bothers to check Peake's room for weapons because he's been nonfunctional for sixteen years. Crimmins cues Peake that the time's right; Peake sneaks up on Dollard, cuts his throat, leaves on the staff elevator. Dollard was a perfect target: Lax about the rules. And if he was involved in a drug scam with Crimmins, that would be another reason to hit him. You asked Swig if Dollard had access to the drug cabinet, so you were thinking the same thing. Or maybe Crimmins sneaked in and did the cutting himself. Showed up on the ward during the staff meeting, knowing he had only Dollard to contend with.'

'What drug scam?' said Banks.

Milo explained the theory, the cars in the driveway that

had bedeviled Marie Sinclair. 'What's better than pharmaceutical grade? Dollard's the inside man, Crimmins works the street. That's why Dollard got so antsy when we kept coming back. Idiot was afraid his little side biz would be blown. He shows his anxiety to Crimmins, tips Crimmins that he can't be counted on to stay cool, and signs his own death warrant. Crimmins has a history of tying up loose ends, and Dollard's starting to unravel.'

'This,' said Banks, 'is . . . colorful.'

'Lacking facts, I embroider,' said Milo.

'Whatever the details,' I said, 'the best guess is that Crimmins managed to get Peake down in that elevator. I think he entered the hospital grounds tonight through that cut in the fence, made his way across the rear yard, maybe hid in one of the annexes. Easy enough, no one uses them. Coming in through the foothills wouldn't be much of a problem. Crimmins used to race motocross. He could've brought a dirt bike or an off-roader.'

'Where does your vic come in?' said Banks. 'The Argent woman?'

Milo said, 'She could've come across the drug scam. Or found out something from Peake she wasn't supposed to.'

'Or, she was part of the drug scam.'

Silence.

'Why,' said De la Torre, 'did Peake start prophesying?'

'Because he's still psychotic,' I said. 'Crimmins made the mistake of divulging what he was going to do, figuring Peake would keep his mouth shut. Don't forget, Peake's been mum for sixteen years about the Ardullo murders. But recently something – probably the attention Claire paid him

– opened Peake up. He got more verbal. Started to see himself as a victim – a martyr. When I brought up the Ardullos, he assumed a crucifixion pose. That could make *him* a threat to Crimmins. Maybe the role Crimmins has in mind for him is victim.'

'Not if he's the one sliced that woman up on the I-Five.'

'Not necessarily,' I said. 'In this case monster and victim aren't mutually exclusive.'

Banks ran his hands down his lapels, looked up at the helicopters.

'One more thing,' said Milo. 'That fence wasn't cut tonight. There was some oxidation around the edges.'

'Well rehearsed,' I said. 'Just like any other production. That's the way Crimmins sees life: One big show. He could've come anytime, set the stage.'

'What a joke,' said Banks. 'Place like this and they take keys home.'

'Not that it matters,' said De la Torre. To Milo: 'You ever seen a maximum-security prison that wasn't full of dope and weapons? Other than my mother-in-law's house.'

'Can't stop inhuman nature,' said Banks. 'So now Crimmins and Peake are heading back to the hometown? Why?'

'The only thing I can think of is more theater. A script element. What I don't get is why Crimmins would leave that woman on the freeway. It's almost as if he's directing attention *to* Treadway. So maybe he's deteriorating. Or I'm totally wrong – the escape's a one-man operation and Peake's fooled everyone. He's a calculating monster who craves blood, is out to get it any way he can.'

Banks studied his notes. 'You're saying the Ardullo thing might've been financial revenge. Why kill the kids?'

'You ruin my family, I ruin yours. Primitive but twisted justice. Derrick might have planned it, but at twenty he lacked the will and the stomach to carry out the massacre himself. Then Peake entered the picture and everything clicked: The village lunatic, living right there on the Ardullo ranch. Derrick and Cliff started spending time with Peake, became his suppliers for porn, dope, booze, glue, paint. Psychopaths lack insight about themselves, but they're good at zeroing in on other people's pathology, so maybe Derrick spotted the seeds of violence in Peake, put himself in a position to exploit it. And it was a no-risk situation: If Peake never acted, who'd ever know the brothers had prodded him? Even if he said something, who'd believe him? But he did follow through, and it paid off, big-time: Carson Crimmins was able to sell his land; the family got rich and moved to Florida, where the boys got to be playboys for a while. That's one big dose of positive reinforcement. That's why I called Peake a major influence on Crimmins.'

'Crimmins didn't worry about Peake blabbing back then,' said Milo, 'but now it's different. Someone's listening.'

'Maybe Claire *was* involved in the drug scam,' I said, 'but unless we find evidence of that, my bet is she died because she'd learned from Peake that he hadn't acted alone. And she believed him. Believed *in* him. Because what she was really after was finding out something redeeming about her brother. Symbolically.'

'Symbolically,' said De la Torre. 'If she suspected Crimmins, what was she doing getting in that Corvette?'

'Maybe she got involved with Crimmins before Peake started talking. Crimmins held himself out as a cinematic hotshot, a struggling independent filmmaker trying to plumb the depths of madness or some nonsense like that. He calls his outfit Thin Line – as in walking the border between sanity and insanity. Maybe he asked her to be a technical adviser. The guy was a con; I can see her falling for it.'

'Something else,' said Milo. 'If Peake's blabbing to Claire, he's telling her about Derrick Crimmins. The guy she knows is George Orson.'

That made my heart stop. 'You're right. Claire could've told Crimmins everything. Fed him the very information that signed her death warrant.'

'Eye wounds,' said Milo. 'Like the Ardullo kids. Only *he* sees. No one else.' He rubbed his face. 'Or he just likes carving people's eyes.'

'Evil, evil, evil,' said Banks, in a soft tight voice. 'And no idea where to find him.'

The helicopters' sky-dance had shifted westward, white beams sweeping the foothills and whatever lay behind them.

'Waste of fuel,' said De la Torre. 'He's got to be on the road.'

35

MILO AND the sheriffs did more cell-phone work. Better suits and they might have looked like brokers on the make. The end result was more nothing: No sightings of Peake.

Milo looked at his watch. 'Ten-fifty. If any reporters are playing with the scanner, this could make the news in ten minutes.'

'That could be helpful,' said Banks. 'Maybe someone'll spot him.'

'I doubt Crimmins has him out in the open,' I said.

'If he's with Crimmins.'

Milo said, 'CHP says the vic from the freeway was transported. I thought I'd hit the morgue.'

'Fine,' said Banks. 'Let's exchange numbers, we'll keep in touch.'

'Yeah,' said Milo. 'Regards to Petra.'

'Sure,' said Banks, coloring. 'When I see her.'

In the past, Milo had sped through the eucalyptus grove. Now he kept the unmarked at twenty miles per, used his high beams, glancing from side to side.

'Stupid,' he said. 'No way they're anywhere near here,

but I can't stop looking. What do you call that, obsessive-compulsive ritualism?'

'Habit strength.'

He laughed. 'You could euphemize anything.'

'OK,' I said. 'It's canine transformation. The job's turned you into a bloodhound.'

'Naw, dogs have better noses. OK, I'll drop you off.'

'Forget it,' I said, 'I'm coming with.'

'Why?'

'Habit strength.'

The body lay covered on a gurney in the center of the room. The night attendant was a man named Lichter, paunchy and gray-haired, with an incongruously rich tan. A Highway Patrol detective named Whitworth had filled out the papers.

'Just missed him,' said Lichter. The bronze skin gave him the look of an actor playing a morgue man. Or was I just seeing Hollywood everywhere?

'Where'd he go?' said Milo.

'Back to the scene.' Lichter placed his hand on a corner of the gurney, gave the sheet a tender look. 'I was just about to find a drawer for her.'

Milo read the crime-scene report. 'Gunshot wound to the back of the head?'

'If that's what it says.'

Folding the sheet back, Milo exposed the face. What was left of it. Deep slashes crisscrossed the flesh, shearing skin, exposing bone and muscle and gristle. What had been the eyes were two oversized raspberries. The hair, thick and light brown where the blood hadn't crusted, fanned out on the steel table. Slender neck. Blood-splashed but undamaged; only the face had been brutalized. The eyes . . . the slash wounds created a crimson grid, like a barbecue grilling taken to the extreme. I saw freckles amid the gore, and my stomach lurched.

'Oh, boy,' said Lichter, looking sad. 'Hadn't looked at it yet.'

'Look like a gunshot to you?'

Lichter hurried to a desk in the corner, shuffled through piles of paper, picked up some stapled sheets, and flipped through. 'Same thing here . . . single wound to the occipital cranium, no bullet recovered yet.'

Gloving up, he returned to the gurney, rolled the head carefully, bent, and squinted. 'Ah – see.'

A distinct ruby hole dotted the back of the skull. Black crust fuzzed the edges and black dots peppered the slender neck.

'Stippling,' said Lichter. 'I'm just a body mover, but that means an up-close wound, right?' He released the head carefully. Another sad look. 'Maybe she got shot first and then they used a knife on her. More like a hatchet or a machete – a thick blade, right? But I better not say more. Only the coroners have opinions.'

'Who's the coroner tonight?'

'Dr Patel. He had to run out, should be back soon with some genuine wisdom.'

He began to cover the face, but Milo took hold of the sheet. 'Shooting, then slashing. Right on the side of the freeway.'

'Don't quote me on anything,' said Lichter. 'I'm not allowed to speculate.'

'Sounds like a good guess. Now all we have to do is find out who she is.'

'Oh, we know that,' said Lichter. 'They pulled prints on her right away. Easy, the fingers were fine. Detective Whitworth said she came right up on PRINTRAK – hold on.'

He ran back to the desk, retrieved more papers. 'She had a record . . . drugs, I think . . . Yup, here we go. Hedy Lynn Haupt, female Caucasian, twenty-six . . . arrested two years ago for PC 11351.5 – that's possession of cocaine for use or sale, right? I know it by heart, because we get lots of that in here. Got an address on her, too.'

Milo covered the distance between them in three strides and took the papers from him.

'Hedy Haupt,' I said, leaning down for a look at the face.

Putting my face inches from the ruined flesh. Smelling the copper-sugar of the blood, the sulfur of released gases . . . something light, floral – perfume.

The skin that unique green-gray where it wasn't blood-rusty.

Most of the head had been turned into something unthinkable, the mouth kissed by a smear of blood, the upper lip split diagonally. Yet the overall structure remained somewhat recognizable. Familiar . . . freckles across the nose and forehead. The ear that hadn't been hacked to confetti, an ashen seashell.

I peeled back the sheet. Plaid blouse. Blue jeans. Even in death the body retained a trim, tight shape. Something protruded from the breast pocket of the blouse. Half a loop of white elastic. Ponytail band.

'I think I know who this is,' I said.

Milo wheeled on me.

I said, 'Hedy Haupt, Heidi Ott. The age fits, the hair's the right color, the body's the right length – look at the right jaw, that same strong line. I'm sure of it. This is her.'

Milo's face was next to mine, exuding sweat and cigar residue.

'Oh, man,' he said. 'Another cast member?'

'Remember what big Chet kept shouting at us?' I said. 'Both in group, and as we walked across the yard? "Cherchez la femme." Search for the woman. Maybe he was trying to tell us something. Maybe maniacs are worth listening to.'

36

MILO WANTED to examine the body closely and to go over the paperwork in detail. Figuring I could do without either, I left, bought scalding, poisonous coffee from a machine, and drank it out in the waiting area facing the autopsy room. The coffee didn't do much for my stomach, but the chill that had taken hold of my legs started to dissipate.

I sat there, thinking about Heidi, executed and mutilated on the I-5.

Everyone associated with Peake and Crimmins was being discarded like garbage. It stank of a special malevolence.

Monsters.

No; Peake's moniker notwithstanding, these were people, it always came down to people.

I pictured the two of them, bound together by something I was really no closer to understanding, stalking, severing, hacking, shooting.

Crimmins's production, the worst kind of documentary. For the sake of what? How many other victims lay buried around the city?

Crisp, rapid footsteps made me look up. A perfectly groomed Indian in his forties passed me wordlessly and entered the autopsy room. Dr Patel, I assumed. I found a pay phone, called Robin, got the answering machine. She was asleep. Good. I told the machine I'd be back in a few hours, not to worry. I finished the coffee. Cooler, but it still tasted like toasted cardboard sautéed in chicory gravy.

Heidi. A narcotics record. That started me off in a whole new direction.

Viewing life through a new set of glasses . . . The door swung open and Milo shot out, wiping his forehead and waving a sheet of paper full of his cramped, urgent handwriting. Body-outline logo at the top. Coroner's gift-shop stationery.

'Heidi's home address,' he said. 'Let's go.'

We headed for the elevator.

'Where'd she live?' I said.

'West Hollywood, thirteen hundred block of Orange Grove.'

'Not far from Plummer Park, where we met with her.'

'Not far from my own damn house.' He stabbed the elevator button. 'C'mon, c'mon, c'mon.'

'Who's in charge?' I said. 'Sheriff or Highway Patrol?'

'Highway Patrol on the killing itself,' he said. 'I reached Whitworth at the scene. He said feel free to check out her house. He's staying there, wants to make sure they scrape whatever physical evidence they can off the road before traffic thickens up.'

'They shot her and butchered her right there on the freeway?'

'Turnoff. Wide turnoff. Far enough and dark enough for cover.'

'Crimmins would know the road well,' I said. 'Growing

up in Treadway. But still, it was risky, right there in the open.'

'So they're loosening up – maybe losing it, like you said. Peake's massacre wasn't exactly well thought out. He left goddamn bloody footprints. Maybe Crimmins is starting to freak, too.'

'I don't know. Crimmins is a planner. The escape says he's still pretty organized.'

He shrugged. 'What can I tell you?' The elevator arrived and he threw himself in.

'Did the coroner have anything to add?' I said.

'The bullet's still in there, he'll go digging. Ready for me to drop you off now?'

'Not a chance,' I said.

'You look wiped out.'

'*You're* not exactly perky-fresh.'

His laugh was short, dry, reluctant. 'Want some chewing gum?'

'Since when do you carry?' I said.

'I don't. The attendant – Lichter – gave me a pack. Says he started doing it for any cops who come in. Says he's gonna retire next year, feels like spreading good cheer and fresh breath.'

Outside the morgue, the air was warm, thick, gasoline-tinged. Even at this hour, the freeway noise hadn't abated. Ambulances shrieked in and out of County General. Derelicts and dead-eyes walked the street, along with a few white-coated citizens who didn't look much better off. Above us, on the overpass, cars blipped and dopplered. A few miles north, the interstate was quiet enough to serve as a killing ground.

I imagined the car pulling abruptly to the side – not the yellow Corvette; something large enough to seat three.

Crimmins and Peake. And Heidi. Riding along.

A captive? Or a passenger.

The dope conviction.

I thought of the meeting at Plummer Park.

My roommate's sleeping, or I would've had you come to my place.

Would a live roommate be waiting for us at the Orange Grove address? Or . . .

My mind flashed back to the freeway kill. Heidi out of the car, surprised, asking Crimmins what was up. Or immobilized – bound, gagged – and terrified.

Crimmins and Peake haul her out. She's a strong girl, but they control her easily.

They walk her as far as they can from the freeway. To the edge of the turnoff, everyone swallowed by darkness now.

Last words or not?

Either way: *Pop*. A searing burst of light and pain.

What was the last thing she'd heard? A truck whizzing by? The wind? The racing of her pulse?

They let her fall. Then Crimmins gives a signal and Peake steps forward.

Blade in hand.

Summoned.

Camera. Action.

Cut.

My guts pogoed as I got in the unmarked, wanting to sort it all out, to make sense of it before I said anything to Milo. He started up the engine, sped through the morgue lot, and turned left on Mission. We roared off.

Orange Grove showed no signs of ever having hosted citrus trees. Just another LA street full of small, undistinguished houses.

The house we came to see was hidden behind an untrimmed ficus hedge, but the green wall didn't extend to the asphalt driveway and we had a clear view all the way to the garage. No vehicles in sight. Milo drove a hundred feet down and we returned on foot. I waited by the curb as he made his way up the asphalt, gun in hand, back to the garage, around the rear of the wood-sided bungalow. Even in the darkness I could see scars on the paint. The color was hard to make out, probably some version of beige. Between the house and the ficus barrier was a stingy square of dead lawn. Sagging front porch, no shrubbery other than the hedge.

Milo came back, gun still out, breathing hard. 'Looks empty. The back door's Mickey Mouse, I'm going in. Stay there till I tell you.'

Another five minutes, ten, twelve, as I watched his penlight bounce around behind shaded windows. A single firefly. Finally, the front door opened and he waved me inside.

He'd gloved up. I followed as he turned a few lights on, exposing a poverty of space. First we did an overall check of the house. Five small, shabby rooms, including a dingy lavatory. Grimy yellow walls; the window shades crazed, gray oilcloth patched in spots by duct tape.

Colorless rental furniture.

Where the space allowed. The bungalow was filled with crisp-looking cardboard boxes, most of them sealed. Printed labels on the outside. THIS SIDE UP. FRAGILE. Scores of cartons of TV's, stereos, video gear, cameras, PC's. Cassettes, compact discs, computer discs. Glassware, silverware, small appliances. Stacks of video cartridges and Fuji film. Enough film to shoot a thousand birthday parties.

In a corner of the larger bedroom, squeezed next to an unmade queen-size mattress, stood a pile of smaller boxes. The labels claimed Sony minirecorders. Just like the one Heidi had used to tape Peake.

'The movie stuff's out in the garage,' said Milo. 'Dollies, booms, spotlights, crap I couldn't identify. Tons of it, piled almost to the ceiling. Didn't see any saws, but they could be buried under all the gear. It'll take a crew to go through it.'

'She was in on it,' I said.

He'd moved into the bathroom, didn't answer. I heard drawers opening, went over to see him remove something from the cabinet beneath the sink.

Glossy white shoe box. Several more just like it stacked next to the pipes.

He lifted the lid. Rows of white plastic bottles nesting in Styrofoam beds. He extracted one. 'Phenobarbital.'

All the other bottles in that box were labeled identically. The next box yielded an assortment, and so did all the others.

Chlorpromazine, thioridazine, haloperidol, clozapine, diazepam, alprazolam, lithium carbonate.

'Candy sampler for a junkie,' said Milo. 'Uppers, downers, all-arounders.'

He inspected the bottom of the box. 'Starkweather stamp's still on here.'

'Uncut pharmaceuticals,' I said. 'It ups the price.' Then I thought of something.

Milo was looking the other way, but I must have made a sound, because he said, 'What?'

'I should've figured it out a long time ago. The missing dog, Buddy. He was sticking in my head because I've seen him before. That day in the park, a tall man in black came by walking a Rottweiler mix. Passed right by where we were sitting with Heidi. Heidi was aware of him. She watched him. He was her roommate. The one she'd claimed was sleeping. Their little joke. They were playing with us right from the beginning. So much for powers of observation. Lot of good it does us now.'

'Hey,' he said, recording the drug inventory in his notepad. 'I'm the so-called detective, and I never noticed the dog.'

'Crimmins stole him from Mrs Leiber. Taking what he wanted. Because he could. For him, it's all about power.'

He stopped writing. 'No sign of any dog here,' he said. 'No food or bowl anywhere in the house.'

'Exactly.'

'Heidi,' he said, suddenly sounding tired.

'It casts a whole new light on her story,' I said. 'Peake's prophecy. Peake's supposed prophecy.'

His hand tightened around his pen. He stared at me. 'Another scam.'

'Has to be. The only evidence we ever had was Heidi's account.'

'"Bad eyes in a box." "Choo choo bang bang."'

'The tape, too,' I said. I led him back to the larger bedroom. Pointed at the stack of Sonys. 'The tape was nothing but mumbles. Unrecognizable mumbles, could've been anyone. But we *know* who it was.'

'Crimmins.'

'Dubbing the soundtrack,' I said. 'George Welles Orson. Like I said, he's an auteur: Produces, directs, acts.'

He cursed violently.

'He murdered Claire,' I went on, 'then set Peake up as a phony oracle to spice up his story line – who knows, maybe he thought he'd be able to use it one day. Write a screenplay, sell it to Hollywood. We took it seriously – great fun, once again he's screwed the Law. Just like he did back in Florida. And Nevada. And Treadway. So when he eliminated the Beatty brothers, he did it again. Used Heidi, again. Once again, no risk; nothing he does with Peake bears any risk. No one's heard Peake talk in almost two decades – who's to say it's not his voice on the tape? When we met Heidi, she let us know she was going to quit the hospital. That allowed her to do you a favor by sticking around. Gave her instant credibility – personally invited by the police. From that point, no one was going to suspect anything she did with Peake.'

'Except maybe Chet.'

'"Cherchez la femme,"' I said. 'Maybe Chet noticed something – something off about Heidi. Maybe the way she related to Peake. Or he saw her steal dope from the nursing station. Or get a little handoff from Dollard. But once again, who'd pay attention to *his* ramblings? Heidi was free to continue as Crimmins's inside woman. She was there in the first place because Crimmins wanted her – she joined the staff right after he left. He gave her multiple assignments: Work with Dollard to keep the drugs flowing, make sure Dollard didn't rip them off, and attach herself to Claire so she could report back what Claire was saying about Peake. Because he *had* to have discussed Peake with Claire. That was the basis of *their* relationship.'

'"Cherchez la femme,"' he said. 'The guy collects *femmes*.' He looked around at the piles of contraband. 'Heidi traveling with him and Peake tonight probably means she was in on the escape. Her being the inside woman would *smooth* the escape, wouldn't it? Yesterday, the last time we ran into her, she was walking Peake right near that service elevator. Dry run for tonight.'

'Has to be. She and Crimmins needed to rehearse, because whatever the state of Peake's psyche, he'd been cooped up for sixteen years, was unpredictable. It's also possible the timetable for the escape was sped up because you were getting too close. Remember when you asked Heidi if Peake had mentioned Wark's name, and she hesitated for a second. Probably shocked that you'd gotten on to the alias, but she stayed cool. Said it was a funny name, didn't really sound like a name. Edging us away from Wark and diverting our attention to Dollard by letting us know he'd been fired for malfeasance. Because Dollard had become a liability. He'd always been the expendable member of the dope scam.

Crimmins and Heidi came up with a kill-two-birds plan: Get rid of Dollard and break Peake loose. Something else: Right after Heidi told us about Dollard, she returned the conversation to Wark, started asking questions. Who was he, was he actually Peake's friend? Why would she care? She was trying to find out exactly what we knew, and we didn't notice because we saw her as an ally.'

'Actress,' he said.

'Calm under pressure – a very cold young woman. The moment we were gone, she was probably on the phone to Crimmins. Informing him you were on to his alter ego. He decided to act.'

'Cool head,' he said. 'Lot of good it did her head.'

'Cool but also reckless,' I said. 'A coke conviction didn't stop her from stealing dope at Starkweather. Flirting with danger was also behind her attraction to Crimmins. She told us she was a thrill seeker. Rock climbing, skydiving off power stations – making sure to let you know that was illegal. Think of it: Telling a cop she'd committed a crime. Smiling about it. Another little game. Getting off on danger is probably also the way she hooked up with Crimmins in the first place. Castro told us Derrick and brother Cliff were thrill chasers, liked speed. Derrick and Heidi probably met at some kind of daredevil club.'

'Going for the adrenaline rush,' he said. 'Then it gets old, so they move on to a different kind of high.'

'Crimmins's crimes have a profit motive, but I've been saying all along that thrill's the main ingredient. Crimmins's thing is creating a twisted world and controlling it. He scripts the action, casts the players, moves them around like pawns.

Gets rid of them once they've finished their scenes. For a psychopath, it would be pretty damn close to heaven. Heidi had similar motivations, but she wasn't in Crimmins's league. It was a fun ride for her, but her mistake was thinking of herself as a partner when she was just another extra. She must have been confused when Crimmins pulled off the I-Five and told her to get out.'

I didn't feel like laughing, but there I was, doing it.

'What?' he said.

'Just thought of something. If Crimmins had been lucky enough to really break into Hollywood, maybe none of this would've happened.'

He took in the room and I followed his eyes. Cramped, dingy, nothing on the walls. For Heidi and Crimmins, interior decorating had meant something else, completely. Cruel puzzles, bloody scenes, embroidery of the mind . . .

'Let me sort out the escape,' he said, very softly. 'Double entry to Starkweather: Crimmins enters the grounds from the back, through that hole in the fence; Heidi drives right in through the front gate, like she would any other night. She waltzes right on to C Ward, heads over to Peake's room, gets him ready. All the techs are at the weekly meeting, except Dollard, who's patrolling. Heidi lures Dollard into Peake's room – no big challenge, all she has to do is tell him Peake is sick, or freaking out – assuming the Jesus pose again. Dollard goes in, locks the door behind him – basic procedure – goes over to check on Peake. Maybe Peake jumps him, maybe not. In either case, Heidi gets Dollard and cuts his throat. Or *she* distracts Dollard and *Peake* does the cutting . . . She makes sure the coast is clear, hustles Peake over to the staff elevator, no floor guide to tell anyone where it's going . . . Down to the basement, over and out.'

'And Crimmins, hiding in one of the annexes, or nearby, meets up with them,' I said. 'Heidi and Crimmins lead Peake out the back fence. Heidi returns and leaves the hospital the way she came in, through the front, while Crimmins and Peake escape into the foothills, where they've got a vehicle waiting that can handle the terrain. Peake's not in great condition, but Crimmins is a climber, already knows the hills; it wouldn't be a problem dragging Peake along. Heidi as Dollard's cutter would also explain why the artery was only nicked, not slashed clear through. She was a strong girl without much of a conscience. But if she'd never actually cut anyone's throat before, her inexperience could've showed. It takes will to saw through someone's neck. And there's the gush factor. She would've wanted to avoid getting bloodstained, had to coordinate cutting and stepping back in time – I can see Crimmins rehearsing her. So she wounded Dollard just deeply enough to open the carotid. Dollard collapsed, so she thought she'd finished him off. He went into shock, lay there draining. Once again, they were lucky – no one found him soon enough to save him.'

'Crimmins seems to have lots of luck.'

'No sin unrewarded,' I said. 'That's why he keeps doing bad things.'

'The nick could also mean Peake did it,' he said. 'Atrophied muscles from all those years in the loony bin.'

'Not if he chopped up Heidi's face. Those gashes took force. What do you figure, a hatchet?'

'Patel said that, or some kind of cleaver. Yeah, you're probably right . . . Heidi cut Dollard, and Peake cut Heidi.'

'Her murdering Dollard would serve another purpose: No need to hide a weapon in Peake's room, risk discovery. Techs carry. You just proved that.'

He pulled out his phone, called Ron Banks, told him about the drugs and the stolen goods, Heidi's involvement. 'Yeah, looks like she was . . . Listen, I'm gonna snoop around her house some more, but it's West Hollywood, so you might as well get some of your guys over here to tape it off. Tell 'em I'm here, what I look like, so there's no misunderstandings . . . Thanks. Anything new over there? . . . Yeah, sometimes the job is boring . . . Yeah, I think I will. Chippie's still over there . . . Whitworth. Michael Whitworth.'

Milo started to search in earnest. The bedroom closet held blue jeans, blouses, and jackets in women's small and medium sizes, and men's black jeans, 34 waist, 35 length, black XL T-shirts, sweaters, and shirts.

'Home sweet home,' he said, shining his light on the floor. Three plastic cartons full of rumpled underwear and socks sat next to a jumble of battered running shoes and several pairs of thick-soled, dirty-looking boots. In the corner were four olive-drab packages the size of seat cushions, festooned with straps. US Army stencil. Next to them, scuba gear, a single set of skis, a box of amyl nitrate – poppers. Another box full of polyester hair. Four woman's wigs: Long and blond; short, spiky, and blond; raven black; tomato red and curly. Three male toupees, all black, two curly, one straight. Labels inside from a theatrical makeup store on Hollywood Boulevard.

'Toys,' said Milo. 'When you were over at Fairway Ranch, see any good climbing spots?'

'The entire development is backed by the Tehachapi mountains. But a short walk through foothills is one thing, serious climbing's another. Crimmins would be limited by Peake's condition. Even if Peake's vegetable act's a fake, he's no Edmund Hillary. Also, if Crimmins has returned to Treadway, it's because it has psychological meaning for him. So maybe he'll stick close to home.'

'What kind of psychological meaning?'

'Something to do with the massacre – maybe he's reworking it. For his movie. Rescripting – *reliving* – a major triumph. Back when he lived there, Treadway was essentially divided between the Ardullo and the Crimmins ranches. Wanda Hatzler told me the Mexican girl Derrick and Cliff threw out of their car ran toward the Ardullo property. On the north side. That could narrow things down.'

'But which way would he go? To the Ardullo side because that's where the massacre went down, or to his daddy's place?'

'Don't know,' I said. 'Maybe none of the above.'

'What's there now? Where the ranches were.'

'Homes. Recreational facilities. A lake.'

'Big homes?' he said. 'Something that might remind Crimmins of the Ardullo place?'

'I didn't get that close a look. It's an upscale development. Whether or not that will trigger anything in Crimmins's head, I can't say.'

'Any obvious place to hide out?'

'It's pretty open,' I said. 'Two golf courses, the lake. If they break into someone's home, there'll be plenty of cover. But even if Crimmins is loosening up mentally, that seems downright stupid . . . Maybe outside the development. Somewhere at the base of the Tehachapis. If Derrick climbed as a kid, he could have a special hiding place.'

Milo got back on the phone, called Bunker Protection. Once again, his side of the conversation was tense. 'Idiot rent-a-cops. No sign of any disturbance, no disreputables have driven through tonight, yawn, yawn . . . OK, let me toss the rest of this palace.'

The second bedroom, the space where Heidi and Derrick Crimmins had slept, was narrow, also devoid of personal touches, with barely enough space for the queen-size mattress and two cheap nightstands. In the top drawer of the stand on the right were a half-empty box of tampons, three gold-wrapped Godiva chocolates, two energy bars, a baggie of marijuana. The bottom compartment held woman's underwear, an empty Evian bottle, some white powder in a glassine envelope.

'The 11351.5 didn't make much of an impression,' I said.

'First offense – she probably got probation. If that.'

'More fuel for her confidence. Coke and poppers would've helped, too.'

He checked under the mattress, in the pillowcases, moved around to Crimmins's nightstand. Pack of Kools, two foil-wrapped condoms, two matchbooks, and a thin red paperback book entitled *Finding Fame and Fortune in Hollywood: Writing Your Screenplay*, 'by the editors of the Fame and Fortune Series.'

The publisher was an outfit called Hero Press, POB address in Lancaster, California. The flyleaf said others in the series included *Buying Real Estate with Nothing Down*, *Options and Commodities Trading with Nothing Down*, *Start Your Own Business with Nothing Down*, and *Live to 120: The Herbal Way to Longevity*.

'The scammer finally gets scammed,' said Milo, kneeling in front of the lower compartment.

Inside was a black vinyl looseleaf. He pulled it out, turned to the title page.

Typed at the top was

BLOOD WALK

A TREATMENT FOR A MAJOR MOTION PICTURE

By
D. Griffith Crimmins***

***PRESIDENT AND CEO, DGC PRODUCTIONS,
THIN LINE PRODUCTIONS, ENTERPENEUR,
DIRECTOR, PRODUCER, AND CINEMATOGRAPHER

The next page, soiled and smudged, bore several upslanting lines written in ballpoint. Curious, sharp-edged penmanship, full of angles and peaks that reminded me of hieroglyphics.

Equip. No prob. Obviosly.
Casting: Wrd of mth? Ad? Pickups? Special effects: Fakeout, double-bluff

Figure out the cameras or use video? Worth the hassle?
Viedo can work good enough
Titles: Blood Walk. Bloodwalkers. Walk of Blood.
Bloodbath. The Big Walk
Alternetive titles: 1. The Monster Returns 2. Bagging the Monster 3. Daredevil Avenger – justice for all. 4. Saturday The 14th 5. Return of the Moster 6. Horror On Palm Street 7. Maniac 8. Psycho-Drama 9. The Ultamite Crime 10. Genius and Insanity 11. The Thin Line – whos to say whos crazy and whos not.

'Another plot outline, just like in Florida,' I said. 'Reads like a twelve year old's diary – look at the third alternative title. "Daredevil Avenger – justice for all." Superman fantasies. He sees *himself* as a risk taker, is thinking of himself as the hero who saves the world from Peake.'

Milo shook his head. 'Number eleven's the one he actually used for the name of his company – who's to say who's nuts, asshole? I say. And you *are*.' He turned to the next page. Blank.

'Guess he ran out of ideas,' he said. 'This kind of brilliance, he *definitely* could've gotten a legit job at the studios.'

The light changed in the room. Something yellowing the window shades.

Headlights. A car idling next to the house. In the driveway.

I thought of Marie Sinclair, cranky and paranoid. Pays to listen to everyone.

Milo moved quickly, killing the room lights, replacing the looseleaf, pulling out his gun.

The headlights dimmed; the engine dieseled for several seconds before quieting. The whoosh-and-click of the car door closing. Footsteps scraping the driveway.

Diminishing footsteps.

Milo raced through the house, made it to the front door, said something to me.

Stay put, he explained later, but I never processed it and I stayed on his heels.

He cracked the door, looked outside, flung it open, ran.

In the driveway sat a lemon-yellow Corvette.

We ran past the ficus hedge. A man was fifty feet up the street, to the north. Walking casually, arms swinging.

Tall man. Thin. A too-big head – much too big. Some kind of hat.

Milo set out after him. Closed the gap, bellowed.

'*Policefreezedon'tmovepolicefreezefreeze!*'

The man stopped.

'*Stay right there hands behind your head.*'

The man obeyed.

'*Lie down slowly face to the sidewalk – get your hands back there again – up up behind your head.*'

Total compliance. As the man lay down, his hat fell off.

In a flash, Milo had his cuffs out, was bending the man's arm behind his back.

That easy.

Time for someone else to have some luck.

'Where's Peake?' Milo demanded.

'Who?' High, tight voice.

'Peake. Don't fuck with me, Crimmins—'

'Who—'

Keeping his gun trained on the back of the man's head, Milo fished out the penlight and tossed it to me. 'Shine it on his face – lift up your face!'

Before the man could respond, Milo grabbed a handful of hair and helped him along. The man gasped in pain. I moved around in front and aimed the beam at his face.

Thin face. Framed by long blond hair. He had hat head from the watch cap that lay a few feet away on the pavement.

A few lights went on in neighboring houses, but the street remained quiet.

Milo held the man's chin as I illuminated scared pale eyes. Weak chin, cottony with fledgling beard growth.

Pimples.

Adolescent acne.

A kid.

37

HIS NAME was Christopher Paul Soames and he had ID to prove it.

An obviously phony California Identification Card and a student card from Bellflower High, dated three years ago. He'd been a sophomore then, with shorter hair and clearer skin. Had dropped out the following summer, because 'it sucked and I had a job.'

'Where?' said Milo. He'd dragged Soames onto the lawn behind the ficus hedge, emptied the boy's pockets.

'Lucky's.'

'Doing what?'

'Box boy.'

'How long did you work there?'

'Two months.'

'After that?'

Soames's shrug was inhibited by the cuffs.

He had a twenty-dollar bill in his pocket, a marijuana roach, a partially crushed bag of Peanut M&M's, no driver's license. 'But I know how to, my brother taught me before he went into the Marines.'

Milo pointed to the Corvette. 'Nice wheels.'

'Yeah – can you take these off me, man?'

'Run your story by me one more time, Chris.'

'Can I at least get off the grass? It's wet, I'm getting my ass wet.'

Milo lifted him by a belt loop and hauled him over to the bungalow's front porch. The interrogation had been going on for nearly ten minutes. No sign of any sheriff's cars yet.

Soames shifted his shoulders. 'These hurt, man. Lemme loose, I din't do nothin'.'

'Didn't steal the car?'

'No way, I tole you.'

'You didn't find an address in the car and drive over to rob the house?'

'No way.'

'How'd you get the keys?'

'Dude gave 'em to me, I tole you.'

'But you don't know the dude's name.'

'Right.'

'Dude just hands you the keys to his 'Vette, just like that.'

'Yeah.' Soames sniffed. A bony knee started shaking.

'Where'd this fairy tale take place?' said Milo.

'Ivar and Lexington, like I tole you.'

Hollywood back streets. The boy had a hollow-cheeked look that screamed too much Hollywood.

Milo said, 'He just came up to you on the corner and gave you his keys.'

'Right.'

'What were you doing on Ivar and Lexington?'

'Nothin'. Hangin'.'

'And he drove up in the 'Vette and—'

'No, he walked up. The 'Vette was parked somewhere else.'

'Where?'

'Coupla blocks away.'

'So you figured him for a john.'

'No – I don' do that shit. That's all that happened, man.'

'What'd the dude look like, Chris?'

'Don' know.'

'Dude gives you his car keys, and you don't know what he looks like.'

'It was dark – it's always dark there, that's why— Go look for yourself, it's always dark there.'

'Dude you don't know and whose face you can't see just hands you the keys to his 'Vette, tells you to drive it home for him, gives you twenty bucks for the favor.'

'That's right,' said Soames.

'Why would he want to do that?'

'Ask him.'

'I'm asking you, Chris.'

'He had another car.'

'Ah,' said Milo. 'Something you forgot to tell me the first time around.'

'He— I—' Soames's mouth snapped shut.

'What, Chris?'

'Nothing.'

'Part of the twenty was the dude told you not to say anything to anybody, right?'

Silence.

'Did he say anything about bailing you when you get busted for grand theft auto?'

Silence.

Milo got down on one knee, eye level with Soames. 'What if I told you I believe you, Chris? What if I told you *I* know what this guy looks like? Tall, skinny, big nose like a bird's beak. Dresses all in black. Black hair, or maybe light brown. As in, wig.'

Soames blinked.

'How'm I doing?'

Soames looked away.

'What if I told you you're a very lucky kid, Chris, because this is a very, very, *very* bad individual and you might be mixed up in something extremely heavy.'

Soames's nose wrinkled. Dried snot crusted one nostril. His eyes were runny. His clothes smelled dirty, old, strangely metallic.

'Something *unbelievably* heavy, Chris.'

'Right.'

'Think I'm kidding you, Chris? How else would I know what he looks like? Why do you think I'm here at his house?'

Soames gave another abbreviated shrug.

'Accessory to murder, Chris,' said Milo.

'Right.'

'Hundred percent right. This guy likes to kill people. Likes to make it hurt.'

'Bullshit.'

'Why would I bullshit you, Chris?'

Soames said, 'You – he— You better be bullshitting.'

'I'm not.'

Soames's eyes had turned wet. His lip was shaking.

'You know something, Chris?'

'You *better* be bullshitting,' Soames whined. 'I let him take *Suzy*.'

Susanna Galvez. Female Hispanic, black and brown, five-two, 116. A DOB that made her fourteen years and seven months old. Missing-persons report filed eighteen months ago at the Bellflower substation.

'Parents suspect she's with her boyfriend,' said Milo, pocketing his phone. 'Male Caucasian, blond and blue, six to six-two, a hundred forty-five, goes by the name of Chris. No last name.'

To Soames: 'So, Mr No Last Name, she ran away with you when she was twelve?'

'She's fourteen now.'

Milo grabbed his collar. 'You want her to make fifteen, tell me the rest of it, Chris. *Now*, you stupid little shit.'

'OK, yeah, yeah, I've seen the guy before, but I don' know him, that's the truth, man. Not a john, that was true, he just usually cruises. No name, he never told me no name.'

'No name and he cruises Hollywood in the 'Vette,' said Milo.

'No, no,' Soames said impatiently. 'Not the 'Vette, never saw the 'Vette before, the other car, this black Jeep. Suzy and I used to call him Marilyn, like Marilyn Manson, 'cause he's tall and weird-looking like Marilyn Manson.'

'What's he cruise for?'

Soames's nose bubbled. Milo pulled out a handkerchief, wiped it, took hold of Soames's face again and stared into the boy's eyes. 'What's his business, Chris?'

'Sometimes people – not me – score dope from him. Pills.

He's got boocoo pills, prescription shit. Not for me, Suzy either. I just seen him sell pills to other dudes. He has this girlfriend, white hair, all punked up, they both sell pills—'

'What happened tonight?'

'Me and Suzy were hangin' out, what time I don't know, we don't have watches, don't give a shit about time, had a couple burgers at Go-Ji's, we were headed back to this place where we camp – no B&E, it's like an empty squat, we camp there all the time, this guy Marilyn comes up and says he needs me to drive the 'Vette to his house, he knows I'm straight he can trust me, he just wants me to drive it there, put the keys in the mailbox, and take the bus back to 'Wood. Twenty bucks now and fifty more when he sees me tomorrow morning at Go-Ji's.'

'What time tomorrow morning?'

'Ten. He's gonna meet me in the parking lot and give me the fifty and also give Suzy back.'

'Give her back from where?' said Milo.

'I don't know,' said Soames. He whimpered.

'He just took her and didn't tell you where or why?'

'He borrowed her, man.'

'To make a movie, right? Guess what kind of movies he makes?'

Soames's shaking knee locked. He began to cry. Milo shook him out of it. 'What else, Chris?'

'Nothing, that's it – you think he really could hurt her?'

'Oh, yeah,' said Milo. 'So think back, genius. Where did he say he was taking her?'

'I don't know! Oh, man!' said Soames. 'Oh man, oh man – after we arranged about the 'Vette, he looked at Suzy and said she was real pretty and he could use her in this movie he was making, he's a producer. He didn't say nothing about where, I thought, *Oh, man, her dad's gonna kill me.*'

'Why?'

''Cause a the movie – you know.'

'You assumed he was making a fuck film,' said Milo.

'No,' said Soames. 'I wouldn'ta— He said, "Don't worry, no one's gonna mess with her, it's just a movie."'

'What kind of movie? You handed her over and didn't ask him *anything*?'

'I— He— I think he said it was a thriller, she was gonna be like a main character, he needed to film her at night. 'Cause it was a thriller. He was gonna give us – her – a hundred bucks.'

'In addition to the fifty?'

'Yeah.'

'Generous.'

'He said it was a big part.'

'And he said he'd give you every penny of it, right?'

'It was for both of us, man. We hang together, but Suzy don't hold no money, I'm more responsible.'

The deputies finally arrived. Milo let them take custody of Soames, and he and I hurried to the unmarked.

He pulled away fast, sped north.

'Two cars means two drivers,' I said. 'Before the escape, Crimmins and Heidi arranged a meet. Somewhere in Hollywood. But Crimmins knew Heidi wouldn't live out the evening, and with her out of the way, he needed someone to drive the second car. Most Hollywood streets have parking regulations; he couldn't risk a ticket. Also, the 'Vette's conspicuous.'

'Why would he trust an idiot like Soames to transport it?'

'The idiot followed through, didn't he? Like I said, Crimmins is good at reading people. Or maybe he didn't care – was finished with the 'Vette.'

'Just like that? He walks away from a car? And why would he be finished with it?'

'Because tonight marks a new stage in his life,' I said. 'And money's not his thing, it never was. The moment he has any, he lets it slip through his fingers. He grew up with fast toys, easy come, easy go. Easy to replace, too. He steals movie equipment, boosting another car's no big deal. The Jeep's not registered under any of the names we know about, either. For all we know, he's got a fleet stashed somewhere.'

'Supercriminal. Daredevil Avenger.'

'Let's face it, Milo, you don't have to be a genius to get away with felonies in LA.'

He growled, raced to Sunset, turned right. I closed my eyes and sat back, knowing exactly where he was headed. Moments later, I felt the car swerve, opened my eyes to see a freeway signpost. The 101 North. Very little traffic this late, and the I-5 interchange was only minutes away. He pushed the unmarked up to ninety, a hundred.

'Susanna Galvez,' he said. 'That Hatzler woman told you Derrick and his brother had a thing for Mexican girls.'

'Nostalgia,' I said. 'Exactly. This whole thing's about reliving the good old days.'

38

THE SPOT where Heidi Ott had been executed wasn't hard to find.

The rosy incandescence of Highway Patrol flares was visible half a mile away, starbursts fallen to the horizon.

As we got closer, a tapering row of red cones cordoned off the right-hand lane. Milo drove between them, showed his badge to a uniformed officer, received a wary appraisal. Two CHP cruisers, a CHP bike, and a sleek, nonregulation Harley-Davidson were parked on the turnoff.

The officer said, 'OK.'

'Mike Whitworth?'

'There.' A thumb indicated a huge man in his thirties standing near an embankment. Several arc lights cast focused glare on a taped-off area. The white body outline was at the far edge of the turnoff, inches from the merging of asphalt and dirt embankment. Full-scale version of the morgue gift-shop logo; life imitates art.

Whitworth stood just outside the cones. Young and in good shape, but he looked tired. His ruddy baby-face was centered by a small, blond mustache. His hair was buzzed so short the color was hard to determine. He wore a peanut-butter-colored leather jacket, white shirt, dark tie, gray slacks, and black boots, and he carried a motorcycle helmet.

Milo introduced himself.

Whitworth shook his hand, then mine. He pointed at the ground. Several ruby blotches, the largest over a foot wide. 'We found some bone bits and cartilage, too. Probably part of her nose bone. We get gore all the time, plenty of bad stuff in garbage bags, but this kind of damage . . .' He shook his head.

Milo said, 'I think the guys who did her are about to do another one.' He gave Whitworth a breakneck account of Derek Crimmins's history, Peake's escape, Heidi's possible involvement, ended with Christopher Soames's account. The recruitment of Suzy Galvez.

'Out in the Tehachapis?' said Whitworth.

'Best guess. The Tehachapis behind his hometown. It's a place called Fairway Ranch, now. Know it?'

'Never heard of it,' said Whitworth. 'I live in Altadena, do most of my work closer to the city. Before Grapevine or past?'

'Right there,' I said.

'Crimmins probably has some climbing experience,' said Milo, 'but Peake doesn't, and if they've got the girl with them, it's not gonna be any Everest thing. They could even be right on the development – commandeering someone's house. The private cops who patrol Fairway say no, but that doesn't convince me. If they *are* in the mountains, I'm figuring right at the base, maybe some kind of sheltered spot – a cave, an outcropping. Either way, we've got to take a look.'

'Who're the private cops and what's their problem?' said Whitworth.

'Bunker Protection, out of Chicago. Every time I try to convince them there's something to worry about, they don't wanna know. Keep handing me this public relations crap – "Nothing ever goes wrong here."'

'Till it does,' said Whitworth, massaging his belt buckle. 'OK, let's get going. I don't know about the jurisdictional aspect, but to hell with all that.' He glanced back at the body outline. 'We're just about wrapped up, so I can get you these four troopers right now, call for more with ETA's of less than half an hour. I'm on my bike – I was going off duty when the call came in; I'll ride solo, meet you there. If the Bunker yahoos give you a hard time, we'll bulk-intimidate them. What about choppers?'

Milo turned to me. 'What do you think? Would noise and lights stop him or egg him on?'

'Depends what's in the script,' I said.

'The script?' said Whitworth.

'He's following some sort of story line. In terms of how he'll react to a direct threat, the problem is we don't know enough about his arousal level to predict safely.'

'Arousal? This is a sex thing?'

'His general physiological state,' I said. 'Psychopaths tend to function at a quieter level than the rest of us – low pulse rates and skin conductance, high pain thresholds – except when tension builds up. Then they can be extremely explosive. If we confront Crimmins when he's still relatively calm – scheming, planning, taking control – it's possible he'll fold his tents and run, or just give up. But if we catch him at a peak moment, he might just go for the big ending.'

'Pull a Koresh,' said Whitworth. 'How old's that girl?'

'Fourteen.'

'Course, there's nothing to say he hasn't already done her.'

Milo said, 'Put the choppers on standby. Get me two, three more cars. Along the same lines, we drive into Fairway quietly, no lights, no sirens.' To me: 'Where do the Bunker people hang out?'

'There's a guardhouse right past the entrance.'

'OK,' he said to Whitworth. 'Meet you at the main entrance. Alex, give him directions. You're the only one who's actually been there.'

39

THE MEN in the powder-blue shirts weren't happy.

Three guards, surprised as they sat in the mock-Spanish guardhouse. Soft music on stereo. The shirts freshly pressed.

Neat, clean building, outside and in, cozy interior: Spotless kitchenette, oak table set with four matching chairs, blue hats on a rack. On the table were the remains of takeout Mexican food. Taco Fiesta, Valencia address. Next to a half-eaten burrito, a Trivial Pursuit® board. Three little plastic pies, blue, orange, brown, the last half-filled with tiny plastic wedges.

The door had been unlocked. When Milo and Mike Whitworth and I entered, all three guards had stood up, grabbed for guns that weren't there. Across the room, a metal locker said WEAPON DEPOSITORY. Next to it was a plaque with the crossed-rifles logo of Bunker Protection.

Now we were all outside in the peach-scented air, under a sky surprisingly deprived of stars. The Bunker guards kept their eyes on the CHP cruisers that blocked the entrance to Fairway Ranch. Inside the cars, the barest outline of men behind night-darkened windshields.

As we'd driven in, Milo had eyed the low white fence, muttered, 'No gate. They could've cruised right in.'

Moments later, Mike Whitworth coasted up on his Harley and said something to the same effect.

'So you haven't searched yet,' Milo said to the tallest guard. 'E. Cliff.' The one who'd protested loudest until Milo hushed him with a scolding index finger.

'No,' he said. 'It's past two in the morning, we're not going to wake up the residents. No reason to.'

'You'd know if there *was* a reason?' said Whitworth.

'Absolutely,' said Cliff. Adding a barked '*Sir.*'

Whitworth stepped closer to him, using his size the way Milo does. 'The way you're set up, anyone could get in – is it Ed?'

Cliff tried to smile as he backed away. 'Eugene. *Not* correct. Anyone entering can be spotted from the guardhouse.'

'Assuming the drapes are open.'

Cliff's head jerked toward the building. 'They usually are.'

Milo said, 'I'm *usually* charming.' He moved in on Cliff, too. 'So tell me, what category would two murderers driving right past you fall into? Sports and Leisure? Arts and Entertainment?'

'Sir!' said Cliff. 'There's no reason to get disrespectful. Even with the drapes closed we see headlights.'

'Assuming there *were* headlights – I know, there usually are.'

'There's no reason—'

Milo stepped closer. Cliff was over six feet, but reedy, an elk confronting bears. He looked at the other two Bunker guards. Both just stood there.

Milo said, 'There's *every* reason to search the premises, friend, and we're going to do it, right now.'

'I'm sorry, sir, in terms of your jurisdiction . . .' Cliff began. Milo's nose moved a half-inch from his, and the voice tapered. 'At the least, I'll have to clear it with headquarters.'

Milo smiled. 'In Minneapolis?'

'Chicago,' said one of the other guards. Nasal voice. 'L. Bonaface.'

'Call,' said Milo. 'Meanwhile, we start. Give me a map of this place.'

'There isn't one,' said Cliff.

'None at all?'

'Not a real map, with coordinates. Just a general layout.'

'Jesus,' said Milo. 'This isn't arctic exploration, hand it over. *Before* you call.'

Cliff looked at Bonaface. 'Go get it for him.' Bonaface went inside the guardhouse and returned with several sheets of paper.

'I brought a bunch,' he said.

Milo grabbed the maps and distributed them. A single page of crude, computer-generated diagram. English street names printed in Gothic, the shops and golf courses, Reflection Lake dead center. No indication a mountain range loomed to the east.

Whitworth said, 'Except for the golf courses, it's a small area – that's in our favor . . . Already divided into six zones, and I've got five officers plus me. How's that for karma?'

'Karma's for believers,' said Milo, 'but yeah, do the golf courses first, then the public buildings and the lake, then door-to-door at each residence. Prioritize any place with anything Jeep-like parked nearby. If the vehicle's got any film equipment in the back, get really careful. If we're right about Crimmins trying to film something, there may be telltale lights.'

I said, 'In his notes he debated learning how to use the film cameras or sticking with video. He's not one for honest labor, so I'll bet on video. That means he may just be using a handheld cam, keeping it very low-key. Also, I doubt he'd be on either of the golf courses. Too open.'

'Assuming he's even *here*,' said Cliff.

'*I'm* assuming you've got golf carts,' Whitworth told him.

'Sure, but they're the property of—'

'Law enforcement.' Whitworth turned to Milo. 'You're doing the mountains?'

'If I can get out there. We'll stay in radio contact.'

'How're you going to travel?'

'Got a four-wheeler?' Milo asked Cliff.

The guard didn't answer.

'Hard of hearing, Eugene?'

'We have basically one Samurai, over behind the golf shop, with the carts. It's a relief vehicle, just in case.'

'In case of what?'

'In case we have to go out back. Like an old person getting lost. But that's never happened yet. We don't use it, I can't even say if the tires have air or if it's gassed up—'

'So you'll inflate and siphon,' said Milo. 'Bring it over.'

Cliff didn't respond.

Milo bared his teeth. 'Pretty *please*, Eugene.'

Cliff snapped, 'Go,' at Bonaface. Again, Bonaface hurried away.

Milo asked Whitworth the helicopters' estimated time of arrival.

'I could only get one,' said Whitworth. 'They're holding it at Bakersfield – five, ten minutes.'

'Eugene, is there a road leading from Fairway out to the mountains?'

'Not much of one.'

'*How* much of one?'

Cliff shrugged. 'It's maybe a quarter-mile long. It was supposed to be for hiking, but none of the residents hike. It goes nowhere, just ends, and then all you've got is dirt and rocks.' He gave a small smirk, decided to hide it by covering his mouth with his hand.

Whitworth drew Milo and me away from him. 'The Ott girl was shot, so they've got some kind of firepower. We have vests; how about you?'

'One,' said Milo. He looked at me. 'None for you. Sit this out.'

'Love to,' I said, 'but you'd better consider using me. It's a hostage situation with two hostage takers, each with a different psychological makeup, in both cases poorly understood. I'm as close to an expert on Peake and Crimmins as you're going to get.'

'Makes sense,' said Whitworth. 'I think we've got an extra vest.'

Milo shot him a sharp look.

Whitworth said, 'Not that I want to tell you how to—'

'I've been through worse,' I said, knowing what was going on in Milo's mind. An undercover situation last year had gone very bad. He blamed himself. I kept telling him

I was fine, the worst thing he could do for me was treat me like an invalid.

'Robin will kill me,' he said.

'Only if I get scratched. Right now it's Suzy Galvez who's got something at stake.'

He looked up at the sky. Out past the development at high, black, unknowable mountains.

'Fine,' he finally said. 'If there's a vest.'

Whitworth trotted over to one of the cruisers, returned with a bulky black package. I slipped the vest on. Scaled for someone Milo's size, it felt like a giant bib.

'Stylish,' said Milo. 'OK, let's get going.'

'One place you might check right away,' I told Whitworth, 'is Sheriff Haas's trailer. Jacob and Marvelle Haas. He arrested Peake for the original massacre, is a major link to the past.'

'He lives *here*?'

'Right over in Jersey.' I pointed south. 'Charing Cross Road.'

Whitworth said to Eugene Cliff, 'Get me the exact address – no, take me there personally.'

Cliff jabbed his own chest. 'What about me? No protection?'

Whitworth looked ready to pound him into the ground. 'Take me within fifty yards and scram.'

'All of a sudden I work for *you*?'

Whitworth's arm shot up and for a second I thought he'd hit Cliff. Cliff believed it, too. He recoiled, raised his own arm protectively. Whitworth's arm kept going. Smoothing his buzz cut. He jogged to his bike, pulled another vest out of the storage box, and slipped it on.

Cliff's mouth was still trembling. He forced it back into smirk mode. 'Big-time SWAT attack.'

'You find this funny?' said Milo.

'I find it a waste of time. And I'm calling Chicago, now.' He took a step, waited for debate, got none, and walked away. The remaining guard followed. Ten steps later, Cliff stopped and looked back. 'Remember: These are seniors. Try not to give anyone a heart attack. They pay a lot to live here.'

'And look where it gets them,' said Milo. 'Just a little mindless violence, and gracious living bites the dust.'

The Samurai was open-roofed, powder blue, and noisy. An after-market roll bar arced over the front seats. Bonaface left the motor chugging and got out. 'It's got half a tank. But hell if I'd use it out there. Makes a shitload of noise, and your lights'll be spotted a mile away.'

Milo checked the tires.

'Those are OK,' said Bonaface. He had a smooth pink face, blond hair, monkey features, big blue eyes. 'Wouldn't use that buggy out there: Too easy to spot.'

Milo straightened. 'You know the area?'

'Not this exact area. Grew up in Piru, but out to the mountains it's the same thing all over. Full of rocks and pits. Plenty of shit to tear up the undercarriage.'

'Any caves at the base of the mountains?'

'Never been out there, but why not? So who are these guys, and why would they be here?'

'It's a long story,' said Milo, getting behind the wheel and adjusting the driver's seat. I climbed in next to him.

Bonaface looked miffed. 'You're using headlights?' He

turned at the sound of his name. Cliff barking from the doorway of the guardhouse.

'Asshole,' muttered Bonaface. He stared at the vest. Smiled at me. 'That thing's way too big for you.'

40

WE DROVE through the center of the development, passing the gentle swell of Balmoral, the northern golf course behind twelve-foot chain link. Moving slowly while trying to keep the Samurai as quiet as possible. Tricky, because low gear was the loudest.

I could hear the low hum of the golf carts, but the vehicles were invisible, except for an occasional suggestion of shadows shifting on the green. Headlights off. Same for the Samurai. The Victorian streetlights glowed a strange, muddy tangerine color, barely rescuing us from depthless black.

We reached the end of the road: The pepper trees that rimmed Reflection Lake. The growth here was luxuriant, fed by moist earth. Miserly light from a distant quarter-moon turned the foliage into gray lace. In the empty spaces, the water was still and black and glossy, a giant sunglass lens.

Milo stopped, told me to stay put, took his nine-millimeter in one hand and his flashlight in the other, and climbed out. He walked to the trees, looked around, parted a branch, and peered through, finally disappeared into the gray fringe. I sat there, absently rubbing one thumb against the warm wooden stock of the rifle he'd placed in my lap. No animal sounds. No air movement. The place felt vacuum sealed. Maybe another time I'd have found it peaceful. Tonight it seemed dead.

I was alone for what seemed like a long time. Then scraping sounds from behind the trees tightened my throat. Before I could move, Milo emerged, holstering his gun.

'If anyone's out there, I can't see them.' He looked at the rifle. Unconsciously, I'd raised the weapon and pointed it in his direction.

I relaxed my hands. The rifle sank. He got behind the wheel.

When we were rolling again, he said, 'It's pretty open once you get past the trees, just some reeds and other low stuff on the other side. No Jeep or any other car in sight; no one's filming.' Grim smile. 'Unless it's an underwater shoot – new twist on *Creature from the Black Lagoon* . . . For all we know, they've already been here and gone, did what they wanted to do, dumped the girl in the water. Or they never came here in the first place.'

'I think they did,' I said. 'No other reason to kill Heidi on the route that leads straight up to Fairway. And Crimmins paid the Soames kid to take the Corvette home – just a mile or two from Hollywood. If he was in the city, he could've driven the Jeep home himself, walked back in half an hour, and gotten the 'Vette. Why bother with Soames unless he was planning to be far away?'

'Because he has plans for Soames? Nice little screen test?'

'That, too. Tomorrow morning. But there'd be no reason to entrust him with the car.'

'Why'd he kill Heidi?'

'Because he had no more use for her,' I said. 'And because he could.'

He chewed his lip, squinted, lowered his speed to ten miles per. The map had indicated a service road that hugged the southern end of the White Oak golf course and led to the rear of the development. The streetlamps were less frequent now, visibility reduced to maddeningly subtle shades of gray.

Milo missed the road, and we found ourselves at the sign marking the entrance to Jersey. Lights out in all the mobile homes. I remembered the street bisecting the subdivision as freshly asphalted. In the darkness, it stretched empty and smooth, so perfectly drafted it appeared computer generated. Resumption of the tangerine light. Deep orange on black; every night was Halloween.

'This is where Haas lives?' he said.

'First street to the right. I can show you the trailer.'

He cruised past the trailers.

'Up there is parking for visitors,' I said. 'No visitors tonight . . . There's Charing Cross. Haas's place is four units in. Look for a cement porch, a Buick Skylark, and a Datsun truck.'

He stopped two houses away. Only the truck was parked in front, backed by Mike Whitworth's Harley.

Lights out. No sign of Whitworth, and I saw Milo's face tighten up. Then the Highway Patrol man came out from behind the trailer and headed for the bike.

Milo stage-whispered, 'Mike? It's Milo.'

Whitworth stopped. Turned toward us, focused, came over.

'In the neighborhood,' said Milo, 'so we dropped by.'

If Whitworth was offended by being second-guessed he didn't show it. 'No one home, nothing funny. I spotted some unopened mail on the table – a day's worth, maybe two.'

'One of their cars is gone,' I said. 'They have family in Bakersfield. Probably traveling.'

'You see any justification for breaking in?' said Whitworth.

Milo shook his head.

'I'm not comfortable with it either. OK, let me go see if any of my guys hit a hole in one. You ready for the mountains yet?'

'On our way,' said Milo.

Whitworth looked out at the black peaks, barely discernible against the onyx sky. Country skies were supposed to be crammed with stars. Why not tonight?

'Must be pretty during the day,' said Whitworth, kick-starting the Harley. 'Sure you want to go it alone?'

'I'd better,' said Milo. 'Gonna be hard enough to avoid being spotted with one vehicle.' He brandished his cell phone. 'I'll keep in touch.'

Whitworth nodded, took another glance at the Tehachapis. Keeping his engine low, he rolled away.

Turning the Samurai around, Milo drove back through Jersey. Lights went on in one of the mobiles as we passed, but so far we'd avoided attracting undue attention. Milo coasted without gas, looking for the service strip. Almost missing it again.

Unmarked, just a car-wide break in the peppers, topped by arcing branches.

Letting the Samurai idle, Milo got out and shined his light on the ground. 'Hardpack . . . maybe degraded granite . . . tire tracks. Someone's been here.'

'Recently?'

'Hell if I know. Jeb the Tracker I ain't.'

He got back in and turned onto the road. The passage was unlit and lined on the north side by more chain link, on the south by a high berm planted with what looked and smelled like oleander. The Samurai traveled well below the berm level, as if we were tunneling.

The four-by-four rode rough, every irregularity in the road vibrating through the stiff frame, Milo's head bouncing perilously close to the roll bar. Nothing changed for the next half-mile: More chain link and shrubbery. Then the road ended without warning and we were faced with the sudden shock of open space, as if tumbling out of a chute.

No more gray, just black. I saw nothing through the windshield, wondered how Milo could navigate. He began wrestling with the wheel. Pebble spray snare-drummed against the undercarriage, followed by deeper sounds, hollow, like hoofbeats. Larger rocks. The Samurai began swaying from side to side, seeking purchase on the grit. Beneath the floorboard, the chassis twanged.

The next dip slammed Milo's head against the bar.

He cursed and braked.

'You OK?' I said.

He rubbed his crown. 'If I had a brain in here I might be in trouble. What the hell am I doing? I can't drive like this. Visibility's zilch; we hit a big enough rock, this thing flips and we break our goddamn necks.'

Locking the parking brake, he stood on the seat and stared over the windshield.

'Nothing,' he said. 'Whole lot of nothing.'

I took the flashlight, got out, faced away from the mountains, cupped my hand over the lens, and tried to examine the ground with the resultant muffled light.

Dry, compacted soil, inlaid with sharp-edged stones and desiccated plants. Matted flat and embroidered by chevron-shaped corrugations. 'The tracks are still going.'

He got down beside me. 'Yeah . . . maybe someone went off-roading. That wild ol' California lifestyle.' He laughed very softly. 'They're supposed to be the crazy ones, but they probably did it with headlights, or at least low beams. Meanwhile, I blind myself. And even without lights we're vulnerable. All the empty space, this thing's probably audible clear to the mountains.' Standing, he squinted at the Tehachapis. 'How far does that look to you?'

'Two miles,' I said. 'Maybe three. You're saying it's time to go it on foot?'

'I don't see any choice. If you're up for it, that is – scratch that, stupid question. Of course you're up for it. You're the one who thinks running is fun.'

He tried to call Whitworth, got no connection, walked a hundred feet back, tried again, same result. Switching off the phone, he put it in his pocket along with the car keys. The flashlight went into another pocket. He took the rifle, gave me the nine-millimeter.

'Handing a civilian my gun.' He shook his head.

'Not just any civilian,' I said.

'Even worse. OK, let me get rid of this thing.' He yanked

off his tie and tossed it in the car. 'And this.' In went his jacket. Mine, too.

We began walking, trying to follow the tracks.

Moving on leather-soled shoes ill-equipped for the task. Nothing to guide us but the hint of the crisp peaks I'd seen during my daytime visit. The quarter-moon looked sickly, degraded, a child's rendering erased here and there to tissue-paper consistency. Set high and well behind the mountains, the filmy crescent appeared to be fleeing the galaxy. What little light filtered down to earth offered no wisdom about anything below the mountaintops.

The lack of spatial cues made it feel as if we'd entered a huge, dark room as big as the world; every step was tinged by the threat of vertigo.

Reduced to stiff, small movements, I edged forward, feeling the rocks rolling under my shoes. Larger, sharper fragments caught on the leather, like tiny parasites attempting to burrow through. As the stones grew progressively larger, contact became painful. I got past the discomfort but remained unable to orient myself. Clumsy with indecision, I stumbled a few times, came close to falling, but managed to use my arms for balance. Several feet in front of me, Milo, encumbered by the rifle, had it worse. I couldn't see him but I heard him breathing hard. Every so often the exhalations choked off, only to resume harsher, faster, like a labored heart making up for skipped beats.

Ten more minutes seemed to bring us no closer. No lights up ahead. *Nothing* up ahead but walls of rock, and I started to feel I'd been wrong about Crimmins returning to the scene. A fourteen year old in his grasp, and we were baby-stepping toward nothing.

What else was there to do but continue?

Three times we paused to risk a quick, cupped flash-lighting of the path. The tracks endured, and immense boulders started appearing, sunk deeply into the ground, like fallen meteorites. But no rocks directly in front of us, so far. This was a well-used clearing.

We kept moving at a pitiful pace, shuffling like old men, enduring the loss of orientation in angry silence. Finally, the moonlight obliged a bit more, revealing folds and corrugations in the granite. But I still couldn't see two feet in front of me, and each step remained constricted, tension coursing up my tailbone. Finally, I got a handle on walking by pretending I was weightless and able to float through the night. Milo's breath kept cutting off and rasping. I got closer behind him, ready to catch him if he fell.

Another hundred yards, two hundred; the peaks enlarged with a suddenness that shook me, as if I'd taken my eyes off the road and were headed for collision.

I reassessed the distance between Fairway's eastern border and the Tehachapis. Less than two miles, maybe a mile and a half. In daylight, nothing more than a relaxed nature stroll. I was sweating and breathing hard; my hamstrings felt tight as piano wire, and my shoulders throbbed from the odd, stooped posture that maintaining balance had imposed on me.

Milo stopped again, waited till I was at his side. 'See anything?'

'Nothing. Sorry.'

'What are you apologizing for?'

'My theory.'

'Better than anything else we've got. I'm just trying to figure out what we do if we get there and it's still nothing. Head straight back, or trail along the mountains just in case they dumped a body?'

I didn't answer.

'My shoes are full of rocks,' he said. 'Let me shake them out.'

A few thousand baby steps. Now the mountains were no more than a half-mile away, reducing the sky to a sliver, dominating my field of vision. The contours along the rock walls picked up clarity and I could see striations, wrinkles, dark gray on darker gray against black.

Now, something else.

A tiny white pinpoint, fifty, sixty feet to the left of the track.

I stopped. Squinted for focus. Gone. Had I imagined it?

Milo hadn't seen it; his footsteps continued, slow and steady.

I walked some more. A few moments later, I saw it again.

A white disc, bouncing against the rock, widening from sphere to oval, paling from milk white to gray to black, then disappearing.

An eye.

The eye.

Milo stopped. I caught up with him. The two of us stood there, searching the mountainside, waiting, watching.

The disc appeared again, bouncing, retreating.

I whispered, 'Camera. Maybe she's still alive.'

I wanted to run forward, and he knew it. Placing a hand on my shoulder, he whispered softly but very quickly: 'We still don't know what it means. Can't give ourselves away. Backup would be great. One last try to reach Whitworth. Any closer and it's too risky.'

Out came the phone. He punched numbers, shook his head, turned off the machine. 'OK, slow and quiet. Even if it feels like we'll never get there. If you need to tell me something, tap my shoulder, but don't talk unless it's an emergency.'

Onward.

The disc reappeared, vanished. Circling the same spot to the left.

Focused on what? I yearned to know, didn't want to know.

I stayed close behind Milo, matching my steps to his.

Our footfalls seemed louder, much too loud.

Walking hurt and silence fed the pain. The world was silent.

Silent movie.

Images flooded my head: Herky-jerky action, corseted women, men with walrus mustaches, mugging outrageously over a plinkety-manic piano score. White-lettered captions, framed ornately: 'So it's carving you want, sir? I'll show you carving.'

Stop, stupid. Keep focused.

Fifty yards from the mountain. Forty, thirty, twenty.

Milo stopped. Pointed.

The white disc had appeared again, this time with a tail – a big white sperm sliding along the rock, wriggling away.

Still no sounds. We reached the mountain. Cold rock fringed with low, dry shrubs, larger stones.

Holding the rifle in front of him, Milo began edging to the left. The nine-millimeter was heavy in my hand.

The disc materialized overhead. White and creamy, bouncing, lingering, bouncing. Gone.

Now a sound.

Low, insistent.

Flash. Whir. Click.

On. Off.

No human struggle. No voices. Just the mechanics of work.

We moved along the mountain undetected, got to within twenty yards before I saw it.

A high, ragged rock formation – an outcropping of sharp-edged boulders, sprouting like stalagmites from the base of the parent range. Clumped and overlapping, ten to fifteen feet high, pushed out twenty feet.

Natural shield. Outdoor studio.

The sound of the camera grew louder. We crept closer, hugging the rock. New sounds. Low, unintelligible speech.

Milo stopped, pointed, hooked his arm, indicating the far end of the boulders. The wall had acquired convexity, continuing in a smooth, unbroken semicircle. No breaks in sight, meaning entry had to be at the far north.

He pointed again and we edged forward inch by inch, bracing ourselves with palms against the rock. The wall curved radically, killing visibility, transforming every step into a leap of faith.

Twelve steps. Milo stopped again.

Something jutted out from the rock. Square, bulky, metallic.

Rear end of a vehicle. From the other side of the granite wall, *flash*, *whir*. Mumbles. Laughter.

We edged to the vehicle's rear tires, squatted, swallowed breath.

Chrome letters: Ford. Explorer. Black or dark blue. Sand spray streaked the rear fender. No license plate. A partially shredded bumper sticker commanded: ENGAGE IN RANDOM ACTS OF KINDNESS.

One-third of the vehicle extended past the rock walls, the rest nosed inside. Milo straightened and peered through the rear window. Shook his head: Tinted. Crouching again, he secured his grip on the rifle, moved around the Explorer's driver's side. Waited. Pointing his rifle at whatever was in front of him.

I joined him. The two of us remained pressed against the truck.

Partial view of the clearing. Plenty of light now, from a spotlight on a pole. An orange extension cord connected the lamp to a gray battery pack. The bulb was aimed downward, well short of the fifteen-foot walls that created the staging area.

Forty-foot stage, roughly circular, set on flat gray earth rimmed by the high, seamed rock. A few boulders were scattered in the corners, like sprinkles of pebbles where the mountain had given way.

Natural amphitheater. Derrick Crimmins had probably discovered it as a youth, driving out with his brother to stage God knew what.

The good old days, when he'd designed sets for his stepmother, acquired a taste for production.

Tonight, he'd gone minimalist. Nothing in the clearing but the single light, a tackle box, and several video-cassettes off to the side. Three white plastic folding chairs.

The chair to the left was off by itself, twenty feet from its neighbors. On it sat a young, brown-skinned, plain-faced girl, arms and legs bound by thick twine, dark hair tied in pigtails. Pink baby-doll pajamas were her sole costume. A pink spot of blush on each cheek, red lipstick on a frozen mouth. A wide leather belt secured her to the chair, cinching her cruelly at the waist, pushing her rib cage forward. Not a belt – a hospital restraint, the same kind they used at Starkweather.

Her head hung to the right. Livid bruises splotched her face and breasts, and dried blood snaked from her nose down to her chin. A shiny red rubber ball was jammed into her mouth, creating a nauseating cartoon of gee-whiz amazement. Her eyes refused to go along with it: Open, immobile, mad with terror.

Staring straight ahead. Refusing to look at what was going on to her left.

The center chair held another woman captive: Older, middle-aged, wearing a pale green housedress torn down the middle. The rip was fresh, fuzzed by threads, exposing white underwear, loose pale flesh, blue veins. Auburn hair. The same kind of bruises and scratches as the girl's. One eye purple and swollen shut. Red ball in her mouth, too.

Her other eye undamaged, but also closed.

The gun jammed against her left temple was small and square-edged and chrome-plated.

Next to her, in the right-hand chair, sat Ardis Peake, holding the weapon. From our vantage, only half his body was visible. Long white fingers around the trigger. He had on his Starkweather khakis. White sneakers that looked brand-new. Big sneakers. Oversized feet.

Tormenting the auburn-haired woman, but showing no sign he enjoyed it. His eyes were closed, too.

Beyond enjoyment into reverie?

The man holding the video camera prodded him. Handheld camera, compact, dull black, not much larger than a hardcover book. It sprayed a beam of creamy-white light.

Peake didn't budge, and the cameraman gave him a sharper prod. Peake opened his eyes, rolled them, licked his lips. The cameraman got right in front of him, capturing each movement. *Whir*. Peake slumped again. The cameraman let the camera drop to his side. The lens tilted upward and the beam climbed, hitting the upper edges of the rock and projecting the eye-dot onto the mountainside. The cameraman shifted and the dot-eye died.

Milo's jaw bunched. He edged around to get a fuller view. I stayed with him.

No one else in the clearing. The cameraman kept his back to us.

Tall, narrow, with a small, white, round, shaved head that glowed with sweat. Black silk shirt, buccaneer sleeves rolled to the elbows, black jeans, dusty black boots with thick rubber soles. Some kind of designer label ran diagonally across the right patch pocket of the jeans. From the left patch dangled the butt of another chrome automatic.

Milo and I sidled farther. Froze as gravel spat under us. No reaction from the cameraman. Too busy mumbling and cursing and prodding Peake.

Manipulating Peake.

Sitting Peake up straighter. Poking Peake's face, trying to mold expression. Adjusting the gun in Peake's hand.

Adhering to Peake's hand.

Strips of transparent tape bound the weapon to Peake's spindly fingers. Peake's arm was held unnaturally rigid by a tripod that had been rigged to support the limb. Tape around the arm.

Forced pose.

Milo narrowed his eyes, raised his rifle, aimed, then stopped as the cameraman moved suddenly.

Half-turning, touching something.

A tight, downslanting line that cut through nightspace.

Nylon fishing filament, so thin it was virtually invisible from this distance.

Running from the gun's trigger to a wooden stake hammered into the dirt.

Slack line. One sharp tug would force Peake's finger backward on the trigger, propel the bullet directly into the auburn-haired woman's brain.

Special effects.

The cameraman ran a fingertip along the line, stepped back. Peake's gun arm remained stiff but the rest of him was rubbery. Suddenly a wave of tardive symptoms took hold of him and he began licking his lips, rolling his head, fluttering his eyelids. Moving his fingers just enough to twang the line.

The cameraman liked that. Focused on the woman. The gun. Back to the woman. Seeking the juicy shot.

Peake stopped moving. The line sagged.

The cameraman cursed and kicked Peake hard in the shins. Peake didn't react. Slumped again.

'Go for it, fucker.' Low-pitched gravel voice. 'Do it, man.'

Peake licked his lips. Stopped. His legs began to shake. The rest of him froze.

'OK! Keep those knees going – don't stop, you psycho piece of shit.'

Peake didn't react to the contempt in the cameraman's tone.

Somewhere else, completely. The cameraman walked over and slapped him. The auburn-haired woman opened her eyes, shuddered, closed them immediately.

The cameraman had stepped back, was focused on Peake. Peake's head whipped back, bobbled. Drool flowed from his mouth.

'Fucking meat puppet,' said the cameraman.

The sound of his voice brought a whimper from the auburn-haired woman. The crepe around her uninjured eye compressed into a spray of wrinkles as she bore down, struggling to block out the moment. The cameraman ignored her, preoccupied with Peake.

No other movements in the clearing. The brown-skinned girl was in a position to see us, but she showed no sign of recognition. Frozen eyes. Fear paralysis or drugs or both.

Milo trained the rifle on the back of the cameraman's

head. Thick fingers around his trigger. But the cameraman was only inches from the fishing line. If he fell the wrong way, the gun would fire.

Tucking the camera under his arm, the filmmaker positioned Peake some more. Peake's arms dangled; he threw his head back. More drool. He inhaled noisily, coughed, blew snot through his nose.

The cameraman yanked the camera up and filmed it. Slapped Peake again, said, 'Some monster you are.'

Peake's head dropped.

Unbound. Free to leave the chair, but constrained by something stronger than hemp.

The cameraman filmed, shifting attention from the woman to the gun to Peake, still inches from the rigged line.

More lip-licking and head-rolling from Peake. His eyelids slammed upward, showcasing two white ovals.

'Good, good – more eye stuff, give me eye stuff.'

The cameraman was talking louder now, and Milo used the sound for cover, charging out into the clearing, raising his rifle.

The cameraman's right thigh nudged the line. Made it bob. He realized it. Laughed. Did it again, watched the pull on Peake's hand.

Peake was able to pull the trigger, but even tardive movement hadn't caused him to do so.

Resisting?

Again, his head dropped.

The cameraman said, 'Where's good help when you need it?' Taking hold of Peake's ear, he shoved Peake's head upward, filmed the resultant gaping stare. Caressing the line with his own index finger as the camera panned the length of Peake's body, moving slowly from furrowed skull to over-sized feet.

Disproportionate feet. *Puppet.*

I understood. Insight was worthless.

I readied my gun, but stayed in place. Milo had inched closer to the cameraman, fifteen or so feet to his rear. With exquisite care, he lifted the rifle to his shoulder, trained it once again on the cameraman's neck. Sniper's target: The medulla oblongata, lower brain tissue that controlled basic body process. One clean shot and respir-ation would cease.

The cameraman said, 'All right, Ardis, I've got enough background. One way or the other, let's *do* the cunt.'

The auburn-haired woman opened her good eye. Saw Milo. Moved her mouth around the red ball, as if trying to spit it out. I knew who she was. Sheriff Haas's wife – Marvelle Haas.

Mail on the table, one day, maybe two. One car gone, the wife left alone.

She began shivering violently.

The young girl remained glazed.

The cameraman turned toward Marvelle, gave us a full view of his profile. Deep lines scored the sides of a lipless mouth. Grainy, tanned skin, several shades darker than the white, hairless head. The head accustomed to wigs. Small but aggressive chin. Beak nose sharp enough to draw blood. No facial fat, but loose jowls, stringy neck. Forearms wormed by veins. Big hands. Dirty nails.

Derrick Crimmins was turning steadily into his father.

His father had been a sour, grasping man, but nothing said he'd been anything other than a flawed human being.

Here in front of me was monstrosity.

Yet open him up and there'd be unremarkable viscera. Bouncing around the vault of his skull would be a lump of gray jelly, outwardly indistinguishable from the brain of a saint.

A man – it always came down to just a man.

Marvelle Haas closed her eyes again. Whimpers struggled to escape from behind the red ball. All that emerged were pitiful squeaks. Milo crouched, ready to shoot, but Crimmins was still too close to the line.

'Open your eyes, Mrs Haas,' said Crimmins. 'Give me your eyes, honey, come on. I want to catch your expression the moment it happens.'

He checked the tape around Peake's hand. Adjusted the gun barrel so that it centered on Marvelle Haas's left temple.

She squeaked.

He said, 'Come on, let's be professional about this.' Moved toward her. Away from the fishing line.

'Used to fish,' he said, arranging her hair, parting her housedress. Slipping a hand under the fabric and rubbing, pinching. 'Look what I caught here.'

Still within arm's reach of the line.

'Back when I fished,' he said, 'a tug on the line meant you'd caught something. This time it means throwing something away.'

She turned away from him. He moved to the left, focusing, filming.

Away from the line. Far enough away.

'*Don't move! Drop your hands! Drop 'em drop 'em now!*'

Derrick Crimmins froze. Turned around. The look on his owlish face was odd: Surprised – betrayed.

Then the flush of rage. 'This is a private shoot. Where's your pass?'

'*Drop your hand, Crimmins. Do it now!*'

'Oh,' said Crimmins. 'You talk so I'm supposed to listen, asshole?'

'*Drop it, Crimmins, this is the last time—*'

Crimmins said, 'OK, you win.'

He shrugged. The lipless mouth curved upward. 'Oh, well,' he said.

He lunged for the fishing line.

Milo shot him in the smile.

41

THE EXPLORER showed up on a Hollywood Division want list. Stolen from a strip mall at Western and Sunset two months before. In the rear storage area were five sets of license plates, three phony registrations, two video-cams, a dozen cassettes, candy wrappers, soda cans. Wedged in the spare-tire case, barbiturates, Thorazine, methamphetamine.

Hedy Haupt was traced to a family in Yuma, Arizona. Father's whereabouts unknown, Welfare Department clerk mother, one brother who worked for the Phoenix fire department. Hedy had earned a B average during her first three years at Yuma High, played a starring role on the track and basketball teams. After she 'fell in with a bad crowd' during her senior year, her grades had plummeted and she'd dropped out, earned a GED, gotten a job at Burger King, run away. During the ensuing eight years, her mother had seen her twice, once for Christmas five years ago, then a one-week visit last year, during which she'd been accompanied by a boyfriend named Griff.

'Had a bad feeling about him,' Mrs Haupt told Milo. 'Carried a camera around and did nothing but take our picture. Wore nothing but black, like someone died.'

Milo and Mike Whitworth found the tapes while excavating the mounds of stolen goods in the garage at Orange Drive. Sixteen cassettes in black plastic cases, buried under thousands of dollars' worth of motion picture gear that Derrick Crimmins had lacked the will, or the ability, to master.

Sixteen death scenes.

The first recognizable victim was the fourth we viewed. Richard Dada, young, handsome, talking animatedly about his career plans, unaware of what lay ahead. Cut to the next scene: Richard's head yanked back by the hair, exposed for the throat slash. The body bisected with a band saw. The dark-sleeved arms of the murderer visible, but no face. The camera was stationary, making it possible for one person to murder and film. Other tapes featured a roving lens that necessitated two killers. The log on the tape said Dada had been killed at one A.M.

Ellroy Beatty's tape featured two segments, an initial shot of the homeless man sucking a bottle near the train tracks, then, four months later, Beatty prone and unconscious on those same train tracks, followed by a long shot of an approaching express. Poor technique; the camera jumped around and the moment of impact was just a blur. Next came brother Leroy, also in two installments. Smiling drunkenly as he talked about wanting to be a blues singer. Four months later, a similar smile, cut short as a black hole snapped onto his forehead like a decal and he collapsed.

Both brothers killed the same night. Ellroy first, his death mandated by the train schedule. Leroy's turn two hours later.

Midway through the stack was Claire Argent's final day

on earth: Like the others, she'd been unprepared. Crimmins had filmed her in front of a bare white wall. Whether it was her own living room couldn't be determined. She talked about psychology, about wanting to learn more about madness, made allusions to the project she and the cameraman would be starting soon, then said, 'Oh, sorry, I'm supposed to forget you're there, right?'

No answer from the cameraman.

Claire talked more about the origins of madness. About not jumping to conclusions, because even psychotics had something to tell us. Then she smoothed an eyebrow – primping for the camera – and smiled some more. Five seconds of shy smile before she was smothered by a pillow. Long shot of her motionless body. Close-up on the straight razor . . .

Twelve other home movies, unlabeled. Seven females: Five teenage girls with the haunted look of street kids, two attractive blond women in their thirties. Five males: A painfully thin goateed boy around sixteen or seventeen and four men, one Asian, one black, two Hispanic.

Folded into an empty box were two sheets of paper.

Title page: **The Monster's Chosen. He Canot Be Stopped.**

Second page: **Cast**

We worked on that for a long time.

The 'fag actor' was most likely Dada, the 'old-maid profesor,' Claire. Other designations included 'the wino twins (Monster finds a perfect match)' and three headings – 'pompos businessman,' 'coke whore,' and 'girl shopping' – for which no conforming tape could be found. 'Greaser farm-chick' matched Suzy Galvez, 'the sheriff's hotblooded wife' Marvelle Haas. The 'teenage pimp' could've been the goateed boy stabbed in the chest, then dismembered. But he fit 'street punk,' so my guess was Christopher Soames. Never had his audition, lucky lad.

At the bottom of the page: 'More?????? definitly. how many????????????'

The job of identifying the unnamed victims was assigned to a six-detective task force from LAPD and the Sheriff's Department. After two months, three of the teenage girls had been matched with runaways on various missing persons rosters; all the girls, it was believed, had been living on the streets of Hollywood. Hedy Haupt would've understood that scene. Two girls and the goateed boy remained nameless, as did the younger of the blond women, probably the 'stripper,' and the black man (the 'nigger stud'). 'Greaser 1' and 'greaser 2' turned out to be Hernando Alas and Sabino Real, cousins from El Salvador seeking work as laborers by standing outside a paint store in Eagle Rock. Contractors seeking cheap labor cruised the store daily. No one remembered who'd picked up Alas and Real, but family members living in the Union District finally stepped forward to make the identification.

A Korean-American salesman named Everett Kim, bludgeoned with a baseball bat – the 'chink' – was traced to the Glendale-based skydiving club where Derrick Crimmins and Hedy had first met. The ex-wife of another member, a dental hygienist from Burbank, turned out to be Allison Wisnowski. 'The nurse.'

Four months later, no new ID's and only one of the bodies had been found: One of the runaway girls, a sixteen-year-old named Karen DeSantis, discovered by hikers in Bouquet Canyon.

One additional tape was found in the Explorer, the scene barely discernible because of poor light: Hedy Haupt aka Heidi Ott, getting out of the four-wheeler, smiling uneasily. Handing the camera to someone off screen, then turning her back and cocking her hip. Moving slowly, seductively. Vamping. Smiling as she turned to look back.

Saying, 'How'm I doing – sexy enough?' just before her head disappeared in a flash. No designation on the list. Perhaps Derrick Crimmins had conceived her as 'coke whore,' or maybe he had yet to dream up a designation.

Creating characters, killing them off.

Folded in a pocket of Crimmins's black silk shirt was a copy of the *Blood Walk* title page we'd found in his nightstand. On the reverse were several handwritten paragraphs in the same sharp-edged hieroglyphics used for the production notes:

The Monster: Combenation of extreme evil-madness and supernatural psychic abilitys to tell the future and to get into peoples heads. Locked up in the high security asylem just like Haniball Leckter he also cant be stopped like Leckter, can go through walls, beam himself around change his moleculs like a StarTrek alien. Exits at will, goes around killing at will. Various people, all types just cause he likes it, gets off on it, not crazy all the time this is just what he does, his job, his callin in life, no one will ever understand it because theyre not in the same dimension. And he canot be stopped anymore than Jason or Freddie Kruger or Michael Meyers.

Except by The Daredeveil Avenger. Who understands him cause He grew up with him and Hes also got the psychic powers but for good not evil. Once He was a kid now He's a man, tall and muscular and silent, a real John Wayne Dirty Harry type but with a sense of humor. True Lies meets James Bond. Doesn't waste action except when it counts. Women love him the same as James Bond but He has no time for them because only He knows what The Monsters really capible of, so only he can stop The Blood Walk which otherwise would be inevatable.

He wears Black but He's the Good Guy. Keep it different, creative. The actions in the end always between him and the Monster. Prime-evil battle. Only at the end can we know how it turns out. In the last scene the Monster dies the worse death of all. Maybe burning, maybe grinded up in some kind of hamburger machine. Or acid. Either way, he's dead.

Or maybe not.

If it works there's always a sequel.

42

'WHAT THE hell was he planning to do with it?' said Milo. 'Take a meeting with some studio scrote?'

He stuffed pretzels into his mouth. No answer expected.

We were sitting in a bar on Pacific Avenue on the south end of Venice, not far from the Marina. Jimmy Buffett on tape, sun-roughened faces and zinc noses, sports talk, the pretzels. Mostly calls for beer on tap.

It was Thursday. I'd spent the afternoon just as I had every day this week. Out in Bellflower with Suzy Galvez, trying to break through. Milo had offered my services right after the rescue. Mr Galvez, a landscaper with a vicious scar running from his left ear to his shoulder blade, had turned him down, growling, 'We handle our own problems.'

Three weeks later, I got the call from Mrs Galvez. Meek, halting, slightly accented voice. Apologetic when she didn't need to be. Suzy was still waking up with screaming nightmares. Two days ago, she'd started wetting her bed and sucking her thumb; she hadn't done any of that since the age of six.

I drove out the next day. The house was a brown box behind freshly painted white pickets, too many flowers for the space. Mr Galvez greeted me at the door, a scar-faced, muscled keg of steam. Shaking my hand too hard. Telling me he'd heard I knew what I was doing. Handing me a mixed bouquet, cut fresh from the garden, when I left.

Marvelle Haas was rumored to be seeing a therapist in Bakersfield. Neither she nor her husband had returned anyone's calls. The task force was still looking for bodies, contacting departments in other cities, other states, trying to figure out how many people Derrick Crimmins had murdered. Cases in Arizona, Oklahoma, and Nevada seemed promising. Evidence on Derrick's brother's motorcycle accident was sketchy, but Cliff Crimmins's name had been added to the victim list.

Milo snarfed more pretzels. Someone shouted for a Bud. The bartender, a black-haired Croatian with four rings in his left ear, palmed the tap. We were drinking single-malt scotch. Eighteen-year-old Macallan. When Milo asked for the bottle, the Croatian's eyebrows lifted. He smiled as he poured.

'What the hell was it all for?' said Milo.

'That's a real question?'

'Yeah, I've used up my ration of rhetorical.'

I was sorry he asked. I'd thought about little else, had answers good enough for talk shows but nothing real.

Milo put his glass down, stared at me.

'Maybe it was all for fun,' I said. 'Or preparation for the movie Crimmins convinced himself he'd write one day. Or he was actually going to sell the tapes.'

'We still haven't found any underground market for that kind of crap.'

'OK.' I sipped. 'So eliminate that.'

'I know,' he said. 'There's an appetite for every damn bit of garbage out there. I'm just saying nothing's turned up linking Crimmins to any snuff-film business deals, and we've looked big-time. No cash hoard, not a single bank account, no meetings with any shifty types in long coats, no ads in weirdo magazines. And the computer Crimmins had in the house wasn't hooked up to the Internet. Nothing but basic software, no files. Our guy says he probably never used it.'

'Technologically impaired,' I said. 'No sweat. Video's as good as film.'

'All I'm saying is it doesn't look like he was after the money. Stole all that gear but never tried to sell it. We figure he was probably living off dope sales.'

'And Heidi's salary,' I said. 'Till she became superfluous. No bank accounts means the two of them spent everything as it came in. They weren't living like royalty and they avoided paying rent, so a good deal of it probably went up her nose.'

'His, too. Coroner found some coke in his system. A little meth, too. And something called loratadine.'

'Antihistamine,' I said. 'Doesn't make you drowsy. Maybe Crimmins was allergic to the desert, needed to keep his energy level up for the big shoot.'

Milo refilled his glass. '*Blood Walk*.'

'Whatever his specific motivation,' I said, 'and he may have had several, in his head it was a major production. It was the process he loved. He got hooked on playing God sixteen years ago.'

He downed the scotch. 'You really think Crimmins did the Ardullos by himself.'

'By himself or with his brother. But not with Peake. Peake was set up. I'll probably never be able to prove it, but the facts support it. Think about Peake's blood test: Just a residue of Thorazine. Heidi'd been weaning him off his meds for a while. Just as Claire probably had. But Claire's motive was to get Peake to talk about his crimes. And, unconsciously, she wanted to find some virtue in his soul because that might say something about her brother. Heidi wanted Peake sufficiently coherent so he could cooperate in the escape and – more important – perform on film. Killing Marvelle and Suzy on camera – the Monster finally reveals itself. But it didn't work. He didn't perform. You saw his condition. With or without Thorazine, he's extremely low-functioning, has been for years. At his prime, he had no more than a borderline IQ. Adolescent paint- and glue-sniffing and alcohol knocked off a few more points. Thorazine and tardive dyskinesia numbed him further. He was never in any shape to plan and conduct a crime spree, even the disorganized massacre Jacob Haas found at the Ardullo house. He had nothing to do with Heidi's death or Frank Dollard's. No motive, no means. Same for the Ardullos.'

'The Ardullos were your basic senseless crime,' he said. 'Maniac on the loose, no need for a motive.'

'That's what Derrick wanted everyone to think,' I said. 'And he got his way. But there's always some kind of motive. Psychotic or otherwise. Peake's no criminal superman, just pathetic. Derrick plotted it all out. Good against evil; Derrick gives, Derrick takes away.'

Another drink poured. Milo said, 'Daredevil Avenger.'

'On some level, Derrick probably started believing his own

PR. Peake as surrogate monster, Derrick as angel of deliverance. But Peake just doesn't fit any type of psychotic killer. He's never shown any indication of a delusional system, bloody or otherwise, never acted violently before the massacre or since. He's a retarded man with advanced schizophrenia, organic brain damage, alcoholic dementia. Crimmins called him a meat puppet and that's exactly what he was, right from the beginning. Derrick and Cliff got him drunk, borrowed his shoes – they were able to even though they were much taller, because Peake's feet are disproportionately large. One or both of them walked through the Ardullo house slashing and bludgeoning. Two killers would have made it easier, quicker. The sneaker prints pointed to Peake and led to his shack. With that kind of proof, why bother looking any further? And don't forget who was in charge: Haas, a part-time cop, absolutely no homicide experience. Then the FBI came in and did an after-the-fact profile.'

Milo had two more shots.

'One other thing,' I said. 'That night, when Peake had his hand taped to the gun, he was experiencing plenty of tardive symptoms. Lots of movement; you'd think he would've pulled the trigger just by chance. But he didn't. And I swear there were times, looking at him, that he seemed to be resisting. Forcing himself to hold back.'

He pushed his drink away. Swiveled on his stool and stared.

'He's a hero now?'

'Make of it what you will.'

Another shot. He said, 'So what are you going to do about it?'

'What can I do? Like you said, no proof. And one way or the other, Peake's going to need confinement. I suppose Starkweather's as good a place as any.'

'Starkweather in the post-Swig era,' he said. 'I heard his uncle found him a job on someone else's staff.'

'Swig was a mediocre man trying to do a wizard's job. There're no easy solutions.'

'So Peake stays put.'

'Peake stays put.'

'You're OK with that.'

'Do I have a choice?' I said. 'Let's say I do raise a stink, somehow manage to free him. Some do-gooder will see that he gets out on the street, which'll turn him into just another homeless wretch. He can't take care of himself. He'd be dead in a week.'

'So we're putting him away for his own good.'

'Yes,' I said, surprised at the harshness in my voice. 'Who the hell said life was fair?'

He stared at me again.

'That day in his room,' I said, 'when I talked to Peake about the Ardullo children and he began to cry, I misjudged him. I thought it was all self-pity. But he was feeling real pain. Not just at being blamed for it. At what happened. Maybe he revealed some of that to Claire, and that's what kept her going with him. Or maybe she never saw it. But it was real, I'm sure of it. Right after that is when he jumped up, assumed the Jesus pose. He was telling me he'd been martyred. Suffered for someone else's sins. Not sorry for himself. At peace with it.'

'Telling you,' he said. 'Severely low-functioning, but he's worth listening to?'

'Oh, yeah,' I said. 'It always pays to listen.'

We sat in silence for a long time. Someone else replaced Jimmy Buffett, but I couldn't tell you who.

I threw money on the bar. 'Let's get out of here.'

He lifted himself with effort. 'You going to see him again?'

'Probably,' I said.

Devil's Waltz

Jonathan Kellerman

AN ALEX DELAWARE NOVEL

It's a living hell

Twenty-one-month-old Cassie Jones has spent most of her short life in and out of Western Paediatrics Hospital. Cassie is persistently, seriously, ill and when no amount of testing can identify the cause, her doctor is led to a disturbing diagnosis – Cassie's mother could be making her daughter deliberately sick.

Child psychologist Alex Delaware is brought in to make an independent assessment of the Jones family. But Alex's attempts to find the answers and save a young girl's life will reveal a terrifying circle of corruption, abuse and murderous hatred.

Praise for Jonathan Kellerman

'Has vampiric grip' *Guardian*

'Sophisticated, cleverly plotted and satisfying psycho-drama' *Sunday Telegraph*

978 0 7553 4291 4

headline

Bad Love

Jonathan Kellerman

AN ALEX DELAWARE NOVEL

No good will come.

It starts with a tape delivered to psychologist Alex Delaware's house – a recording of a soul-sickening scream followed by a twisted, childlike voice chanting 'Bad love. Bad love. Don't give me the bad love . . .' Alex heard that phrase a decade ago, at a symposium for Dr Andres de Bosch and his work with troubled teens; why is he hearing it now?

Then there are strange phone calls, a horrific act of vandalism and the discovery that other symposium delegates have been murdered. Unless Alex can make sense of the mind games being played he will be next . . .

Praise for Jonathan Kellerman

'Convincing psychiatrics; stylish, solidly characterised and salted, as usual, with Kellerman's distaste for the LA landscape' *Literary Review*

'His portrait of lotus land under siege, with its underclass of sickos, addicts and no-hopers, is precise and convincing' *Observer*

978 0 7553 4292 1

headline